To my friends Julie and the legendary Don Paco.

Enjoy

Wayne Flanary

8-12-14

GABRIEL

DENNIS FLANNERY

Copyright © 2013 by Dennis Flannery
First Edition – September 2013

ISBN
978-1-4602-2677-3 (Hardcover)
978-1-4602-2678-0 (Paperback)
978-1-4602-2679-7 (eBook)

All rights reserved.

No part of this publication may be reproduced in any form, or by any means, electronic or mechanical, including photocopying, recording, or any information browsing, storage, or retrieval system, without permission in writing from the publisher.

Produced by:

FriesenPress
Suite 300 – 852 Fort Street
Victoria, BC, Canada V8W 1H8

www.friesenpress.com

Distributed to the trade by The Ingram Book Company

ACKNOWLEDGEMENTS

My thanks to my primary copy editor and dear friend, Janet Ford, who spotted many a gaff in structure, time and space.
And
My son, Sean, also an excellent editor. He spent a great deal of time making intelligent suggestions and tidying things up.
And
To my treasured friend Lesley whose two cents worth was worth a great deal more.
And
Last, but far from least, my wonderful wife, Zelia, who's encouragement, editing and love have kept me at it.

Our angels Aidan and Eryn, you will always be in our hearts. We miss you.

CHAPTERS

1	HANLY JORDAN NEWS HOUR
4	THE STUFF
12	THE BODY
15	THE HONOR
18	TRANSFERENCE
27	GABRIEL MANSION
33	PIG SHIT
39	A NEW MAN
45	FIRST LOOK
61	ANNOUNCEMENT
64	ALL ABOARD
70	VOLUNTEER
76	TWO BY TWO
78	COMPLETION AND LAUNCH
83	NORMAN DATE
92	HE'S GONE
98	FIRST PLANET
106	FIRST TIME IN ORBIT
117	A WALK OUTSIDE
123	THE SEEDING
130	LET IT GROW
154	RESURRECTION

169	GET TOGETHER
183	THE CAVE
189	HARVEST AND SEED
197	HOME SITES
201	BUILDING MATERIALS
204	KIDS AND CLONES
213	VANCE AND LARA
219	VISITORS
229	LET'S TALK
248	GOLD
253	PLANNING FOR MALIC
257	THE MALIC ARRIVE
269	GREAT LOSSES
273	THE VOUT RETURN
275	HERE COME THE YASSI
281	THE RESCUE
303	BACK TO GABRIEL
306	THE GATHERING
312	LITTLE RAT BASTARDS
322	WORLD WIDE NEWS HOUR
335	EPILOGUE

AUTHOR'S NOTE

GABRIEL is a sequel to my novel, The WGC. A sequel can, at times, be difficult to follow if its predecessor has not been read. The following glossary is an attempt to answer What the hell? When the hell? and Who the hell? before the questions are asked.

Glossary

ALEXANDER GABRIEL: A brilliant 43-year old investment broker who, following a skiing accident in 1997, found himself inexplicably hurled back thirty-five years in time to 1962, and ultimately forced to begin his life over at the age of eight. However, Alex had retained his immense knowledge of the future investment world and, over the next few decades, used this knowledge to amass a vast fortune.

TEDDY: Teddy Oldaker was Alexander Gabriel's best friend in both of Alex's lives. In their first lives, they grew up next door to each other and were as inseparable as two friends could be, until the Oldaker family moved to Arizona just after the boys graduated from high school.

In Alex's second life, Teddy Oldaker became a major movie star before being tragically killed by street thugs in 1985. Alex insisted that Teddy's DNA be preserved, and twenty years later this DNA was used by the scientists at Norman Research to create a clone. Teddy's clone was born to surrogate parents on August 18, 2005. The second Teddy, Teddy Stoddard, was known as Teddy Jr.

NORMAN RESEARCH: A large research facility named after Alexander's scientist father, Norman Gabriel. Norman Research employed the finest minds ever assembled. The original facility was located in Southern California, but its headquarters was relocated to Mariana. This is the location where the world renowned and beloved Dr. Dale Isley led his team to the discoveries that changed the world and, in time, they would change the galaxy.

THE WGC: World Guidance Council. A governmental body formed by Alexander Gabriel and the leadership of Gabriel Industries and Gabriel International. These companies possessed nearly unlimited resources. Their combined value was so great that it could not be accurately calculated.

The leadership of the WGC realized that the world was on a downward spiral, and without massive intervention would self-destruct within the next six decades.

In 2010, the WGC, through the threat of economic manipulation and the use of an extraordinary weapons system, took control of all of the world's governments. To demonstrate the power of their new weapon, and their resolute sincerity, the WGC immediately executed over a 150,000 of the world's most vile people. Murderers, serial rapists, and corrupt, vicious heads of nations all perished. No matter where they were or what they were doing, these evil people could not escape this weapon. During the cleansing process, no property was damaged, and not a single innocent person was harmed or killed. Once the world's governments were convinced that there was nothing they could do to defeat the WGC, they reluctantly accepted this new world government. They had no choice.

AURATRON: A device invented by Dale Isley that reads the electrical/biological signals of an individual. After two years of concentrated effort, the employees of Gabriel Industries were able to record over a million auras ranging from murderers to politicians. The Auratron was used as an aiming device for the particle cannon that executed over 150,000 evil people in the first day of the WGC world takeover.

MARIANA: The island nation, formally known as Sao Tome & Principe, is located in the Gulf of Guinea off the west coast of Africa.

Alexander Gabriel bought the island from its citizens and renamed it after his mother, Marian. He then proceeded, over the next few years, to transform it from a tiny third world country into a shining jewel on the world's stage. Mariana became the seat of the WGC and the world's capitol.

WEC: World Economic Currency. The WEC, pronounced "weck", replaced the world's myriad of currencies. The huge mistakes made with the introduction of the Euro were corrected. The WEC would remain a stable and secure currency.

FOREWARD
(An excerpt from The WGC)

CENTRAL OREGON
April 12, 1997
8:15 a.m.

The two men and two women, all fashionably dressed in colorful ski gear, flew in single file over a small rise, propelling clouds of fresh powder into the crystalline air. As they headed down a wide open, untracked slope, they separated and skied four abreast, leaving in their wake four snake-like grooves in the virgin snow. They were two hundred yards above the tree line when they came to a stop. They were smiling broadly while catching their breath and taking in the beautiful view of the Cascade Mountains. Within seconds the shorter man, Alex, gestured downhill. "Last one to the bottom buys lunch today." Without another word he turned his skis around and sped off.

The two young ladies laughed as they quickly followed. The second man, Jason, standing a good three inches taller than Alex, called after them. "I'll enjoy that free lunch." He smiled to himself and confidently waited another moment before starting down the slope.

Two hundred yards below, in the cover of trees, were three sloppily dressed young snow-boarders or "shredders" as they called themselves. They weren't shredding at the moment; they were passing around a small glass pipe. One of them, after taking a last pull off the pipe, dropped it in a pocket and bent over to attach his bindings.

"Okay, chicken shits, let's get some air this time." He flipped his board around and took off through the trees at a suicidal speed. The two others quickly followed.

A little further up the hill, Alex was about fifty yards in front of his three companions as he raced down the groomed run between the small forests of trees. He was still smiling as he looked back to see if he was maintaining his lead when, without warning, a stoned shredder came flying out of the trees a good six feet in the air, clipping Alex on the side of his head, throwing him wildly off balance. Alex's sunglasses shattered and flew off as he shot directly toward a large tree. Further up the hill, a sickening thud was clearly heard by his companions.

"ALEX!" Jason screamed in alarm.

INGLEWOOD, CALIFORNIA
April 12, 1962
8:20 a.m.

Prairie Avenue was still damp from sporadic spring showers. The smell of wet pavement and exhaust fumes mixed to create a special freshness unique to such a day. Despite the seasonal rains, traffic was moving at a normal pace until just after 8:20 a.m. when the routine flow on this active avenue was abruptly interrupted as an ancient pickup truck came to a screeching, side-sliding stop, effectively blocking the two southbound lanes.

Within a second, a frail old man in baggy, paint-stained white overalls threw open the dilapidated truck's door and all but fell out of its cab. "He ran right out in front of me!" he cried out as he headed on wobbly legs, back in the direction he had come; leaving his old truck right where it had stopped.

Immediately horns began honking, tentatively at first but gaining in urgency as the seconds passed. Gusting breezes were blowing what appeared to be school papers and crayon drawings from one side of the road to the other, a few sticking to the shallow puddles the rains had created on the asphalt.

On the far side of the road, about a hundred feet north of where the old pickup had come to its dramatic stop, a young boy, maybe seven or eight years old, was lying on his back just a foot or two from the curb. He wasn't moving. His clothes were wet, torn, and stained with small amounts of blood mixed with grime from the road. His right shoe was missing and that sock was half off, exposing a small white heel and a nasty looking road scrape on the anklebone. The only movement was an occasional twitch of the half-covered foot.

A girl, maybe a year or so older than the boy, after precariously dodging four lanes of traffic in her effort to reach the stricken boy, quickly knelt beside him.

"ALEX!" she cried.

GABRIEL

PROLOGUE

HAMAH, SYRIA
August 18, 2016
1:30 a.m.

It was a moonless, starless night-- as dark as it gets. A well-worn panel truck was quietly making its way through the nearly empty streets of Hamah. After a series of turns, it slowed, and then came to a stop in an alley behind a nondescript two-story home in a middle class neighborhood. After a moment, the driver's side door opened and a middle-aged man, with a long gray beard and dressed in the simple clothes of a workman emerged, leaving the door ajar. He paused for a moment and casually looked around while listening to the sounds of the night. At that late hour, there were some dogs barking in the distance and the faint noise of a few TV sets still on. Satisfied he walked to the garage door, unlocked and opened it, and returned to the truck. After sliding into the driver's seat, he deftly backed it into the garage, got out and closed the garage door from the inside. Within seconds, five men in black robes, toting large, heavy-looking duffel bags stepped out of the rear of the truck and entered the home.

GABRIEL MANSION
MARIANA
THE HANLY JORDAN NEWS HOUR

August 21, 2016
6:45 p.m.

After a commercial break, the television picture returned to a live shot of Dan Jordan and Bob Hanly sitting behind their desk on the set. Hanly was checking his notes; Jordan was looking into the camera. Within two seconds, the screen changed to a solo shot of Dan Jordan.

"Now, we're going to switch to the Gabriel Mansion on the island nation of Mariana for the scheduled news conference," said Dan Jordan.

The picture changed to a dramatic zoom shot, starting at water's edge and quickly traveling three hundred meters up an expansive and magnificently manicured grounds to a wide marble stairway that led to a large, elegantly crafted granite veranda located on the west side of the Gabriel mansion—the seat of the World's government.

The activity on the veranda consisted of a dozen or so men and women in the process of saying goodbye. Many had personal cameras and were posing with the other dignitaries while assistants or waitstaff took a lot of pictures of them shaking hands and or hugging. All seemed to be in a good mood.

"We're waiting for this monumental meeting, this historical moment, to conclude before we can begin our news conference," stated Bob Hanly in split screen. The other half of the screen was filled with the comings and goings on the veranda. "The World Guidance Council or The WGC as its commonly known, has apparently just accomplished another one of its major goals."

"We'll wait for the announcement," said Dan.

"Not hard to spot Jason Gould in the crowd," said Bob.

"No, I'll say not. Even at sixty he doesn't seem to have shrunk much. Still a good six four, I'd guess, and pretty slim. Mr. Gabriel has jokingly said that Chairman Gould always reminded him of a Lebanese basketball player because of his height, weight and dark complexion."

"That dark hair is mostly gray now."

"I can relate to that."

"The man is actually smiling."

"That's a rarity. He is normally quite stoic, at least in public."

"It's interesting to note that he and Alex Gabriel have been partners, collaborators and close friends since their early twenties," said Bob. "And together they built financial and media empires that are second to none."

"There is no second place for any of their endeavors," said Bob, "they are just too far ahead of the pack."

"Mr. Gabriel is the financial genius and Chairman Gould is unmatched in his brilliance in manipulating public opinion. His manipulation of the news media during the WGC's world takeover allowed that extraordinary undertaking to succeed with little worldwide panic. A panic could have resulted in considerable loss of life."

"There's Alexander Gabriel saying goodbye to the British Finance Minister," said Dan.

The shot on the split screen went to Alexander Gabriel. Alex was now 62. His blond hair was thinning and graying. He too was smiling. His extraordinary blue eyes had an extra gleam today.

"That man is still universally regarded as the most powerful man in the world despite the fact that he no longer holds any formal rank in the WGC," said Dan.

"When you control that much money you don't need rank," responded Bob.

"I just spotted Douglas Ito, the Treasurer of the WGC … just off to the left of Chairman Gould."

A camera picked up the short, impeccably dressed white haired Asian man. He was shaking hands and speaking to an older well-dressed lady.

"That man has not aged since I've been in the news business."

"I believe Mr. Ito will be 90 on his next birthday."

"He's timeless… and I might add, shrewd, cunning and a numbers wizard."

"Oh, yeah."

"There's Alexandra Greenwood, the WGC's President," said Dan.

"She, as everybody knows, is Alexander's cousin and by all accounts, an extremely capable person."

"If she weren't, she wouldn't be here."

"No, no she wouldn't."

"It's hard to tell which one is more stoic, Jason Gould or Alexandra."

"She is certainly straight laced and some say, almost humorless."

Bob smiled, "You'd almost expect her to wear her hair in a tight bun."

"It's said that she doesn't wear any makeup, but she is still a rather striking woman. Handsome rather than beautiful like her mother," remarked Dan.

"Nobody, and I mean nobody is as beautiful as her mother," said Bob.

Dan smiled, "You've always had a crush on Colleen Gabriel."

"Me and about two billion other men on this planet."

"And Joan Hocket has just walked out on the veranda," said Dan, "The head of the WGC's International Social Programs. Quite a gal."

The screen switched to a picture of a dignified handsome black woman in her late sixties. Her gray hair was cut short and tidy.

"She certainly has an interesting background," added Bob.

"There's a woman who went through a massive ideological conversion many years back."

"Indeed, she started out as a liberal Berkeley graduate and set off to right the wrongs she felt society was imposing on the less fortunate minority groups. Dr. Hocket was so effective, after just five years, she was appointed the Director of Social Services for the State of California. After a few years, according to her autobiography, she became disenchanted with the welfare system. She tried to change the policies that, according to her, were not helping those they were charged to help, but were actually destroying whatever hope they may have had. It was about that time that she was introduced to Alexander Gabriel."

"She was the major player in putting the social system and society together on the island nation of Mariana. Now it's considered one of the garden spots of the world. Then Mr. Gabriel put her in charge of doing the same thing for the remainder of the planet."

"The rest is history, as they say."

"There he is," exclaimed Bob.

"Hard to miss," said Dan.

The picture switched just in time to see Vance Youngblood walk out of the interior of the mansion onto the veranda. Vance wasn't much taller than five ten but he was wide – at least at the shoulders. There were few men in the world who could match the bulk of Vance's delts. They seemed somewhat unnatural. Below those shoulders was a large muscled chest, a relatively narrow waist and tree-trunk legs. This was one powerful looking human being. Nearing the age of 70, Vance's body wasn't as massive as it had been in his prime, nevertheless it could still evoke envy in an athlete half his age. His cold brown eyes still held considerable menace. His hair was now nearly white, but still lay thick and low on his forehead.

"Other than Alex Gabriel himself, Vance Youngblood has to be the most recognizable person on the planet."

"People are just beginning to realize that Vance isn't just a physical power behind Alex, but has a keen mind to boot. This man carried a 4 point average throughout high school and college. Joined the navy, became a SEAL, was highly decorated in a couple of well-known conflicts and retired as a Seal captain."

"He's been in charge of security for Gabriel Industries and the WGC for over 38 years."

"It is well documented as to what he did after Alex's parents were kidnapped and tragically killed by terrorists. Fanatics have stayed clear of the Gabriels ever since. You don't want to upset this man."

"Well, if I needed security that's certainly the man I'd want in charge of it."

"Looks like the news conference is about to start. The WGC members are taking their seats."

The picture then switched to a close-up shot of those six people sitting at a long, simply decorated table in the shade of the veranda. There were four cameras covering this event, but just a single reporter, Lara Lions. One camera was on Lara; the others covered the six people at the table. These cameras fed worldwide to all the major networks and the networks, in turn, provided access to all local and regional stations.

Lara was just 23 when she went to work for FOX News and had, in two short years, become the world's most watched news personality. Lara had a quick wit to go along with her charming personality, and a professionalism normally associated with a much older reporter. The fact that she was a very attractive redhead was a bonus.

After a glut of requests from hundreds of news sources worldwide asking to embed a news team on the island, the leadership of the WGC determined that their island nation was too small to house and feed such an army of reporters. They elected to have one reporter represent all of the networks. To determine who should hold this coveted post, the WGC hierarchy took a poll; Lara Lions received all of the votes.

About the time she turned 25, she was offered the much-coveted position of being the exclusive news reporter for the WGC. The major networks grudgingly approved her selection for the job. . . they had little choice. Lara's position was not as press secretary, but rather she performed the job traditionally carried out by dozens of reporters from all over the world. In effect and in a small way, the leadership of the WGC changed the way news conferences were conducted, at least on their island. Lara was fair and would not only ask her own questions, but also the best selection of questions submitted by the networks.

These six at the table had just concluded a major world economic conference and were now ready to hold the news conference to announce the completion of a foremost goal of the WGC.

The television picture narrowed in on Jason Gould's face.

"We are extremely pleased to announce that after four years of concentrated effort, the world has, as of today, completed the changeover to the WEC, pronounced Weck (World Economic Currency). As of October 1, 2016, it will be the only legal tender accepted worldwide.

We predicted it would take three years to make this change, but it's been closer to four. The lessons learned after the euro's introduction in 1999 exposed a multitude of deficiencies in planning. These deficiencies were, of course, taken into consideration and corrected in our development of the WEC legal tender. Runaway unearned benefits, or so-called entitlements, will not be tolerated by the WGC. All nations will provide exactly the same social benefits, including health care, pensions, and retirement benefits based on an individual's lifetime contributions to those programs. And all health care and retirement programs will be fully funded as part of an employee's compensation package. Given that is now the law, the value of the WEC cannot be affected from nation to nation, as the euro was in the past." Jason paused for a moment. "The international use of the WEC will provide all peoples of the world a strong, stable and secure currency." Again Jason paused, looked at Lara and smiled. "We will now take your questions, Lara."

"Thank you, Chairman Gould. Is this WGC's last major goal?"

"It's the last major goal to be accomplished. We're still in the process of building the hospitals and medical facilities required to serve all peoples of this planet and we believe that massive task will be completed by the end of next year. And, of course, we're still trying to get the world's population under control."

"Will there ever be an end to that endeavor, sir?"

"Yes."

"Yes? That's it, Mr. Chairman?" Lara smiled.

"I'll just add that there will be several countries changing leadership within the next six months."

"Would you care to name those countries?"

"They know who they are," said Jason. "And, for the sake of diplomacy and expediency, there will be no more questions today on that subject." Jason smiled slightly.

Lara knew enough to drop the subject. None of the people sitting at this table would tolerate being badgered. It was quite clear when no meant no. "May I direct my question to Mr. Youngblood?"

"Of course," said Jason.

Lara turned to Vance. Although he was forty years her senior, it was clear to any observant person that she was smitten by this extraordinary man. There was certainly some chemistry between them.

"Mr. Youngblood," the camera switched to Vance, "although terrorism has been reduced to less than 5% of its past highs, there are still a few active cells in the Mid-east. Can you tell me, sir, will you ever be able to completely stop terrorism?"

Vance smiled at Lara. *If I were thirty years younger I would sure take a run at this gal,* he thought. But what he said was, "Oh, hell yeah. There are just a few crazy sumbitches out there stirring up trouble and killing innocent people, but just a few. Those bastards are having trouble recruiting new crazies because of our policy of feeding their worthless carcasses to pigs. The head dipshits can't seem to convince the lesser dipshits that they will still get their 72 virgins, even if they are turned into pig crap." Vance said seriously.

Everybody laughed, including Lara, the cameramen, and the members of the WGC. Vance was always a favorite of reporters because of his complete candor. You could always depend on him to use colorful language. To anyone's knowledge, Vance had no real sense of humor, but he didn't seem to mind if his statements got an occasional laugh. However, no one—but no one—would ever think to laugh at Vance. But then again, laughing at his way of stating his opinion didn't seem to bother him.

"Thank you, sir, for that descriptive answer," said Lara as she all but winked at Vance. "I would like to ask Mr. Gabriel a question if I may?"

Vance politely nodded.

"Mr. Gabriel, it's been ten years since you resigned your chairmanship of the WGC and arguably turned the power over to Chairman Gould. How do you feel about the progress of the world since that time?"

"First, there is no argument as to my turning the leadership of the WGC over to Chairman Gould. He is the boss, and I might add, a great one. For all practical purposes, Chairman Gould and I have been partners in nearly every facet of our lives since we were in our early twenties. We think alike and all our decisions, major and minor, throughout this time, have been made in concert."

"Although you don't hold a formal title in the WGC, would you agree that you still wield a great deal of influence over the decisions and actions of the WGC?"

"No, I don't agree. When I retired from the WGC, I retired from the WGC. I rarely get involved in any of the decisions or actions taken by the WGC. I give my opinion only when asked."

Lara smiled and turned back to Jason Gould. "Mr. Chairman, do you agree with Mr. Gabriel's assessment of his relationship with the WGC?"

Jason smiled. "Without question, Lara. As a matter of fact, unless we ask him for his opinion, we're not going to get it. Mr. Gabriel has an uncanny mind for simplifying the seemingly complicated and his foresight is astounding. Given all that, we still try to hold our requests to a minimum."

"Well, that should put to rest any opinions to the contrary." Lara turned back to Alex, as she nodded in acknowledgment of the truth of Jason Gould's statement. "So, Mr. Gabriel, how do you feel the world is progressing under the leadership of the WGC?"

"The state of the world and its record answers that. The condition of the planet and its people is currently in a place that could not have been conceived of two decades ago. Quite literally, the world has become a place where all its peoples have gained a much brighter future. I am extremely proud of what the world, under the guidance of the WGC, has accomplished."

"As well you should be, sir. However, this reporter cannot believe that you, Alexander Gabriel, the man that led the WGC in the complete takeover of the world's governments is just sitting around in a rocking chair watching time go by."

"Well no, I've got other projects that occupy my time. I'm still putting in some pretty long days."

"Would you like to share with the world what those projects might be, sir?"

"Not at this time, Lara. Loose lips, as they say. But, in a year or two we might have something exciting to share."

"Can you give us a hint?"

"Not yet. It's been my experience that once a hint is given, the questions never stop, so we'll wait a year or two before we let this cat out of the bag."

"Then, I guess we'll have to wait. Thank you, sir." Lara smiled as she turned toward Joan Hocket. "Madam Secretary, how would you describe the state of the social programs that you and the WGC have instituted over the past decade?"

"Over all," started Joan, "I'm extremely pleased. We have all but eliminated starvation in all corners of the world. In parts of the Middle East and parts of Africa, there are still a few people living in the Stone Age whom we can't seem to convince to take the offered help. But, they amount to less than 3% of the world's population.

Worldwide unemployment is at an all-time low. Health care is at an all-time high and improving daily. A good education is now available to 81% of the world's children. We have some work to do in a few Islamic countries. Slowly but surely, as they say." Joan all but rolled her eyes. "Aid to the truly needy has improved dramatically since we eliminated most aid to the world's freeloaders. So, to repeat myself, I am extremely pleased."

"Thank you, Madam Secretary." Lara turned to Alexandra.

"Madam President, you had some massive shoes to fill with the retirement of your cousin. And by all accounts, you have filled them with great skill and wisdom."

Alexandra smiled which made her look even more like her beautiful mother, Colleen. "I have not had to run the WGC all by myself. Chairman Gould and the rest of the WGC leadership and I work in concert, as was the case with my cousin. My success was ensured when you combine that fact with the reality that all my life I've had the best role models and environment imaginable. I was not only raised and nurtured by my wonderful parents, but by these incredible people sitting here with me today. Some of their knowledge and abilities were bound to rub off on me." Alexandra smiled again, "I don't think anyone could ever fill my cousin's shoes. But thank you for suggesting that might be the case."

"Not at all, Madam President. It is clear to me, and I'm certain most of the world, that you have inherited another Gabriel trait—humility."

"I don't know what to say to that."

"No response is required, ma'am. Thank you." Lara smiled and turned to her right. "I would like to direct my last question to Secretary Ito."

The cameras moved to frame the white haired gentleman on the left side of the table. Douglas Ito's eyes, even at his advanced age, still held a bright sparkle of wisdom.

"Mr. Secretary, it has been widely reported that over the past several years, vast amounts of money, all supplied by Alex Gabriel, have been spent in the construction and reconstruction of nearly half the world's nations. So much money, in fact, that Gabriel Industries and Gabriel International may be close to bankruptcy. Would you care to comment on that?"

A rare smile crossed Douglas Ito's face. "Although it's true that Mr. Gabriel has provided an unimaginable amount of money to the world, estimated at one point at nearly three quarters of his fortune, I am smiling because he still has a couple of WECs left in the bank. Gabriel companies have no chance of becoming insolvent and never have had. As a matter of fact, now that the heavy spending has tapered off, Mr. Gabriel's fortune is actually rebuilding at a steady pace."

Lara smiled. "That is good news." She turned to Alex. "Can we assume that you will continue to provide the funds necessary for the world to continue its remarkable rebuilding?"

"Yes." Alex paused for a moment. "I've been blessed with the skills and knowledge to make a great deal of money over my lifetime. I never really considered that fortune as truly mine. I always felt that someday I would be required to do something remarkable with it. In these past few years, I realized that the wealth I accumulated has always been and will continue to be earmarked for the benefit of the world." Alex smiled, "I, however, will maintain the right, along with the members of the WGC, to spend it as we see fit."

"I humbly offer my personal thanks, as well as those that come from the vast majority of this planet's population, for all you've done and are doing for our betterment."

"Thank you."

"You are a remarkable man, sir. Thank you and the members of the WGC again for all you've accomplished." Lara turned to one of the cameras. "Back to you, Dan and Bob."

The picture returned to the studio and to the set of the Hanly Jordan News Hour.

"Well Dan, I still remain amazed at the consistent candor of the leadership of the WGC. I find it refreshing, even after all these years."

Uniformed staff stood in the background, ready to pour more liquid refreshments or remove empty plates as the moment dictated.

"A toast," Jason raised his glass of tea, "To the WEC, the world's only currency."

All raised their glasses and smiled as they toasted this monumental event.

"It's been a trying four years," said Alex.

"If the Stone Age Muslims had pulled their heads out of their asses sooner, the transition would have been completed a year ago," added Vance. His dislike for anything Muslim was common knowledge.

"They did slow things down a bit," agreed Douglas Ito.

"A bit?" said Vance, "If we hadn't cut them off from all international commerce, they never would have switched over… ignorant bastards."

"On a much lighter note," said Alex changing the subject, "Teddy Jr. is going to be 11 years old in three days."

"No way," responded Vance.

"Time flies… as they say," said Jason with a smile.

Vance was clearly perplexed, "Shit! I forgot. I've got to get something in the mail to him."

"We've been a bit busy," said Alex.

Teddy Oldaker grew up living next door to Alex and since they were toddlers, had been best friends. In 1985 Teddy was killed in a random act of violence by street thugs. But, before his death, Teddy's wonderful ebullience and sense of humor greatly influenced Vance's stoic personality. No one had seen Vance laugh prior to meeting

Teddy but after that first encounter, Vance's personality seemed to have lightened up considerably.

Teddy was a natural born entertainer who went on to become an international movie star and was posthumously awarded an Oscar for best actor.

Vance's deep affection for Teddy transferred to his clone, Teddy Jr. or Junior, as he is now called. This fondness was never understood by anyone, since from all appearances, they seemed to have nothing in common. But, there was no doubt in anyone's mind that Vance would give his life for this boy, regardless of whether he was a clone or not.

"His mom tells me that Junior loves old movies. And old big band music," offered Alex.

"Oh?"

"And there are several sights on the Internet that have such items for sale."

"Thanks, Alex, I'll…"

A quiet chime interrupted the conversation.

"Excuse me," said Vance, breaking off the conversation. He reached into his shirt pocket and retrieved his phone.

"Vance here."

He listened for a moment before asking, "How reliable is this intel?" Vance's eyes narrowed as he listened for another moment. "Transfer your file to my computer and be in my office in 15 minutes." He pushed a button and returned the phone to his pocket.

"Important?"

"Could be. Another spotting of bin Shajea. This time in Syria."

"That is one elusive bastard," said Jason as he took a sip of iced tea. "So elusive," he continued, "that we haven't been able to get an Auratron fix on him in all these years. The man is truly crafty."

"If we had his aura recorded, the rat bastard would have died a long time ago," said Vance.

"No doubt," said Alex.

"It's probably just another case of someone trying to collect the million WECs reward. It's probably a case of mistaken identity, but I have to check it out." Vance wiped his mouth and hands with his napkin and stood up. "I'll let you know how it goes." With that he turned and headed through one of the four doublewide French doors that gave access from the veranda into the mansion.

8:05 p.m.

"Looks like there might be something to this latest spotting of bin Shajea," Vance said as he walked into Alex's private living room.

"Oh?"

"I'm going to head out in about an hour and fly to Damascus. I have to pick up some people and equipment." Vance sat in an overstuffed chair close to Alex.

"He was spotted in Damascus?"

"No, he was spotted in Hamah, quite a way north of Damascus." Vance paused for a moment. "Had three different reports from three unrelated sources."

"Really?" Alex was surprised.

Sheik Muqbel bin Shajea was the most wanted and by far the most hated man on the planet, including by the majority of the Muslim world. After he kidnapped and killed Alex's parents, he managed not only to avoid capture for nearly four decades, but continued to incite a few younger radical Muslims to continue terror attacks in the Middle-East, killing thousands over the intervening years. He was clearly brilliant and clearly a sociopath.

Alex's brow furrowed. "It concerns me that he's been spotted by so many people. It's not like him to be spotted at all."

"We're on the same page on that thought," agreed Vance. "I'm betting there's a rat in the crackers here."

"You be careful, my friend. Shajea may be getting older but that slimy piece of shit is cagey beyond belief."

"We're about the same age, ya know and I'm still pretty cagey myself," Vance smiled, gave a mock salute, turned and left.

Upon returning to his office, Vance made two phone calls. The first was to Captain Sam Maniscalco, his right-hand man. Sam would get the ball rolling on transport and logistics. The second call went to Jeep Hatch, his comrade-in-arms for over forty years. Jeep was now in his late seventies, yet there were few people Vance trusted more to have at his side in any conflict.

"Bin Shajea was spotted by three different people?" asked Jeep.

"That's the intel."

"Well, that's some kind of bullshit. The fucker's up to something."

"Agreed. But what?"

"Something horrible would be my guess," Jeep said sincerely.

"No doubt," agreed Vance. "I'd like you and ten of your best to meet me in Damascus tomorrow evening. Sam will arrange transport. I'll email what I want you to put together in an assault package."

"Yes, sir."

"Jeep?"

"Yes, sir."

"We need to get the fucker this time."

"Yes, sir, we do."

Vance hung up and leaned back in his chair. He began mentally reviewing all he knew about this evil man. What he knew was simple; Bin Shajea was cunning, charismatic and he was a sociopath. This man was truly evil, probably one of the most evil in history, certainly the worst in the past half-century. This animal was responsible for tens of thousands of deaths and many times that many maiming's and mutilations.

Men, women and children are all the same to him, thought Vance. *Just five years ago this piece of shit took control of a grade school for girls in Afghanistan and decapitated all the girls. Girls as young as six years old. Over 80 of them. The son-of-a-bitch…over 80 of them,* Vance repeated in his mind. Tears formed at the thought. *He is also the slimy piece of pig shit who kidnapped Alex's folks, who were two of the warmest and most giving people I've ever known.*

Marian Gabriel, Alex's mom, headed Gabriel Relief International for Alex. GRI was created by Alex and Marian and financed by Gabriel International. Its purpose was to bring relief to the world's most downtrodden in third world countries; those people from countries ravaged by drought, famine, diseases, and civil wars. GRI provided health care for the sick and injured, food for the poor and hungry and as much security as feasible for many of the war ravaged, poverty stricken areas of the world. Untold thousands of people were helped in countless ways by the GRI organization.

A huge job, but she ran it like a well-oiled machine, Vance remembered fondly. *She was a natural leader.*

Norman Gabriel was a rocket scientist. Before his retirement, he worked for Scientific Aerospace Research Corporation (SARC). His area of expertise was pressure hull design and he was the best in his field. Norman was a low-keyed gentleman who Vance loved and respected more than he ever admitted to anyone.

Norm turned out to be one of the bravest men I've ever known, Vance recalled with great sadness.

Bin Shajea demanded a half a billion dollars ransom for their return, and after much discussion and trepidation, Alex paid the ransom.

Within an hour of receiving word that the ransom was transferred into a Swiss account of his designation, Bin Shajea ordered the execution of both Marian and Norman. The hangings were videotaped along with the unspeakable atrocities perpetrated on their corpses after they were dead.

Within hours of learning of the Gabriels' deaths, Vance led the team that retaliated against the terrorists. All of the terrorists who were directly involved and still in the hangar that held the Gabriels were killed outright or taken captive. No matter where they lived in the world, any other terrorists who had been involved with the murders in any way were killed within three months. Bin Shajea managed to escape to Yemen, went underground and disappeared.

It was Vance who found the bodies of Marian and Norman still hanging from a makeshift gallows. It was Vance who cut them down and gently carried their mutilated bodies to a waiting aircraft to be returned to the States. It was Vance who even now, as he remembered, had tears streaming down his cheeks.

DAMASCUS, SYRIA
August 22, 2016
7:36 p.m.

The Gabriel Falcon 80 jet with a WGC logo on its tail landed at the Damascus International Airport at 7:36 p.m. and taxied to a private hangar located on the opposite side of the runway from the main terminal. The door opened and the stairs unfolded. Within seconds, a tall, tough looking man with an Uzi machine pistol at the ready appeared in the hatchway. He quickly scanned the immediate area, ignoring the older man who stood at the base of the stairs. Finding no threat, he proceeded down the stairs. Vance came down just behind him.

An older man with piercing gray eyes, huge white eyebrows and a head as bald as a tank helmet, quickly stepped forward and gave Vance a sharp salute, "It does these old eyes good to see you, sir."

"Hey, likewise, Jeep. It's been too many years." Vance smiled as he returned the salute. Then they shook hands.

"Time passes too quickly," Jeep lamented. "Hey, Sam, nice to see you again, too."

"Good to see you, sir. It's been a while."

The two shook hands as Vance looked up at the early evening sun. "It's real fucking hot here, Jeep."

"I'd like to say you get used to it, but that would be bullshit." He nodded toward the hangar. "Air conditioned in there, and it's where ten of our best are putting together the requested equipment."

Without further conversation, the three headed for the hangar.

"I'm looking forward to seeing the guys," said Sam.

"They're just as crusty as ever," remarked Jeep.

"Let's get that ordinance loaded on the plane and fly outta this fucking frying pan," said Vance.

GABRIEL

HAMAH, SYRIA

8:15 p.m.

A gaunt man of indeterminate age sat cross-legged on a large cushion. He was stroking his gray beard as he read a note that had just been delivered by a young courier. There were five other men in this dismally decorated, cluttered room. Four had black beards of varying lengths and one had a beard dyed red; all were dressed in black, well-armed and looking "mean to the bone."

The middle-aged man observed, "They have landed in Damascus sooner than we thought, but it matters not, we are ready."

"Praise be to Allah," said the five younger men.

Bin Shajea gave an evil smile, "Now, we will see how the satanic Vance Youngblood dies."

10:03 p.m.

The 13 men exited the Falcon 80 onto a much cooler tarmac at the Hamah airport. Vance and Jeep led the other eleven as they walked to the delivery truck that had pulled up to the cargo compartment of the jet.

"Let's get the truck loaded up and get out of sight, ASAP," ordered Jeep.

Two of the men jumped into the cargo hold of the plane and two jumped into the back of the truck. Four others formed a line to the truck and transferred the bundled weapons and related gear hand over hand to the men in the truck. All equipment was loaded efficiently and quickly. Jeep and Vance got into the truck's cab and the ten men jumped into the rear. The last man shut the cargo door and headed for the driver's side of the cab.

August 23, 2016
4:15 a.m.

Just two blocks from the supposed residence of bin Shajea, seven black clad, heavily armed men gathered around a table in a hotel room. A rough mockup of the private residence sat in the middle of the table.

"We have all three exits, including the garage and outside stairway, covered with two men each." Vance pointed out the exits on the mockup. "They're already in place… five of us will be going in here at 04:45. Jeep, I want you and Sam to remain as backup in the van right about here." Vance put his finger on the map. "You'll be able to provide additional cover on the outside stairs and garage from there."

"Wish you would let me or Sam take the lead here, my friend," Jeep said sincerely. "This bin Shajea is an evil sumbitch. Five times, over the past three decades, we've had a shot at him and five times he's managed to kill some of our team and escape."

"That's why you and I are taking this one," smiled Vance.

4:46 a.m.

Exactly 60 seconds after Vance and his team entered the home, large explosions were set off near the three exits. The explosions did not occur right at the exits; the explosives were well hidden in the best places where the WGC teams would cover the exits. These explosions killed six of Jeep's men instantly. At the moment of the explosions, Vance and his four-man team had just cleared the bottom floor and were at the head of the stairs on the second floor. A much smaller explosion destroyed the inside stairway, effectively trapping the five on the second floor.

"Trap!" yelled Vance.

The five went into a defensive mode. Two kicked in a nearby door only to be faced with a hail of automatic gunfire. They were dead before their bodies were flung backward into the hallway.

Vance, without hesitation, pulled the pin on one of his hand grenades and lobbed it into the room. The explosion blew the kicked-in door back out and off its hinges. Vance and his remaining two men dove into the room. That was a mistake. The hand grenade fragments had failed to touch the terrorists inside. They were safely hidden behind heavy sandbag bunkers. They rose up and killed Vance's two remaining teammates. A half a dozen bullets tore into Vance's body. Three were stopped by his body armor. One hit on the left side of his neck, just missing the carotid artery but damaging his third vertebrae, another managed to slip under his body armor at the side and smash into his lower spine and the last hit a glancing blow to the back of his head as he fell face first with his right arm pinned under him. The shooting stopped. The silence was deafening.

4:49 a.m.

"Well, what do we have here?" asked smiling bin Shajea as he entered the room from another door. "Can this be the indestructible Vance Youngblood?" He walked over to Vance's body and gave it a hard kick. There was no movement.

"Turn him over, I want to see this blasphemer's face."

One of the black-dressed terrorists set his AK-47 on top of his sandbag bunker as two of the other four left their shelters and gathered around Vance. The first terrorist bent down and grabbed Vance's body armor and pulled him over. That was a mistake. In Vance's shaking right hand was his Glock 50 automatic.

Then all hell broke loose again. There was another sustained blast of automatic gunfire, but this time it came from outside the room. Bullets tore through the black cotton robes of the three exposed terrorists, spewing shredded meat and bone on the far wall. Another shot was heard, but this one sounded different. It came from Vance's Glock. It struck bin Shajea's right knee, shattering it. Screaming, he collapsed on top of one of Vance's dead team members.

The two uninjured terrorists, who had stayed behind their bunkers, directed their return fire to outside the room.

"Take me out!" bin Shajea screamed in pain.

One terrorist continued a suppressive fire through the doorway and adjoining walls as the other jumped over the bunker and grabbed bin Shajea's robe and dragged him through the second door. The remaining terrorist continued firing as he ran to follow bin Shajea and his fellow terrorist out of the room. His progress was stopped cold as another report from the Glock tore off the back of his head.

4:51 a.m.

A full two minutes passed in silence before their panel truck could be heard shattering the garage door and rapidly leaving the scene.

"Vance, can you hear me?" yelled Jeep from outside the room.

No response. Jeep looked at Sam as if to confirm that the worst had happened. Through the smoke and dust kicked up by the firefight, Sam's eyes stayed riveted on the doorway and into the room as far as he could see.

"Vance!" Jeep repeated.

"Jeep," an almost inaudible voice came from inside the room. "Clear here," the weak voice said.

Jeep jumped up and ran into the room. He was at Vance's side two seconds later. He could see the blood pulsing from the hole in Vance's neck. He quickly reached down and applied pressure on the wound. "Sam," he yelled, "Get the chopper here, now. Land on the roof."

PART 1
DISCOVERIES

CHAPTER 1

THE HANLY JORDAN NEWS HOUR
MARIANA
June 30, 2020

The familiar theme music played as the picture turned from the Hanly Jordan News Hour logo to a live shot of the two news anchors in their normal seats on the set. The camera zoomed in on Dan Jordan as he began talking.

"This is truly a day to remember. . . celebrations are being held in thousands of cities and towns around the world. All celebrating the tenth anniversary of the WGC's world takeover. A day that will certainly live on in history as long as there is history."

The picture switched to Bob Hanly. "No one can deny that, Dan. It was a day that scared the hell out of about half the people on the planet, including me. A day, ten years ago, that changed the world in ways that no one would have thought possible. A day that ended all wars. A day that ended most crimes. A day that began an evolution to a peaceful, productive planet."

"In the past ten years, all nuclear bombs and most armies have been dismantled," added Dan Jordan. "Other than the WGC's small but extremely effective elite force, most nations have just small volunteer reserve armies, mainly for emergencies."

"Worldwide pollution is now down 31%; that's remarkable. And when was the last time we ran a story about starvation anywhere in the world?"

"It's been four years since the WEC became the worldwide currency, which certainly simplified doing business in what has become a truly free-trade world."

"In addition to those remarkable accomplishments, a new study was just completed showing that as many as 43% of the prisons worldwide have been shut down, mostly in the United States. Some are being torn down, some are being turned into decent living quarters for lower income folks, and some are actually being converted into luxury condos." As Bob Hanly continued speaking, the picture switched to an outside view of Alcatraz Island showing landscaped gardens, lawns, swimming pools and several bayside restaurants overlooking the yacht harbor. "You can see why there is a waiting list for a condo on both Alcatraz and San Quentin," Hanly smiled, "seems these are the new yuppie pads. Location, location, location, as they say."

The picture switched to Dan Jordan, "And almost everyone can travel any place in the world without fear of being kidnapped, maimed, or killed. The exception to this freedom would be Alexander Gabriel and the leadership of the WGC. They still have to exercise caution when traveling."

"Notwithstanding all of these improvements, the world is still far from perfect. Although the birthrate is down 14% from what was projected prior to the WGC's takeover, and that's a significant percentage, population control still vexes the WGC. The continuing problem is mainly found in the Muslim and Hindu populations. It's an ongoing battle, but the WGC continues to fight the fight... they have to. They know that, particularly with this population, if an inch is given to any group, then all groups will demand the same inch."

"Although there are fewer nowadays, Muslim terrorists are still trying to disrupt any and all progress being made in Islamic countries." Dan Jordan's face saddened, "It's been four years since Vance Youngblood was cut down in an ambush."

CHAPTER 2

THE STUFF
MOUNT NORMAN
RESEARCH FACILITY
July 1, 2020

The rapidly descending elevator still gave Alex a queasy feeling even after all these years. He involuntarily reached for the handrail. "Damn thing's nearly free fall."

"Yes, sir," Vance's attendant agreed.

Vance grunted acknowledgement, but said nothing else.

Alex turned his head to his right and looked down at his dear friend. Vance's head was supported with an extensive neck brace that was screwed to his skull in four places. His once massive shoulders were still unnaturally broad, but reduced to little more than the bones of an old man. The fingers of his right hand had a slight tremor as they rested on the short control lever at the end of the armrest. His left arm and both legs were useless and looked to be just skin and bone. Vance seemed to be all but bolted into his high-tech wheelchair. He was seventy-four years old; but because of his condition looked a decade older. His white hair had thinned considerably, his hairline had receded a full inch. His light brown eyes were no longer cold and certainly didn't hold the menace they once displayed.

Never a complaint from this man, not one, thought Alex, *not in the four years since the ambush… not a single complaint*, Alex finished his thought. *I doubt even Teddy could make him laugh. . . well, maybe Teddy could. . .*

Vance had become a near total recluse following his paralyzing injuries, allowing less than ten people to visit, and only half of those people he saw regularly. Lara Lions was one person he refused to see under any circumstances. He did not want her to see the cripple he had become. For the first year, Lara put in a request every week for an audience with Vance, but it wasn't to be.

They waited in silence for the elevator to come to a relatively smooth stop and the doors to slide open. Alex motioned for Vance and his attendant to exit first, and then followed them out. They turned right and headed down a wide hallway lined with glass walls and doors on both sides. Lab techs were busy with their projects. In the labs where hazardous materials were used there were two sets of double-sealed doors and HazMat signs were prominently posted. One lab contained radioactive materials and also had solid walls and a double-sealed door. This lab was off limits to most in the complex. The three men stopped in front of a door at the end of the hall; the door slid open automatically. Vance's attendant took up a station just inside the door and Alex and Vance entered and approached a workbench in the middle of the lab where Dale Isley, Chuck Kroll, and four other individuals were standing. The other four were members of Dale's team: Dr. George Beitzel, a biochemist who had been with Norman Research for three years; Dr. Amanda Patrick, a mechanical engineer, who'd been part of the team for just over two years; and two newcomers to the lab, Dr. Jer Liedeker, a neuroscientist, and Dr. Orlando Savy, an orthopedist.

Dale had remained quite dapper over the years; he didn't seem to age much. Just a few gray hairs at the temples gave any clue to his age; to anyone's knowledge, he led a clean life and didn't have any vices. Research was his only passion and he was still considered the finest mind on the planet. It was widely believed that Dale's acumen was well ahead of his peers worldwide in the areas of physics and microbiology.

Chuck, on the other hand, had put on a good 30 pounds and his hair was reduced to a dark ring around a bald dome. Alex himself looked a bit younger than his chronological 66 years. Other than the 11 pounds he'd put on in the past decade and thinning gray hair, he seemed to be in good condition.

Chuck spotted the two first, "Ah, here they are." The five others turned to greet the two newcomers.

Alex and Vance shook hands with the six. Following the usual pleasantries, Alex said, "I know from years of experience that you two don't call me to your lab unless you and your teams have come up with something special," Alex smiled.

"You're welcome anytime, Alex," smiled Chuck. "We'd just like to have some advance notice so that we can put the booze away and hide the girls! But you're right, our friend Dale has done it again." Chuck turned to Dale, "I'll turn this demonstration over to you."

"What have you got?" asked Alex.

"Some new stuff that I think you'll find interesting."

"I have no doubt."

Dale nodded toward the back of the lab, "Let's head over there and we'll give you a show and tell."

Dale led the way and the rest followed him across the lab to a small stainless steel table at the rear of the lab. The seven gathered around, leaving room for Vance's wheelchair. This table was uncluttered—unlike most of the other work areas. It held a spool about four inches in diameter and six inches high, wrapped about half full with what appeared to be light brown wire about the thickness of a kite string. A foot long piece of this wire was sitting on a glass tray that sat next to a small transformer. Protruding from one end of the transformer were two thin wires about three feet long with alligator clips attached.

"This is the stuff." Dale picked up the piece of wire and handed it to Alex.

"Oh," Alex seemed surprised. "I thought this was wire, but it doesn't feel like it. Feels funny."

"Let me have it for a second." Dale took it back and attached an alligator clip to either end and handed it back to Alex. "Hold the clips between your thumb and forefingers."

"This going to shock me?"

"Shouldn't," Dale smiled.

"Shouldn't?" Alex smiled as he took the wire and held it by the alligator clips.

"Put just enough tension on it to take out the sag," suggested Amanda.

Alex complied and pulled the ends apart until the wire was straight.

"Ready," Dale asked with a smile.

"Shoot," replied Alex.

Dale reached over and pushed a button. One clip pulled out of Alex's fingers and dropped to the lab table. Dale took his finger off the button.

"Hey," said a surprised Alex, "let me try that again... now that I know what to expect."

Alex picked up the dropped end and took out the slack, "Hit it."

Dale pushed the button. Alex held on this time. "This has some pull to it."

Alex continued to hold the wire against the pull.

"Okay, let it pull your hands toward each other."

Alex let the wire pull his hands together. The wire shrank to about half its length as it increased in diameter.

"You're looking at a synthetic muscle fiber." Dale announced with a big smile on his face. "Actually a bit stronger. That pull you felt was created with just one 10,000th of a volt."

"That's impressive. What's it made of?" asked Vance.

"It's an entirely new compound which is made up of 30% of a super ferrous new metal, bound with a really interesting material. We extrude these fibers using a modified pasta-making machine, believe it or not. Then we just run it through an insulating dip, which is only about a micron thick and then we roll it on a spool. We can then cut them to any length we want. Once cut, each separate strand gets a high intensity magnetic charge that permanently fixes the magnetic molecules in line with the poles. The fiber and insulation, among other things, are tougher than a boot. Take a look over there." Dale pointed to another stainless steel workbench. On it were five different pieces of equipment, each active. "This stuff is being put through every fatigue regimen we can devise."

Alex could see the small machines pulling, twisting, rubbing, freezing, and heating the fiber strings.

"They have been working that way for a month now. We had a couple of failures at first, but with a simple adjustment to the formulas, it fixed them."

"Well I'm sure you have a use in mind for this magic stuff?"

"Oh yeah! It is our intention to duplicate actual muscles using these synthetic fibers."

Alex was intrigued, "And?"

"That's the best part. We're going to use it as a base to create prosthetic limbs that hopefully have the same agility, range of motion, and strength as a natural limb."

"What?"

"Yes, sir," Dale was quite serious. "We are going to build a prostheses as close to a natural limb as possible. Every fiber, muscle, tendon, cartilage, bone and skin will ideally look and work as a natural limb."

"Skin too?"

"If we're right, this new compound will do amazing things. It has incredible properties. I don't think we have even begun to see its potential."

Alex and Vance were quite intrigued and said nothing for a few moments.

"Have you got a name for this magic compound yet?" asked Alex.

"We have," answered Chuck, "but Dale is resisting."

"Well," said Dale, "I'm not the only one responsible for the creation of this stuff."

"Really?" said Amanda, "Without you, this material would not exist. Without any of us, it would. It just might have taken a little longer, but I doubt it."

"Okay, so what's the disputed name?"

Five of the six scientists in unison said, "Isleium!"

"Ah, geeze," responded Dale.

"Perfect," said Alex. "Isleium it is. End of debate." Alex paused for a moment then asked, "What can we do to help you?"

"We'd like to expand our research... considerably."

Alex looked at this genius, his friend. The man whose brilliant inventions and insights made it possible for The WGC to take over the world's governments ten years ago.

Alex didn't give it a moment's thought, "You have, at your disposal, unlimited funds... you always will have."

Dale smiled. "Thanks, Alex. I'll try to give you your money's worth."

"If you don't, it will be the first time."

Vance had remained silent throughout this dialog, but he was paying close attention. "How will it be powered?" he broke his silence.

"Right now, we're thinking about putting rechargeable power cells inside the artificial bone, where the marrow would normally be."

"We've come a long way on storage batteries," offered Chuck. "We can store a lot of power in a small space."

"Gabriel Industries is making a lot of money on that technology," Alex smiled, "Thank you very much."

"What makes it work? How does it know to move?" It was clear they had Vance's attention and it was also clear he didn't care one bit about the profit Gabriel was making on batteries.

"We're working on that major challenge."

"Any ideas?"

"Oh, sure, we've got a couple of good ones. Actually there is one idea with two approaches. First one is to have micro transmitter-receivers attached to the nerve endings that lead to the severed limb. The prosthesis also has a similar transmitter/receiver. We're thinking that if the brain is still sending signals via the nerve, there is a possibility that we can read that signal and transmit it to the prosthetic."

"That would be bridging the gap in severed nerves," Vance observed.

"Exactly," Dr. Beitzel answered, "And that brings us to our second approach." Beitzel paused for a moment. "This one could change everything." Beitzel looked at Dale. "I believe you should cover this."

Vance and Alex turned toward Dale. "You have our undivided attention," said Alex.

"It may be possible for the stuff… 'Isleium' to simulate nerves as well as it does muscles and… maybe at the same time," said Dale. "We think the stu… 'Isleium' might be ultra-programmable."

"Kinda like stem cells without the reproduction. . . we think," injected Beitzel.

If Vance's head could have snapped around, it would have. Neither he nor Alex said a word. The enormity of what was just said was taking a moment to settle in.

"We have just begun working with it as a possible nerve." Dale was quiet for a moment. "It might be possible to have an Isleium nerve cluster meld with the natural nerves bridging the gap and…" He abruptly stopped talking for a moment and then turned to Vance. "I know what you must be thinking, but you need to understand there are no promises here. We may be just jousting at windmills."

"I do understand, but the hope you just gave me for a future will keep me going." Vance's voice had a positive tone, something no one had heard since the ambush that crippled him.

Alex turned to Dr. Savy, "Do you envision that it will be attached by straps the way prosthetics are now?"

"No. Let's say in the case of an entire arm replacement our idea is to actually create a ball for the existing shoulder socket, elbow or wrist joints, and then replace the old bone with a lightweight titanium one. We'll attach the Isleium muscles to the shoulder or elbow in the same manner as natural muscles. It becomes their arm. We think we can use natural skin to cover as much as possible of the prosthetic. From that point on then the prosthetic has artificial skin with maybe a small band or a tattoo to cover the seam."

"So the new limb is never removed?"

"That's our intention," answered Beitzel.

"We think by putting the Isleium fibers together, just as actual muscles are banded, we can create natural movement," Dr. Beitzel went on. "We hope to connect the muscles with artificial ligaments and tendons to the real bones or titanium bones with an adhesive so strong that they almost fuse with the material it is bonding. By the way, everything described up to this point, including the adhesive is based on this same material, Isleium."

Vance looked pensive for a moment and then asked quietly, "Could you make an entire body this way?"

It didn't take this group of geniuses to know what Vance was thinking. Dale looked Vance square in the eye. "We've been thinking about that."

CHAPTER 3

THE BODY
Year 2024

The hologram was showing a computer simulation of a life-size figure of a man with the skin removed. All bone, tendons, veins and muscle were clearly visible in great detail, but the image was not the familiar image of the inner workings of the human body. It was different and unnatural.

Viewing the unusual image were Vance, Alex, Chuck, Dale, and Drs. Liedeker, Beitzel, and Patrick. Other scientists were busily working in additional areas of this large lab.

"The bones are made of a titanium alloy. The muscles and nerves are, of course, Isleium." Dale pointed his laser at an intersection of muscle, tendon, and bone. "Over the past three years, the adhesive at these connecting points has worked perfectly; we've had no failures in any of the prosthetics."

"To the prosthetic users of this world, you genuinely have become a saint," Alex said.

"Helping those who have lost limbs or have had paralysis has been the most rewarding achievement of my life," Dale said sincerely.

"Tens of thousands. . . actually, I believe the number approaches 200,000," added Alex.

"Except for a small percentage," said Dale sadly.

"Under five percent," said Alex.

Dale looked at Vance, "I'm sorry Vance, Of all the people I wanted to help…"

"Shit happens, my friend." Vance paused for a second, then smiled, "You can make it up to me by building me a whole body."

Dale returned the smile, "We're going to try."

"I will point out that what you've already accomplished is nothing short of spectacular," said Alex.

"We owe that success to my brilliant team and to you, Alex. There's no way we could have accomplished this without the best minds and whole lot of WECs."

"The automated manufacturing of these prosthetics is almost as remarkable as the prosthetics themselves," remarked Chuck. "Few could afford one of these sophisticated prosthetics if they had to be handmade. The programming for the computers that run the manufacturing machines is the most extensive I've ever seen or heard of . . . to say nothing of the machines themselves."

"We had 34 of the best programmers in the world working for over a year on this project… incredible accomplishment," added Beitzel.

"Nobody else could have done it, even with all that," remarked Alex. "So let's see what you've come up with."

Dale nodded in acknowledgement and turned back to the hologram. "Computer, remove the front rib cage." The hologram's image instantly changed to show the inside of the chest.

Vance moved his joystick and his chair moved forward a little closer to the hologram. Alex stepped forward in tandem and stood next to Vance.

"See these?" Dale used his laser to point to two odd-shaped objects about 4 inches in diameter and 6 inches long located on either side of a sophisticated-looking contraption taking the usual position of a human heart. "These are actually bellows, lungs of a sort. We don't need oxygen but the air circulation helps cool this small fission reactor," Dale pointed to the reactor. The reactor was somewhat larger a normal heart. It was festooned with two large tubes, a dozen or so smaller tubes and wires of every color. "And here," Dale pointed to a smaller object, "is a circulation pump which simulates a heartbeat and serves as an integral part of the cooling system for the reactor. It distributes the heat around the body, and acts as a radiator in much the same manner as the human body. In addition, we hope that it gives our creation a real life feel."

"I suppose the respiration and heartbeat increase as the workload increases?" said Alex.

"Yes sir, that's the plan," answered Dale.

"Really? I was kidding."

"No point in using fuel while at rest."

"Of course not," Alex smiled. "How long before you can actually build one of these?"

"At our current rate of progress, we're thinking just about two years."

CHAPTER 4

THE HONOR
THE HANLY JORDAN NEWS HOUR
2026

Dan Jordan was on camera as he shuffled some papers in front of him.

"Okay, it looks like we're ready to switch to a live feed from the mall in Washington D.C. Take it away, Lara."

"Thanks Dan. We are just a minute away from the president's unveiling of a monument-size statue of Dr. Dale Isley. I can't wait to see it; I've had the pleasure and honor of spending some time with Dr. Isley over these past eight years and I can tell you there is not a nicer or more caring person in the world." Lara gestured around her. "As you can see, this occasion is being given the interest it deserves."

The shot of Lara was pulled back to reveal additional cameras and crews reporting their stories live for the four major networks. Lara was the only reporter used on the island of Mariana because of the WGC mandate, but news stories in other parts of the world were reported on by whomever wanted to cover the story. This was clearly one of those occasions. In addition to the press, there were thousands of spectators sitting in the temporary stands and standing behind the restraining ropes. A good percentage of those in attendance were clearly the beneficiaries of Dale Isley's brilliant discoveries. These grateful people identified themselves by wearing a green armband to honor the man who made their bodies whole again.

The cameras switched back to a large covered statue with a dozen dignitaries sitting in front of it. Along with the President of the United States sat Alexander Gabriel, Dale Isley, Jason Gould, Alexandra Gabriel, and the Secretary of the Interior. The camera moved back to Lara.

"I believe that this man will be remembered as one of the great geniuses in history. His name will be held in great esteem along with Einstein, Newton, Da Vinci, Galileo, Beethoven and the like. This statue, to be dedicated today, is probably just the first of many yet to come. The world's nations have historically honored their great men and women with great works of art. Few in history could claim a more significant contribution than Doctor Isley. He is responsible for hundreds of thousands of amputees and paralyzed individuals regaining a complete life again."

The camera view became a split screen with Lara on the left and Dan Jordan on the right side.

"And what a humble man," added Dan. "I guess it was all they could do just to get him to attend the dedication ceremony."

"That's right, Dan; even then he argued that most of the credit goes to his team for the research and work and to Alex Gabriel for the funding."

"Well, despite his patently humble personality, I suspect, as you've stated, this clearly will be the first of many statues to honor this brilliant man," said Dan.

"Absolutely," agreed Lara. "There are already dozens of statues of Alexander Gabriel around the world. And he, like Dr. Isley, remains humble and reclusive." Lara looked at the podium. "And now, here is the President of the United States."

The picture switched to the President. "We are gathered here today to honor a man who has literally changed the world in so many ways that they are hard to enumerate. But today, we are honoring this man for his contribution to the betterment of hundreds of thousands of disabled human beings around the world. I could go on singing this man's praises. . . but that is not why you are all here today. So without further ado, I give you Dr. Dale Isley."

As the President pulled the cord, the large cloth cover seemed to float off the statue, landing at its base. On top of a ten-foot tall marble pedestal was a 20-foot tall bronze statue depicting Dale Isley in a lab coat slightly bent over as he helped a smiling young man out of a wheelchair. It was magnificent and clearly a work of love. It was a perfect depiction of Dale and his work.

The crowd, in unison, gave a loud "Awe," then applauded and whistled in appreciation. Along with the thousands of people in attendance, the President was smiling and clapping enthusiastically. The applause went on for a full minute. As the applause began to abate, the President held up his hand to signal he was about to talk.

"This stunning piece of art," the President began, "was created by a master sculptor from Italy, Sergio Mattiola, whose own daughter lost an arm in an accident while helping her father put together a sculpture in his studio. She has since received her new fully functional arm. Mattiola refused any payment for his work on this incredible statue."

CHAPTER 5

TRANSFERENCE
NORMAN RESEARCH CENTER
MARIANA
July 21, 2027

Vance had been on edge for almost two weeks. His robot was in the final stages of completion, and time was dragging. He had a short temper and was snapping at everyone around him. Had he acted this way when he was full bodied and menacing, there could have been a serious problem. As it was, he had three attendants quit in the past week. Dale finally had to request that Alex intervene and ask Vance not to visit the lab until Dale told him it was time. Vance reluctantly acquiesced. Of course, they had already tried Isleium nerve replacement therapy on Vance and unfortunately, he was one of the 5% whose nerve damage could not be corrected. It was the most heartbreaking failure Dale had ever experienced.

August 2, 2027

"Vance, my friend, could you come to the lab tomorrow morning?" Dale said over the phone.

"It's ready for me?" Vance asked; his excitement couldn't be masked.

"Yes, sir. We believe we have the bugs out of it," Dale paused for a moment, "I'm certain that Beitzel has already told you that this is going to take some time. Maybe a month of working two or three hours a day."

"I have plenty of time, Dale... plenty." Vance paused for a second, "I can't wait to see my robot."

Dale smiled. "We came up with a better name than robot or android or cyborg. We've named it a SLF, an acronym for SYNTHETIC LIFE FORM," said Dale, "pronounced "Self" not S.L.F. Your SLF is extremely lifelike, if I do say so myself. We'll all probably feel like packing guns once we put some hair on it."

"Music to my ears."

Dale smiled again, "We've been using a physically fit associate, actually he was a world-class athlete in college, spend two hours a day wired to your SLF while running, lifting, punching, jumping, twisting, dancing, and touching all manner of textures with all parts of this body. We're trying to put the entire human physical coordination into its system prior to you assuming control. Don't want you flopping around like a fish out of water. When we transfer all of your knowledge, emotions, reflexes, and a thousand other things we haven't yet thought of, be prepared that we may have to put your new mind and body through each process again in order to get everything coordinated."

August 3, 2027

Vance motored himself into the dedicated lab at 8:00 the next morning; his new attendant waited outside. Inside, waiting for him, were Dale Isley, George Beitzel, Orlando Savy, Jer Liedeker and three computer techs. As he wheeled toward the other men, Vance's eyes were darting around the totally uncluttered lab. He was visibly nervous. He soon spotted what looked like a big man sitting on a chair covered with a white sheet just past the other men. His wheelchair stopped immediately.

"Can I see my SLF?" asked Vance without preamble or humor.

"You can," said Chuck, "but so you realize, it is not complete cosmetically. We can't put in the eyelashes, brows and hair yet. It... you will look much better when we're done."

"Show me," Vance all but commanded.

Beitzel walked over and removed the sheet. The SLF was dressed in dark blue sweat pants with nothing above the waist. Its skin tone looked as if it were alive. Veins, muscles and tendons were quite visible and life-like. Dozens of electrodes were attached in various places to the chest, neck and back. The SLF's eyes were shut as it sat ramrod straight on the stool.

Vance's eyes displayed mild surprise but did not stray from the sitting figure before him. He said nothing as he scanned the entire body. Then he drove his chair slowly around the sitting SLF. He took in every inch of the thing.

Dale said, "What do you think?"

Vance said nothing for a full minute as he made another turn around the SLF. Then, surprisingly, he smiled through the tears that had formed in the corners of his eyes, "I think I'm one big, handsome sumbitch."

There was an almost audible sigh of relief.

"I'm pleased you think so," said Dale to the affirmative expressions of the others.

The scientists had built this prototype SLF to Vance's exact specifications, as he was when he was in his prime. The huge shoulders, large chest and arms, the relatively narrow waist, muscled abs, and tree-trunk legs were all there.

"You're going to look a lot more like your SLF in a few minutes," smiled Dale. "We've got to shave your head smooth so this cap makes perfect contact." Dale picked up a wig stand. On it was what looked like a shower cap with thousands of tiny wires, almost as numerous as hair, protruding from it. All the wires were collected at the back of this cap, which looked like a covered ponytail and led to a large computer consol.

"Get to shaving," responded Vance.

While a lab assistant was shaving Vance's head, Dale and Liedeker were fitting the SLF with an identical cap.

For three weeks Vance sat in the lab at least three hours a day hooked up to his SLF. It was mentally exhausting work. They had him blinking, winking with both eyes, frowning, smiling, yawning, raising eyebrows, whistling, talking, yelling, growling, singing, and so on, all while being wired to his SLF brain. Liedeker's team of techs sat at their computers making adjustments to the SLF's functions as they requested specific movements from Vance. Sometimes he was asked to repeat the same movement more than a dozen times. They were monitoring the SLF's face. Once the expressions or movements on both faces matched exactly, they went on to the next one. No matter how many times he was asked to repeat a movement, Vance complied without a single comment or complaint.

August 24, 2027
9:00 a.m.

Vance was on his last scheduled visit to the lab. Again, he was hooked up to the SLF. An hour into this session, he abruptly stopped complying with the requests coming from the techs.

"What the hell?" said Chuck who was sitting at his station in front of the EEG monitor.

All turned toward the monitor and all could see there was definitely no brain function, nothing but flat lines. There was a stunned silence. This was not expected to happen.

Beitzel, after a brief moment, quickly bent over Vance and checked for a pulse. . . none. Respiration… none. Beitzel stood upright with an alarmed look on his face. He turned to the others, "He's dead!"

"Oh my God," exclaimed Dale. His head snapped around to look at the SLF. It sat motionless, still attached to hundreds of wires.

"Oh, shit!" said Chuck as he adjusted the dials on the monitor.

"CPR, NOW!" screamed Beitzel. "Get him out of that chair and on this table." With a sweep of his arm he sent an array of equipment scattering to the floor.

Chuck ripped the wired cap off Vance's bald head and dropped it on the floor. Liedeker quickly did the same with all the sensory leads attached to Vance's body. Two techs quickly grabbed Vance by his boney arms and pulled him out of his wheelchair. A third tech took him by the ankles and the three had no trouble lifting and lying Vance on the table.

"Oxygen mask and defibrillator are in my lab. Bill, go get them." Beitzel yelled as he leaned over Vance's lifeless body and began pumping his chest.

It seemed like an eternity before the tech returned with the oxygen and defibrillator—but it was less than two minutes.

Beitzel quit his CPR and attached the oxygen and defibrillator. He turned the oxygen on then set the dials on the defibrillator. "Stand clear!"

The jolt of electricity barely caused Vance's body to move. Beitzel put his stethoscope to Vance's chest and listened. After a brief moment he turned to the defibrillator and increased the voltage. "Clear!"

Again there was little movement and again Beitzel leaned over and applied the stethoscope. He detected no heartbeat. He repeated this three more times before he looked up at his colleagues and slowly shook his head, "He's gone."

"Oh, no, no, no," cried Dale. "No, no." Tears began forming in his eyes. He turned to the sitting SLF but he just stood looking down at it, clearly not knowing what to do next.

Thirty seconds passed before anyone said anything. Only the soft beeping of a monitor could be heard.

"Lots of activity in the SLF brain," said Chuck whose eyes were now glued to the SLF's monitor.

Dale's head snapped around. "What?"

"There's a lot going on in that head,"

Now everybody turned to look at the SLF's monitor. The EEG was chaotic; it was showing wild spikes and valleys, and a lot of 'em. Nothing like an EEG of a human.

"Oh, Jesus," said Beitzel.

"Oh, Vance, what have I done to you?" Dale said softly. He had clearly taken responsibility for Vance's death.

As if on cue, the SLF started twitching, just a little at first but within seconds the twitches began turning to spasms.

"Grab him," yelled Beitzel, "Hold him into the chair."

The techs jumped into action, two grabbing the SLF's upper arms and a third wrapping his arms around the tree trunk legs. Quickly, it became all they could do to keep the SLF from falling out of the chair. But within a few seconds the spasms dwindled back to mild twitching, then all movement stopped.

"Jesus!" one of the techs uttered as he released his grip.

"Look here," said Cuck.

The SLF's EEG was changing. It was slowing down. The spiking lines began to round and soften. A cohesive pattern started shaping up.

The six men stood mesmerized as the pattern displayed on the EEG monitor began to resemble that of a human.

A low growling sound started from behind the six. They all spun in unison to face the SLF.

"What the…"

The SLF's eyes began blinking rapidly. Its head began moving from side to side. Then both motions suddenly stopped as it looked up at Dale.

A full minute passed before…

"I am here, gentlemen" came an unnaturally low-pitched voice from the SLF. "All of me… I'm all here."

Not a sound came from the stunned scientists; none even drew a breath until Dale screamed, "YES!" as tears flowed freely from his eyes.

10:15 a.m.

The scientists were in the middle of removing all electrodes and the skullcap while the Vance SLF was carrying on a conversation with Dale and Chuck.

"Thought we'd lost you," said Dale for the third time since Vance became animated.

"I know you did," said Vance with considerable tenderness.

"I was so overwhelmed with grief, I couldn't think. It was the most horrible feeling I've ever had." Dale started to tear up again.

Vance looked at Dale. "I saw you crying, my little friend. I'm sorry I scared you."

Dale just nodded.

"Can you tell us what went on in your mind?" asked Chuck.

"No, not really. It seemed my head was full of loud static that seemed to last for a very long time. But it started becoming quieter and then things started clearing up—and they still are, I might add." Vance paused for a moment before continuing. "Once I started hearing words, things came into focus quickly. Took a while to find my voice."

Chuck was taking a last look at the EEG monitor before the techs removed the leads. "It's amazing. Your EEG is well patterned, but certainly not human; got some of the same waves, but there's a couple extra in there."

"Is that a problem?" asked Vance.

"Wouldn't have the slightest idea. We have no data, nothing for comparison. Your mind seems to be operating extremely well, so we'll assume it's fine."

Vance nodded and then asked, "Where's the top to this outfit?" He looked down, "Let's get me dressed, I want to take this body for a ride."

"Vance," said Dale. "We need to conduct a few tests to see how everything is working way before you go anywhere."

"Can that wait?" asked Vance.

"No," said Dale without hesitation.

Vance nodded. "Okay, let's get to it."

"I might point out that Vance's voice is quite a bit lower, deeper if you will, than the "original," said Beitzel. "We can adjust that. How's your hearing?"

Vance stopped talking for a moment and moved his head around. "Loud enough, maybe a little brassy."

Beitzel made notes on his electronic pad.

"Sight?"

Again Vance moved his head looking all around the lab. "What's the best you can have?"

"Perfect is considered 20/20 but 20/10 is not unusual and I've heard of 20/5 once," answered Liedeker.

"Well then, if I have to guess I'd say 20/5, if not better. I can see everything."

"Smell?" asked Beitzel.

"Too good – like a Bloodhound. There are a couple of people in here who need to change their deodorant."

"It's been a tense day," said Beitzel.

"That sure sounds like something the old Vance would say," Chuck said with a smile.

"This is the old Vance, Chuck, just a new shell," said Vance.

"Fair enough," said Chuck with a smile.

"Okay, let's see how you can move," said Beitzel.

"Roger that," responded Vance.

"Let's start easy," suggested Dale.

"Raise your right arm straight out in front of you," said Beitzel.

Vance paused for a brief moment and then raised his arm to shoulder height.

"Left arm?"

Vance raised his left arm up to parallel the right.

"Both straight over your head."

Vance complied with no problem.

"Bring them down to shoulder height and spread them wide."

"Okay, bring 'em down into your vision and make a fist with both hands."

Vance again complied with ease. He smiled broadly as he watched his left hand make a fist several times. Then he folded his arms across his chest. "How am I doing?"

"So far… great!" said Dale, "Perfect, actually."

"Okay, stand up."

Vance nodded, "I can do that."

"Take your time, we're not in a hurry," suggested Beitzel.

"No sweat."

As Vance stood he wavered a bit, but corrected quickly. "How's that?"

"You tell us," said Beitzel.

"It was easy."

"Sit back down, please," said Liedeker.

Vance complied, but sat down hard. Without another word, he stood back up and sat down again, this time slowly and controlled.

"Good," said Beitzel.

"Are you ready to go for a walk?"

Vance looked Beitzel in the eye. "I've been ready. . . for a very long time," he said quietly.

The truth and emotion of that statement was clear. Dale and Amanda looked a little choked up. This was no longer a synthetic being. A living, feeling man was here in this new body.

Vance stood up and took his first step in 11 years.

1:25 p.m.

The team completed all the scheduled tests and Vance did much better than expected. He was easily able to perform physical movements, including running, jumping, and skipping rope. He could even do handstands; his balance was perfect.

Following the physical tests, Liedeker made adjustments to Vance's hearing, voice, and corrected a dozen other minor glitches. The team then pronounced Vance as fit as could be. "Super fit," said Beitzel.

"Hold off on telling Alex what has happened here today," said Vance. "I want to surprise him."

"Okay," said Chuck.

"No sweat," agreed Dale, "But I want to be there."

"Me too," said Chuck.

"You got a deal," agreed Vance. "How long is it going to take to make me pretty?"

"We'll call in the techs right now if you're not too tired. Lots happened here today."

"Gentlemen, I'm not tired at all. I feel as if I've just gotten the best rest I've had in my life… times ten."

CHAPTER 6

GABRIEL MANSION
August 24, 2027
7:22 p.m.

Alex pushed the button on his earpiece. He had a puzzled look on his face.

"What's up?" asked Jason.

Alex didn't answer for a second. "That was Vance."

"Yeah?" Jason didn't see why Alex was confused.

"Well… he sounded different. I'm trying to figure out… his voice seemed a little strange… but upbeat. Had a lilt to it."

"Lilt?...Vance?"

"He said he'd be here in 20 minutes."

Jason looked at Chuck and Dale, "You know anything about this?"

"Couldn't say," answered Chuck.

Jason looked askance at Dale.

"I'm with Chuck," Dale said without being asked.

7:40 p.m.

The four were waiting in Alex's study when Jonathon, the evening butler, walked in visibly upset and on shaky legs to announce, in a quivering voice, that Mr. Youngblood was there to see them. Alex and Jason looked at each other as if to say—why would Vance want to be announced? He had the run of the place. And why did this occurrence shake up Jonathon?

They both quickly glanced at the two scientists before Alex responded to the butler, "Well, Jonathon, show him in."

"Yes, sir." Jonathon turned and left the room only to return in a few seconds. "Mr. Youngblood, sir."

In walked Vance dressed in expensive black slacks and a beautiful pearl gray short-sleeved pullover shirt that did nothing to hide his impressive upper body. His eyelashes were nearly black; his hair and eyebrows were the same with a little gray mixed in. He looked young, healthy, and powerful.

Alex and Jason's jaws hit their chests as they slowly stood without taking their eyes off Vance. They looked like they either wanted to run or rejoice. Chuck and Dale sat quietly with knowing smiles.

Vance was beautiful. He stood with his feet slightly apart as he smiled broadly at the four men. "I wish you could see your faces."

Alex's eyes filled with tears to the point of overflowing. He remained speechless.

Jason's eyes remained dry, but he too was mute.

Vance held his arms out to the side and did a slow turn. "Everything works."

Alex, slowly gaining a little composure, walked over to Vance, put his arms around his friend and squeezed.

8:30 p.m.

While the five were sitting on overstuffed chairs talking about Vance's SLF, Vance would, every couple of minutes or so, get up and walk around the room touching various surfaces, feeling and lifting everything he could reach while continuing the conversation.

"Can't seem to sit still," he explained to Alex and Jason. "Got a real need to feel everything."

"That's interesting," said Dale.

"Hey, you keep on moving and feeling if that makes you happy. We're not having any problem keeping tabs on you," remarked Jason.

"Your voice is almost perfect. It's amazing," said Alex.

"They couldn't get Isleium to work as a voice box but they managed to get a base to treble sound out of it. The actual words come from three speakers located in my throat. The combination sounds good, huh?"

"Sounds great! And seems quite normal. If I hadn't been hearing your voice for the past few decades, I wouldn't know the difference."

"Good, I was kind of concerned about that."

"How do you feel in general?" asked Alex.

Vance walked back to his chair and sat. "I feel free. . . clean."

Alex's brow furrowed slightly, "I'm going to need a little more here."

"It will probably be hard to understand, but I feel euphoric. I have no pain, no… concerns, if you will. The feeling is clean."

"I doubt Alex and I will be able to grasp what you are feeling right now. You have, today, gone from a near totally disabled man to what looks to be a perfect physical specimen. And damned intimidating, I might add," said Jason.

"It's more than that," said Vance. He sat for a full minute obviously in thought. "I didn't realize until now, but most of the physical aches and pains that we are subjected to throughout our lives, don't actually go away. They seem to but they don't . . . they accumulate. They are masked by our mind. It must be true with memories, too. They fade but they're still there, in our subconscious. This mind isn't masking anything. This body has never experienced pain. I have memories of the bad and horrible things I have been a part of or witnessed, but there is no negative drain on me; I just feel clean."

"So," smiled Alex. "You would recommend a SLF mind and body for everyone?"

"I'll hold off on that answer for a while. I've only had a few hours experience. But, I can tell you that of all the thought I've given to how this. . . this body and mind would work, and I have imagined thousands of scenarios, this beats any I imagined by many times. There is no way to describe it. I'm just ecstatic."

Vance looked over at Dale for a moment before walking over and standing in front of Dale's chair. "Would you mind if I gave you a hug?" Vance said softly.

"No, I don't mind." Dale stood. "I would like to caution you about squeezing too hard. I'm not sure you realize your strength yet."

Vance wrapped his impressive arms around the diminutive Dale and squeezed very gently. "There are no words to thank you for what you've given me. You've given me everything. I'll never forget."

The five men sat in silence for a minute, reflecting no doubt on what Vance just said.

Dale broke the silence, "Well, I don't believe we're going to build a lot of these, they're a bit pricey."

Alex looked at Dale. "Apparently, you have some idea what an SLF costs."

"Douglas came by the labs the other day to check out what we had spent a lot of your money on," said Chuck. "He let the cat out of the bag."

"And how much was that cat?" asked Alex.

Chuck looked over at Dale then back at Alex. "Just over 100 million."

"For just one?" asked a shocked Jason.

"Well yeah, but prototypes always cost more. I think we can probably build an SLF now for a tenth of that, and in time, half of that," said Chuck.

"The six million dollar man was a pussy," said Vance with a big smile. He got up and started walking around the room again. The four men watched him move, saying nothing, all wrapped up in their own thoughts.

Jason spoke first, "Not to throw a damper on the moment, but what's your biological body doing?"

"It died about nine this morning," Vance said in a conversational tone as he headed back to his chair.

"What?" Alex sat forward in his chair, clearly shocked.

"Died," Vance repeated as he sat down.

Jason looked over at Dale and Chuck then back to Vance. "Jesus, how do you feel about that?"

"Relieved."

"That's it ... relieved?"

Vance took a moment. "My body has been gone for 11 years. And for 11 years, I've had to endure all sorts of indignities and a myriad of negative emotions because of that body. Now I have my healthy mind and what seems to be a great body. I won't miss the old one."

"Well, that's pretty hard to argue with," Jason said quietly.

"I've got to admit I have mixed emotions here," said Alex. "The original Vance was my dear friend and an invaluable member of the WGC. Not to mention my protector for nearly 40 years. He was as brave, tough, loyal, and resourceful as they come. He gave his all for the world and me. I'm quite sad. I grieve for him."

"I'm still here, boss, really, I'm still here," said Vance.

Alex looked at Vance. "Intellectually I know… I know. But, emotionally I'm having a bit of trouble."

"Me, too," said Jason, "but I'm sure that will pass with a little time. Hell, I'm already getting used to the big lug."

The five smiled at that and sat in silence for a few seconds.

"What would you like done with your old body?" Alex suddenly asked.

Vance knew the answer to that question. "Over the past month, I've given that a lot of thought and I would like it cremated and I would like to bury the urn beside Teddy's grave in Forest Lawn," he said sincerely.

"Really?" said Jason.

"I would. The thought of that makes me feel warm for some reason. I can't explain it."

The deep and binding connection between Vance and Teddy had never been understood by anyone. Vance was truly the hardest, toughest man any one of these men had ever known. And as far as they knew, he had no discernible sense of humor. Teddy, on the other hand, was without question the kindest, warmest, funniest man alive. At one time, Jason admitted that he fully expected Vance to throw Teddy off the cliff at the Gabriel mansion in Newport Beach, but within minutes of their meeting quite the opposite was the case. Seemingly within seconds, the two became fast friends. Prior to that meeting, so many years ago, nobody had ever heard Vance laugh. But Teddy had him doubled over in hysterical spasms for most of the evening. Teddy had a way about him—he could charm any soul; he quickly discovered what amused an individual and, from that point on, they were going to be entertained.

When Teddy was killed, Vance was thrown into a deep depression. At the trial of Teddy's killers, three of the skinheads responsible for his death were acquitted. Afterwards, it was suspected but never pursued that Vance found them, beat them, and hung them in their gang's garage. Not long after that event, the two convicted skinheads were raped and killed in prison. Anyone who suspected Vance had any hand in those killings kept their suspicions to themselves.

"No need to explain anything," said Alex. "Since Teddy's folks have passed on, I guess we're as close to family as there is. I can't see any reason not to bury your body next to Teddy's."

"I'll make the arraignments if you want," offered Jason.

"If you'll get the cremation done, I'd appreciate it, but I'll take the ashes and bury them myself. I'd like to have a little visit with Teddy anyway."

A visit with Teddy? Thought Alex. *That's not something the old Vance would consider. Maybe he'll snap out of it when the newness of this incredible experience wears off. Don't know how I'll be able to handle a "sensitive" Vance.* Alex smiled to himself, but said nothing.

"There is something else," said Alex. "I have thought, for the past couple of years, about the various consequences resulting from the development of this incredible technology. The concern that keeps popping up in my mind is—whether or not the soul, if any, is transferred along with the mind."

Vance looked Alex straight in the eye. "I was not aware of my SLF, at all, until the instant I died. In that instant every last vestige of me, all that I was, transferred here." Vance pointed at his chest. "That absolutely would include my soul… if any."

CHAPTER 7

PIG SHIT
SAUDI ARABIA
October 23, 2027

A WGC elite force of 12 men had just landed in Abha, Saudi Arabia, a small dusty, sun-drenched city about 70 miles north of the Yemen border and just a few miles east of the Red Sea. After 15 years, this area remained about the only area in the world that offered any semblance of protection for those who practiced radical Islam. It's where the worst of the worst went to hide and regroup. It's the place Sheik Muqbel bin Shajea finally made a mistake.

It had been 36 years since bin Shajea masterminded the kidnapping and murder of Norman and Marian Gabriel, and 11 years since the ambush that all but killed Vance. But now he was caught, ratted out by one of his own. The huge reward of ten million WECs offered by the WGC to capture him finally paid off. He was an old, sick, one-legged terrorist who now sat on a filthy floor in what was serving as a jail cell in the basement of the Abha city hall.

The WGC force made no attempt to hide their arrival. Quite the contrary, their pending trip was broadcast on worldwide news a day before they got there. This was huge news. The most infamous and evil man in the world was finally in custody. The world speculated on what exactly the WGC would do?

Two dozen news cameras followed the WGC light cargo plane as it arrived. Twelve men dressed in the military uniform of the WGC exited the plane via the front hatch. One of the twelve men was different. He wore large sunglasses and had a deep hood over his head so that his face could not be seen, but he was clearly in charge.

A modern flatbed truck pulled up to the rear of the boxy plane. Two exceptionally large metal crates were rolled down the lowered rear ramp. The WGC men watched as the truck driver expertly operated the small crane attached to the front of the truck's bed. One at a time, he lifted the metallic crates and set them on the bed facing backward. There was a God-awful racket being emitted from inside the crates. And what the hell was that smell? Once the heavily built crates were loaded and strapped down, the WGC men got into two separate white vans. One van headed for the city center and the other, leading the flatbed truck, headed for a small sports arena just outside the city.

ABHA CITY HALL

Eighteen minutes later, one of the white vans pulled to a stop in front of the Abha city hall. Three men dressed in WGC uniforms and the man in the hooded jacket emerged from the van and headed toward the entrance of the building. The entire time, their trained and experienced eyes continually shifted as they checked the security of the surrounding area.

There were a dozen well-armed Saudi police standing guard at the main entrance and an equal number stationed around the entire perimeter of the building. In addition, four light mechanized fighting vehicles were manned and ready at strategic points around city hall. The Saudis were clearly taking no chances that this evil man might escape their custody. That would not be good for anyone concerned.

The four WGC men were not questioned nor impeded as they entered the city hall. A distinguished and flustered middle-aged man met them in the small central lobby. This was the mayor of Abha, and beside him stood two assistants.

"I will see bin Shajea by myself," said the man with the hood without preamble or introductions. The mayor looked as if he'd lived a hard life but didn't seem as intimidated as his two assistants were by the presence of the WGC. All three Saudis were dressed in the Gelabah garb, the traditional clothing of the region. The mayor was clearly used to giving orders, not taking them, but he knew he no authority over the fit and armed men wearing the WGC uniforms.

"Yes, sir. If you'll follow me, please."

It was obvious the mayor wanted nothing to do with any of this. He cursed the day bin Shajea was brought to him for restraining. He knew that nothing good could come of it.

The four WGC men followed the mayor and his assistants to his office where the hooded man silently signaled the other three to take up defensive positions within the office. The three moved into position with their weapons at the ready. The mayor and his assistants didn't need to be told these were hard men; a quick glance confirmed it.

The mayor said something in Arabic and his assistants quickly moved to their work stations and went about their business. They were nervous and frightened, but kept their eyes glued to the real or imagined tasks on their desks.

"Follow me, sir," said the mayor as he turned to a door at the back of his office.

He led the hooded man through two doors and down a flight of stairs. "He is in there," said the mayor as he pointed to a padlocked door with two Saudi policemen with automatic rifles standing guard on either side of the door.

"Key," said the hooded man as he held out his hand.

The mayor reached into his pocket, produced a key and handed it to the hooded man.

"All of you leave, and leave the doors open on your way out."

"Yes, sir." The mayor signaled the guards to follow as he turned quickly and started up the stairs with the police close behind.

The hooded man waited until the mayor and policemen were gone before unlocking the door and throwing it open. He stepped inside the small dank room.

Bin Shajea was sitting on the dirty floor. He had no choice; there wasn't a stick of furniture in the room and just a single bright bulb hanging from the low ceiling. "Who are you?" asked bin Shajea with contempt, making no attempt to rise.

The hooded man said nothing as he turned his back and removed the light jacket containing the hood and tossed it aside. He removed his sunglasses and put them in his shirt pocket and turned around to face bin Shajea.

Bin Shajea's eyes got huge with terror and he started screaming.

Vance stood with a smile that would curdle fresh milk. "Can your God bring a dead man back to life?"

Bin Shajea kept screaming while trying to scurry away like a three-legged crab. He was desperate to put as much distance as he could between him and the terrifying apparition that stood before him.

"This is going to be a bad day for you," Vance smiled broadly. "A real bad day."

Vance walked over, reached down and grabbed bin Shajea by his long white beard. He turned, and as effortlessly as carrying a briefcase, dragged the screaming bin Shajea through the door, up the stairs, and into the mayor's office where he dropped the old terrorist. "Is everything ready at the arena?"

"Yes, sir," said the WGC captain.

The mayor and his two assistants gasped in disbelief and were transfixed. They could not take their eyes off Vance. One assistant dropped down on his knees and went into a prostrate position. The mayor thought he had seen and lived through it all, but he clearly hadn't. He and his assistant backed up to the farthest wall, the shock clearly etched in their faces.

"Let's load up this pig shit and head out."

"Yes, sir." With that, two uniformed men grabbed the now crying bin Shajea by the arms and dragged him out to the waiting van. The news cameras recorded the whole thing, including Vance as he walked out into the daylight. The reporters went wild. They thought they were in on the biggest story of the year, but now here was a fully resurrected Vance Youngblood with the man who crippled him years ago. This was going to be the biggest news story of the decade. "Holy Shit!" and many other creative expletives could be heard among the reporters.

The two WGC men unceremoniously threw bin Shajea into the back of the van as if he were a sack of garbage. The reporters were crawling all over themselves trying to get pictures as they yelled out questions. The four WGC men said nothing as they got into the van and drove off toward the arena. The news crews ran to their various camera trucks and cars and sped off in close pursuit.

When they arrived at the arena, where the other van and flatbed truck waited, the four WGC men exited to the flash of dozens of cameras recording the event. Questions yelled from the many reporters were ignored. The scene was nearly chaotic.

Two WGC soldiers pulled bin Shajea out of the back of the van and ripped his clothes off leaving him lying naked and whimpering in the dirt. Vance walked over and again grabbed bin Shajea by the beard, hauled him through a gate into the center of the small arena, and dropped him. He then turned and walked back to the exit of the arena as a throng of reporters converged on him like a pack of jackals. The questions came from every angle. Vance held up his hand until the questions stopped.

"I will make a statement to explain what we are doing here today, but there will be no questions. I realize you also have dozens of questions about me personally, but rather than trying to answer them in this setting, there will be a full disclosure next Friday evening on the worldwide news." Vance paused for a moment before beginning his statement.

"In this arena sits the most evil man alive in the world. This piece of shit is responsible for the deaths and maiming of tens of thousands of innocent human beings. He murdered people in all corners of the world. The pain and suffering he caused over the past four decades is immeasurable. He is without soul or conscience. He epitomizes the term 'sociopath'," Vance stopped for a moment, then resumed. "The entire world knows that when he dies he will surely go to hell, but the crazy bastard probably thinks Allah is smiling on him. We want him to know, before he dies, that he will spend the rest of eternity in the lowest level of hell screaming in terror and agony."

The questions started immediately but Vance ignored them. "You may want to direct your cameras into the arena."

Many cameras were already on bin Shajea but within seconds all but one or two had every angle of the arena covered. Most were recording this scrawny one-legged old terrorist as he sat weeping in the dirt of the arena. A couple of cameras remained concentrated on Vance.

The flatbed truck was backed up to the gate in the wall that surrounded the arena. Its crane picked up one crate at a time and placed them over the gate pointing the doors toward the center.

Bin Shajea's terrified eyes became glued to those crates. He began to whine like a hurt dog.

Vance nodded to his captain. Six WGC men turned to the five-foot high wall with their automatic rifles trained on the crates. Two WGC men opened the arena gate, entered, and closed and locked the gate behind them. They climbed on top of the metal crates, pulled the locking bolts and lifted the sliding doors straight up.

Out bolted two of the largest, meanest looking wild boars ever to roam the earth. It was estimated later that these boars must have weighed over nine hundred pounds apiece. If their thick black hairs were any coarser, they would have been quills. Their razor sharp tusks curved a good fourteen inches out of their upper jaw. They were drooling as they whipped their heads around looking for either an escape route or food. In a few seconds, they spotted bin Shajea and started trotting in his direction.

"Oh my God," one horrified reporter managed to get in before the air was filled with expletives from the crowd of reporters. But over this noise could be heard the reverberating cacophony of deep chesty grunting and pounding of cloven hoofs coming from the twin boars barreling toward bin Shajea.

Bin Shajea started screaming, praying, and crying all at the same time. He held out his hands to ward off the coming attack... those were the body parts the boars took first.

CHAPTER 8

A NEW MAN
November 5, 2027

Similar to most of the news conferences over the years, the podium was set up on the front lawn of the Gabriel mansion. Again, there were the standard four cameras and the one reporter, Lara Lions. Lara was now in her early thirties, but appeared several years younger.

Lara looked up from her notes just as three men walked out from the entrance to the Gabriel mansion. In the lead was Alex followed by Vance and Dale. They walked straight to the podium where Alex took the center position and was flanked by his two companions.

Lara was transfixed on Vance. Her mouth was slightly agape. Even after the three settled in at the podium, she continued to keep her eyes on Vance.

It didn't take Alex long to see that there was a problem. "Lara?"

The picture changed to Lara, as she remained focused on Vance.

"Lara? Would you like to get this news conference started?" Alex asked.

Lara's head snapped around bringing her back to reality. "Oh, I'm so sorry, sir. I guess I'm... I'm in shock along with the rest of the world."

"I can see that," responded Alex. The camera shot returned to Alex. "But I'm going to give you a pass on this one. We had a similar reaction when we first saw Vance in his present state. Quite frankly, I still do a double take when he walks into a room."

Lara looked over at Vance. "You look great Van… Mr. Youngblood." There was a little gleam in her eyes. But she wasn't on camera now… Vance was.

Vance smiled slightly and nodded.

Lara resumed her professional demeanor and turned back toward Alex. "I again apologize, Mr. Gabriel. Please go ahead with your statement."

"Thank you, Miss Lamb," Alex smiled. "There has been considerable speculation as to how Mr. Youngblood managed to recover from his near total paralysis and become forty years younger in the process. And, I might add, some of the speculation is quite accurate. All credit and kudos must be given to Dr. Isley and his team." Alex turned to Dale and nodded. "The world is aware what this man and his remarkable team have done for the people suffering from paralysis and amputation. He made their lives whole again through the development of revolutionary new prosthetics and nerve replacements."

"Dale has taken his extraordinary invention Isleium to another level: the making of an entire body. And whose body is better to duplicate or a person more deserving than Vance Youngblood?" Alex smiled and looked over at Vance. "A man who had his body destroyed at the end of his decades-long quest to make the world a safe place. It took Dale and his team just two years to create and build this completely new body for Mr. Youngblood. This body is called a SLF. That acronym stands for Synthetic Life Form. Mr. Youngblood's brain is also made of Isleium but all the memories, emotions, thoughts, needs, compassion, personality, likes and dislikes are Vance's. Through an ingenious process, everything that embodied the organic Vance was transferred to the brain and body of his SLF. And as you can see he operates perfectly. We will now answer a few questions."

Lara went straight to Vance. "Mr. Youngblood," Lara started, "to say the world is startled at your revival is the greatest of understatements. Sir, to have you standing in front of the world's cameras looking like the young, powerful, handsome man you were forty years ago is incomprehensible. In case nobody noticed, I am clearly flummoxed, bewildered, flabbergasted—I have so many questions flying around in my mind, I'm having trouble picking one out."

Vance smiled as he leaned into the microphone. "Just take your time, Lara, we'll wait. Hell, we three were just going to spend the morning sitting around the pool knocking back a few beers anyway." Vance started drumming his fingers on the podium as he stared at Lara with one eyebrow up. Alex and Dale actually laughed.

Lara was further confused by Vance's lighthearted response.

"Oh my God… I… I guess the first question I would ask is, how do you feel?"

"Right now I feel like a comedian."

"Right now I feel like an amateur," Lara responded.

That caused Vance to laugh good-naturedly.

"All right, I'll get serious," said Vance. "I feel wonderful. This SLF body is every bit as good as my original body when it was in great shape. I have no aches or pains at all. My coordination and balance are better than they ever were. And my endurance is far superior."

"Do you feel… human?" Lara was getting into her stride.

"I do. My mind, as far as I can tell, is exactly as it was. Thought patterns, likes and dislikes, ability to think and reason, memories; they're all there."

"It sure seems that way, plus you seem to have added a sense of humor."

"I don't know where that came from," Vance paused for a second. "I really don't."

"On a more technical note, may I ask what your power source is?"

"Nuclear. Got a dandy little reactor residing in my chest, again thanks to Dr. Isley and his remarkable team."

"How long before it runs out of power?"

"We're thinking maybe two-hundred years."

"Really?"

"Yep."

"Do you eat and drink?"

"Don't eat and I have to admit, I really miss that. But I also don't get hungry. I do drink a little. Need some moisture for various functions. Just water mainly."

"Is your SLF body fully functional in all ways?"

Vance smiled again. "Are you asking me out?"

The shot turned to Lara, catching her deep blush.

". . . Ah. . . I hadn't thought about that. . . But now that you bring it up, sure I am." She smiled brightly.

Vance returned her smile, "You have a date."

"Well, that little exchange ought to make the news highlights," said Alex. "Is there any way we can get back to the part that the world is actually interested in?"

"I suspect the world will find that interesting," said Vance.

Alex nodded in agreement.

"Boy, I've broken several unwritten rules in the past five minutes. I apologize, sir," Lara said sincerely.

"We'll live," responded Alex.

"Thank you, sir. I'll endeavor to keep it professional from now on." Lara turned back to Vance.

"How long have you been… reborn?"

"Just over two months."

"You've managed to keep this a secret for two months?"

"Clearly, we have."

Lara glanced down at her notes.

"Is your SLF body as strong as a human body?"

"And then some. We estimate a nearly 50% increase in strength and speed."

"Really?"

"Yes. And in addition there seems to be no end to my endurance. I do not tire."

"That's astounding, but then so is everything else concerning your SLF."

"We, especially me, could not be happier with this SLF body."

"I cannot even imagine. For you to go from nearly completely disabled to super human is incomprehensible."

"I agree. It is to all of us as well."

Lara shook her head in amazement before continuing. "If you don't mind, I have a few mundane questions that were submitted for me to ask?"

"Ask them."

"Do you require sleep?"

"No, but I can and do shut myself off during the night to keep from being bored."

"Does your hair grow?"

"No. It is made from yet another form of Isleium and is very tough, very durable."

"Do you take showers?"

"I do. This SLF body doesn't sweat and it has no discernible odor, but dust and grime can stick to it. Aside from that, like most people I enjoy showering. It's invigorating."

Lara smiled and looked down at her notes. "Thank you, Mr. Youngblood, for your candid and forthright answers. I doubt the world has been as curious about anything since the WGC's takeover 15 years ago." Lara smiled at Vance. "Now, if I may, I'd like to ask Mr. Gabriel a few questions."

Vance nodded.

"Mr. Gabriel, I have a question that has come up from several news organizations concerning the high cost of the Isleium prosthetics. Many in the world seem to feel that these prosthetics should be provided at no cost to the recipients or at the very most, at cost. Would you care to remark on that?"

"Well, I'm a little surprised by that question, but since it has been asked, I'll answer it. First, as you know, almost everyone on this planet now has and pays for health insurance according to their abilities and location in the world. All health insurance policies are required to provide coverage for Isleium prosthetics and nerve replacement, this despite the fact that in the majority of cases the need itself is a preexisting condition. Because of the cost of the prosthetics, worldwide, health insurance premiums, are higher by just under 1%. That means that nearly everybody in the world is sharing the cost of this expensive technology, despite the fact that they are required by only a very small percentage of people. But there was no other practical way to do it.

We at Gabriel Industries, the developers and manufacturers of Isleium prosthetics and nerve replacements, sell these prosthetics and technology at a reasonable profit to thousands of doctors and hospitals around the world. This is called capitalism." Alex paused for a second. "Capitalism is not a dirty word. Without capitalism, the world might still be in the Stone Age, or medieval times at best. Because, Lara, without the expectation of profits, few will invest time or money for any new technology or business. Why would they? Without the profits made by Gabriel Industries over the decades, there would be no Isleium prosthetics."

"We have invested over a billion WECs in this technology. At the price we've set, it will take a full decade just to recoup that initial investment. Had this technology failed, we would have lost those billion WECs. I'm quite certain the world would not take up a collection and return our investment money. The risk of capital loss is the downside of capitalism. Without capitalism the world would be at best where it was 15 years ago before the WGC takeover and quite probably considerably worse off. Does that answer the question to your satisfaction?"

"Yes, sir. And then some."

"Good."

"Another question, if I may?"

"Of course."

"Are there plans to build more SLFs?"

Alex paused for a moment before answering. "There are two more being built as we speak."

"Can you tell us for whom they are being built?"

"Not at this time. I can tell you that we are donating one at no cost to the recipient. A person of great mind and weak body."

"Wow. That ought to get the world started on speculation."

"No doubt." Alex smiled.

"May I ask what a SLF body costs?"

"Let's just say that they're quite expensive."

PART 2
THE SHIP

CHAPTER 9

FIRST LOOK
June 25, 2028

"That's a nice looking neighborhood," remarked Teddy as they passed over the coastline. He was looking down through one of the ten large windows in this ultramodern helicopter as it headed inland. Teddy happened to be on Mariana visiting between movies and jumped at the offer to accompany Alex to this small island 25 miles to the north of Mariana.

"That's the project's bedroom community, just shy of 400 homes. Everyone working on the ship lives there," informed Alex. "That's actually a complete town. It's got everything."

"Lots of pools, it looks like Malibu from up here."

On the helicopter with Teddy and Alex were a contingent of scientists and engineers from around the world, and one scientific reporter who was there to do a continuing story on the progress of this massive project.

About a minute after they passed over the coast, the helicopter started making a wide right turn allowing, passengers on the right side of the craft to see the huge orb that was a starship in the making. They could also see the research facility that curved around the ship on three sides like a horseshoe. The majority of this facility was only four stories tall, the exception being the large elevator shaft located at the top of the horseshoe. That shaft rose ten stories to meet the ship just under the midway point. Compared to the size of the ship, the research facility looked quite small. But it was a modern high-tech research and manufacturing facility that fabricated many of the multitude of smaller parts required to build the ship. It did not manufacture the large essential parts for the project, such as the massive structural beams and pentagon-shaped hull plates. Those were manufactured in other parts of the world and shipped to Mariana.

"Oh my God!" said Teddy.

"Impressive, don't you think?" said Alex. "it's 325 feet or a hundred meters in diameter—a perfect orb. My dad's design," he said proudly. "Right now it kind of looks like a massive bronze golf ball with the top 25% chopped off, doesn't it?"

"More like a Faberge egg with. . . what is the shape of those hull sections?"

"Pentagon, five sided, like the pattern on a soccer ball."

"Oh, yeah, like the military building."

"Yep, that's it."

"Anyway, it looks like a Faberge egg with pentagon dimples to me," smiled Teddy.

"Sculptured dimples. Pentagon inside a pentagon, for strength."

"Cool looking, really cool." Teddy was like a wide-eyed kid.

Alex's memory shot back to 1968 when the first Teddy visited the Gabriel Building in Newport Beach. *Sixty years ago. We were only fourteen then. Now I'm seventy-four and Teddy is twenty-three…hum. But the original Teddy was completely awestruck; he'd never been in a building like that before.* Alex thought sadly, *I really hurt his feelings that day. He was hurt when I told him I owned that forty-story skyscraper. . . Still do, I guess. I shouldn't have kept that part of my life from him for so long.*

"Can't believe anything that size will be going into space."

"What?" Alex snapped out of his brief nostalgia.

"I said I can't believe that big soccer ball is going into space."

"It had better. We're two and a half years into its construction and a whole bunch of WECs." Alex pointed to the left, "The framework is supposed to be completed this week. See those structural beams protruding from the inside? They'll curve in to complete the circle. The bottom 75% already has its outside hull."

"Looks like it's made of gold."

"For what it's costing, it may as well be," smiled Alex. "The hull is actually a composite made of a thin layer of a super ferrous alloy bonded to a thicker layer of an aluminum alloy which, in turn, is bonded to a new, very tough ceramic/plastic about 12 inches thick. It's tricky manufacturing, actually. During the bonding process, the pieces must be molded to form the ship's curve. But when everything is completed and installed, those pentagon sections insulate and add greatly to the structural integrity of the ship. It's the outer skin that gives it kind of a bronze or brassy tint."

As they circled closer, they could clearly distinguish two huge cranes lifting one massive curved structural beam into place. They could see men standing inside the ship guiding the cranes. On the outside were a couple of dozen men on scaffolding, installing the pentagon shaped sections to the completed upper framework.

"How big are those sections, anyway?" Teddy's eyes were glued to the window.

"Nine feet on a side. It takes just over 1,000 of them to make up the hull."

"It's going to take a lot of really big rockets to get that thing off the ground," Teddy observed.

"No rockets at all," said Alex. "New propulsion system. That's what some of your fellow passengers are here to accomplish. They're the experts; they're going to start putting the star-drive together."

"Star-drive? You've got warp engines?"

"Oh hell no—not possible. What we do have is an incredible new propulsion system. It combines two new technologies. The first is called a Synthetic Mercury Plasma Eliminator, shortened to SMPE. This technology will, or is supposed to, eliminate mass."

"Ah – nope, that didn't sink in," said Teddy.

Alex smiled. "On Earth it would be considered anti-gravity. In space it renders whatever is in its field massless. The ship won't have the mass of a speck of dust."

"You gotta be shittin' me."

"I hope not," Alex said sincerely. "The original theory was based on natural mercury, but we couldn't use it because its mass was too great. We're using a synthetic mercury that Dale and his team created—it has twice the desirable qualities and half the mass." Alex could see Teddy's eyes were starting to glaze over but he decided to continue.

"The synthetic mercury will be in five two-foot diameter conduits that run the full circumference of the ship at the midway point. The synthetic mercury is accelerated within the conduit at an incredible speed, which creates a Magnetic Vortex Field, or MVF. This creates antigravity, if you will. We then combine the SMPE with the other new technology, a Magnetic Variance Accelerator, or MVA, which provides thrust and enables the ship to move at incredible velocity.

"My head is starting to turn into a vortex field with all these letters 'n stuff," said Teddy with a confused look on his face.

Alex laughed before continuing. "At any rate, this ship will weigh close to 12,000 tons when complete, but the SMPE will render it weightless."

"Really?"

"Yep, and theoretically this propulsion system will accelerate the ship at 1g up to 98% of light speed."

"1g?"

There was a tap on Alex's shoulder. "May I, sir?"

Alex looked over his shoulder at the gentleman, in his sixties, sitting just behind them.

"Oh, by all means, Doctor," said Alex.

"First," started the doctor, "let me say you have extraordinary knowledge and understanding of this ship. And you explain it well. To be honest, my interruption was mainly an excuse to meet this young man with you."

"Oh, sure," said Alex, "Teddy, I would like you to meet Dr. Chris Garcia, the most highly regarded physicist and expert on SMPEs in the world. Dr. Garcia and Dale Isley are the lead designers of the SMPE and MVA drive that we're going to use in this ship. Dr. Garcia, this is my dear friend, Teddy."

The doctor smiled, "I know who Teddy Stoddard is. You are my favorite actor, young man."

The two shook hands.

"I'm flattered, Doctor, thank you," Teddy said warmly. "I didn't realize you eggheads had time to see movies," Teddy gave his big toothy smile.

"Some don't, I suppose, but I really enjoy them. This is very exciting for me," said Dr. Garcia. "Wait until I tell my children and grandchildren whom I met today—very exciting."

"I'm flattered," said Teddy sincerely. "But compared to what you've accomplished, I'm nothing but a bit player."

"Oh, no," responded Dr. Garcia. "You bring happiness and entertain the world in such a fine way; you're a joy to watch."

"Well, that is the nicest complement I've ever had. Thank you so much," Teddy said sincerely.

"It's quite true, young man."

The helicopter came in for a landing on a pad just ten meters from an entrance to the research facility. Everybody unbuckled and got ready to exit the rear of the craft.

"Why don't we walk together, doctor," suggested Alex. "You can fill in your new friend on the propulsion system."

"Agreed," said Dr. Garcia, "Very exciting."

Teddy raised one eyebrow and gave Alex a look as they stood to leave the helicopter. As they walked down the stairs, they gazed up at the ship.

"Holy shit!" said Teddy. "That thing is really, really big… my God! Didn't see those legs from the chopper… they're really big too."

"Landing gear," said Alex. "Takes six of them connected to those enormous pads to hold the weight." Alex looked over the ship. "I haven't been here for a couple of weeks myself," he said. "They've come a long way."

A paved road led to a large open ramp at the bottom center of the ship. Small, specially designed electric trucks were delivering building materials into the center of the ship.

Dr. Garcia had his hands on his hips, leaning back as far as he could in order to see as far up as possible. "Well, I have to admit this is probably the most impressive thing I've ever seen. You must be very proud, sir."

"I sure will be—if it actually flies."

"If it doesn't, you can always turn it into a real pretty 5-Star hotel," Teddy joked as he continued to look over the ship.

"Okay, and we'll name it "Alexander's Folly."

They, along with most of the passengers from the helicopter, stood for a few more minutes looking at the ship.

"Shall we?" They all started walking as Alex motioned toward the entrance.

"Where were we?" asked Dr. Garcia.

"One-g acceleration," said Alex.

"Oh, right. You see, Teddy, a 1g acceleration simply means that what you feel right now, the gravity that is holding you to the surface of this planet is 1g, or one force of gravity. If you leave the gravitational pull of Earth you are weightless. So 1g acceleration feels like you're still on Earth."

"That doesn't seem like you would be accelerating very fast."

As they approached the entrance door, it slid open; they walked into an air-conditioned interior.

"Well it's actually 9.8 meters per second per second," Dr. Garcia continued, "Or about 32 feet per second per second, if you'd rather."

"Ah… I'm gonna need a little more info here."

The doctor smiled. "Okay, at that acceleration, for every second that you are moving at one g, you accelerate 32 feet per second faster than the second before. As an example, in three seconds, you accelerate from 0 to 96 feet per second, in another second you are traveling at 128 feet per second, and in one more second you are traveling at 160 feet per second and so on."

"I get it. Wow!"

"And that adds up fast," said Alex.

"As a matter of fact, my new friend," added the doctor, "at 1g acceleration for a year, the velocity would reach 77% of light speed."

"And that would be?"

"About 143,000 miles a second."

"No way!"

"Yes, sir. And at that speed you could leave Earth, circle the moon and return to Earth in under two seconds. Or you could fly around the world over five times a second."

"Wow! Really?"

"Indeed."

"So how long is it going to take to get where you're going?"

"Depends on where we're going," said Alex.

"You don't know where you're going?" Teddy said with complete astonishment.

"Not yet, but we're working on it."

"Working on it?"

They continued to follow the scientists, who were guided by a research staff member. Some were directed to labs on the route, most of the party continued down the long curving hall toward the ship's access elevator. When they arrived at the elevator, there was already a small group waiting and most were wearing lab coats or white overalls. As Alex and Teddy approached, the group looked at Teddy and recognized him immediately. Teddy had become a big Hollywood star in the past two years, just as he was in his previous life.

They entered an elevator with an extra-large capacity, at seven meters square. It transported passengers, building materials, and equipment of every description. It could and did lift tons at a time. On this trip, there were only passengers. When the doors slid open, there were already a half a dozen people inside. Alex, Teddy and the others walked on and the doors slid shut.

"Mr. Stoddard," said a young man in a lab coat. "I wonder if you would give me your autograph."

"Be my pleasure," Teddy responded. "But I don't have a pen."

"Here you go," said Dr. Garcia as he handed Teddy one of the many pens stuck in the top pocket of his jacket.

"Thanks, Doc." Teddy turned to the young man. "Where would you like me to sign?"

"How about the lab coat?"

"No prob."

During the slow trip up to the ship's hatch on Deck 9, Teddy was signing autographs and enjoying banter with all of the passengers. As they exited the elevator, Teddy continued the banter for a few minutes on the ramp just outside the open hatch. For his part, Alex just stood aside and let the scene play out. He didn't mind the time taken for his employees to enjoy his favorite person in the world. He loved to watch the interaction between Teddy and others. Teddy was magical with people; he really cared for everyone he met and they all considered him a close friend within just a few minutes, which was remarkable.

After a few more minutes, Alex tapped Teddy, "We have a lot of ground to cover. Better break it off and get to it."

"Okay, no sweat." Teddy turned to his new friends, "Been great jawing with you pilgrims, but the boss and the doc here want to show me this here contraption," Teddy said in his best John Wayne impression. He got a big laugh. Teddy shook hands with everyone, using their names, before saying "See ya later."

With that, they turned and everyone entered the interior of the ship. The employees headed in different directions, either in pairs or by themselves, most still laughing as they ventured into the heart of the ship. Inside was abuzz with activity.

"Holy crap," Teddy looked wide-eyed around the interior. "It looks even bigger from the inside."

Alex looked at Dr. Garcia, "I believe the deck above is your purview, doctor. Give us your best."

"Certainly. Let's take these stairs up a deck."

Teddy and Alex followed the doctor up to the next deck. As they stepped onto Deck ten, they were in a huge round room with a ceiling height of nine meters. There was a four-meter diameter tube running vertically in the exact center.

"That's the main elevator," Alex pointed out. "It runs to all 20 decks. A bit of an unusual design. It not only goes up and down but sideways on the seven center decks. Travels horizontally out 20 meters on those floors in six different directions like spokes on a wheel. Helps carry heavy loads and shortens walking time."

"Are we going to ride on it?" asked Teddy.

"Just the up and down is on line right now," said the doctor. "But if you're going to see the other decks that would be the way to go."

"Still a lot to see on this deck before we head up or down," said Alex.

"Look over there," said Dr. Garcia, "Those folks are just finishing up the installation of the supports and cradles for the synthetic mercury conduit. Massive, aren't they?"

"Massive is right," said Teddy. "And a lot of them. There are so many it looks almost solid."

From where they stood they could see several technicians directing the extensive use of lasers to set heights and angles.

"This is the SMPE deck," said Alex. "The center of this deck will house the main MVA. It's massive also."

"Everything about this ship seems to be massive," said Teddy.

"They're supposed to be ready for the conduit at the end of the week," said the doctor. "The conduit is the trick here. Must be perfectly round and perfectly polished on the inside. That fluid is going to be hauling ass, excuse the expression, and the seams in the conduit can't be much more than a micron off." The doctor looked around and nodded in satisfaction. "Your engineers have developed a fabulous way of doing the inside polishing."

"We have the best," said Alex.

"No question," the doctor agreed.

They spent another thirty minutes on this deck before the doctor suggested they drop down to Deck 17. They headed for the elevator.

As they stepped off the elevator, the doctor explained, "This is the guidance room. In here will be an array of gyroscopes and another MVA, but this one will be much smaller. It's designed to direct the ship like a rudder. Unlike the main engine above, it will tilt in all directions, turning the ship. It can also be used to increase or decrease speed, if necessary, but for most of the journey, it will remain idle."

"We'll start installing this MVA in about a month. You can see some of the hydraulics that will be used to tilt it." The doctor pointed at four places where huge hydraulic cylinders were already in place.

"This deck has a higher ceiling than the one for the main MVA," Alex pointed out, "in order to allow for the tilt of this one."

"Indeed." Dr. Garcia looked around and involuntarily nodded his head. "They are making fine progress. Would you mind if I leave you now? There's a lot I need to review."

"Not at all," said Alex.

"Hey, Doc, thanks for the info. You're a good teacher, I learned a lot," said Teddy as he shook hands with the doctor before giving him a nice hug.

"Well, you're a fine young man. I can't wait to tell my children—very exciting."

The doctor walked off toward the center of the ship. Alex and Teddy spent another quarter hour strolling around this deck, seeing what could be seen and stopping occasionally to ask a question of a technician.

"Let's head to the bridge," suggested Teddy.

"No bridge yet. That will be on Deck 4. We'll head up to the living quarters, or what will be the living quarters, on Deck 5."

"The bridge is on Deck 4? Seems like it should be on the top of the ship."

"The top two decks are going to be packed with so many sensors, telescopes, and technology that there won't be room to even change your mind up there. Deck 3 is the medical deck; it will be equipped like a small hospital."

The elevator door slid open and they stepped onto Deck 5. From this level, they could clearly hear the construction activity going on above them.

This deck was much smaller than the center decks, closer to 50 meters in diameter. They walked directly away from the elevator down a long hall. The hall was intersected every 12 meters by other corridors and then dead-ended in a T-shaped hallway. There they took a left turn and headed down that last corridor.

Alex explained, "In this area, there are forty pie-shaped living quarters that range in size from five meters in the center to eight meters on the outside."

"Let's take a look inside one," suggested Teddy.

"Okay." There were no doors installed so Alex turned right into the next outside room.

There wasn't much to see, just a good-size empty room. It was partitioned for a closet and bathroom, but there were no doors or portholes.

"Not too plush, I'm thinking," joked Teddy.

"Got a way to go before furniture is installed."

"No windows?"

"Portholes, no. No need for them. These rooms won't be used until the ship has reached its destination. Until then, all the passengers will be in stasis. This ship will serve as a home until the colonizers have settled in and built their own homes. Might take years, or possibly decades."

Teddy stopped in thought for a moment and then turned to Alex. "What exactly do you expect to find on another planet?"

"It's not exactly what we expect to find, but what we require of a planet."

"Oh, okay, what do you require?"

"There are some absolute requirements that must be in place before we'll land. They begin with water, a lot of water. Without that, a planet is just a big dead rock as far as we're concerned. The temperature has to be within a certain range to support life as we know it, so we have to be in the Goldilocks Zone."

"Goldilocks Zone?"

"Too close to a star is too hot, too far from a star is too cold. Somewhere in between is just right, hence, the Goldilocks Zone."

Teddy smiled, "I get it."

"So, the temperature is determined by its distance from its star and the type of star."

"There are different types of stars?"

"Oh, hell yes. Huge ones, tiny ones, old ones, new ones, hot ones, cool ones, red ones, white ones, and many more in between. Stars are classified and alphabetized from A, F, G, K, and M. Our Sun is a class G star, but only about 7% of stars are categorized as G class, making them rather rare. For our purposes, the best chance for this colonizing mission is a class K star, because 90% of stars are Class K."

"Didn't know that."

"No reason you would," Alex smiled. "Another requirement is the planet's mass. Mass creates gravity. So again, it has to be in a certain range. We think the colonizers, and most life forms we plan on introducing to a new planet can survive from 90% to 105% of Earth's gravity. Better less than more, but we can live with more. And we'll require a molten iron core."

"Oh, oh. Say what?"

"Did you know that the Earth has a molten iron core?"

"If I did, I've forgotten. Not too interested in science stuff, until now."

"Not your thing, my friend."

"No, I'm pretty much tied to the impractical aspects of life," Teddy smiled. "So why the iron core?"

"Our iron core creates our magnetic field, that's why we have a North and South Pole. Without that field, we would be bombarded with nasty stuff from space. Gamma rays are the worst. We couldn't survive without that shield."

"Damn! That's a lot of requirements. Do you think you'll find one?"

"Well it's estimated that there are about 60 billion planets in our galaxy and if just 1% fit our criteria that equates to 600 million prospects. Of that number, we can eliminate over 80% because of various factors, size and lack of water being the obvious eliminators."

"600 million!" Teddy smiled. "Have you found any that might work?"

"Believe it or not, there are tens of thousands that demand a closer look. And because our sensor technology is improving damn near daily, we have dozens of planets that hold great interest. We're committed to identifying at least three strong candidates that are found in the same basic trajectory. As we approach the first planet in the line, our onboard sensors can give us all the data we need to know. If the first one doesn't fit the bill, we'll go on to the second, and so on."

"Not leaving much to chance, are you?"

"There had better not be anything left to chance! Let's keep moving."

The two left the room and headed back to the elevator and then down to Deck 8. As the door slid open, they stepped out.

"This is the incubation deck," said Alex.

"You're taking chickens?"

Alex laughed. "As a matter of fact, yes, along with thousands of other birds and animals. The deck above will store animal embryos and the eggs of birds, fish, reptiles and insects along with spoor and seed for the animals, such as oysters, clams, mussels and so forth."

"Two by two, as they say," Teddy gave a big smile. "I was in a play once about the Ark. Going to be changing your name to Noah?"

"Not changing my name, but the principle is the same as the Ark. We'll have everything from earthworms to elephants."

"Well, this is a good-size deck," Teddy said as he looked around, "but I don't think you're gonna get elephants in here."

"Embryos, mostly embryos."

"You're going to grow elephants from embryos?"

"That's the plan. On this deck and the one below, there will be nearly a hundred incubation chambers of all sizes. Of course, we'll have seeds and spoors from every desirable plant, such as grasses, grains, trees, flowers, bushes, fruit, vegetables, even moss and mold, you name it." Alex paused for a moment, "And insects."

"Insects? You're going to be taking flies and spiders?"

"We have ongoing studies to determine what to take. Flies serve a purpose, as do spiders. But we will not be taking every species, that's for sure."

"You're, in effect, taking this entire planet with you."

"Just the good stuff."

Teddy went silent for a while as they walked around this deck. Here, as with many of the other decks they'd visited so far, extensive plumbing and wiring was visible coming from bulkheads, ceilings and floors.

Teddy stopped for a moment before asking, "What about people?"

"That's a much bigger challenge. We are going to have 20 humans aboard, 16 female, all taking the trip in stasis. These people will be young and well educated in their fields, and as mentally and physically perfect individuals as we can find. On top of that, we'll have thousands of near perfect human embryos frozen for what may be hundreds of years."

"Apparently, you're not opposed to thinking ahead."

"Apparently not," Alex smiled.

"How long is this trip going to take?"

"Don't know, but the trip, no matter how far, is going to take a long time. At the minimum it will be 20 years, probably closer to 40, maybe a great deal longer." Alex paused a second, "And that is the time required just to get there. Depending on what we find on our new planet, some work will inevitably need to be done. We're figuring forty to sixty more ship years to develop the planet."

Teddy cocked his head, "Ship years?"

"The ship will travel at over 97% of the speed of light and at that speed, for each year on the ship, ten years will pass outside the ship."

"Ah…"

Alex could see by the expression on Teddy's face the concept would take a while to explain. "Let's not get into that right now. Time, speed, and space get pretty complicated."

"Okay. Being a man of simple mind, that's probably a good idea."

"No matter what," Alex smiled, "it's going to take a lot of time. So, the colonizers will be placed in stasis and will stay in stasis for the whole trip."

Teddy changed the subject, "Where are you going to find these perfect people who agree to take this trip?"

"We're already putting out feelers to every college in the world. We think we'll get hundreds, if not thousands of volunteers."

"No way."

"We think so, yes. The trip, as far as a colonist is concerned, will seem like a matter of minutes, maybe just seconds. It will be like going under general anesthetic for an operation and waking up after it's done."

"What if something goes wrong when everyone is asleep?"

"Then the voyage will probably be over. Even if we had one or two people trained for possible problems, they almost certainly couldn't be brought out of stasis quickly enough to correct the problem. But, at this time, we do plan on having one man rigged to wake up if such an event occurs. But once brought out of stasis, he'll have to stay out, and it could be years before a suitable planet is found. That's an unacceptable scenario." Alex paused for a moment. "This is a huge problem, not only in case of an emergency but when considering dozens of other tasks that cannot be done with mechanization or technology."

"Pitch black for 40 years by yourself—yeah, that might work on a man's mind."

"That won't work for all sorts of reasons, but we're thinking about an alternative."

"Such as?"

"Can't say right now. It's kind of sensitive."

"Okay." Teddy had a puzzled look on his face.

"But we're building in all the safeguards possible. As an example, on Deck 1 there will be a compliment of 12 nuke-tipped missiles.

"You're going to have nukes?"

"Yes, but hopefully we won't need any of them. But we'd rather have them and not use them than not have them and need them."

"You're expecting an intergalactic war?"

"Not on our minds, no, But asteroids or meteors could be a problem. We'll have the most sophisticated scanning and detection devices ever assembled. At the planned speed of travel, there is no time for a human to react to an impending collision. If something has the potential for a collision and we don't have time to alter course, it must be destroyed within microseconds. The MVF will create a magnetic field that surrounds the ship and actually extends out thousands of meters."

"No way!"

"Oh yeah! It will be similar to the Earth's magnetic field, only much stronger. Theoretically, it will be able to deflect smaller objects, maybe as big as a small car away from the ship. But something larger will have to be blown into smaller pieces that can be deflected. That's where the nukes come in."

"At hundreds of thousands of miles a second or whatever, good luck with that," said Teddy.

"We'll be looking billions of kilometers ahead."

"These speeds and distances are starting to boggle me a little."

"It's hard to comprehend sometimes."

CHAPTER 10

ANNOUNCEMENT
THE HANLY JORDAN NEWS HOUR
February 5, 2030

The familiar theme music played as the picture turned from the Hanly Jordan News Hour logo to a live shot of the two aging news anchors in their normal seats on the set. The camera zoomed in on Dan Jordan as he began talking.

"This is a special addition of our nightly news," said Dan Jordan. The picture switched to a shot of Alex Gabriel as he started up a short flight of stairs that led to a podium erected in front of the starship. In a voice-over, Jordan continued to talk. "Within minutes, we believe that Alexander Gabriel will announce that their scientists, after nearly a decade-long search, have found three planets viable for colonization. The announcement is scheduled for 6:05 p.m. Eastern standard time, just two minutes from now."

"This is a very exciting day for the human race, Dan," said Bob Jordan as the camera switched to him. "Just look at that ship, will you? That's incredible."

The picture switched to a shot of the massive ship that filled the screen. After a few seconds it switched back to Alex at the podium. A dozen other people were now on the podium and stood behind and to the sides of Alex. He began to talk.

"We have picked today to christen this ship and to make a monumental announcement. We'll start with the christening. As most of the world knows, my father, Norman Gabriel, designed this incredible ship. When he was designing this ship, he had no clue that his design would be incorporated into the largest spaceship ever built. He had no idea that his design would be responsible for taking the best life this planet has to offer to another far-off world. However, I know it and I'm very proud of my father's accomplishment. Consequently today we honor his legacy by christening this ship, The NORMAN."

There was a round of enthusiastic applause.

Alex turned and walked to an extension of the platform that jutted out to within a meter of the NORMAN's hull. A lab assistant handed Alex a bottle of champagne that was attached to a long golden chain. A temporary gold plated panel of steel was attached to the hull to protect it from damage from the champagne bottle.

"I proudly christen this magnificent ship, The NORMAN." With that Alex swung the bottle toward the NORMAN's hull. It exploded against the steel plate showering the people on the podium with drops of champagne. A great cheer went up from those on the platform and all the spectators in attendance. A smiling Alex turned and walked to the podium. He waited for the applause to subside before speaking.

"Earlier this week, the scientists at Norman Research have at long last put the third and final planet on the list of possible destinations for our ship. This last planet is approximately 42 light-years from the planet Earth; it is the furthest of the three selected planets. All three planets are positioned in the same directional coordinates in our Milky Way galaxy." Alex smiled, "We of course hope that the first planet in line fits the bill perfectly. That planet is only 23 light-years away. Or, if you'd rather, about 14,000 trillion miles." Alex paused and looked behind him, then turned back to the many cameras in front of the podium. "The brilliant people standing here with me are the brains behind this monumental project." Alex smiled, "We, of the duller intellect, only provided the funds."

"The world has been kept abreast of this project almost from the beginning of construction, so I will not bore you with lots of technical details. Millions of people, around the world, have been following the ship's progress throughout its construction. Specifically, this planet is the second planet the NORMAN will reach during the voyage. As we see it now, this planet seems our best prospect."

Alex smiled brightly. "We are pleased to announce that our planned launch is scheduled for October 30th of this year."

Huge applause, whistling, and cheering arose from the few hundred people assembled in front of the podium.

Alex waited until the applause stopped. "We will keep the world informed of our continued progress. Thank you for all your well wishes."

"Well Bob, it looks like humankind will be reaching out to the stars. What an extraordinary day. I, at my old age, actually have chills. Wow!"

"You're certainly not alone there, Dan. I'll bet millions of the world's citizens are feeling the same way. This tops all of the science fiction that has been written over the generations, and all of the science fiction motion pictures ever produced. This is exciting. This is real!"

CHAPTER 11

ALL ABOARD

September 8, 2030
2:30 a.m.

Vance was alone on the bridge of the NORMAN. However, at this early hour, on other decks of this incredible ship, were dozens of people feverishly working. Vance had been sitting in the captain's chair for over an hour. He was in a reflective mood, and his emotions were running the gamut from jubilation to trepidation to sorrow. He recalled sitting in Alex's living room one evening, just over two years ago, having the conversation that brought him to this moment…

July 4, 2028

"Alex, I have a request, or actually maybe it's an offer," said Vance.

"Anything, you know that," Alex responded.

Vance nodded solemnly and paused briefly before saying. "I want to captain the NORMAN."

Vance's sudden offer took Alex by surprise; a welcome surprise to be sure. This was the best answer to the majority of unsolvable problems plaguing the voyage of the NORMAN. He knew Vance was the only one who could do the job; he had known it almost from the beginning of the project, but had never spoken of it to anyone. He looked at Vance for a moment before responding to this statement. "I'm not going to insult you by trying to talk you out of this. We both know that you are, by far, the best man for the job, so I'm going to accept your offer before you change your mind," Alex said sincerely. "You've taken a massive weight off my back. I haven't told anyone this, but I was about to order another SLF to be built for me, so I could assume that role."

"Really?"

Now it was Vance's turn to be surprised. That possibility hadn't occurred to him.

"I believed it would be necessary. I, along with you and Dale, know more about the ship, its capabilities, and its objectives than anyone. But because of your temperament and experience, you possess capabilities that I'll never have. You are the best man for the job." Alex paused for a moment. "The project will fail without a SLF aboard."

"Agreed, but it scares me, Alex. It's such a huge thing."

"It gives new meaning to the words, 'into the vast unknown.'"

"For sure." Vance paused for a second, "We also know you would never have asked me to do it."

"No, I wouldn't have. I thought about it countless times since the beginning of the project. There were too many problems that our brightest minds just couldn't solve, things that could put the whole project in jeopardy. A SLF is the only answer," Alex stopped for a moment, "but it was too big a thing to ask of anyone, let alone one of my best friends."

"I figured."

Both men sat in silence for a moment.

"I'll tell you this," said Alex, "with you aboard, the chances for complete success have gone up immeasurably." Alex paused and reflected for a moment. "You know, all that this planet has become would not have been possible without your actions over the years. Your presence aboard the NORMAN and on a new planet will mean the difference between success and failure." Alex paused, "I'm overwhelmed here with conflicting emotions." Alex looked away for a moment before turning back to face Vance. "I'm relieved and overjoyed knowing that the NORMAN now has a real chance for complete success, but conflicted by knowing that I'll be losing one of my dearest friends. That is no small thing to me."

"Alex, you are the best thing that ever happened to me. You are the best thing to ever happen to this planet. You have made my life relevant. You have saved this world from self-destruction. It's you who have led the way on everything."

Alex shook his head and paused for a long moment. "You need to hear a story. I feel that maybe now I can tell you… just you. It's a story that I've only been able to tell to one person in all my life. That person was Teddy and I was only able to tell him on the day before he died."

Alex had Vance's attention. "Oh?"

"Yes. Over the years, I suspect that somewhere in the back of your mind you may have suspected that what you are about to hear might actually be the case."

"To say that I'm all ears would be a mild understatement."

Alex took a deep breath. *Please let me do this…* Alex pleaded in his mind. He began, "On April 12, 1997, I was skiing with Jason on Mount Bachelor in central Oregon. I was 43 at the time, and Jason was 41. We were partners in a very successful investment brokerage company and were making a lot of money," Alex smiled, *I'm going to be able to tell it, thank you.* "We were actually considered the Golden Boys of the West Coast.

"It was a beautiful day on the mountain and we were skiing full tilt down a run when a snowboarder came flying out of the trees, hit and knocked me off balance. I apparently skied directly into a big tree." Alex paused. Vance said nothing, just waited for Alex to continue.

"I regained consciousness on a wet street in Inglewood, California in the year 1962."

"What?" Vance leaned forward in his chair.

"Yes, 1962. I was taken to a hospital to treat my injuries. The terror and confusion that overwhelmed me when I found out the year and discovered I was only eight years old is indescribable."

"Holy shit," Vance said quietly.

Alex nodded, "At first I thought I must be having a nightmare, hallucinations, or suffering from brain damage. But everything seemed to be perfect for that time in history. I mean everything.

But I could not accept the circumstances. How could I? Being shot back 35 years in time is, of course, impossible. I would not accept my parents. I knew they had been killed in a plane crash six years before in 1991..."

"1991?" interrupted Vance.

"Yes," said Alex, "and on the same date."

"No." Vance knew all too well that Muslim terrorists hanged Marian and Norman Gabriel on June 16, 1991. "Jesus, Alex, I can't imagine how that must have affected you."

"Seeing my mother nearly sent me off my rocker. I was convinced that I had severe brain damage. It took several days before I managed to force myself to accept this new life scenario. At any rate, after accepting my parents, I tried to tell my mother what had happened, but could not. No matter how hard I tried I couldn't. But, even then, it took months before I came to the realization that I was going to have to live my life over, starting as an eight-year-old."

"How in the hell did you remain sane?"

"I was given tranquilizers," Alex smiled. "They certainly helped me get through the initial shock." Alex stopped for a second, "The key to this entire story is that I had retained all my memories. I knew everything about the future investment world."

"Holy shit!"

"Holy shit is right. So I'm not the genius everybody has given me credit for all these years, I simply have a great memory."

Vance was clearly dumbfounded. "Give me a moment here."

Alex nodded in understanding.

Vance got up from the cushioned chair and walked over to a large window overlooking the Gabriel estate. He stood silently at that window for a full two minutes while Alex waited for him to process this mind-boggling story. Vance turned back to Alex.

"I'll tell you this; you are the genius that we all believe. You may have had a crystal ball when it came to investments and such, but the way you've handled and used that vast amount of money over the past... what... 68 years, shows true genius. Look at the organizations you've built, the foresight to build and develop Gabriel International, Global Media, Norman Research, GRI, the nation of Mariana, and now a ship to take life to another star system. You didn't do all that with a great memory."

"You're giving me more credit than I deserve. Look at all the people who have had a huge hand in everything you've just named. Jason, a true media genius, Dale—what can you say about Dale—there are no words—and you, my dear friend, just to name a few. Without your powerful hand, we would have long since been destroyed."

"Maybe. But, it was you who put the best people together, provided them with everything they needed to do their jobs to the best of their ability, and demanded vision. Now that's genius."

Alex said nothing for a moment. "Clearly I was picked to be put in this position by something or someone back in 1962. Why me, I don't know."

"You're right there. Since you related the story of your folks' visitation, just after they were killed, I knew it would be inexplicable. No doubt about it. I remember on our fishing trip just before the WGC took over the world, you told us there were two incidences that convinced you that we were in some way being controlled or influenced by some intelligence far greater than ours. The visitation by your folks was one, and you have just told me the other."

Both men sat in silence for a while before Vance smiled.

"You know, I'm feeling much better about going on this voyage now. I think this is something that we're supposed to do. I should have realized it sooner."

———

So, as Vance sat alone in his captain's chair at this early hour, he reflected on the circumstances and the path that put him in this chair. He smiled a little, *it all started with a bodyguard job back in… 1978. Walter Gabriel… Uncle Walt had called me to talk about protecting his rich young nephew. Who would have thought it would lead to this chair? Who would have thought? It's been an extraordinary ride these past 52 years.*

Vance was clearly the only individual who could captain the NORMAN, simply because of his unique makeup and abilities. He was the only one who could effectively put himself in stasis for any length of time. A week, a month, a year, it didn't matter. When in stasis, he could be wakened in an instant and spring into action. In addition, because of his Isleium brain, Vance could store and use massive amounts of data about the NORMAN.

Vance looked over his shoulder at a bulkhead that Alex had told him about six months ago. There was a secret compartment in that bulkhead, and what it contained was on a need-to-know basis. Vance was glad to be on the list of those with a need to know. The knowledge gave him some comfort.

CHAPTER 12

VOLUNTEER
THE HANLY JORDAN NEWS HOUR
October 1, 2030

"And now our cameras shift to the Gabriel Mansion for a scheduled special announcement," said Dan Jordan. "It's all yours, Lara."

The picture switched to Lara, "Thank you, Dan. I think we're about to hear a surprising announcement from Alex Gabriel. And it looks like they're ready."

The picture changed to Alex Gabriel and Vance Youngblood standing at the familiar podium on the lawn in front of the mansion, and then the camera went to a close-up of Alex.

Alex began, "I am announcing to the world today that Vance Youngblood has volunteered and will captain the spaceship NORMAN on its maiden voyage." Alex paused briefly to let this information sink in. "This decision was actually made over two years ago at the request of Mr. Youngblood. We have kept it under our hats, as they say, to keep the press from hounding him until the day of the launch."

"Mr. Youngblood's presence aboard the NORMAN immeasurably increases the chances of success for this project. Mr. Youngblood, because of his unique physicality, temperament, and experience is the only person in the world who could do this job." Alex paused for a moment. "Lara, we will take a few questions."

The camera switched to Lara. The normally smiling and upbeat young woman was clearly less upbeat.

"Mr. Youngblood, this is quite a surprise. All of you at the WGC certainly can keep things under your hat! You never let on."

"We can keep a secret," Vance smiled.

"Yes you can."

Vance, before volunteering for this monumental task, had discussed it with Lara with the understanding that she would also keep the secret. She was now feigning ignorance; giving the impression she knew nothing about this revelation.

They had been a couple for over two years at the time. She deserved to be the first to know his intentions. She didn't take the news well, and had been nearly inconsolable for the next week.

Vance, standing in front of the microphone looking at Lara, was now momentarily reliving that evening, *"I understand what you want to do and why you're doing it,"* she started, but within seconds her emotions took over. *"You're leaving me forever,"* and she began crying. Until that moment, Vance hadn't realized how attached he and Lara had become. He was, in fact, leaving her forever, which was the worst part of his decision. He would miss all of his friends, in particular Alex, and Dale, the gentle little man who had given him his life back. But Vance had never been in love before. There were many girlfriends in his lifetime, but none reached for and grabbed his heart like Lara Lions.

"Your intelligence, bravery and skills are legendary," said Lara, "Would you tell the world what prompted your decision to captain such a voyage?"

"There are a host of reasons, Lara, not the least of which is a spirit of adventure. I challenge anyone to imagine a greater adventure. Imagine being the first person to walk on a new world. Imagine being the person who has been charged with and given the honor of creating a living environment for a multitude of humans and thousands of other species."

"I can't think of anything greater," said Lara sincerely.

"However, as Mr. Gabriel stated, the main reason is my unique set of abilities. No human could endure such a trip, even if all of the necessities of life were provided. The amount of food required to feed a single human being for forty or more years would take up most of the ship's storage. As you know, I don't eat, I drink very little, and under normal circumstances my power source will last up to two hundred years. Also, additional fuel for me will be aboard the ship."

"Any other reasons?"

"May I?" Alex interrupted.

"Yes, sir, of course."

Alex looked at Vance and then back to the camera. "Without Mr. Youngblood at the helm, this project has little chance of an acceptable success. We would probably be able to find land and start life growing on a distant planet, but wouldn't be able to colonize humans or any living mammals. Mr. Youngblood is fully aware of that and it is the main reason he volunteered. My dear friend tells you the truth about his spirit of adventure and abilities, but he leaves out the courage and loyalty that were the driving forces behind his decision."

"Thank you, sir. I'm sure you're going to miss your friend."

"You have no idea," answered Alex.

"Me, too. He's one of my favorite people." Lara actually looked to be on the verge of tears. "I know tens of millions of people around the world will also miss him. He's been a Guardian Angel for the multitudes."

Vance leaned into the microphone, "I appreciate that sentiment, Lara, but fortunately the world doesn't need as much guarding as it once did. However, the life that will be aboard the NORMAN certainly will."

"They will be in great hands," said Lara.

"Without question," added Alex.

Lara, after a brief pause, got back on the subject. "It's our understanding that this trip will take a minimum of 22 years and probably closer to 40 years to complete. How, sir, are you going to endure 40 years alone?"

"One of my unique abilities as an SLF is to switch off and go to sleep, for any length of time desired. If I get bored, I'll switch off for a year or two. I can assure you I will not be awake for 40 years. I'll also have Mr. Gabriel and Dr. Isley to keep me company and help solve any problems that come up."

"But many would consider them computer programs, not actual humans."

"They are no more a computer program than I am." Vance smiled slightly, "I'm not a human, Lara."

"You are to me."

"And they will be to me." Vance looked into the camera's eye. "There have been rumors floating around the world for several months that this beautiful young lady, Lara Lions, and I are in a romantic relationship. I believe this is a good time to put an end to those rumors. I want the world to know that I love this woman as I never have loved anyone before." Vance paused for a brief moment. "To leave her, to be without her forever is the only truly sad thing about this pending voyage."

The picture quickly switched to Lara. Her face displayed her true feeling for this extraordinary man. Without a doubt, she was a woman in love.

If that statement doesn't bring tears to everyone in the world, nothing will, thought Alex.

After a moment Vance continued, "That being settled, I'll go on. Mr. Gabriel and Dr. Isley will be as real as I am, they simply won't have a SLF body. Their computer generated images will look as real as I do standing before you." Vance looked at Alex, "With that, I'll turn this announcement back to Mr. Gabriel."

"Thanks Vance. I believe that is all the information you need today. We'll keep you informed as to our progress for the next few weeks prior to liftoff."

The camera switched back to Lara who was still clearly affected by what Vance had revealed about their relationship. Within seconds, she regained her composure.

"Another major announcement by Mr. Gabriel and Mr. Youngblood. Back to you, Dan and Bob."

"Well, Dan, what the 'Norman Project' gains by Vance Youngblood's presence is this planet's loss. As tough and uncompromising as he is, Vance will be missed by billions on this planet."

"None will miss him more than Lara," added Bob.

"Maybe not," said Dan, "but I'll bet a month's pay that Alex Gabriel comes in a close second."

October 2, 2030

Right after the announcement that he would be the NORMAN's captain, Vance had made a personal request of Alex. A request he had thought about for the past year.

"I want to take a clone embryo of Lara with me on the trip, if that's all right with you."

Alex looked at Vance and smiled. "Been waiting for two years for you to ask that question. Of course you can. As far as I'm concerned you're in charge of this trip. Whatever you want, you get."

"Thanks boss," Vance said with a smile. "I haven't run this by Lara yet."

"She'll be thrilled."

"Hope so… I am."

"Hi, gorgeous," Vance said into the phone, "would you care to join me in the garden in about an hour?"

"Well, I don't know Hon, are you going to give me some bad news?"

"I'd rather take a beating."

There was a pause on the other end. "I know you would," Lara said softly.

"Is it a date?"

"It's my intention to spend every possible minute with you until you leave the planet, you big lug. Of course it's a date."

"See you in an hour." Vance smiled to himself as he hung up.

Vance's tropical garden lay on the north side of his 14-acre estate, which was about a half a mile south of the Gabriel Mansion. Vance's home was a great deal more rustic and considerably smaller than the Gabriel's. It was constructed of heavy wood, native stone, and steel; it suited him to a tee. It sat on a bluff with a wall of windows pointing west to take in the spectacular view of the cliffs and ocean. All in all, it was a very warm and inviting home.

Vance was waiting for Lara on the bench in the middle of the garden where he and Lara had sat so many times over the past two years. The smell of dozens of fragrant flowers and fruit blossoms permeated the warm humid air. It was a beautiful evening.

Lara walked into the garden exactly on time.

Vance stood up as Lara approached.

"Hello, Hon," she said with a smile.

"Hey gorgeous." With that, Vance took her into his arms and gave her a big kiss.

After a moment they parted a few inches. "I don't ever want to stop doing that," she said in a whisper.

"Me, neither." Vance stood to one side and motioned her to sit. "Let's plant 'em for a minute."

They sat holding hands.

"I want to ask you something," said Vance.

Lara turned and looked at Vance. "Okay."

"How would you like a future you to come along on the trip?"

Lara didn't say anything for a moment. "Do you mean as a clone?"

"I do."

"Then the answer is yes, absolutely. Thought you'd never ask."

"I can't tell you how much that means to me, to know that you'll be with me in the future."

Lara put her hands on either side of Vance's face. "That is probably the most romantic thing you've ever said to me."

CHAPTER 13

TWO BY TWO
October 15, 2030

Over the past three weeks, there had been a fever of activity in and around the NORMAN. The last of the supplies were being loaded, stored, and categorized. Thousands of items from varieties of seeds, grasses, grains, vegetables, flowers, bushes, and trees were brought aboard and stored. Beneficial fungi, spoors, and mold were loaded. All the beneficial and necessary insects had been placed in their compartments. Fertile bird eggs by the thousands were placed in stasis. Thousands of embryos from thousands of animals were stored in a deep freeze along with a few mature mammals that were to be kept in a cryogenic state. The last of the well thought-out and required elements to be placed aboard were the humans who agreed to undertake this amazing voyage.

As Alex predicted, there had been no problem getting volunteers to go on this unprecedented trip. Of the thousands that applied, only 20 people were selected to take the trip. They comprised the best of the best. A chance to colonize, to be the first humans in a new world, was a strong incentive. There were four "Adams" and 16 "Eves" selected. The honor, challenge, and adventure drew these young people from all corners of the world. Many who were not chosen to go were offered an opportunity to have their genes take the trip in the form of sperm, eggs, and embryos. These embryos would become part of the new world population in the centuries and millennia to come. Thousands readily agreed. Lara Lions had now agreed to be among the hundreds of embryos of exceptional human beings to be taken on the trip, including clones of Teddy, Alex, Jason, Dale, Chuck, Colleen, Walt, Marian, Norman, Lara and Vance.

As a precautionary measure, it was decided that once every two generations, Alex and Vance's clones would be carried to term by a surrogate mother. If the new planet, for whatever reason lacked leadership, the intention was that these two alpha males might step up to provide that guidance and direction. Before and after that decision was made, there were several weeks of animated discussions around water coolers and at social gatherings about the thematic debate of nature versus nurture.

CHAPTER 14

COMPLETION AND LAUNCH
October 30, 2030
(Launch minus 60 minutes)

The world was poised on the brink of the most momentous event in history. This occasion nearly rivaled the WGC's world takeover that occurred some two decades before. Dozens of reporters and camera crews from around the world were on the island. The ocean around Mariana was all but clogged with cruise ships, yachts, and boats of every size and description.

From sea level, the top two thirds of The NORMAN were clearly visible as it sat gleaming just 400 meters inland.

For the past three years, the progress of the spaceship NORMAN had been continually reported on by most news organizations. There was also a dedicated website for the NORMAN where those individuals who wanted more detailed information could follow the construction and its progress.

The final preparations had been made and the NORMAN was now complete. The interior was a sparkling testament to modern technology; the exterior was truly awe-inspiring in its sculptured simplicity.

In this last hour before launch just a handful of people were still aboard. These were technicians doing final checks on all major systems, from the NORMAN's five nuclear generators, to the cryogenics deck, to a dozen or so other major and minor details. Additionally, the NORMAN had been placed in a sterile mode for the last two weeks to ensure that no unwanted organisms were taken along for the ride.

All aboard, except Vance, were dressed in sterile suits. Alex, Lara, and Dale were on board to see Vance off. All his other friends had said their goodbyes the day before, including Teddy, who had received an extra strong hug from Vance. This was a solemn occasion. Through their visors, tears could be seen on both Alex and Lara's faces as they bid goodbye to this brave and loved man.

"Goodbye, you big lug," said Dale with way more humor than he felt.

"You have given me life," Vance said to Dale. "Now maybe I can help take life to another world. Thank you, my dear little friend." With that Vance gave Dale a big long gentle hug.

"Ah, gee," Dale responded and quickly turned and walked toward the hatch.

"I think we've said all we need to say," said Alex. "Our lives will be over centuries before you get to where you're going. We'll keep in contact for as many years or decades as we can, but our centuries will pass as the decades pass for you and this fine ship."

Vance nodded.

"I'm going to thank you for my protecting my life all these years and for the protection you will surely provide for all the lives aboard the NORMAN. And, my dear friend, I'm not going to cry… at least until later on. Goodbye, Vance." Alex grabbed Vance in a bear hug and squeezed.

"I'll get your ship to the perfect planet for you. That's a promise. Don't give it another thought," Vance smiled and patted Alex on the back.

Alex nodded through his tears, let go of his friend, turned and followed Dale's path to the hatch.

Lara came next. She put her arms around Vance and held on. Nothing was said for a full minute. "You have the best adventure in the universe," she choked out. "You protect the life aboard this ship. And you tell the future me about me when I grow up on that new world. You love me then as you do now." Lara quit talking for a moment.

Vance said nothing he just held on to her.

She looked up into his eyes, "Oh hell, Hon, I'm so sad."

Vance was choked with emotion. "I'll always love you," he managed to get out.

LAUNCH

Vance sat in the captain's chair. He was scanning the multitude of instruments that were in his line of sight. The main MVA and guidance MVA were beginning their startup and the SMPE had begun accelerating the synthetic mercury in its tubes to 22,000 rpm. There was no discernible sound on the bridge. All systems were well within tolerable limits; 95% were reading right on the mark.

Due to Alex's famous penchant for punctuality, The NORMAN was scheduled to lift off on the exact second, rise to 160 meters and stop to retract the landing gear. It would then continue to 800 meters and stop again for a few tests, then rise within a minute to 1,600 meters and hover for five minutes. This would give the world a perfect last look at the great ship and give enough time for the technicians to check all the systems in flight. If there was a malfunction, they could land and handle the problem.

"T minus 60 seconds," said the launch master over the intercom.

Alex sat in the shaded viewing stand located just 100 meters from the NORMAN. With him were Dale, Teddy, Lara, all of the scientists and engineers on the project, the officers of the WGC and Gabriel Industries, and the extended families of the 20 young colonists aboard. Also, there were dozens of construction workers who had helped build this magnificent ship and everyone who had a hand in its development. There were close to nine hundred people in the stands.

"T minus 30 seconds."

Without question, for someone who had already had a lifetime of spectacular experiences, this was one of the most emotional moments in Alex's life. He was about to witness the beginning of the greatest achievement in human history. Gabriel Industries, through Norman

Research, had been responsible for a multitude of incredible technical breakthroughs and inventions over the past four decades, but this was the topper. There was no future profit to be made here, this was pure expense, pure adventure. Fully a quarter of Alex's vast fortune was represented in the spaceship NORMAN.

Alex was about to lose one of his best friends. Even before the NORMAN left the ground, he felt the pangs of loss. What would life be like without Vance watching his back? As he sat on pins and needles waiting for the launch, Alex felt exposed, almost insecure.

"T minus ten, nine, eight..."

"Let this work," Alex said under his breath.

"...three, two, one."

"It's moving," someone shouted.

And it was. Slowly the huge orb was rising.

Others joined in with shouts of encouragement and joy.

Alex stood up, followed instantly by everyone in the stands.

"It's going to fly!" Alex yelled and began to laugh. "It's going to fly!"

The NORMAN lifted above their heads. What an incredible sight! It was almost impossible for the human mind to comprehend. This massive bronze object was floating silently above the Earth. At 160 meters, it stopped and the six huge landing struts withdrew slowly into the bottom of the NORMAN, then disappeared. The NORMAN continued its upward movement to 800 meters and stopped again.

"The NORMAN is now at 800 meters. All systems are 100%," said the launch master's voice over the intercom system.

The NORMAN did a slow 360-degree turn and stopped.

"Go, Vance, go," said Alex to no one in particular.

The NORMAN began to rise again. It went to the prescribed 1,600 meters and stopped for the last time. The NORMAN was awe-inspiring as it hovered motionless in the sky above this small island. Its beautiful bronze hull fairly sparkled in the morning sun. At that moment, it was a sight being recorded for history by thousands of cameras on the ground, at sea, and in the air.

Despite such a relatively small crowd, the yelling and cheering created a huge din.

All of a sudden, a familiar voice could be heard over the noise. It was Vance. The crowd went silent in order to hear what this brave man, this modern explorer, had to say.

"Ladies and gentlemen of the world. This is Vance Youngblood. I want to wish you all the best on this planet Earth. We here aboard this ship will never again walk among you. But we will be setting foot on a new world in the future. We have aboard this ship the finest the Earth has to offer. We will cultivate our new planet with our love and labor. We bid you farewell."

The NORMAN began to rise once more. It seemed slow at first, but as the seconds passed it clearly was beginning to accelerate. The sun shining on its bronze hull made it look like a small sun itself. Within two minutes its glitter began to diminish and it became a tiny speck of light. Then it was gone.

PART 3
THE VOYAGE

CHAPTER 15

NORMAN DATE
November 11, 2030

All was going as planned. The NORMAN's main MVA and the SMPE were running smoothly while maintaining 1g of acceleration. The guidance MVA had done its job in directing the initial liftoff flight and was shut down on schedule. All systems were on autopilot and would remain on auto throughout the trip. Vance would only intervene if something went wrong. At this moment in time, twelve days into the voyage, the NORMAN was traveling at over ten million meters per second, over 35 million kilometers an hour.

Vance was on the cryogenic deck making a final systems check before opening this deck to space. This specifically designed move would subject colonists and the other living things on this deck to absolute zero and create a complete vacuum. At absolute zero, time stops completely. From this point on the colonists would not age a single second until they were brought out of stasis.

Creating a vacuum and dropping the temperature was a delicate action that required extreme caution. The pressure had to remain constant in the cryo-capsules until the deck was completely frozen and a perfect vacuum. As a precaution, prior to and during their initial freeze, the colonists were hyper-oxygenated to allow a slow spark to re-animate their brains and bodies as they were being brought out of stasis. These cryo-capsules also served as specialized, sophisticated microwaves. When the time came, the space hatch would be closed, the deck re-pressurized and brought up to a normal temperature. Then, one at a time, the colonists would be subjected to microwaves in their capsules and brought out of stasis. Vance would be on hand to assist in the thaw. His presence, at this crucial time, would make the difference between success and a complete failure.

All seemed to be in order. Vance took one last look through the clear canopy on each capsule. He had gotten to know each of these 20 people during their training over the past nine months. In that short period of time, they had become a close-knit family…

January 2, 2030
Ten months earlier

The 36 prospective young colonists from around the world had all arrived within a day of each other and been assigned a cot in one of the five dormitories located on a remote ranch in southeastern Oregon. The 36 were composed of 8 males and 28 females. These were the best of the best. All of their lives, these brilliant young people had been high achievers and had always gone the extra mile, doing whatever it took to accomplish their goals. They not only excelled in their chosen academic studies, but displayed extraordinary physical prowess in various athletic endeavors. Of these 36 candidates, only 20 would be selected to travel on the NORMAN. They all were passionate about being selected to take the trip. Competition was extremely high, bordering on fierce.

Before they arrived, Vance extensively studied the comprehensive resumes and psychological profiles of each of the individuals. He made copious notes on each individual, with special emphasis given to any possible weaknesses in their intelligence, character, or physical abilities.

Vance was in charge of the training camp and he elected to more or less run it as a military boot camp—with a number of twists. To begin with, each morning the candidates were woken at 5:00 am with a different loud noise. One morning it might be the sound of a jet taking off. The next maybe an explosion, then fingernails on a blackboard, a roar of a lion, a scream of a woman, a quack of a duck—always different, always loud.

Breakfast was served at 5:30 am right after a bout of light calisthenics. Each day, the breakfast was designed to be as different as the cooks could make it. One morning it might be oatmeal and toast, the next pork chops with mashed potatoes and gravy, the following mixed fruit, then steak and eggs. The cooks were encouraged to be creative. The only stipulation was that it be nutritional. These were some of the subtle ways that Vance used to train his charges to become accustomed to surprises, and to never assume anything.

After breakfast, the specific training got under way. The majority of the training revolved around learning agricultural practices. How to plant, fertilize, harvest, and care for every manner of foods. They were taught to field dress all types of animals, fish, and birds. They were taught to properly butcher large and small game, and to fish with conventional tackle, as well as tackle they had to make from available materials. They learned to make fish traps, nets and spears, and even fish hooks from seashells. They were required to know and operate all of the extensive equipment carried aboard the NORMAN.

In order to conduct this specialized training, top experts in all required fields were brought in from all over the world. In the allotted nine months of training, each young person was taught to hunt with every conceivable type of weapon; some conventional, such as rifles, shotguns, pistols, and bows and arrows, as well as some they were trained to make, such as spears, clubs, and boomerangs. They were taught to build traps and snares with whatever was available in the wild, and to know what type of trap or snare was best for each animal. They were taught to read animal scat and signs. They learned a little about the subtle differences in tracks made by different animals: a wolf, dog, coyote, deer, elk, antelope, squirrel, raccoon and skunk.

Their instruction included learning to start fires with whatever was available; to make quick shelters, even to make soap. They spent two weeks participating in the building of a log cabin.

They were all extensively trained in emergency medical treatment; how to stitch wounds, treat shock, and to assist with delivering a baby.

Even if all electronics failed in the future, the colonists could still access any and all necessary intelligence via the ship's extensive library, which contained thousands of how-to books on just about every subject, such as building log cabins and boats, mining and refining ore, and making medicine from available plants and elements.

All of these lessons involved hands-on training, and each prospective colonist was graded in their proficiency. These scores were then added to the observed abilities of each individual to work well with others, their leadership qualities, endurance, and temperament.

Two young ladies and one young man were sent home early in the training because Vance had serious misgivings about each of their abilities to get along with others, their mental state, and their questionable capacity to handle unexpected tasks. Vance's judgment was the final word and was not questioned.

At the end of the training, three young men and ten more young women were eliminated from the ranks and sent home. That left the remaining 20 very special young people chosen to become the new world's first colonists.

November 11, 2030

Vance knew that he wouldn't see these animated and brave young people again for at least 40 years, likely a great deal longer, and he was reluctant to leave this deck. "Goodbye. See you in a few decades," he said as he turned and stepped through the hatch. He turned back and pushed the close and seal button on the hatch. As he headed toward the elevator, he heard the reassuring sound of a thunk and a hiss indicating the required vacuum seal was achieved.

Once back on the bridge, he sat in the captain's chair and did nothing for a few moments before speaking aloud, "Alex, Dale?" Immediately, life-size images of both men appeared on the 7-meter wide by 2-meter high viewing screen, which displayed images in three dimensions. It was almost a hologram and required no special glasses to view.

Both Alex and Dale spent weeks downloading their intelligence, creative abilities, personalities, voices, thoughts, and physical images into separate Isleium computers. Just about every bit of information that made them who they were. Dale and his team had made the corrections in the program, allowing this massive download to be programmed into separate Isleium brains, without having the original host die as happened in Vance's case. The ship's main Isleium computer remained separate from the Isleium brains of the two men, but Alex and Dale retained a direct link to the main computer.

Their incredibly lifelike images were generated on the viewing screen. The computer automatically linked them to a setting appropriate to the conversation they were in with Vance. The majority of the time that Vance communicated with them, their images looked as if they were on the bridge. But the location or backdrop for their images was not restricted to the bridge. They might appear to be sitting when they were called, or walking around the bridge checking on systems. If Vance were talking to them in a lab, the two friends appeared to be in the lab with him. The images of "Dale" and "Alex" were as brilliant as the original men and fully capable of abstract and creative thought. Vance could speak to either one or both at the same time; all he had to do was say their name to bring them on line. When Alex and Dale designed it, they knew that this system, over time, would be a great comfort to Vance. "Hey, Dale open the line to the base please," he said.

"Right away, Vance. Did all go well in cryo?"

"Seemed ok, yes. I'm ready to open the space hatch."

"The ship's computer agrees," said Dale.

The NORMAN was experiencing a time delay that was growing by the second in contacting the Earth base on Mariana. Due to the Doppler Effect, words coming through on the intercom stretched out to the point of not being understandable. At the NORMAN's present velocity, a simple sentence took up to two minutes to reach its terminal point. To offset this phenomenon, all of the computers on the NORMAN and at the Mariana base were programmed to condense a message into a micro blast, or 'squib,' which allowed the message to be received at a normal cadence. As the ship's speed and distance increased, the computer automatically adjusted the speed of the squib's blast to account for this time delay. Conversely, however, the interval for a returning message to be received was now up to 20 hours. This time delay would continue to lengthen from hours, to days, to weeks, to months, until finally it would be lost in time.

"You may make your report now, Vance," said Dale.

"Thanks, Dale."

"Mariana base, this is Vance. I have just completed the final inspection of the cryo deck and found everything within tolerances. As we talk, readings are being transmitted. I will now open the deck to space. The NORMAN is operating perfectly, and after this operation, I will shut myself down for thirty days. Wake me anytime, I'll be here," Vance smiled.

"It looks to me, my friend, as if this trip isn't as hard on you as we thought it might be," said the smiling image of Alex.

"No it isn't. It's surprisingly peaceful and the visuals are incredible. Your insistence on putting this huge viewing monitor on the bridge makes a big difference. There is almost no feeling of claustrophobia. A little screen wouldn't have done the job. What a view!"

"I thought maybe that would be the case. Perhaps you should communicate that to base; it will relieve the minds of all of your friends back there. It sure does mine."

"Roger that. NORMAN to Mariana base, Alex suggested that I let you know that life aboard the NORMAN is not too bad. . . actually it's quite nice. I'm enjoying the peace and quiet and the views are indescribable. The view changes quickly at over 35 million kilometers an hour. It's hard to take my eyes off the panorama. Please, keep me abreast of what's going on down there. Vance out."

EARTH

November 12, 2030

"A communiqué is coming in from the NORMAN," reported the tech.

These messages were automatically relayed to all of the major networks; there was no censorship. It was the network's choice to either interrupt programs in progress or delay the message for a later broadcast. Most chose to interrupt. A majority of citizens, worldwide, wanted to immediately know about the voyage. Millions of people went further and maintained a direct link to receive all the communiqués from the NORMAN. There were only a scant few equipped to send messages to the NORMAN. These included the chiefs at the Mariana base, Alex Gabriel, and any people he selected.

12:50 p.m.

NORMAN, this is Alex at Mariana base. Hi Vance. I can't tell you how happy we, particularly me, are with your apparent ease and comfort aboard the NORMAN. That was one of my biggest concerns. We received your report and are pleased with the NORMAN's progress. I thought that you would want to hear about our progress. We've had quite a breakthrough on population control as of late. Four of the six nations that were adamantly dragging their feet, have now fallen into step with us. Massive sterilizations have begun. We still won't meet our goals, but this means that we will only be off by approximately 15% by the end of next year. All other WGC goal projections are being realized on a timely basis. This planet is shaping up nicely.

You are now 26 hours younger than you would have been on Earth. Soon you will be years, then decades younger and we, your friends on earth, will be long gone. Have a nice nap and we'll talk to you in 30 days.

"Always good to hear from Earth," said Dale.

"Good to hear they are getting the population under control," added Alex.

"I'll say," agreed Vance. "We're going to have the opposite problem on our new planet. We'll be short of humans for hundreds of years."

"True," responded Alex.

"Okay, my friends, I'm going to take a nap for a spell. If anything fun happens, give me a shake."

"We'll keep an eye on things for you, sleep tight," said Alex.

Vance got up and walked to his private room just off the bridge. His bed was an unusual design; instead of a flat mattress it appeared to be more like a big mold, shaped like a deep imprint of Vance's body. All of the cryo capsules were constructed in this manner, shaped and customized to the individual's form.

Vance stripped off the overalls he was wearing and put on what looked like a blue shape-fitting body sock. He lay down, adjusted, and shut himself off.

NORMAN DATE
December 30, 2030
8:00 a.m.

Vance's eyes opened exactly at the preprogrammed time. Just above his bed were a small array of sensor terminals. Vance looked up and saw nothing but green lights.

Good, he thought. *Nothing broke*. He got up, changed into his work overalls, and went to the bridge. "Alex, Dale." The view screen immediately held the images of both Alex and Dale.

"Good morning," said Alex.

"Sleep well?" asked Dale.

"Just gone for a second," said Vance. "Anything exciting happen while I was out?"

"No, sir," answered Dale.

Vance sat in the captain's chair while checking the sensors.

The speed indicator now showed over 86 million kilometers an hour.

"Jesus," said Vance.

"We are moving right along," said Alex.

"Main screen, forward view," said Vance.

Six high-tech exterior telescopes, each equal to the power of the old Hubble telescope, but just a quarter of its size were evenly spaced at the "equator" of the NORMAN. All were able to point in any direction, but were facing forward for the majority of the voyage. They not only provided an incredible exterior dimensional view, but also served as the major visual detection for the nukes on board. They could see light years ahead.

The main screen instantly came on. Stars seemed to be flashing by like tracer bullets. "Wow! Now that's a light show."

"Didn't imagine it would look like this," added Dale.

Vance watched the show for a full five minutes before saying, "Rear view." The screen switched to the aft cameras. It looked almost like the NORMAN was firing the tracers. "Without doubt, the recordings of this will be enjoyed by our young colonists."

CHAPTER 16

HE'S GONE
GABRIEL MANSION
EARTH DATE
December 30, 2043

A middle-aged Lara Lions was standing in front of the news cameras delivering her report to the world. Lara had aged gracefully and remained beautiful over the decades, but today she looked closer to her actual age of fifty-two. Today, there was a palatable sadness about her.

It was the third continuous day of rain, not a heavy rain, but a chilling drizzle falling out of a low overcast sky. Occasionally, the soft boom of far off thunder could be heard like a sad omen. It was the third day since the news that Alexander Gabriel had fallen gravely ill.

"We've been informed by Mr. Gabriel's doctor, Thomas Snider, that Alexander Gabriel has been diagnosed with a particularly aggressive form of leukemia." It was clear that Lara was in distress herself. She paused for a moment to gather her emotions. "Dr. Snider told us that he believes that Mr. Gabriel has just a few days left." Lara stopped again and looked away from the cameras. A full ten seconds went by before she turned back to the cameras and resumed. "This is the toughest thing I have ever had to report; the world is about to lose the man who literally saved it from self-destruction. He is a wonderful man, a kind and a compassionate man and a dear friend. Mr. Gabriel is just shy of 90 years old but he always seemed to possess the wisdom of someone much older than his years. He is the last of the original WGC members. Nineteen years ago, we lost Walter Gabriel, four years ago, both Douglas Ito and Joan Hocket were taken from us, and last year Jason Gould passed on. Thirteen years ago, Vance Youngblood left Earth, and by the latest reports he is still alive and on the dedicated mission to colonize a planet with the Earth's best." Lara looked back toward the mansion and then back to the camera. "We are about to lose the last of these extraordinary people. . . this is terrible." Lara stared into the camera for a moment. "We will keep you posted as to the condition of Mr. Gabriel. In the meantime, back to you Dan and Bob."

Inside, the Gabriel mansion was permeated by a deep gloom. Alexandra Gabriel-Greenwood, Alex's cousin and now Chairman of the WGC, was his closest relative. At the moment, despite being known for her stoic personality, she was an emotional wreck. She had been wandering about the mansion for three days. She was unable to sit, even for a moment.

Teddy was sitting at Alex's bedside holding his dear friend's hand. He had been there continuously for two days. Without Alex, Teddy would not exist and the world would have been deprived of one of its finest entertainers. When Teddy was lying near death at Cedars Sinai hospital in December of 1985, Alex had convinced his parents to let the doctors remove and freeze some of his DNA. At the time, cloning was not possible, but Alex knew that it could be done in the future—he would see to it. So, Alex was literally responsible for Teddy's life. This Teddy was Alex's son in every way, except biologically.

Teddy Junior, as his grandparents had called him, was now 38 years old. Whereas the original Teddy had been posthumously awarded an Oscar for best actor, Teddy Junior had been awarded two Oscars, a Golden Globe, and a Tony. He was at the top of the entertainment world.

When the word came that Alex had fallen gravely ill, Teddy was in the middle of making a movie in northern Canada. Without hesitation, he ran off the set, chartered a jet, and was at Alex's bedside on the other side of the world nine hours later. He spent every minute there while Alex was awake, and left only for brief periods while Alex slept. When Alex was awake, the two men talked continuously.

"Teddy, I need to tell you a story a story about me and your namesake," said Alex. "I'm not sure I'll be able to tell it, but I'm going to give it a try."

"I know I'm a clone of Teddy Oldaker, Alex. I've always known that. Hell, everyone knows that."

Alex smiled, "You are Teddy Oldaker. You've been my best friend for 124 years."

Teddy's expressive face turned to one of puzzlement. "You mean 80 some years, don't you?"

"No, 124 is correct."

"But…"

"I've had two lives and you were part of both of them."

"You're a clone too?" Teddy was clearly shocked and his expression showed it.

Alex smiled slightly—had he been in good health, he would have laughed. "No. That's not nearly as intriguing as what actually happened to me."

"Oh?"

"Listen up."

An hour later Teddy's mouth was agape. Alex was able to tell his story for just the third time in his life, first to Teddy Sr. on his deathbed, second to Vance before he left, and now to Teddy Junior.

Teddy, after a few moments, managed to find his voice. "I… I don't know what to say. That is the most incredible story I've ever heard. I never suspected anything like that."

"Why would you?" Alex was fading. "It's impossible… impossible," his voice trailed off.

"You're not looking good, Alex. I'll go get some help."

Alex's mind flashed back to his childhood, actually to his second childhood when he first saw Teddy after the accident that sent him back 35 years in time. At that moment, Alex was in pain and the eight-year-old Teddy could see it. "*It doesn't look like you're havin' much fun. I'll go get your mom,*" he had said.

"Teddy," said Alex, his voice barely audible, "I want you to get all the help you need and get me to my rock."

"Your rock?"

"Yes, on the little island just off the north shore. You know, I took you..."

"Hell, Alex do you think you should move?" Teddy's face displayed deep concern.

"Teddy, I haven't much time no matter where I am. And I sure don't want to be here in bed when I die. So go make arrangements . . . quickly."

Within ten minutes, Alex was on a stretcher heading to an ambulance parked right by the front door of the mansion.

Alexandra was holding his right hand and Teddy was holding his left, as the attendants were about to place the gurney into the back.

Lara was there, standing off to the side, tears streaming down her cheeks. Alex spotted her.

"Wait," said Alex weakly.

They stopped.

Alex raised his hand and beckoned Lara over.

She went quickly over to his side. "Oh, sir." It was all she could do to get the words out.

Alex took her hand, "I gotta go. But I wanted to thank you for loving my friend, Vance. You were his first and only true love. Thank you… I gotta go."

The attendants efficiently loaded him into the back of the vehicle. Teddy and Alexandra got in with him and the ambulance took off quickly.

Lara sat down on the steps and bawled.

When they arrived at the small dock just two miles away, a 42-foot launch was waiting with the engines running.

After rapidly removing the stretcher from the back of the ambulance, the attendants ran the length of the dock to the launch, loaded and strapped the stretcher in the back to the deck. Without hesitation, the launch took off to the north.

"Go, go, go," Alex, whispered. He started inhaling in rapid short breaths.

Teddy and Alexandra held his hands on his last trip to his rock. He began smiling as the sea mist touched his face.

"Cousin," said Alexandra.

"Shhh," said Alex. "Faster."

The boat could go no faster, it was flat out. It had only been twelve minutes when the boat pulled up to the small dock on Alex's personal little island. During that time, Alexandra gave the attendants instructions. Even before the launch had finished tying off, the attendants quickly took the stretcher off the boat and, as carefully as possible, raced down the narrow path to Alex's rock. Alexandra and Teddy followed.

At the base of the outcropping, the attendants unstrapped Alex and gently carried him to the seat that Jason and Vance had cut into this huge rock so many decades ago. At Alexandra's signal, they gently sat him down and retreated back to the dock.

Alex smiled as he looked across the narrow passage to the island nation of Mariana. He could see the waves crashing against the base of Mt. Norman. He could see the lush fields of crops and orchards to the east of the mountain. This was his nation. His creation. He continued to smile as he looked to his left and right. He spotted something in the sand just above the water line. He pointed, "Get that."

Teddy hurried down, retrieved a coconut and brought it back to Alex. Alex turned it over in his hands and smiled. After a few seconds, he gently sat the coconut down beside him.

He smiled at Alexandra, then at Teddy. "I love you two." Then he looked back at Mariana, smiled once more, "Hi Mom, hi Pop," he said softly. Then his head slowly dropped forward and he was gone.

SHIP DATE

August 2, 2033

"Getting a communiqué from Earth," announced Dale.

"Let's hear it," said Vance.

"We are sad to inform you that Alexander Gabriel passed away this morning, on the Earth date December 31, 2043, after a short bout with leukemia. He was 89 years old. The world is in mourning. He was considered the savoir of humanity and was among the greatest leaders in history. His presence on this planet will be sorely missed."

Vance was stunned. He said nothing, just stared blankly at the viewer. The images of Dale and Alex remained silent.

After a few minutes, Vance quietly said, "I should have been by his side. I'm... I'm in trouble here."

"Do you remember, my dear friend, when your body died?" asked Alex. "Do you remember I grieved for you?"

Vance nodded once. "I remember."

"I'm still with you, my friend. Right here." Alex's image on the screen pointed to his heart.

CHAPTER 17

FIRST PLANET
June 25, 2048

"Wake up, Vance," said Dale.

Vance's eyes instantly popped open. He instinctively looked at the sensors above his bed. All green.

"We're coming into the sensor range of Planet 1," said Dale.

"Right on time, about four light-years out," responded Vance as he rose from his prone position. "How's it looking?"

"Too soon to get all the readings. I can tell you that it has water and some atmosphere. But we knew that before we started."

"Present speed?" asked Vance.

"97% of light."

"How many Ks an hour is that?"

"Just over a billion per. We've been coasting for over two years now," said Dale.

July 21, 2049

The NORMAN was now only three light-years away from the first planet to investigate for possible colonization. Both Alex and Dale were on the viewing screen. The NORMAN's speed remained at just over 97% of the speed of light.

"Coming up on full sensor readout," said Dale.

"Let's put it on the screen," said Vance.

The viewing screen filled with the image of Planet 1. It didn't look very hospitable. It had the appearance of a big gray round rock.

"How's it looking?" asked Vance.

"Great so far… wait, oh, oh."

"I don't want to hear oh, oh."

"Ah, hell. The planet's surface is only about 27% water and the dry land is made up of iron, copper, and about 90% solidified magma. Core is iron all right, but nearly solid. A magnetic field is there, but very weak. It would take thousands of years to terraform this rock into something that is livable."

"Shit!"

"This is real disappointing," said Alex.

Vance sat for several minutes saying nothing, just watching the screen. "Any reason to take further readings?"

"No, not really," answered Dale.

The three said nothing for another five minutes. They knew that Planet 1 probably wouldn't be the one chosen, but the reality was quite depressing nonetheless. It had been a long trip already.

"Release me," said Vance. The restraint holding him in his chair retracted. Vance grabbed the secure railing that ran around the bridge and pulled himself closer to the screen. "How much longer to number two?"

"From here," said Dale. "About 12 light-years."

"That's about thirteen for us," Vance's sprits were understandably down.

"However, since we've eliminated it, we don't have to continue to number one, so we can make a turn now and cut a year off the time," offered Dale.

"Sorry, Vance," said Alex. "We were hoping to get you on some solid ground, sooner rather than later."

"Hey, I can handle it. Maybe I'll just turn myself off for the next decade or so." Vance smiled. "Well, let's get the SMPE and MVAs up and running."

"Better get back in the chair during the startup," suggested Dale.

Vance pulled himself over to the chair and sat.

"The SMPE and MVAs are starting their windup," said Dale. "Two minutes to full power."

"I'll line up the trajectory," said Dale. "Ready for power?"

"Let her rip," responded Vance.

The gravity came back at about 75%, not because of forward thrust, but due to sideways thrust. The thrust from the guidance MVA turned the NORMAN eighteen degrees on its axis while the main MVA was on full power. The NORMAN was making a huge arc at over a billion kilometers an hour. The guidance MVA would remain on at full power for two hours to put the NORMAN on the proper trajectory for Planet 2.

PLANET 2

February 5, 2059

After coming out of a two-year stasis, Vance sat down in the captain's chair. "Alex, Dale," he said.

The two images appeared on the screen.

"How are we doing?"

"Just over three light-years out," Dale reported.

"Sensors getting any detailed readings yet?"

Planet 2 was displayed on the right side of the viewing screen. Alex and Dale's images occupied the left. This planet, even to the naked eye, looked different than Planet 1. It had a distinct blue tint. And instead of the land being gray, it seemed to be multicolored. Even at this extreme distance, the telescope array on the NORMAN was showing what could be clouds.

At the speed they were traveling, the planet appeared to be spinning nine times faster than it actually was. At their present speed, a year on the NORMAN equaled over nine on the planet.

"We're getting great readings. And I like what I'm seeing."

The viewing screen blinked and then a color view of the planet was displayed.

"Oh, my," said Dale.

"Look at that," added Alex.

"We're home," said Vance with a smile in his voice.

On the viewer before Vance was an image of a beautiful blue marble. Water, land and clouds were all there. From this great distance, it looked very much like Earth.

As the planet turned and the image constantly changed, the three said nothing.

"Go to close up," said Vance.

The picture changed and filled the screen with an 8,000 square kilometer panorama of the surface, clearly showing that the land masses were multicolored. Various shades of green bordered what was certainly water. Browns, grays, oranges, and red made up most of the remaining view.

"High percentage of water," said Dale. "Ice caps at each pole. That green fringe around the water has to be plant life of some kind. Atmosphere is similar to Earth's, with much higher carbon dioxide and nitrogen, and much lower oxygen levels. The trace gasses detected are similar to Earth's."

"Look at the shape of that continent," said Vance. "Wow."

"Not hard to tell something really big smashed into it," said Dale.

"Damn near round," said Alex.

"Is that a moon?" asked Vance.

"It sure… there's another. Two moons," said Dale.

"I'd better send a communiqué to Mariana Base—not that it's still being manned."

"Channel open," said Alex.

Vance thought about what he was going to tell Earth about what they found and what they were going to do. "Mariana Base, this is Vance Youngblood. We have found the planet we were looking for. It is the number 2 planet. It looks to be perfect for our purposes. We expect to arrive there in approximately three ship years, 27 Earth years. We know you won't receive this message for 24 years, if at all. Just in case anyone still cared, we wanted to report that, in all likelihood, humans will be colonizing another planet. Vance Youngblood out."

"Do you think they are still monitoring our communications?" asked Dale.

"If the planet Earth is what we'd hoped it would become, it will be monitoring our progress. The only thing that makes me a little queasy is that we haven't heard from them in over a year."

"They could have sent hundreds of messages over the past year, but we won't receive them for over 20 years," responded Dale.

"Time and space," said Alex.

"Speaking of which, I'm going to shut off for a while. Wake me when we are about a month out from number two."

April 7, 2060

"Wake up, Vance," said Dale.

"How's it looking?"

"We're not approaching the planet yet," said Dale.

"Oh? So why?"

"A communiqué coming in from Earth," said Dale.

"Really? Thought we'd heard the last from them."

"Let's listen," said Alex.

"Vance and the starship NORMAN, we have horrific news to relay to you. A massive asteroid has entered our solar system and will impact Earth in fourteen months, ten days and six hours, or in the Earth year 2540. We will not be able to stop it. It is one quarter the size of the moon. It is a planet killer. We have nearly completed three starships and will launch them in just over a year from now. One will be heading your way. The other two will head in another direction hoping to find a suitable planet out of the fifteen excellent possibilities we have identified. We will preserve as much of Planet Earth's life as possible. Earth will be gone long before you receive this transmission. Good luck and God speed. Earth out."

All three men aboard the NORMAN were stunned. The planet Earth was no more. It was hard to comprehend.

"Well," Alex started, "I... don't know what to say. You'd think that in the past 500 years, they would have discovered the technology to disintegrate anything."

"Hum," muttered Dale.

"What?"

"Maybe the people of Earth became so passive that it didn't occur to them to develop a destructive device on such a massive scale, or maybe any scale."

"Or, it may be that there was nothing that could be built that could divert or destroy something a quarter the size of the moon," said Vance.

"That's probably a better answer," said Dale.

The three remained quiet for a few more moments.

"I'll turn our telescopes toward Earth," said Dale.

Vance nodded, "Yes."

It took thirty seconds to re-orient the telescopes before the image came into sharp focus.

"That can't be right," said Alex, "What the hell?"

"Give me a second here," said Dale. "Need to filter the sun's glare."

The brilliance of the Sun was reduced to allow a clear picture. Now they could see the Earth's sun and surrounding space. The picture was shocking. The sun now had an unusual set of rings around it. Almost like a halo in its glow, but quite faint. It was a startling image, but at the same time quite beautiful.

"That is our sun," said Dale. "And I assume those rings are what's left of the Earth, and I think Venus too. Maybe all of the inner planets and moons."

"Jesus," said Vance.

Nothing more was said for fifteen minutes while the three looked at the incredible image displayed on the viewer.

"How soon could the ship they sent get to Planet 2?" Vance suddenly asked.

"They would have launched about 25 years ago, so all things considered they could be there in as little as four of our years at our present speed, and their technology," offered Dale. "Once we land, however, that time will stretch out to hundreds of years."

"Their technology should be far greater than ours, one would think," suggested Alex.

"For sure," said Vance.

"But they couldn't travel any faster," concluded Dale.

January 5, 2062

"Time to wake up," said Alex.

Vance's eyes instantly popped open. As he always did, he looked at the array of sensor terminals above his bed. All green.

"Anything exciting happen during my nap?"

"As a matter of fact, just over a minute ago a nuke was fired," answered Dale.

"No shit?"

"Yes, and the readings show that we just passed through the radiation and debris field."

"I didn't think we'd use any of them. I'm surprised," added Alex.

"Had to be a small asteroid. We're going so fast that it's going to be tricky to analyze. The debris field was already over 13,000 kilometers in diameter as it went through that part of space…in about a millisecond. This will take a few minutes," said Dale.

"But it worked," said Vance. "No damage to the ship?"

"Not a scratch that we're aware of," said Alex.

"Your insistence that we leave nothing to chance may have just paid off big," said Vance. "I do recall that there were a lot of arguments against taking nukes."

"That's odd," said Dale.

"What's that?"

"All I got was a minuscule reading on the debris, but it's reading like some sort of alloy… along with the nuke's radiation."

"Really? Probably an old Earth probe… like Voyager maybe," suggested Alex.

"No chance. At the speed that any of the Earth's probes could go, they wouldn't get this deep into space for tens of thousands of years. Even if one of Earth's satellites had made it this far, nothing was sent out that was big enough to cause a nuke to fire. I'd better check the firing parameters protocol."

"And what are the chances that we would run into our own probe in space?" asked Vance.

"There's not enough zeros after the decimal point to calculate that," answered Dale.

"Doesn't make sense," added Alex. "Are you sure it was an alloy?"

"No, not really. The reading could be altered because the atomic blast changed the molecular structure of whatever it blew up."

CHAPTER 18

FIRST TIME IN ORBIT
May 12, 2062

The ship's braking gravity was at 1g and had been for just over two years.

"Slowing to 41,000 Ks per hour, Captain," said Dale cheerfully.

As the NORMAN approached at a relatively slow speed, the planet filled the screen. Its appearance was mostly blue, much to the delight of those aboard the NORMAN. Over the past three years, in conjunction with the ship's main computer, Dale had made as many determining calculations about the makeup of the planet as was possible from extreme distances. A lot of data was now stored, and would be added to the data acquired from orbit and surface sensors.

They would now slide into orbit at the planet's equator and make extensive studies of their new home. They required copious amounts of information regarding the composition of this planet in order to assure its livability for all of the life forms presently housed inside the NORMAN.

"Close the cryo deck's hatch," said Vance.

"Hatch closing," reported Dale.

"We have three moons," said Alex.

There on the view screen was the third moon. It was diminutive, less than 650 kilometers in diameter.

"Pretty little thing," said Alex.

"That's going to make for a beautiful night sky," suggested Vance.

"And maybe some interesting tides," added Dale.

"How about naming them Faith, Hope, and Charity?" asked Alex.

"That works for me," Vance responded. "We can always rename them if the need or want comes up."

The NORMAN slipped into the planet's orbit at a mere 30,000 kilometers an hour. The SMPD and main MVA were shut down, but the guidance MVA remained online to change and set the NORMAN's attitude. The main sensor arrays on the top deck were pointing at the planet's surface. These actions produced zero gravity, but only Vance was affected.

The ship's remaining sensors were set in motion. As many cameras photographed the surface, the huge array of sensors measured, weighed, and analyzed the chemical makeup, recorded temperatures, and gathered data and other critical information.

"We have a strong magnetic field," reported Dale.

"Copy that," Vance responded.

"Deploying weather satellites," said Dale. "We need to know weather patterns, temperature, where the rain falls, and where the storms occur."

"Copy that."

The planet's surface was made up of thousands of islands ranging in size from a few acres to six major continents. It contained three times the number of islands found on Earth. Only two of the six continents were connected. These two linked continents were approximately the same size, and both were roughly oblong in shape. One lay in the southern hemisphere, the other in the north. They were connected by a 30 by 1,300 kilometer landmass that ran diagonally from northwest to southeast, straddling the equator. From space, the two connected continents looked like a gigantic warped dumbbell. Both the southern and northern continents came within a few hundred kilometers of their respective poles. Unlike on Earth where only the South Pole is a continent, each pole here was a small continent, and both were covered in thick ice.

Ninety-five hundred kilometers to the west of the "Dumbbell Continents" sat the largest continent. The equator dissected this huge landmass at about 1,200 kilometers north of the continent's geographical center. The continent was nearly 8,300 kilometers from east to west and 6,600 kilometers from north to south, making it a bit larger than the African continent on Earth.

"That is a big body of land," said Alex.

"I'll say," agreed Dale.

"Vast, to say the least," Vance added.

They were about a third of the way across the continent, traveling from west to east, when they crossed a colossal volcanic mountain range that spanned nearly the entire continent from north to south. More than 100 of the mountains peaked above 7,000 meters; three went above 8,000. They almost made the Rocky Mountain range on Earth look like foothills. From orbit, they could clearly see the calderas of hundreds of extinct volcanoes. They counted 33 volcanoes in the northern hemisphere, which appeared active; to the south, the volcanoes all seemed to be dormant, if not extinct. Some of the calderas in the dormant volcanoes were deep blue lakes filled with water, while others remained dry.

"It's a good sign, those volcanoes," said Dale. "Got to have a molten core to create them."

East of the volcanoes looked like a huge expanse of nothingness. In that dry barren section of land, they could see dozens of massive dust devils, many as tall as 3,000 meters, and the tops of the cones reached up to a half-kilometer wide. For hundreds of kilometers, these enormous whirlwinds were cutting a zigzag pattern from west to east across that territory.

"Holy crap, that doesn't look like a friendly environment," said Alex.

"Don't think we'll be setting up camp there," said Vance.

As they continued their orbit across this continent, they observed rainstorms varying from small showers to full-blown thunderstorms. As they passed over the east coast, a huge storm was battering the southeast coastline. From their vantage point, it looked like it could be a Category 6 hurricane, maybe even bigger.

"Looks to be wet and windy down there," remarked Vance.

"It's an active planet, that's for sure," said Alex.

"That storm is more than 1,630 kilometers wide," remarked Dale. "This planet looks like it gets a lot of rain. Just look at the storms over that ocean."

For 4,800 kilometers east of that vast continent, they passed over a grouping of volcanic islands approximately 1,200 kilometers in length. They counted ten islands in all, ranging from just below the equator to 1,100 kilometers north of it. These volcanic islands varied little in size or in the distance between them. From orbit, they looked like a black pearl necklace because of the distinct curve of the chain of islands.

"It's not hard to tell where the continental plates collided," said Dale. "Those are still active, still expanding."

As they rotated, a fourth continent came into view approximately 2,660 kilometers to the east of the Black Pearl islands. This was the continent with an unusual shape. It was round and shaped much like a massive engagement ring.

"So this is what it looks like up close," said Alex.

This continent's body, or "ring", was composed of a comparatively thin landmass that surrounded a massive freshwater inland sea. The ring's "band" ranged from 478 kilometers wide on the west coast, and gradually increased to just over 662 kilometers wide as it circled to the north and to the south, forming an almost perfect circle nearly 5,240 kilometers in diameter. The east side of the continent had an 830-kilometer bulge that resembled the setting on a ring. This bulge was formed by a sizeable mountain range that ran parallel to the continent's ring. This "setting" included dozens of mountains that were dominated by six mountain peaks ranging in height from 3,700 to 4,200 meters. These mountains did not appear volcanic, as those located on the "Vast" continent, but they were clearly huge pressure ridges. The six tallest were snowcapped. Scattered around the ring's "setting" were dozens of small islands making them appear almost as if they were sparkles emanating from a diamond. There was little doubt that in its distant past this continent was formed by a collision with a huge asteroid or meteorite. Lying within the ring's band was a massive inland sea containing approximately seven million square kilometers. Two thirds of the ring lay north of the equator. The three aboard the NORMAN immediately named it the "Ring Continent." Sixty-five hundred kilometers of ocean lay between the eastern coast of the Ring and the western edge of the North Dumbbell. The six continents, including the north and south poles, seemed to balance the large landmasses evenly around the planet.

On their fifth orbit Dale gave a report, "Sensor readings are quite interesting, Vance," said Dale.

"Give me some highlights," Vance responded.

"The surface is covered with approximately 80% water, nearly 90% of that is salt and the huge sea within the Ring is fresh. Gravity is within 1.05% of Earth's. The planet's size is 100.7% that of the Earth's. At the equator, the planet is spinning at 2,010 Ks per hour, which correlates to a 20-hour day based on our sixty-minute hours. I'm just guessing a little here, but it looks like it circles its star approximately every 400 days."

"Our clocks and calendars are going to be of no use here," said Vance.

"Based on locating an acceptable planet and its size, we already have a protocol in place to recalibrate minutes, hours, days, and years, as well as speed and spin. We'll do that once we get that information down to the thousandth of a second."

"I'll leave that to you," said Vance. "Any real negatives here?"

"Not with all that. We couldn't have expected better," answered Dale. "Over land at the equator, the average temperature ranges from 75°-110° Fahrenheit, night to day. The hottest temperature we recorded during this orbit was the interior of the "Vast" continent, at 130° during the day and 90° at night. The coolest, other than the planet's poles, seems to be at the northern hemisphere of the Ring, with temperatures of 60° during the day and 20° at night. At the equator, the sensors indicate that over the oceans, it's in the high 80s during the day and high 50s at night."

"We can live with any of those temperatures. It has to be cooler to the north or south."

"For sure. From what I can see here we can pretty much pick our climate," said Dale. "Also this planet has a slight tilt to its axis. Not quite as much as Earth's but enough to create climate changes."

"Our Earth's sensors were right," said Alex.

"We hit the jackpot as far as I'm concerned. There likely are perfect planets out there somewhere, but where and how far?" questioned Dale.

Vance sat for a moment tapping his fingers on the arm of his chair. "Okay, what's the downside?"

"A shortage of oxygen. Compared to the air on Earth, at 7.68% of the atmosphere, it's going to be really hard to breathe. That fix is going to take time," said Dale.

"That's a lot more oxygen than we originally anticipated," said Alex.

"True," agreed Vance. "We weren't expecting much, if any."

"It's still not enough—it's equivalent to the amount of oxygen at 8,600 meters, similar to being on the top of Mt. Everest on Earth. The good news is that atmospheric nitrogen is at 89.22%, 10% higher than Earths, and the carbon dioxide count is .3091, ten times that found on Earth. All the other gases are similar to Earth's."

"How can such a high count of carbon dioxide be a good thing?"

"With these nitrogen and carbon dioxide levels, plants will grow. Really grow. And as the plants grow, they absorb that nasty CO_2 and turn it into oxygen."

"I knew that," Vance smiled.

"Also, without a great increase in oxygen we won't have an ozone layer. Without ozone, not much will be able to live on the surface."

"I didn't know that."

"Here's something else I'll bet you don't know. This solar system is probably fifty million years younger than the Earth's."

"That's good?"

"Can't hurt. But because of its relatively young age, this planet may be a great deal more prone to earthquakes."

They were coming up on the west side of the long narrow landmass that connected the Dumbbell continents. One-hundred and fifty kilometers north of the equator, on this already narrow landmass, it thinned dramatically. It looked as if the two continents might have shifted at that point. This slender stretch of land appeared to have been broken, creating more than two dozen small islands at the area of the fracture. However, a narrow isthmus no more than 16 kilometers wide still connected the two continents.

"That's interesting," said Dale as he commanded the sensors to concentrate on the isthmus. "Looks like a future canal location to me."

"It does, all right," agreed Vance. "But not for the next millennia or two."

In 20 minutes, they again approached the western edge of the Vast Continent.

"Looks like a good place to put the African animals," said Alex.

"Hopefully in a few hundred years," answered Dale.

An hour and a half later they passed over the narrow west side of the Ring Continent. They could clearly note the difference between the water contained within the Ring and the water seen on the rest of the planet. It was light blue and so crystal clear it appeared shallow; you could see the bottom in most places. Nevertheless, the sensors showed it to be deep, up to 2,000 meters in the middle. The oceans were a darker shade of blue, with a slight tint of purple when the sun's reflection was just right.

Wherever water met land, on all coasts, lakeshores, and riverbeds, something was growing. Visibly, the green belt went inland eight kilometers in some places, but just one or two in others. It was the same around all of the tens of thousands of lakes and rivers that dotted the islands and continents. On the other hand, the vast majority of this planet's land mass seemed to hold no life. From orbit, the multitude of colors spread across the barren land held the promise of a large variety of minerals.

"Looks like we have an abundance of iron, tin, and a lot of other minerals. Wait a second," Dale said. "If I'm not mistaken, we have gold. . . and quite a bit of it."

"Gold?"

"Yes, sir."

"Gold is rare on Earth, but apparently not here. It all depends on what was in the neighborhood when the planet was formed. There seems to be as much gold on this planet as we had copper on Earth."

"That's good, I assume?"

"Oh, hell yes. Gold is the most versatile and durable of all metals. Great qualities. Great."

The NORMAN remained in orbit for another week studying the planet. They set the NORMAN's guidance system to slightly alter its orbit for each revolution. By the end of the week, they had passed nearly straight over every kilometer of the planet. The sensor memory banks recorded size, shape, depth, and temperature of every ocean, lake, river, stream, and creek on the planet. They recorded the height, width, and mass of every mountain and hill. They also recorded the location and size of all major mineral deposits, from iron to gold to zinc. They mapped the entire topography of this new world. They also recorded a number of fairly symmetrical holes on all of the continents that seemed strangely out of place. During this mapping time, Vance, Alex, and Dale made short and long-term plans. In the short term, Vance was going to be busy. He would be working 20-hour days in an effort to single-handedly seed the entire planet.

As one might expect with so many years of planning, many scenarios had been created for bringing a hypothetical new planet to life. These studies began two years before the NORMAN's construction was started. The finest minds in botany, zoology, biology, agriculture, animal husbandry, geography, oceanography, mineralogy, and every other related field worked on the project over the ensuing five years. Once all of the data available on this planet was fed into the computer, the correct first steps and subsequent course of action would be laid out within minutes.

Aboard the NORMAN, on Deck 15, were seven runabout airships, five small and two that were about three quarters the size of a boxcar, all driven by SMPEs and MVAs. It also held five boats, four suited for small jobs, and one for big jobs that was quite large. Both were driven by water-jet propulsion. There were four multipurpose land vehicles, two all-purpose tractors, and a fantastic variety of tandem equipment. Small nuclear reactors, considerably larger than what was embedded in Vance's chest, provided the power for this entire fleet. All of the vehicles were specifically designed to aid in seeding, planting, and introducing animal life to the planet. Because of this, the ceiling of Deck 15's hanger was twice as high as most of the other decks and it had an exterior hatch allowing egress and ingress to and from the outside.

It was agreed that the Ring Continent should be the base camp for the colonists. It contained the largest concentration of fresh water on the planet, and was surrounded by salt water. Its topography ranged from flat planes to snowcapped mountains. The continent also contained thousands of freshwater lakes and rivers, and the soil deposits were as good as they were anywhere on the planet.

About 1,900 kilometers northwest of the equator, on the saltwater side of the Ring, was a beautiful natural bay where the weather was ideal. The mouth of the bay was 400 meters wide, opening up into a protected area encompassing about nine kilometers across and three wide. Two rivers emptied into the bay in the form of waterfalls, one tall and spectacular, and the other 80 meters wide but much lower in height. A third river came from inland, gushing through a narrow canyon, which produced a freshwater bay. The fresh water exited the mouth of the bay, forcing the salt water back a good kilometer before the two mixed.

To the south of the bay, the land flattened out to gentle rolling hills for nearly 80 kilometers. This was to become ideal farming country in the future. Given all these features, everyone believed that this would be the ideal place to begin their new civilization.

"Time to come out of orbit and land this thing," said Vance.

"Agreed," said Dale. "On the south side of the bay?"

"Looks perfect."

"That should be a nice view."

An extensive checklist had to be completed before the descent began. This precaution took the better part of three hours to accomplish.

"That's the last of the list," said Dale.

"Start the main MVA," ordered Vance.

"Buckle up."

Three minutes later, Vance gave the order and the guidance MVA started changing the NORMAN's orientation from top down

GABRIEL

toward the planet to bottom leading in orbit. The MVA then began reducing speed. There would be no fiery entry. The MVA would gradually slow the NORMAN to three hundred meters an hour as it descended into the atmosphere of the planet. At 10,000 meters, the NORMAN began slowing further. The "brakes" would be evenly applied as it approached the chosen landing area. At 2,000 meters, the massive landing gear automatically deployed. The NORMAN slowed to just a few meters per second and nearly stopped just before touchdown.

"We're here," announced Dale.

"Shutdown the MVAs and SMPE," ordered Vance.

"Shutting down."

"Perfect," said Alex. "I'd give the engineers a big bonus if we were back on Earth."

"Without question," smiled Vance. "I couldn't feel it touch down."

The huge bronze orb was now sitting on the top of a broad knoll situated 30 meters above the bay; the first time it had been on land for over thirty-two years.

On the viewer appeared the words, WELCOME TO GABRIEL. Some computer programmer, over three decades in the past, had secretly programmed the main computer to display those words on the NORMAN's landing.

"Very flattering and quite an honor for my family," said Alex sincerely.

"Nothing could be more deserved," said Vance.

"Ditto," said Dale.

"Thank you."

"I'm now recalibrating all the timing and dating devices on the NORMAN to reflect the planet Gabriel's timing. According to the corrected protocols, we're to reset everything to reflect 50-second minutes, 50-minute hours, 20 hour days, and 10-month years."

"I'm going to have a little trouble with that for a while, I suspect," said Vance.

"Me, too," said Alex.

"Actually neither one of you will," said Dale. "You're thinking as if you have a human brain. We'll all get that change downloaded into our SLF brains in an instant and then think no more about it. No sweat."

"You're right. It's the colonists who will have the trouble."

"They'll learn, and it will make life a lot easier for the future generations," added Dale.

"Well, be that as it may, I'm going outside to take a walk," announced Vance with a big smile.

"Take us with you, my friend," requested Alex.

"No sweat, I'll pick up a direct feed camera on the way out. We'll see our new home together."

Vance went into his ready room and changed into some loose fitting denim pants, walking boots, and a cotton shirt. He went to a storage locker and picked up an audio/video camera that was about half the size of a deck of cards. He attached it to a special lightweight rig on his shoulder and returned to the bridge.

"You guys ready?" he asked.

"Can't wait," said Alex.

"Let's head out." With that, Vance walked to the elevator.

It took 23 seconds to ride from Deck 4 to Deck 20, which seemed like an eternity for Vance right now. Vance exited the elevator, walked about ten paces to his left and pushed a button. The huge loading ramp began to lower itself to the ground. Eight seconds later with camera running, Vance walked down the ramp onto the soil of his new home.

CHAPTER 19

A WALK OUTSIDE
May 13, 2062

As Vance stepped onto the tight carpet of lichen and vines, he went to his knees, bent over and kissed the ground. "We are here," he said with deep emotion.

"How's it smell?" asked Alex.

"Delightful," Vance answered after a moment. He was clearly choked up. "Clean, fresh." He stood up, "And look at this view."

He looked left, to the west, where the ocean met the bay. He could see where the fresh water rushing out of the bay caused considerable turbulence where it plowed into the ocean water, forming an estuary 150 meters beyond the entrance to the bay. *Interesting*, he thought. *There must be a lot more water dumping into the bay from the three rivers than is apparent.*

He looked to his right and saw that the hill on which they sat joined the side of a nearly sheer cliff about 300 meters to the east. The cliff itself looked cleaved off from the side of the small mountain, although from Vance's viewpoint, he couldn't see any rubble or boulder field at its base. What he could see at the cliff's base was the mouth of a gigantic cave rising 100 meters or more up the cliff's side. "Are you seeing this?" asked Vance.

"That is one big cave," answered Dale.

"Big is right," added Alex. "What the hell would have caused such a hole?"

"It almost looks like it was carved on purpose, kind of an oval shape. Wonder how far back it goes," said Dale.

"We'll figure that out some other time," said Vance. "Right now I'm enjoying the view."

From where he stood, he could see the entire bay. He could see the mist rising from one of the waterfalls a half kilometer off. The river was rushing into the bay from the far side of the cliff to his right; straight ahead was a gentle slope leading to the mouth of the bay.

"Temperature is 78 degrees," reported Dale.

Vance stood with his hands on his hips and looked around for a full two minutes. "I'm going to walk down to the water."

Without another word, Vance set off straight ahead down the gentle hill. To his right, the land remained quite level until it intersected with the cliff. Then a series of hills, large and small, surrounded and formed the boundaries of the bay.

After a minute of walking on the short green carpet, he came to a short drop-off no doubt formed by the rushing waters leaving the bay. It was easy to climb down the three meters or so by stepping from rock to rock. At the bottom where the vegetation stopped, he walked onto a narrow sandy beach. He stopped, bent over and picked up a handful. "Hmm," he expressed.

"What have you got there?" asked Alex.

"A fine sand, lots of colors in it but mainly off-white."

"Hold it closer to the camera so we can see it," said Dale.

Vance brought his hand up close to the camera's lens.

"Do you know what you've got in your hand, my friend?" asked Dale.

"Sand?"

"Yes, but it's a nifty sand. Looks like it's mainly quartz, volcanic ash, and cinders. The black grains are no doubt iron oxide and the gold grains are… no doubt gold."

"No Shit?"

"No shit."

Vance mulled that information for a moment, "Wait a sec. This continent isn't volcanic, so where does the ash come from?"

"Remember the Black Pearl islands? They've been erupting for tens of thousands of years. This continent is downwind. So there you go."

Vance nodded to himself, "I'll buy that."

He sniffed the sand. "Smells like clean water."

"It should because it looks as if there are few, if any, pollutants in it."

He walked to the water's edge and tossed in the handful of sand. He bent down, washed the remaining sand off his hands, cupped a palm full of water and took a sip. "Had to be the first to do that," he smiled.

"If not you, then who?" responded Alex.

"No one for a few hundred years, I guess." He stood and looked around again, then looked back into the water. "What do you suppose those bumps are?"

"Bumps?"

"In the water, just under the surface."

"Can you get a better picture?"

"Camera's waterproof so I'll wade out and give you a close-up."

He took off his boots and socks, rolled up his pant legs and waded out to about knee deep. He took the camera off its shoulder rig and lowered in into the water a foot from one of the bumps.

"How's that?"

"Good. Back off a little. . . there, that's fine."

"Any clue?"

"By God, they're stromatolites," said Dale, excitedly.

"I'm guessing that's a good thing."

"They are one of the main reasons why Earth was able to create life on the surface. They are oxygen producers. Great oxygen producers."

"These things are alive?"

"Yep, single cell bacteria, a type of algae. They use water, carbon dioxide and sunlight to create their food, like photosynthesis. In turn, they produce oxygen.

"No shit?"

"No shit."

"Got all the pictures you need?"

"Yes, sir."

"Then I'm off to do a little exploring." Vance pulled the camera out of the water and clipped it to the rig. After putting his socks and boots back on , he walked right along the beach toward the back of the bay. He was in no hurry. He picked up rocks, looked at them, put some in his backpack, dropped others, and threw others into the water. He made sure he retrieved samples of all of the native plants he could find, along with soil, water, and rock samples. It felt so good to be outside, to have a sky overhead, and to see beautiful white clouds drifting high above.

As it turned out, there were three varieties of plants growing on the planet. One was very similar to Earth's lichen, a primitive mold that actually digests and thrives on rock. The NORMAN had brought several varieties of lichen on board for just that purpose. It would create soil and oxygen as it ate rock, just what it had already been doing for millennia on Gabriel. This presence of this native vegetation saved those aboard the NORMAN from hundreds of years of terraforming. This was a Godsend.

Another plant was more of a tiny leafed vine that took root in the lichen's leavings and the volcanic ash, and after maybe thousands of years had managed to creep inland. It was possible that this plant might be edible by animals, such as rodents, rabbits, squirrels, groundhogs, and the like. They might thrive on it. Those animals were among the thousands of embryos aboard the NORMAN.

The third plant was a true moss. It was found mainly on the banks of rivers and lakes at higher altitudes, where the lichen had not taken hold. Over the millennia, these plants had managed to make large deposits of organic material in the nitrogen-rich volcanic soil, in some places several meters deep. This was welcome news aboard the NORMAN.

"What could be the origin of these plants?" asked Alex.

"Many theories suggest that all life came from space as seeds and spoors stuck to meteors and other space debris," said Dale.

"That could be," said Alex. "But it all had to start somewhere."

"That study should give the colonists something to do in their leisure time," suggested Vance. "You're planning to give them leisure time?" Alex smiled.

"Not for a few decades, I wouldn't think."

"Let's preserve samples of these plants in a sterile environment for future study," suggested Dale. "Don't want to taint them with what we've brought along."

May 14, 2062

Vance walked down the ramp once again. He wanted to take a look at the topography to the south of the NORMAN, and the large cave that was so close by. They all—Vance, Dale, and Alex—presumed the land to the south would be ideal for farming, so Vance wanted to walk through the gently rolling hills up the winding creek for six or seven kilometers to see if he could discover the source, the headwaters. He could have taken one of the small runabouts, but he wouldn't enjoy that as much.

"Think I'll take a look at the cave first," he said and headed off to his right.

As he walked directly toward the cave, it seemed to grow in height. "Wow, this is big." He continued walking until he reached the mouth. He stopped and took an instrument from his utility belt, switched it on, adjusted a dial, and pointed it straight up. "Jesus, the mouth is 130 meters high." He pointed the instrument to his right, noted the distance and then pointed it to his left. "Just over 200 wide." He walked inside. "Holy crap, this thing is big enough to park the NORMAN in--- several NORMANs."

Half an hour later, Vance emerged from the mouth of the cave. "That looks like a secure place to store almost anything, and a lot of it. Damn thing is nearly a kilometer long before it starts tapering down in size and ends up in a whopping fresh water pool at the back."

"By the measurements you've taken, it looks like the floor of the cave covers nearly fifteen acres," said Alex.

"And the floor is nearly flat, with no debris to speak of. Looks damn near man-made."

"The walls appear to be solid gold-bearing quartz," said Dale.

"What about parking the NORMAN inside" asked Alex, "out of the rain?"

"We'll do some studies on the structure to see if it will be safe. Wouldn't want the roof caving in on the ship," said Dale.

"I think we'll take no chances on that until we have finished taking our time travel trips," said Vance.

"Agreed," said Dale.

CHAPTER 20

THE SEEDING
May 15, 2062

"We'll start with the Ring and maybe get some seeding on the other continents with the leftovers, if any," said Dale as Vance was readying one of the larger runabouts.

"Agreed. Let's get our home continent ready for our kids. The rest of the territory can wait for a millennia if necessary."

Vance's first task was loading the large airship's main hoppers with a mixture of grass seeds and legumes, such as clover and alfalfa, which have the ability to absorb nitrogen from the air and collect it in their root systems. It was a good way to naturally add nitrogen to the soil.

When planning for this eventuality, it was believed that some varieties of seed would fare better where others might fail; a simple survival of the fittest would apply. Some seeds would find the wet areas more to their liking, whereas they might perish in the arid climates. Their knowledge of Gabriel's weather systems was still limited, so broadcasting a mixture of seeds seemed the wiser course. Vance flew at an optimum height and speed, broadcasting the seed mixture sparingly over the western-most edges of the Ring Continent's soil deposits. It didn't have to be seeded heavily; the years, decades, and centuries that followed would spread the grasses through traveling roots, and the prevailing winds would carry the seeds inland. The three other warm continents would also be seeded, but at a more reduced level.

Next, four smaller hoppers would hold other seeds that could be dropped individually or broadcast as the situation dictated. Chief among this group of seeds were trees with fast-growing roots and seed-propagating trees; both would provide food and shelter for future animals. These seeds, along with ferns and mosses were to be dropped at high elevations on the shores of rivers, and creeks. Over the decades, the water flow would distribute the seeds and spoors downstream. Other bins held various bushes, vines, and edible flowers. Others contained seeds of the spruce, pine, and fir trees. These seeds were to be sparsely broadcast high in the mountain ranges. Gravity and wind would distribute their seeds, and eventually these trees would provide the lumber for future building. In the most ideal areas around their chosen bay, Vance, with computer guidance, planted many more lumber trees for easy access to the colonists. It was already planned that a century from now, oak, maple, teak, mahogany, and dozens of other hardwood trees would be planted when the soil was richer.

This was a time consuming job. It took Vance two full months to complete the task. Fortunately, he required neither sleep nor fuel. He never stopped moving and he never complained. He was enjoying himself as never before.

"I've got an unusual reading here," said Vance. He was flying at a low level, parallel to the central/west coast of the Vast Continent, and broadcasting seeds for plants and trees that would thrive in the tropical atmosphere.

"What do you have?" asked Dale.

"Don't know. I'm going to circle around and come over the spot again." Vance did a 180-degree turn and slowed the runabout down to a crawl as he headed back.

"Got it again. Going to land and take a look."

"Good."

Vance set the runabout down on a sandy area about two kilometers inland. His restraining harness automatically released as he pushed the button to open the hatch. He attached his shoulder-mounted camera and walked out into the humid air.

He spotted it immediately. There, 30 meters in front of him, sticking out of the sand, was a fairly large piece of metal. "Jesus! Can you see that?"

"We see it," said Alex.

"Got your compact sensor with you?"

"I do."

"Point it at that thing before you get any closer. Don't want you exposed to radiation or toxins of any kind."

Vance did as suggested. He pushed several buttons in turn and got no negative readings. "Slight radiation count, not a dangerous level. Otherwise, all clear," he reported.

"All the same, be careful," suggested Alex.

Vance walked the 30 meters, keeping his sensor pointing at the object. The object was an untarnished gold in color, about 20 millimeters wide and 3 millimeters thick, with its edges curved in. It stuck up about two meters out of the sand. Vance held the sensor just a fraction of a meter from its surface. "Still just a slight radiation count."

He replaced the sensor in its case attached to his belt and put his hand on the object. He applied some forward force to see how solidly the thing was stuck in the sand. It didn't move. He put both hands on it and tried to lift it out of the sand. It didn't budge. "It's stuck."

"I need all or at least a piece of that thing," said Dale.

Vance tried shaking it. Nothing.

"Rather than cutting off a piece, why don't I try to hook up a cable and pull it out?"

"Agreed."

Vance walked back to the runabout, got in and lifted off then flew the 30 meters back to the object and pushed a button. A cable with a self-locking hook extended from the bottom of the craft just below the cockpit. Vance let out 15 meters of cable, leaving the hook laying just a meter from the object. Then he landed two meters away. He exited the runabout and attached the cable around the object via the hook, tugged on it a couple of times to make certain it was secure, and returned to the runabout. "Here we go."

The runabout rose slowly until it came to the end of the cable slack… then it stopped.

"Going to apply some power." Vance pushed the power lever forward. At first nothing moved, but then with just a bit more power, the object began lifting out of the sand. "It's coming free."

"Copy that," said Dale.

The object came totally free at just under seven meters as it swung below the runabout like a pendulum. Vance carefully lowered the runabout until the object was returned to the ground. He then pulled forward enough to set the runabout down clear of the object. He exited again and walked back to take a look at his discovery. It was a straight piece for its entire length. The end that had been buried five meters under the sand had a jagged edge. It looked like it had been violently ripped from something—the big question was from what?

Vance bent over to see if he could lift it. It was surprisingly light. The whole seven-meter section weighed no more than three kilos. "I can get it into the runabout through the rear hatch. I'll just lay it on top of the bins."

"Roger that," said Dale. "Can't wait to analyze it."

"You'll have to wait until I finish broadcasting this load."

"No problem."

As Vance was storing the object on top of the bins, he stopped suddenly, "Whoa!"

"What?" asked Alex.

"It has some writing on it."

"Any known language?"

There was a long pause, "Not even close."

Eight hours later, Vance pulled into the NORMAN and landed the runabout on Deck 15. As soon as he exited, he walked to the rear hatch and removed the object. The main lab was on this deck so Vance took the object off the top of the bins and headed straight for the lab. He walked over to the bench and sat the object on it. The bench was only four meters long, causing the object to hang over at both ends.

"Here you go, Doc. What do you want me to do?"

"First let me see the writing."

Vance reached up and pulled a camera/microphone that was suspended from the ceiling and pointed the lens at the writing. "Is this close enough?"

"Move up a little."

Vance did so.

"Right there is perfect. Now run the camera down the length of the writing."

Again Vance complied. "What do you think?"

"It's from another civilization. That's what I think."

"That's what I thought."

"Somebody beat us here," said Alex.

"Well that's. . . um, I was going to say interesting but it goes way beyond that," said Vance, "unexpected, shocking, enlightening, frightening, and the list goes on."

"Certainly gives real meaning to the words, 'we are not alone,'" remarked Alex.

"It might also answer some questions about the plant life and the strange unnatural looking holes we've see around this planet," said Vance.

"Could be the answer to the big cave here on Home Bay," said Vance.

"Yes it could," answered Alex.

"Let's see if we can tell what it's made of," said Dale. "Get some filings from the ripped end and put some in the spectrometer and the electron microscope."

Twenty minutes later Vance sat on a bench looking at the object. Dale had just informed him that the object was made up of gold and something akin to aluminum.

"They somehow managed to meld the two, plus something else, into a single molecule. It's lightweight, really strong and noncorrosive. Whoever they are, they are well ahead of our metallurgy technology. This stuff would have made a great skin for the NORMAN."

"Can you tell how old it is?"

"Having some trouble with dating. The metal doesn't lend itself to that; however, the dirt stuck in the ripped section does to a certain extent. I could be off by as much as half, but I'd say it's been stuck in planet Gabriel for less than a year.

No one said anything for a few seconds, before Alex spoke. "Wonder what they were doing here?"

"I wonder what caused something to break," said Dale.

"I wonder if they'll be back," added Vance.

―――――

After completing the Ring seeding, Vance managed to lightly seed the remaining three warm continents and the largest of the islands. The seeds, by necessity, were spread thinly, as little as three tons per continent and just a few hundred kilos on the large islands. As the fields and prairies grew over the years, seeds would be harvested and redistributed wherever needed.

Next came the water plants. Kelp and algae would grow rapidly in the nitrogen-rich waters, so they and other water plants were seeded next, which would provide food for the future tiny plant-eating aquatic animals. Freshwater plants were then seeded. Here, Vance was able to concentrate on a relatively small area just shy of 6 million square kilometers of the Ring Sea. He scattered the seeds around the entire circumference of this enormous body of water in scarcely two days. Next were the vast oceans of salt water that covered the rest of the planet Gabriel. Using a computer-generated model, which took into account the currents, wind, rain, and projected drift, he distributed seeds of larger water plants, including mangrove trees, over the rest of Gabriel. This took nine weeks.

"What comes next? asked Vance as he sat down in the captain's chair. "Can't wait to see how everything grows."

"That covers everything we can do on the surface. Before we leave for ten years, we'll go back into orbit and distribute the satellites," said Dale.

Deck 13 was the satellite deck. It contained 163 sophisticated satellites. Forty-two were loaded with various life forms, and were to be placed in orbit along with three master satellites. The remaining satellites would stay on board until the next phase of terraforming.

The master satellite's sensors would monitor the growth of the plants on land and in water and measure the oxygen levels in both. Once the required levels were satisfactorily established, and the required growth and spread of plant life was reached, the master satellite would give commands to these specialized satellites, and they would drop out of orbit and distribute their contents to one of the 42 preselected spots on Gabriel's surfaces. It was calculated to take between ten and thirty years before the first satellite dropped out of orbit.

In this manner, animals such as plankton, snails, shrimp, and water bugs of every description were to be introduced to Gabriel's oceans and seas. Fifteen satellites would accomplish the same job for the land areas. Bees and other beneficial insects were the only cargo aboard ten of these satellites. The satellites had parachutes designed to provide soft landings for the drop of specialized beehives into the middle of a bloom. The objective was for the beehives, eggs, and chrysalides to thaw before the satellite's doors would open. Under tolerable conditions, the hope was that these insects would, over the years, spread far and wide, and thus provide invaluable pollination and seed distribution for millennia to come.

CHAPTER 21

LET IT GROW
October, 2062

The NORMAN lifted off the surface of Gabriel just shy of five months after it had landed. Vance loved his new home but he was anxious to get under way.

"Check list complete?"

"Yes, sir," responded Dale.

"Our route is programmed in?"

"Yes, sir. We are going to be making one hell of a big circle—hopefully ending up back here at the end."

Vance smiled, "How big a circle, Dr. Isley?"

Dale returned the smile, "Trillions and trillions of kilometers, Captain. And, as a side effect, there will be gravity on board for most of the trip, not just during the acceleration and deceleration phases."

"Why . . . wait a sec, I've got this one," said Vance.

Dale said nothing and waited while Vance mulled over his own question.

"In order to make a circle," Vance paused for a moment, "The guidance MVA is going to remain powered up to apply a sideways thrust while the SMPE and main MVA maintain acceleration. This ship will be on its side with the top facing toward the center of the arc."

"Exactly."

Vance smiled again. "How much gravity?"

"Just shy of a quarter g. It will keep you comfortably in your seat."

Vance nodded in understanding. "Okay, let's get out of here for a few decades," said Vance.

"Ten decades, actually," added Dale.

"How long in ship time?"

"Aboard the NORMAN at full speed, eleven and a half years."

Vance nodded, "Let's get going. I can't wait to see what this place looks like in a 100 years."

The NORMAN went into orbit and spent the following day placing the 42 satellites in their proper orbit. It occurred to the three on board that from now on, no matter what happened to them, Gabriel would be a living, breathing world.

HEADING BACK
January, 2072

With only a year to go before returning to Gabriel, Vance was on the incubation deck overseeing the auto system as it began placing the embryos of dozens of species into the artificial wombs. The wombs were designed to simulate, as closely as possible, the natural womb of the same species. Just as in nature, some of these "wombs" could hold two or more embryos and contained the predicted chemical makeup of the amniotic fluid. The proper temperature and the sound and movement of the pregnant mother were simulated.

Two decks were packed from floor to ceiling with frozen embryos, sperm, and eggs. Every possible known beneficial species on Earth was included. Everyone understood that some of the thousands of species would not survive for various reasons, but it was hoped that the majority would flourish.

Once the planet's statistics and ecology were entered into the computer, a plan of action was produced on how to proceed. All of the systems on the incubation deck were designed to be as automatic as possible, but they still required a certain amount of hands-on assistance.

"The program starts with the herbivores and grazers, which have the longest gestation periods," said Dale. "These are the big animals.

On the Ring there will be deer, elk, moose, mountain goats, big-horned sheep, horses and long-horned cattle. On the Dumbbell continents we'll add llamas, alpacas and oxen to that list. And on the Vast continent, we'll have the African animals like gnus, zebras, and a few varieties of antelope. They are needed to start the large herds of prey animals that the continent will need in the future. The timing for these births starts just after touchdown, and is spaced out enough to allow you to keep up without being overwhelmed."

"Before I even start, it sounds overwhelming," responded Vance.

Dale smiled, "This process is scheduled to take just over two years."

"Got to get 'em off the ship ASAP; otherwise, it'll be a big mess in a hurry," Vance smiled.

"Even at that, my friend, you're going to be a nursemaid for quite a while. We have tons of powdered formula aboard, and you'll be bottle-feeding a lot of critters."

"I'm looking forward to it."

"What the hell happened to the hard case, the calloused badass that we grew so fond of back on Earth?" asked Alex.

"Believe it or not, I've been asking myself that same question," smiled Vance.

"What is your answer?"

"I have no need to be a badass anymore. I don't have to deal with assholes or fucked up circumstances. And besides, I'm loving every minute of this adventure. I feel so relevant again."

"I would say that you are probably the most relevant being in the galaxy right now," Alex said sincerely.

"I doubt that."

"I share Alex's opinion here," said Dale.

Vance paused for a moment, "At any rate, I can't wait to see the animals that we've brought come to life. It will be incredible."

"Your change in attitude is amazing," said Dale. "I'll bet a psychiatrist would love to write your case history."

"No doubt," agreed Alex.

Nothing was said for a second then Dale reinitiated the animal conversation.

"Fortunately there were a lot of forward thinkers working on these projects," he said. "There are a lot of really cool mechanical wet nurses on board. A whole deck is dedicated to them. Some really clever stuff. Heck, most of these animals won't even know that they don't have a real mother."

"I know, it's remarkable. I'll just have to make certain that their mechanical udders stay full."

"And be handy with repair tools," cautioned Dale. "I've never seen anything that can't be broken by a young animal." Dale paused for a moment. "We'll be incubating the smaller critters, rabbits and such, on our next trip. We can't turn fast propagators loose on the vegetation until we have predators ready to control them. They'd breed so fast without predation; they'd devastate the vegetation in just a few years. Consequently, all of the other animals would starve."

"There should be plenty to eat on the Ring when we get back," added Alex.

"We'll be wasting a lot of animals if there isn't," remarked Vance.

"Five of each species to start. Four females to every male and hope nothing happens to the male?" asked Vance.

"Yes sir. But we do have ample supplies of sperm from all relevant species. If the male of a species dies, we can artificially inseminate the females. At some time in the future, we'll be doing that anyway in order to diversify the gene pools. As it is, we're going to have inbreeding for several generations, but that's unavoidable. The naturalists assured us that any related genetic problems should weed themselves out through natural selection over a few generations."

"Yeah, we don't need any three-eyed elk running around the Ring. Wouldn't look right," said Vance.

"Marine life, such as fish, mollusks, and coral will be a lot easier—just eggs and seed, some of which we'll have to hatch and ready for transplant, but most of the eggs will just have to be put in the right place."

RETURN TO GABRIEL

March, 2074

"Look at that," exclaimed Vance as the planet Gabriel came up on the view screen.

It had changed dramatically over the past 100 years; what was once barren land was now 30% covered in vegetation. There were deserts of various sizes outlined on all of the continents except the Ring—because of its unique makeup, it had no really arid areas. Most of the deserts were located in the rain shadows of mountain ranges, but the massive deserts could be seen on the interior of the Vast continent to the east of its volcanic mountain range. There were various shades of green visible from the oceans, seas, and lakes to the highest mountains. The color of the fresh-water sea within the Ring had subtly altered, and was now a darker shade of blue.

"How long before we begin orbit?"

"Three hours," Alex responded.

"Thirty-seven of the satellites have dropped out of orbit," said Dale. "Five haven't."

"We'll soon find out how they worked when we land."

"We will need to bring the five duds back aboard to see why they're still in orbit."

"Agreed."

―――――

"What are the oxygen levels reading?"

"It's now at 17.45%, which is about the level found in Earth's atmosphere at 1500 meters. And because of the increased oxygen and massive thunderstorms planet wide, Gabriel now has an ozone layer at over a half a meter thick around the planet. That will increase as the years pass."

"How thick was Earth's ozone layer?"

"One and a half meters, give or take."

"The key here is that animals can now live on the surface. Because of the rain, carbon dioxide and nitrogen, vegetation has grown exponentially, adding to the oxygen levels, which in turn increase the ozone layer," said Dale.

The NORMAN slipped into orbit three hours later and began a sensor scan of Gabriel. On their first orbit over the Ring, Vance let out a joyous yell. "It's becoming a garden of Eden, for Christ's sake!"

"Zooming in," said Dale.

They could see the tall evergreen trees, now a hundred years old, as they grew in the hills and mountains. A good representation of hardwood trees were close to rivers, ponds, and lakes. Grass and multiple varieties of plants covered a nice percentage of the more arid land.

They could clearly view the aquatic plants thriving in the massive inland sea. As they approached the Ring continent's 'setting,' as they had been calling the bulge on the east side, they could see that the firs, pines, and other softwoods had a good foothold in the tall mountains.

"Gabriel is advancing its evolution at an incredible rate. Its progress in a hundred years is roughly comparable to Earth's progress over a thousand years. It's quite remarkable."

"Guess our efforts have not been in vain."

"That and the ideal conditions on the planet. All it needed was seed. It's like a well-designed and equipped biosphere."

After four complete orbits of intelligence gathering and satellite retrieval, they started their descent. Vance was in a hurry to get back on Gabriel's surface. They went through the same procedure as they had on their first landing.

The second that the NORMAN touched down on the hill above what they now called the Home Bay, and the SMPE and MVAs were shut down, Vance was up and at the elevator.

He once again stepped out onto the surface of Gabriel. "We're back," he smiled as he took in the view. "Wow! Take a look as this, will ya." Vance swung slowly back and forth to give a full view of the bay, the cave, and surrounding hills. The hills were completely covered in shades of green.

"Heading down," said Vance as he started walking toward the bay. Grass and a variety of new plants made walking a little tougher. He had to lift his feet over the foliage, which was crowding out and replacing much of the low-growing native vine. He again walked to the shore and picked up a handful of sand. It looked the same; he sniffed it. "Looks the same, smells a little different."

"We have more life in the water now. That changes the chemistry, changes the smell," said Dale.

"Humm."

"I need to analyze it again," said Dale. "And get a good sampling of the vegetation, particularly the grasses and more of that native vine. I'd like to see if its chemistry has changed any."

"Bees," Vance exclaimed.

"Say again," said Alex.

"Got bees all over the place," answered Vance. "And I see some butterflies."

"Perfect," said Dale. "At least some of the satellites have done their job. The plants are being pollinated and the colonists will have honey."

"Roger that." Vance dropped the handful of sand, rinsed his hands and opened the backpack. He withdrew a small vile and scooped up a couple of ounces of water, then capped the vial. After placing the vial back into the backpack, he took off to walk around the bay.

Vance returned to the ship after six hours of exploring. He beat a big storm by just minutes. In his backpack were samples of every plant he could find, along with soil, rock, and water samples. He went directly to the lab to put his samples into the ship's analyzing systems while they were still fresh. When done, he went to his stateroom and took a shower, then walked onto the bridge.

"Dale, Alex." The images of the two instantly appeared on the main screen.

"Had fun taking the hike with you," said Alex.

"Not as much as I did."

"Analysis nearly complete," said Dale.

"Any bad news?"

"Not so far. Most of the plants seem to have plenty of protein, carbohydrates, and other nutrients. They will be good feed."

"No reason they wouldn't, I guess," said Vance.

"You're going to need to start erecting the pastures and nurseries for the animals soon," said Dale.

"Heading to deck 20 as soon as the analysis is complete."

"All the specs are downloaded on your pad. Just to our south, the flat land with that pretty little creek running through it will be ideal for the construction."

"We'll see if the engineers have done as well on the design of these nurseries as they have on everything else."

Within an hour, Vance drove the specially designed tractor down the loading ramp. The rain was coming down in sheets, but Vance remained dry inside the cab. In case he had to exit the tractor, he had on rain gear that made him look like a Grand Banks fisherman, with a yellow insulated jumpsuit covering his waterproof boots, and a wide floppy-brimmed hat.

Dale had suggested he wait until the rain stopped, or at least let up, but Vance was determined to get the job done quickly. Forty pastures needed to be readied for the forty different species that were in incubation.

The fencing and related equipment were yet another example of the incredible designs provided by the scientists and engineers so long ago. High-tech solar powered fences would contain the animals, and the accompanying high-tech nurseries would shelter and feed them.

"Is this fence going to hold the critters?" Vance asked as he headed back to the NORMAN.

"It will unless they enjoy a jolt of 10,000 volts," answered Dale.

"Time will tell," said Vance.

"We have babies being born," Dale's excited voice came into Vance's earpiece.

"Be there in a few minutes. Break out the cigars," Vance said excitedly.

Within ten minutes, Vance arrived on the incubation deck. He had taken off the rain gear and was now dressed in his normal lightweight jumpsuit. He went immediately to the artificial womb, which displayed a blinking green light. The amniotic fluid was just draining from the capsule into the recycle tank. The twin whitetail fawns were moving within their artificial sack. Vance turned and extracted a pair of surgical scissors and a white cotton towel from their dispensers, then turned back to the fawns. He gently cut the artificial sack open, turned one of the fawns and clipped the umbilical cord, then did the same for the twin. Both started breathing on their own as their long spindly legs stretched out.

"We're watching you, dad" said Alex.

Vance smiled, "How am I doing?"

"You're a natural," said Dale. "Don't forget the scent."

"Got it, thanks." Vance spread out the fluffy white cotton towel on a table, picked up a small aerosol can marked *Whitetail doe* and lightly sprayed the towel that he had used to dry the first fawn, whom Vance quickly named Bambi. As Bambi was trying to stand up, Vance picked up the second… Bimbo.

A few minutes later, Vance had the fawns dried and placed in a small holding pen. He bottle-fed both at once with a double-nippled bottle.

"This is exciting, this is incredible," Vance said quietly. "First mammals born on Gabriel."

After a few minutes, the twin fawns were asleep and cuddling together in a corner of the tiny pen.

"You'd better get back to the artificial nurseries, my friend. You're not going to be able to give personal service to hundreds of animals."

"I'm on it."

Vance spent the next 38 hours setting up nursing stations, working nonstop. The creek that ran through the middle of the pastures would supply the water to a sophisticated filtration system, which would then pump the filtered water to each individual station. The individual stations would add specific enzymes and proteins required for each species. Vance's job was to make certain that the nursing station's bins were constantly supplied with these specialized chemicals. These nursing machines were the key to the successful introduction of animals on Gabriel.

May, 2074

"Jesus!" Vance exclaimed. "I'm thinking we should have brought two of me."

Vance, even before all the incubated animals were born and transferred to the pastures, had been on nearly a constant run just to keep up with maintaining the nursing machines. When that recurring chore was complete, he had to make sure the young animals were able to find their way back into their shelters and, in many cases, put them on the artificial nipples.

"Does it say anywhere how much work these little critters would require?"

"As a matter of fact, it does," said Alex, "It's in the fine print."

Both Alex and Dale laughed. Vance did not.

"Can't believe how fast these animals are growing," said Vance as he walked down the line of pastures, checking and replenishing the nursing bins yet again.

"We can see that. Remarkable."

"Bambi, Bimbo, and their siblings are already agile and frisky. Check 'em out."

Vance made sure the camera attached to his shoulder followed the five fawns as they cavorted around the pasture. Vance could hear Alex and Dale laughing as they watched.

Vance observed. "And, you will note, they stay a good half a meter from the fence line. The fence works, just as the boys back home said it would."

"We can see that," said Alex into Vance's earpiece. "It looks like all are doing well."

"All babies are supposed to be cute, but I've got to tell you, moose are an exception."

"We can see that too. They have a face only a mother could love."

"I'm pretty fond of the homely little shits," Vance responded with a smile that Alex and Dale could not see. "The moose love the water. They wade in the creek more than they stay on dry land."

"That's the nature of the beast," responded Alex.

"It looks like most of the critters are nibbling on everything in sight. Hope the feed lasts long enough for them to get big enough to turn loose."

"It should," said Dale.

"Well, if it doesn't, I'll turn them loose. I'll bet they won't wander far from the nursing stations until we wean them."

"No bet," responded Alex.

Vance spent as much time as he could just watching the baby animals as they ate, played, grew, and slept. He had to tear himself away to get done what needed to get done. He was tireless, putting in 20-hour days, every day. All bitching aside, he was in his personal heaven.

June, 2074

"I have the tanks full of fish and I'll be off in five minutes," said Vance.

"Good. Should take you 18 hours to plant them."

"That's what the computer says. Then I'll be back for more."

Vance started with planting staple fish like krill, shrimp, sardines, mackerel, cod, and a score of other species from the main tanks. These species would feed future generations of larger fish and sea birds. He would plant just a few hundred of each in places designated by the computer program. In addition, as he passed over specific areas he would drop a variety of fish from the smaller tanks. It was hoped that all of these various fish would eat, breed, and migrate from these areas over the following decades.

Quail, pheasant, chucker, wild turkeys, and other seed-eating game birds were hatched out by the dozens, raised to maturity, and planted in the best environments that the Ring and other continents held for them. They would be a food source for the colonists and predators as well as a great help in further seed distribution.

July, 2076

"Time to buckle up, Vance," said Dale.

"I'm on it." Vance walked across the deck and sat in the captain's chair. He looked at the view screen that held the image of the pastureland just south of the ship, the land that had raised hundreds of animals over the past two years; these animals had subsequently been transported to areas on The Ring, the three other main continents, and the largest islands. The pasture fencing and nursing stations were cleaned, dismantled, and restored to the NORMAN. Alex, Dale, and Vance discussed storing these supplies in the massive cave, but didn't want to leave them to the elements for a hundred years, as they expected to use them many more times in the future.

They had already witnessed some of their animals grow to near maturity. Mule deer, moose, elk, big-horned sheep, and a dozen other varieties were also transplanted to their ideal environments. Other grazing mammals were flown to their prescribed continents. Bambi and Bimbo, along with their fellow whitetail, were turned loose on the landing spot. It was as close to an ideal environment for their breed as could be found.

"A hundred more years to brew the planet," said Dale.

"Yeah, but this time we're leaving our animals behind. I'm having a little trouble with it. They'll all be dead long before we get back."

"But hopefully their offspring won't," said Alex. "We should come back to a truly living planet."

"Let's hope," said Vance.

This was the first negative emotion that Vance had displayed since his SLF was created 49 years ago.

"Ready to take off, Dale. Hit it."

June, 2086

Vance stayed in stasis nearly the entire ten years they were in space. He woke up at regularly scheduled times to check the systems and get updates from Alex and Dale, but he didn't spend more than a few hours at it. He wanted the time to fly by, and it did. He spent less than 20 hours awake during that decade.

The NORMAN returned to Gabriel and again completed four intelligence-gathering orbits before landing. They saw, among other changes, where large and small lightning-caused fires had burned forests and grasslands around the planet. Some of the forests had nearly grown back, and others were in the process of regrowing, just as on Earth. The burning of grasslands was a good thing. Fires removed the dead nutrient-starved grasses and plants, while stimulating new nutrient-rich growth. Other than the deserts on all of the continents except the Ring, they could see that a good percentage of the land had vegetation.

"Looks like we have vegetation of some sort covering over 60% of the planet now," said Dale.

The planet also had more cloud cover, snow on its mountains, and ice on its poles. Data stored in their aging weather satellites confirmed this. It had been just over a hundred years since they departed Gabriel, and the planet had definitely changed.

"Atmospheric gasses have altered," said Dale. "We have less carbon dioxide and nitrogen, but more oxygen. And you'll find it interesting to note that we now have methane, a small amount to be sure, but methane nonetheless."

"To detect it at all means that we have a lot of gas-producing animals down there." Vance smiled broadly. "They're alive!"

"That can be the only explanation," said Dale.

"Nice to hear the smile back in your voice, my friend," said Alex.

At orbiting altitude, and even with infrared, it was nearly impossible to spot wildlife, and they didn't try. There was no question that Vance would be in a runabout ASAP after landing to determine the degree of their success.

As they approached their designated landing spot, they found it had grown over with grass, bushes, and trees, but had subsequently been burned, leaving only fresh grass, a scattering of stubby bushes, and a few burnt-out stumps.

"Well, we got lucky. A fire has come and gone on our spot."

"This fire went through about two thousand acres before it stopped."

"Thunderstorms start them and stop them," said Dale.

"Need to make it a policy to leave wild fires alone in future generations. The practice of suppressing wildfires in the 20th and 21st centuries on earth did more harm than good, and was the direct cause of the massive fires that followed for decades," said Alex.

"Agreed," said Vance.

"This place will be designated a historical site in the future."

Vance smiled, "No doubt."

———

"I'm out of here," said Vance without preamble as he got out of his chair. He headed for his room to put on his overalls, boots, and shoulder-mounted camera. He walked down the ramp to a field of grass.

"We're home," he said aloud.

"That we are," responded Alex into Vance's earpiece.

Vance took a deep breath and sucked up the smells of Gabriel. "Smells different… smells alive."

"There's a lot more contributing to the odors than there was," said Dale.

Vance started walking down the hill. "Heading to the bay…" Vance stopped walking and talking. To his right, at the edge of the forest that now blocked the view of the cave entrance, stood a small herd of white-tailed deer. Standing among them was a beautiful buck with a magnificent rack.

"Do you see this?"

"We see."

"Look how beautiful they are. They're checking out the ship and me. That's 15 generations after Bambi and Bimbo by God… just look at them."

The deer didn't seem frightened. They were curious and cautious to be sure, but not afraid. After a moment, with the buck in the lead, they turned and started walking into the forest.

Vance followed after them at a slow pace. He spotted a flock of grouse off to his left, and saw three vultures slowly circling about a half a mile inland.

He returned to the NORMAN after a five-hour hike. It would be tough to find a happier man in the universe.

"We have an abundance of wildlife out there. I've seen dozens of animals and eight different species of birds."

"We've been watching," said Alex.

"Time to get some squirrels, rabbits, and the like turned loose and breeding. Massive amounts of feed out there," said Vance.

"That's exactly what the program calls for," reported Dale.

"I'll get the incubation/gestation started for all the programmed animals before I take a runabout around the Ring."

"Done," said Vance as he walked to the elevator. "I'm going to shower and change before I head out."

"Good," said Dale. "We'll keep an eye on the nursery."

Small animal gestation periods were much shorter than those of large mammals. Also, the small animals were to be raised aboard the ship, not outside. When mature, these small furry critters would be deposited in designated areas around Gabriel. Vance was going to be busy again.

Twenty minutes later, Vance was in the middle of loading fertilized roe into a large runabout's tanks. While on his fact-finding trip around the Ring, he would deposit this roe into the oceans, lakes, and rivers. The sensors aboard the runabout, in conjunction with the ship's computers, would direct the planting of the roe. He would make dozens of such trips before he was through seeding the planet. In the meantime, the incubation/gestation deck was a fever of activity.

Vance returned to the NORMAN 12 hours later. "You've got the data," said Vance as he walked onto the bridge. "We have thousands of animals living on the Ring. Seems like more than we projected, but I'm sure part of that assessment is my exuberance. The herds of elk are amazing. And the mule deer must have been breeding like drunken sailors."

"We are analyzing the data as we speak. Looks as if we are going to need to introduce predators sooner than we thought," said Dale.

"Predators?" Vance seemed reluctant.

"We've got to balance nature or the ecology of the planet will suffer," Dale smiled at Vance's reluctance to the thought that any of "his" animals might be killed.

"I know."

"The predators will eliminate the weak, old, and sick animals as well as help to weed out most of the negatives of inbreeding."

"And if there aren't predators to control the fast-propagating animals like rabbits, they will decimate the planet within a few years," added Alex.

"I know, I know. I got caught up in my protective mode. Sorry. Tell me what to put in gestation."

"As soon as the data is analyzed, we'll know how to proceed. Shouldn't take but a few more minutes," said Dale.

"While we're waiting, I might point out that it's going to take a long time for the predators to propagate large enough numbers to make a big difference to the prey animals, and by that time their numbers will be great."

"Good point," said Vance.

"Data coming in," said Alex.

Mountain lions, bears, wolves, wolverines, coyotes, eagles, hawks and owls of many species were the next to be introduced on the Ring and North Dumbbell continents.

On the South Dumbbell, they were replicating, as close as possible, the South American ecology. Here the predators were jaguars, sun bears, pythons, and birds of prey.

The Vast continent was selected to replicate the African continent, so it received lions, leopards, cheetahs, hyenas, and wild dogs along with many other different birds of prey. It would take many centuries of evolution to perfect the balance, but time really wasn't a problem.

The incubation of these animals required time for gestation, raising, and training. For example, the prey animals needed to be trained to hunt. There were extensive instructions for each species loaded into the ship's computers. Vance, Alex, and Dale knew that even with the most detailed instructions, it was going to be a random hit and miss on success in some of these areas. Vance knew that at least another two years on the planet was required, but he was up to the task. He dove into every chore he was assigned by the computer, no matter how hard.

This was the last major thing to accomplish before leaving Gabriel again, allowing it to evolve for another century.

2089

As it turned out, it was closer to three years before the successful introduction of predators was completed. Failures resulted when trying to introduce two necessary animals, the black bear and the African lion. No black bears survived the first winter on the Ring. Vance had transplanted these bears to the northern part of the continent, which mirrored their natural habitat on the North American continent, but without a natural mother's training in hibernation, the bears either starved or froze. Vance took this failure very hard.

"Should have known we couldn't teach them to hibernate. This time we'll put them in a much warmer climate and let them work their way north over the generations."

They couldn't determine why two of the five lions didn't make it; they could not find the bodies. There was plenty of small prey for the young lions to catch and eat. They suspected that the other three, or perhaps just one rogue killed the two lions. The three survivors were female and that was good. Along with five black bears, they put five more lions in incubation, three females and two males. The three-year-old lionesses were captured and artificially inseminated. They were going to find out how good the lions would be as mothers, without any motherly training themselves.

Vance had personally observed leopards successfully hunting both large and small prey. The instincts of these cats were amazing.

In the past two years, the fish in the oceans, seas, rivers, and lakes began to thrive. By the time the NORMAN would return from its decade in space, 100 years planet time, the numbers should be more than sufficient to turn loose the more predatory species of fish.

2099

The NORMAN again landed on the knoll above the bay, west of the cave; they now had to shift the landing spot about 30 meters south at a clearing in the trees.

Ninety-eight more years had passed since the NORMAN had been here. Again, the planet had evolved dramatically. The vegetation, including grasses, plants, and trees looked to be completely established. Gas levels had changed again. Oxygen was now at a nearly ideal level and methane concentrations were up. The carbon dioxide and nitrogen levels were lower. The planet appeared to have settled into a comfortable ecology, which was everything that the three men could have expected.

Vance was anxious to take his first day's hike before a fact-finding trip in a runabout. How were the predators doing? How was the prey doing? What were their numbers?

He walked onto the bridge dressed in his jumpsuit, boots, backpack and camera. "Let's take a walk."

"With you all the way," said Alex.

"Can't wait," said Dale.

Vance walked down the ramp once again. As soon as his feet hit the soil, he stopped and took a large breath as he took in the view. "Look at what a hundred years can do." The area was now heavily wooded. Oaks, maples, and ash dominated the landscape. The bay could not be seen through the trees.

"Again the smell has changed. More subtle this time."

"The planet is settling in," said Alex.

Vance started walking down the hill, but this time he was forced to walk around trees to reach his destination. He didn't see an animal for the first ten minutes. He saw many species of birds from hawks to quail, but no mammals.

"I don't like this… where's my deer?"

Vance walked out of a thick stand of oak just before he reached the short cliff on the side of the bay. He startled five whitetail deer that were browsing around the water's edge. They began pronging at a fast pace toward a far-off stand of trees.

"I see them, but they're running from me. What the hell?"

"I suspect that they have learned fear and caution because now they're being preyed on," said Dale.

"Well, shit!" said Vance.

"This is actually good news," said Alex. "It means that in all likelihood, the predator animals have survived and flourished and the prey animals have managed to survive despite them. We couldn't have asked for more."

"You're right. Okay, I'm good with it. I must have taught my killers well."

"That's right," said Alex.

Vance smiled to himself as he proceeded on his hike to the bay. He spotted rabbits, both jack and cottontail, and something that looked like a cross between the two. He checked the trees for squirrels as he walked, and he was not disappointed. He saw an abundance of two species. The oaks were a source of food and shelter for the squirrels and birds. Between the browsers and grazers, the grasses and plants were being kept at a healthy level.

As he approached the bay, he could hear geese honking and ducks quacking. "Great! Can you hear that?"

"We can. Sounds like the water fowl are established," said Alex.

"More food for the colonists and predators," added Dale.

As Vance walked over the last rise to the bay, he spotted the water birds. Hundreds of geese and ducks turned to look at him but did not fly off. They seemed to converse with one another, but apparently they didn't feel Vance was a threat. To Vance, the noise was music to his ears.

"Wow!"

"It looks like those species like it here," said Alex.

Vance stopped, put his hands on his hips and smiled. What a view. The bay was beautiful. Trees grew to the water's edge in many places. In some places the huge branches of oak stretched out over the water. In other places, water grasses and sandy beaches dominated the shore. Vance walked over a sandy area to get close to the water's edge. This was a freshwater bay because of the three high-volume freshwater rivers that emptied into it. The presumption was that it would be an ideal area for fish, such as salmon and steelhead that spawned in freshwater and spent most of their lives in saltwater. Vance spotted fish, but he didn't know what species they were. They looked like trout, but they were quite large, maybe four to six kilos.

"Can you see the fish?"

"We can but not too well. Probably steelhead."

"Fun catching—good eating."

Vance continued to walk inland around the bay. In 350 meters, he came to the first river. It was one of the two rivers fed via a waterfall that was about two kilometers east of the bay. The river was clearly down a meter or so from its seasonal high-water level. Muddy banks were exposed, giving Vance a clear view of bear and coyote tracks.

"Bear tracks here," said Vance.

"Give me a close up," said Dale.

Vance removed the camera from its shoulder harness and held it closer to a clear track.

"Black bear," said Dale.

"Yes!" said Vance, clearly pleased, "Got 'em going."

"Get me some shots of other tracks," requested Dale.

"How about these?" Vance held the camera toward what looked like dog tracks.

"Coyote."

"Thought so."

Vance continued to hold the camera as he walked up river. It didn't take long before he spotted six vultures circling 50 meters south of the river. Vance made his way to the spot and discovered a fresh deer kill.

"Black bear, you think?"

"Could be, if it's a big one."

"Might be a cougar or maybe a grizzly," added Alex.

"See if you can spot some tracks or scat. Cougar shouldn't be a problem, but a big grizzly could be."

Vance looked around but saw nothing except a messy kill scene. The grass and plants were flattened and disturbed, and there was blood spread around the carcass of the deer. He reattached the camera to its shoulder harness and walked back toward the river on an established game trail.

As Vance walked around a large thicket of berry bush, he nearly collided with a huge grizzly. The bear stood up on its hind legs, towering a meter over Vance.

"SHIT!" Vance was completely surprised.

The bear didn't hesitate. It took a swipe at Vance's head with one massive paw. Vance's reflexes instantly kicked in and he ducked. The bear took another swing with his other paw and Vance jumped backward to avoid being struck.

The bear advanced on its back legs with its head bowed forward in a classic sign of aggression. Without further hesitation, Vance punched the shaggy behemoth with a powerful straight right just below the rib cage. The bear grunted, dropped down on all fours and backed up a few steps before it stopped. It remained there while making a strange sucking sound. Vance assumed he'd knocked the wind out of it. This massive animal had probably never been challenged by anything in its life. It was not only in some pain but probably confused, but it didn't stay confused for long. It roared and started walking slowly on all fours toward Vance. The bear was pissed. Vance turned a little sideways with his knees slightly bent in a classic fighter's stance. When the bear got within three meters of Vance, it accelerated forward. Vance hit him square on the nose with a massive punch, then rolled to one side to avoid being steamrolled by this huge, pissed-off grizzly. He was back on his feet facing the bear in an instant. But he needn't have bothered; the bear had been stopped in his tracks and set back on his haunches. That punch was all this bruin needed today; blood was pouring from this hapless animal's nose. There was a large rip where the nose was attached to the beast's upper lip. It sat for a full two minutes while making a whining sound before it slowly stood and looked at Vance. It grunted, turned, and trotted off into the brush.

"Shit!" Vance said again.

"Holy Shit!" said Alex. "That scared the crap out of me."

"I… can't… even… talk," said Dale.

"Did ya see the size of that sumbitch?"

Four hours later Vance was back at the NORMAN and heading for the shower.

"Hope that bear will be all right," said Vance, concerned.

"He'll heal," offered Dale. "But he's going to have trouble killing without pain for a while. He'll probably chew on the dead deer for a week or so. Doubt he'll stray far from it in his condition. You might go back and check on him in a week."

"Not without a gun, I won't."

"Doesn't look like you need one," said Alex.

"Got to admit, this SLF body has got some power."

"I'd guess that bear weighed 600 kilos at least. And you all but cold-cocked it. Yeah, you've got some power… and speed."

"We screwed up," said Dale.

"What's that?"

"We should have recorded the auras of all the animal varieties," said Dale. "We didn't do that."

"That's remarkable," said Alex.

"That is a big mistake on our part," said Dale. "For all sorts of reasons, we should have every species' aura on file."

"I'm stunned," said Vance. "I was beginning to think we'd thought of everything."

"This was too obvious, I suppose."

"You designed the Auratron so we could keep track of bad guys on Earth; we didn't think of using it on animals," said Alex.

"Well, be that as it may, we need to get the animal auras recorded," said Dale. "The uses will be many; we can keep track of numbers, locations, movements, and migration patterns, just to name the obvious. And we can avoid dangerous animals, such as grizzlies, lions, and critters like that."

"Can you program the computers for that?" asked Vance.

"Already have a program for humans, so it won't take much to add animals."

"Let's get it done," said Alex.

"Agreed," said Vance. "I have a thought."

"Which is?"

"Make the dangerous ones afraid of humans, as they are for the most part on Earth."

Alex was puzzled, "Why would you want to do that?"

"Because the colonists won't have my strength, my experience, or my training. A colonist would have been killed today."

"Without question," said Alex.

"How do you plan on doing that?" asked Dale.

"Maybe I'll go smack 'em around a little."

There was silence for a moment.

"Rather than you're smacking them around—we can build you a cattle prod or a Taser," suggested Dale. "Something like that would be more consistently effective."

"Now you're talking."

"And we'll have to put human scent on you. Animals rely on scent for identification as much or more than sight. You don't smell human."

"Agreed," said Vance.

"How are we going to record their auras?" asked Alex.

"Auratron," said Dale. "We have a dozen in stock."

"Why?"

"Don't know," answered Dale. "They must have been part of our questionnaires asking what we wanted to take on this trip. As I recall, the list was hundreds of pages long, so I probably just checked them off without much thought."

"Fortuitous," remarked Alex.

"Tell me you don't expect me to run down every animal on the planet to get their aura recorded."

"Of course not. I can program the computer with just one aura per species. Each species will be unique."

"Oh, okay."

"That's still going to take time," said Alex.

"Be like hunting, we'll make a sport of it," Vance smiled. "We'll get the colonists involved when we wake 'em up."

Vance walked back onto the bridge after his shower, dressed in clean overalls and fresh boots.

"I'm going to take the small runabout out while there is still a little light. I'll get a much better idea of what's happening on the Ring."

"Take an Auratron with you."

"Roger that."

2101

The NORMAN was scheduled to leave Gabriel on its final high-speed trip into space, allowing time to flash ahead on Gabriel. Vance had spent the last two months putting some finishing touches on the planet. He distributed seeds, spores, insects, mammals, rodents, birds, small predators, and fish in specific tropical climates. In a hundred years, the rain forests should be alive with all manner of life. The NORMAN continued to store thousands of other seeds from grass to trees and everything in between. It held animal embryos that had not yet been used. Elephants, rhinos, hippos, alligators, crocodiles, monkeys, chimpanzees and gorillas had not yet been introduced to the Vast continent.

The gorilla was the one animal that Vance was anxious to introduce to Gabriel. It seems he had a previously unknown affinity for them.

"Just something about them," he told Alex and Dale. "They are powerful but quite gentle."

Alex and Dale thought it best not to say anything about obvious similarities.

The three men decided to wait until they were permanently settled on Gabriel before incubating any monkeys or apes. The apes in particular required years of personal care before they could fend for themselves, much like human babies. Vance simply did not have the time right now.

Domesticated dogs, cats, horses, cows, sheep, goats, chickens, ducks, and geese would be introduced as wanted or needed by the colonists. From this point on, the colonists would aid in seeding Gabriel with the remaining plants and animals.

CHAPTER 22

RESURRECTION
July 10, 2112

The NORMAN landed once again at the conclusion of their last time-accelerating trip. From this point forward, the NORMAN's time would remain in sync with the time on the planet Gabriel.

In the past hundred years, Gabriel's ecology had continued to mature. The planet would continue to evolve based on its present status, as no more seeding or additional animals were to be introduced on a massive scale. Just a few of the more exotic plants and animals were planned for introduction over the next few years, but none were vital to the planet or the colonists.

"Interesting to note that over the last hundred years, the humidity has increased just under 3%," said Dale as the NORMAN settled onto Gabriel's surface.

"Tropical plants have had an effect, you think?"

"Partly. Vegetation absorbs and breathes moisture and Gabriel has a huge tropic zone now, especially on the Vast continent. The majority of the land is now covered in some sort of vegetation and there are tens of millions of animals breathing."

"We're less than a year out from waking our colonists," said Dale.

"We'll get everything up and working in plenty of time," said Vance. "The plan of action is well laid out. . . thank God. I'll put the horses, cows, sheep, and goats in incubation this week."

"That takes care of most of the domestic animals," said Alex.

"The big ones. We will start the incubation of chickens, ducks, and turkeys in about three months. Our kids are gonna need eggs."

"You've been an easy keeper," said Alex.

"But the kids won't be," said Dale. "They're going to need a lot of food."

"Kids, what can you say?" Alex smiled.

Vance was studying the plan laid out on the computer screen. "According to this, I have to plow about a hundred acres this week, disk two weeks later and cultivate right after that. Need to get the grain planted before the rainy season. Wheat and corn first, it says."

"Of course," said Alex. "Basic staples."

"We have fruit trees well established on our side of the Ring," added Dale. "Apples, peaches, pears, and a variety of nuts to the north. All varieties of citrus and some nuts do well here. Coconuts, papaya, and mangos require a climate closer to the equator," he finished.

"The trees need a lot of care. Right now, a fruit farmer would have a heart attack if he saw the condition of the trees. Our kids are going to be doing a lot of pruning."

"They'll certainly have plenty to do when they wake up," said Alex.

"For sure."

Vance continued to read the computer screen. "Have to break out the desalinator and start stockpiling salt… and the same with the nitrogen converter. We will get a lot more farm produce with the addition of nitrogen to the soil."

"Work doesn't seem to end, does it?" stated Dale.

"Idle hands and minds, as they say," answered Vance.

"In a year from now, you will have so much help around here you may have to take up fishing just to kill the boredom," joked Alex.

"That'll be the day."

April 3, 2114

The time had finally come. It was time to take the colonists out of stasis.

Vance was visibly nervous as he prepared to revive and reanimate these 20 young people after nearly 84 years. When revived, would they have all of their faculties? Would they be able to function at all?

Without them, Vance would be alone forever. The ecology of the planet would be left for nature to sort out. Not a bad thing, but not the plan. Maybe someday other colonists, or perhaps the civilization that had left that unidentified gold alloy object would return to Gabriel. They would never have to leave; they will have landed on a true Garden of Eden.

The first person to be reanimated was a neurologist and medical doctor, Terri Diggs. She was 24, an athletic brunette, brown-eyed, and of average height. She came from a large family, as did most of the colonists. One of the hundreds of criteria used in evaluating prospective colonists was that the colonists came from large families with many siblings. Having the ability to bear many children later in life, without appreciable damage to the mother, was a highly desirable gene and would be a big plus on a planet with so few people. Terri had three sisters and five brothers and her mother was still in excellent physical condition. Aside from her MD degree, she had cross-trained as a veterinarian and had studied animal husbandry. Because of these skills, she was the first selected to come out of stasis.

The cryogenic deck was brought up to a normal temperature with higher than normal oxygen levels. Vance checked all of the cryo chambers twice before standing at the control console in front of Terri's chamber.

"This is the scariest thing I've done on this whole trip, I don't mind telling you."

"We feel the same. This is for all the marbles, as they say," said Alex.

"You gentlemen ready?"

"Yes, sir," said Dale.

Vance reached over and pushed the first of a series of buttons on the control console. A green light went on above the button as the inside of the cryo chamber lit up. Now, Vance could clearly see Terri's face. She looked as she did when he had last seen her 84 years ago, except that her complexion was nearly white. Vance was taken aback for a moment. She looked like a china doll.

He pushed a second button. The chamber that had spent 84 years in a complete vacuum now filled with 100% oxygen and normal atmospheric pressure. The relative humidity was brought up to 78% and the temperature within the chamber rose to eighty degrees. After a moment, a second green light came on.

Vance pushed a third button. A low humming began as the microwaves began bombarding Terri. The number 100 appeared on one of the console screens and began slowly counting down. . . 99. . . 98. . . 97 . . . . Vance's eyes shot to the gauge that displayed Terri's internal temperature; it registered minus seventy-six degrees. The count continued, 94. . . 93. . . 92. . . .

Vance was all but hyperventilating as he watched this critical process. *Please God, let this young woman live again,* he silently prayed. The internal temperature rose to minus forty-one degrees—89. . . 88. . . 87. . .

It seemed the seconds were taking minutes. The humming of the microwaves continued. Vance was tempted to turn away and not watch.

Jesus, I haven't been this scared since they told me I was totally paralyzed. 78. . . 77. . . 76. . .

The temperature was now minus twenty-four. 61. . . 60. . . 59. . .

Please God. Vance's eyes were switching from the chamber to the temperature gauge every two seconds. Her temperature was now plus one degree. 42. . . 41. . . 40. . .

Vance checked the oxygen mask attached to the outside of the chamber. He turned the valve on… it worked… he turned it back off. His eyes went back to the gauge, it registered plus thirty-nine. 36… 35…34…

Vance thought he could see some color coming into Terri's face. *My imagination?*

Her temperature was beginning to rise more quickly. It was sixty-seven and moving up. 29… 28… 27…

As Terri's temperature hit seventy-eight degrees, her recorded brain patterns began transmitting through electrodes located strategically around her head. A green light should have come on by now—but it hadn't.

Vance looked up at the viewer, looking for a reassuring gesture from Dale. There was none. Dale looked puzzled.

Vance was thinking as he checked the console for signs of trouble, *an alarm would sound if anything unexpected happened. . . wouldn't it?* 20… 19…18…

Terri's temperature was at ninety… 5… 4… 3… 2 . . . 1. Ninety-eight degrees. The microwaves stopped, a latch released and the clear canopy cracked its seal, opened up and back, exposing Terri's body. A loud alarm sounded. Beep, beep, beep…

"What the…"

A soft buzzer rang as two preprogramed electrodes connected to Terri's temples sent a mild programed shock through her brain. Nothing happened. Not a twitch from her body. A second buzzer rang as the two electrodes near her heart sent through a larger jolt to that organ. Again, nothing happened.

"Vance," said Dale, clearly alarmed. "Something's wrong."

"No shit! Tell me how to fix it."

"I don't know, I…"

As Vance watched in horror, Terri's face started to turn dark.

"Oh, please Jesus, no."

Vance quickly reached into the capsule and grabbed Terri by the upper arms and shook her; an action clearly triggered by desperation.

Terri's face turned dark blue then the flesh started wrinkling, all within a matter of seconds. Her flesh began to soften in his hands.

As if he received a large jolt of electricity, Vance released his grip. He quickly turned away from the horror decomposing in the cryogenic capsule. This beautiful, gifted young woman was gone. All she would have brought to this new world was gone. The promise of humans colonizing a new world, gone. Vance dropped to his knees and cried. Alex and Dale cried with him.

After a few minutes Vance stood. He avoided looking into the capsule as he walked slowly out of the cryo deck and left the ship. He walked out across the old pasture land to the south and kept walking for hours. He had no communication devices with him, nor did he want any. This was the worst moment of his life. He felt so alone, so isolated. The suffering was overpowering; a sensation he had never experienced before. He, at this moment, felt certain that he would be alone on this new world forever. All was lost, all was for naught.

It was a full day later before Vance returned to the NORMAN. As he entered the Bridge he said, "Dale and Alex."

They appeared. They both looked as sad as Vance felt.

"I'm sorry I left you," said Vance. "I'm…" He couldn't finish the sentence and looked away from the viewer.

"We have some news that might cheer you up a little," said Alex. Vance turned back around. He certainly needed cheering.

"What?"

Terri's capsule had lost its seal," said Dale.

"What?"

"We ran a diagnostic, it definitely wasn't sealed. We don't know the cause."

Vance sat straighter in his chair.

"We think we can discover the reason, but not without your help. We need you to do a physical inspection."

Vance knew part of that inspection would be to remove Terri's remains. Vance had seen a lot of death and carnage in his life, but he knew he would have a horrific time handling Terri's body. It would be nearly overwhelming. But it had to be done.

"Let's get to it." Vance got out of his chair and headed for the elevator.

It took two hours, but Vance found the problem. Something that was less than half the thickness of a BB had penetrated the capsule exactly in the location of Terri's head, right on the seam where the canopy met the capsule. Had the hole been a millimeter or two lower it would have been spotted before reanimation began.

"I believe if we performed an autopsy we would find that Terri's brain was completely destroyed," said Dale. "Whatever hit us, and shot through the capsule, probably was traveling at close to the speed of light."

"How can that be?" asked Alex. "How could it get past our shield?"

"We may never know for sure, and the only possibility I can come up with is that a tiny piece of whatever we destroyed with a nuke fifty years ago, was in the debris field, and blasted through our shield. When we have time I'll be able to calculate where the object hit and where it exited the ship. We'll plug the holes."

Vance was puzzled. "Why wouldn't we have discovered it? Wouldn't the ship's sensors detect a leak?"

"Not that small, no. There are probably bigger leaks in this ship than that one, and there always have been. No matter how meticulous the construction, they are unavoidable."

"We need to check the other capsules," Vance stated.

"Already done," said Dale, "They're as tight as a drum."

After a few minutes Alex spoke, "I know you were really nervous about starting this reanimation process the first time, and I know it's going to be terrifying for us all the next time, but you know it has to be done."

Vance closed his eyes for a moment before opening them and looking at Alex. "Jesus, Alex, I've never been as scared as I am now. Not even close."

"We all are, my old friend, we all are."

"I suggest we take a day or two to gather our nerves," said Dale.

"Yes, please," responded Vance.

April 5, 2114

The process began again, this time it was another young lady by the name of Lesley Carlon. Lesley had similar academic credentials as had Terri; she was a medical doctor, and she was one of Vance's favorites.

Vance's eyes read the gauge, it registered Lesley's temperature at forty-one, the clock was at 35…34…33. Vance was never a praying man but he was praying now.

27…26…25… Vance looked at the temperature again, seventy-nine degrees. As with Terri, Lesley's recorded brain patterns began transmitting through the electrodes attached to her head. A green light came on.

"YES!" yelled Vance.

Lesley's temperature rose to ninety-one…4…3…2…1. Ninety-eight degrees. The microwaves stopped and the latch released. The clear canopy cracked its seal, opened up and back, exposing Lesley's body. No alarm went off.

"YES!" Vance yelled again.

The soft buzzer rang as the electrodes connected to Lesley's temples sent the mild shock through her brain. She twitched.

"YES!" yelled Vance once again.

The second buzzer rang as the electrodes stimulated Lesley's heart.

Her body stiffened momentarily, then relaxed.

Vance looked up at another console screen; it showed her heart beating slowly.

"YES!" Vance could hardly control himself.

Yet another screen began registering some brain waves. Color was returning to her skin, but she wasn't breathing.

Vance grabbed the oxygen mask, turned it on and placed it over Lesley's mouth and nose. *Please, please…* The mask did the breathing for Lesley for a full minute… it seemed like ten times that long to Vance. Lesley suddenly took a deep, shuddering breath.

"Oh God!" exclaimed Vance.

"She's breathing," said Alex.

Lesley's eyes opened. She did not look around. Her eyes were dilated and fixed in one position.

"Lesley," Vance said quietly. No response. "Lesley, can you hear me?" He said louder. No response.

Vance looked up at the viewing screen. His eyes looked at Alex and Dale as if to say, please help me.

"Stay calm, Vance," said Dale. "We had some moments like this with our trial runs in the beginning."

"Yeah, but those volunteers were only left in stasis less than a month."

"But the effect will be the same. Give it some… wait! Take a look at the EEG, it's starting to become more active."

"Oh shit! You're right." Vance's tone went up several notches. He looked at the console's screen. The brain waves were becoming more active by the second. Vance again looked at Lesley. Her eyes slowly closed and then reopened. This time the dilation was reduced and she seemed to be somewhat aware of her surroundings.

"Lesley, can you hear me?"

Lesley's brow furrowed slightly and she blinked three times in rapid succession. She turned her head toward Vance. "Hi, sir," she squeaked out in a raspy voice. "Are we there yet?"

Vance couldn't speak. He was overcome with emotion. His Isleium brain simply locked up for a moment, so he nodded his head twice. If he'd had tears, they would have been flowing.

"You okay?" asked Lesley.

Vance nodded enthusiastically.

"Can I get something to drink?" she managed to squeak out.

Vance paused a moment and then regained his voice. "You bet… wait a sec." Vance shot over to a locker and retrieved a bottle of water, and returned to Lesley. "I'll help you sit up a little while you have a sip."

Vance gently slid his hand under Lesley' shoulders and lifted her to about a 45 degree angle. "Here you go." Vance put the drinking bottle up to Lesley's lips. She took a small sip, swallowed and took another sip. Then she lifted her hand, placed it on Vance's and squeezed.

Vance looked her in the eyes. He could barely talk he was so overcome with emotion. "I can't tell you how much that squeeze means to me," he choked out, "It's been a long time."

Lesley looked at Vance for a long moment. "How long?"

"84 years."

"80… I thought 40… or 50… but 84?"

"I'm afraid so. But I believe you're going to be pleased with what we've done."

"84 years… wow."

"Let's get you to a sitting position."

Lesley nodded and Vance slowly lifted her to a sitting position.

"More water please."

Vance again held the bottle up to her lips. She lifted her right hand to take it.

"Can you hold onto it?"

"I think so."

"Good," Vance smiled. "How are you feeling?"

"Real groggy, but getting better, I think."

"I'm going to lift you out of the chamber and lay you on a therapy bed so we can get your body working, and the circulation going."

"Okay."

Vance slid his right hand under Lesley's knees and placed his left hand on her back. He lifted her effortlessly out of the chamber and gently laid her on the bed on her back. "How's that?"

"Knees are real stiff… everything is real stiff," she smiled weakly.

"We're going to start working on that right now."

"I'm ready."

Two hours later, Lesley was sipping on her third bottle of water as she sat on the side of the bed kicking her legs back and forth. She began moving her head up and down, round and around to warm and stretch the muscles in her neck. She was becoming quite animated.

"I believe I'm going to live."

Vance remembered what a delightful person she was and remembered her sense of humor, sometimes cutting, but always funny.

"Hi Lesley," said Alex from the viewer on the opposite wall.

Lesley looked up and was taken aback for a moment. "Well hello, Mr. Gabriel. I wasn't expecting to see you, sir."

"We can't tell you how thrilled we are to see you up and moving."

"I'm pretty thrilled myself. Wasn't sure if I ever would."

Alex looked at Vance for a moment before turning back to address Lesley. "I've always been in awe of you twenty extraordinarily brave young people."

"We couldn't resist being the first human beings on a new planet."

Alex nodded. "Do you remember this man?" The image of Dale appeared next to Alex."

"Dr. Isley, of course. Nobody would ever forget either of you. How are you, sir?"

"Very well, now that you are up and moving. We've had a lot of challenges on this voyage, but to revive you is our happiest moment. . . by far. We're so glad to see you, Lesley."

"Thank you, sir."

"We'll let you get on with your therapy. We'll have plenty of time to talk later."

"Okay."

"Ready to stand up?" asked Vance.

She hesitated for a second, "Sure, let's give it a go."

Vance stood in front of her and took her upper arms in his powerful hands. She slid down until her bare feet touched the deck. Vance held on to her while she adjusted her balance.

Vance let go with one hand and stepped to her side while maintaining his hold on her left arm.

"Here I go," she said with some concern.

She took a step, balanced, and took another, then another until she was walking pretty well—a little shaky, but well. Vance relaxed his grip.

Lesley stopped moving and looked at Vance. "I'm starving."

"Oh, shit, I'll bet you are. Do you think you can walk to the kitchen or do you want a wheelchair?"

"Let's walk. I can use the exercise."

They walked through the hatch to the elevator and took it to Deck 3.

"Protocol says that you need to ingest a couple of things before you eat."

"I know, Terri and I wrote some of them," Lesley smiled. "I have no enzymes or bacteria in my system. Got to get the juices flowing again."

Vance involuntarily made a small sound. Lesley noticed.

"Are you alright, sir?"

Vance looked at Lesley and smiled, "Standing here talking to you makes me better than alright. Much better." With that he reached over and gave Lesley a long hug. "I can't begin to tell you what this means to me," he said with deep emotion, and then released her from the hug.

"Well I'm pretty damned pleased to be here," she responded cheerfully.

"Then you know that after taking in all the bugs, you're gonna have to wait two hours to eat," said Vance with a lighter tone.

"I know, but damn it… it feels like I haven't had anything to eat for 84 years."

Vance laughed hardily. He hadn't been exposed to humor for a very long time. "Good one," he said.

Lesley smiled.

Four hours later, after Lesley had eaten a light meal and taken a short nap in her stateroom, Vance knocked on her door.

"Come on in, sir."

The door slid open and Vance entered. Lesley had removed the body sock that she had worn for 84 years, showered, and put on a tailored, powder blue jumpsuit. She looked like an angel to Vance.

"You ready to see what we've done?"

"Am I ever! Which planet did we land on?"

"The second one. It was nearly perfect. It is perfect now."

They took the elevator down to Deck 20, walked to the large ramp, and continued down.

"I'm going to hang back a few feet and get a picture of you stepping on Gabriel for the first time."

"Gabriel?"

"That's the name of your new planet."

Lesley nodded approvingly, "Of course."

"Oh my God!" exclaimed Lesley as she stepped off the ramp onto the surface of Gabriel. "Oh my… oh my." Tears formed in her eyes as she brought her hands up to her face. "Oh, sir, you did all this?"

Vance nodded as he looked around. "All the physical stuff, yes. But all the directions came from the computers that really smart men programmed a long time ago."

"Oh my. . . I… in my wildest dreams, never imagined it would look like this… this is Eden."

Vance's face held a pleased and proud look. "I think so too."

"Does the whole planet look like this?"

"To one extent or another. Depends on the climate. Not many areas are as pretty as this one."

Lesley continued to look around as she wiped tears from her eyes. She closed her eyes and took in the air through her nose. "Oh, gosh, it even smells wonderful. Look at the birds!" she pointed off to the left, toward the oak forest.

"Wait till you see what we have here," Vance said proudly.

"How long did it take you?"

"By Gabriel time, we've been planting and cooking for four hundred years, but by ship time, just 50 years."

"You've been doing this by yourself for 50 years?"

"I haven't been alone for a second," answered Vance. "Had my two best friends with me the whole time."

"But they're just computer programs."

"Hardly," said Vance, "They're as real as I am, without bodies of course. They are the same individuals as they were on Earth."

"But. . ."

"You'll see what I mean when you spend some time with them."

"Let's go for a walk," said Lesley.

"We can take a runabout if you want."

"I need to walk for a little while anyway. Can we?"

"As long as you'll tell me when you're tired."

"I promise."

Vance led Lesley first to the bay and they sat on a large boulder while Vance pointed out the many features of the area. Then they walked up the river for a while, stopping often to let Lesley rest.

After an hour they arrived back at the NORMAN.

"Gosh, I think it's time for this little girl to take a nap."

"I'm sure it is," Vance responded. "When you're rested, come on up to the bridge and fetch me. We'll head down to the mess and get you something to eat."

"It's a deal. See you later."

Two hours later Lesley entered the bridge looking refreshed. Vance stood up and walked over to her.

"Mind if I give you another hug?"

"I insist," she said with a big smile. "I cannot imagine being without human contact for 84 years. So you go ahead and give me hugs whenever you want."

"Thank you, I'll probably do that."

Vance gave her a big hug and stood back to look at her. His smile got bigger.

"You must have changed plans a little," said Lesley.

"Why do you say that?"

"Well, it was Terri who was supposed to be reanimated first. But it was me. Just curious as to why."

Vance's smile disappeared and was replaced with one of sadness. "Why don't you sit down over here," Vance said as he led Lesley to the captain's chair.

"Oh, oh," expressed Lesley as she took a few steps and sat. "This is not good."

"No, no it isn't. It's as bad as it gets."

Lesley's eyes filled with tears. "Oh no. Not Terri,"

Vance nodded, "We did try to animate her first but she was already gone."

Lesley didn't need to hear anymore; she broke down and cried. Vance reached down, took her by the shoulders and pulled her into a hug. She buried her face in his shoulder and bawled.

The next person to be revived was the first male, Quinn Noble. The process of his reanimation was nearly a mirror duplicate of Lesley's reawakening. Quinn was a gifted architect and builder. He also had considerable talent on the saxophone and had been a star center on the University of Oregon's basketball team. He was the biggest and most athletic of the colonists. It was assumed that he would become the Alpha male of the group, behind Vance, of course. That assumption was bolstered by the fact that he was also one of Vance's favorites.

Next came Daniel Anderson from Norway. He was a gifted biologist and a pretty good hand with a guitar. Dan was shorter and stockier than Quinn, gray-eyed with strawberry blond hair. His English was perfect with just a touch of an accent.

After Dan came Leda Gonzales. Leda was a nutritionist and an accomplished chef. She was born in Mexico but raised in Los Angeles. She was just a bit taller than five feet and weighed just under one hundred pounds. She had dark hair, olive skin, and large dark eyes. Leda had a charming personality, a radiant smile, and a voice like an angel. She was one of the colonist's favorites.

The reanimation began to go much faster, now that there were others to help Vance revive the remaining sixteen. Within seven days, all of the colonists had been revived. Two people caused a great deal of trepidation, as they took twice as long as the others to come to full animation. But in the end, they seemed to be fine. The single most important mandate for the voyage of the NORMAN had come to its conclusion.

The loss of Terri had been explained to all as a group. Terri had been a true "Miss Congeniality" among the colonists. It was a devastating loss, both on a personal level and because of the loss of her contributions to the planet. It was a loss that would take the colonists a long time to put behind them. Terri's remains were buried in a solemn ceremony on the coast just west of where the NORMAN sat. Her grave sat on a low knoll overlooking the ocean.

Following their reanimation, the colonists were housed in their pre-assigned staterooms. These would be their homes until permanent homes could be built.

CHAPTER 23

GET TOGETHER
April 9, 2114

After that first week of respite, the 19 colonists were told to report to the flight deck at 8:00 a.m. the next morning.

All 19, plus Vance, fit comfortably in the hanger deck of the NORMAN. Soft fold-up chairs were set up in two rows of ten in front of the five small runabouts lined up and down the center of the huge deck. The chairs formed a semicircle around a portable viewer that duplicated the same size and picture quality as the one located on the bridge. On the opposite side of the viewer were the two large runabouts and row after row of attachments for all of the vehicles.

Alex asked Vance to turn the viewer off, but leave its cameras and microphones on so that he and Dale could enjoy watching and listening to the colonists. They felt that if they were visible the youngsters might feel self-conscious.

About half the colonists arrived early, and despite the loss of Terri, upbeat conversations were in full bloom. The din from the conversations increased as more colonists joined them. These young people had become close friends during their nine months of training. To them it had only been a week or so since they'd seen each other. This wasn't an 84-year reunion causing the excitement; this was the pure thrill of being on a new planet. This was their reason for being, and their life from now on.

The appointed time of 8:00 a.m. came and went as the young people enjoyed coffee and cinnamon rolls, rolls that had been baked by Leda earlier from stocks of basic staples held in the ship's stores.

Vance stood to one side while his charges interacted with one another. There was no hurry to get the meeting started. Besides, Vance was enjoying the banter far more than anyone; he had been alone for a long time.

At 8:45, Vance suggested everyone take a seat. When they were all seated, Vance stood in front of the viewer.

"All of you have had a little interaction with Alexander Gabriel and Dale Isley since your reanimation, but I want to formally introduce you to Mr. Gabriel and Dr. Isley." The images of Alex and Dale appeared on the viewer.

There was enthusiastic applause.

"Mr. Gabriel," said Vance, "I turn this first formal gathering over to you." With that, Vance walked over and took a seat that had been left vacant in the middle of the front row; Quinn and Lesley flanked him.

"Thanks Vance," said Alex as he smiled at the 19 young faces sitting before him. "I hope you come to regard Vance Youngblood, Dale Isley, and myself as many things in your life. Leaders, counselors, close personal friends, even surrogate parents. Actually, it is possible that we are as emotionally attached to you as your biological parents ever were. You are everything to us. It's all of you who will make this extraordinary adventure, this journey through time and space, both a success and a pleasure. Without you, this grand voyage would be a great deal less than what we dreamed. Without you, this new planet is little more than a massive wildlife park." Alex paused for a moment before proceeding. "The extraordinary technology that made this voyage possible was, for the most part, developed by the humble man standing here beside me." Alex looked at Dale. "Dale isn't, nor has he ever been a public speaker, but he is and always will be one of the most brilliant men ever born. He is and always has been a very warm, loving, compassionate, and giving man. Now two worlds have benefited greatly because of him." Alex turned to Dale. "Would you like to say a word or two?"

Dale looked at Alex and smiled. "As a matter of fact, I would."

Alex looked a little surprised and Vance's right eyebrow rose a bit.

Dale smiled. "I just wanted to tell everybody how happy I am. . . no, ecstatic would be a better word here. Anyway, I'm thrilled that we are now all here, except the wonderful Terri, and that everyone is fully functional. I cannot say enough about the massive contribution that Vance made toward the development of this planet; it will be the stuff of legends in the history of Gabriel. The development of Gabriel has been a true a labor of love for this man.

"You young people are here and alive on this beautiful place because of Vance Youngblood's passion, courage, and physical dedication—and Alexander Gabriel's foresight and commitment of his wealth. And finally, I want you each to know that I'm available any time you have a question about anything. Please use me as a resource."

Everyone who was assembled stood and applauded enthusiastically.

"Wow," said Alex. "That's the most words in a row that I've heard Dr. Isley say since I've known him." Alex paused for a moment, "I need to add just one or two minor notes to what Dr. Isley just told you. Without Dr. Isley, Vance would not exist. Without Dr. Isley, there would be no starship NORMAN. Without Dr. Isley, those humans still alive would have been living on a vicious, corrupt, polluted, overpopulated Earth. That just begins to give credit to this remarkable man." Alex turned to Dale and applauded as all other in the hanger rose to their feet and joined him.

When the applause stopped, Alex continued. "Finally, when Dr. Isley asks you to use him as a resource, he means it, and my young friends, there is not a better resource in the universe."

"Before we begin showing the development and creation of life on Gabriel, I would like to add to what Dr. Isley said." Alex quit talking as he looked at each of the colonists in turn. "You are, in many respects, our children. You will become the mothers and fathers of all future generations. Your names will be held in awe and respect throughout history," Alex paused again. "To that end I am pleased to tell you that we have picked this day to start a new calendar. This day will be January 1, 0, the beginning of a new history. Your history."

The colonists erupted in applause, yells, and whistles. This was the beginning of modern history. This was an everlasting honor. Alex held up his hand to stop the applause.

"By necessity, we need to refer to four time periods from time to time. No pun intended. Earth Time is designated "ET." We left Earth in 2030 ET. The present year on Earth is 2502 ET. "NT", or NORMAN Time, is used for referring to time that has passed on the NORMAN. Right now it is 2114 NT, which is 84 years after we left Earth. Planet Time, "PT", is for time that has passed on this planet from our first landing on it. It is now 410 PT. The present time, the time that will be used except in references to history, is "GT", or Gabriel Time, and that is now. But, you won't be using the GT designation any more than you used AD after the date on earth. This date is simply January 1, 0."

By the look on their faces, Alex could tell that at least half were confused. "No concern at all for most of you. It simply won't matter. For present and future historians, the time and place are important."

Alex's face turned serious. "You are… the last of the humans and the first of the humans." Alex paused, as he looked each individual in the face. "To explain that statement, I regretfully have to give you some shocking and terrible news." Alex paused for a second, "In the year 2478 ET, some 448 years after the NORMAN left the planet, Earth was completely destroyed by a massive asteroid."

A few involuntarily screamed, some sat stunned, some cursed. Many had tears in their eyes.

Then the questions came rapid fire.

"Are you sure?"

"Could there be a mistake?"

"How did you find out?"

"Were there any survivors?"

Alex held up his hand to stop the questions. "We are sure. After receiving a communiqué from Earth, we turned our telescopes and sensors toward Earth. It was gone. Also gone were Mercury, Venus and Mars. We assume there was a cataclysmic chain reaction. The orbits that they once occupied around the Sun are now a debris field that looks similar to the rings around Saturn." Alex stopped talking to not only let what he'd just said sink in, but also to give these young people all the time they needed to come to grips with this horrible knowledge.

"Any survivors, sir?" Quinn repeated.

"Yes. In their communiqué, we were informed that three starships were nearly complete and would launch safely. Two were going to head away from us toward what they described as 15 excellent prospective planets. One, they said, would be heading to us."

That seemed to brighten up the young people.

"We have to assume that what they regarded as 15 excellent prospective planets are exactly that. They were over four centuries ahead of us in technology. We believe they found a planet that probably didn't require a lot of terraforming."

There was a clear agreement with that statement.

"How long will it take them to get here?" asked Lesley.

Dale took this question. "If we assume that they traveled at the same speed that we did, they could be here in as little as 200 years. If they accelerated faster, say at 1.5-G up to 97% of the speed of light, they could be here a little sooner. We simply don't know what to expect."

"Their trip should take no longer than 30 years, not much different than ours. But you must remember that nearly five centuries had passed on Earth, when only 84 years passed on the NORMAN. Now that we're stable, our time will accelerate as Earth's did when we were at speed."

"This is all very confusing," remarked Aidan.

"You've all had my classes on time and space, but I realize not everyone can wrap their heads around the concept," said Dale. "Look up Lorentz factor on the ship's computer. It will give you some insight as to the cause and effect of speed and time."

"The concern is," said Alex, "that if they were getting close, the assumption is that they would contact us, but that hasn't happened."

"We've had little communication with Earth as their centuries have passed. But we must keep in mind that it's likely that they simply lost interest in us over the centuries. We assume it was a shot in the dark when someone on Earth decided to inform us of their impending disaster. The message itself took nearly 32 years to reach us. What we don't know is whether or not Earth had sent any other starships out over the centuries. I personally would be surprised if they hadn't," said Vance. "They had all the technology they needed. One would assume that they improved on our design over the centuries."

Alex took over. "We encourage you to talk about this to one another. Some of you may simply accept what has happened, others may have trouble with it. Be sensitive to your friends' feelings. If any of you have a real emotional problem with it, please don't keep it to yourself. There is one excellent psychiatrist, Mary, among you; please use her and talk to her if it will help." Alex paused before saying, "I'll turn the meeting over to Vance."

"I would suggest to you that we concentrate on developing this new world of ours. To give this world all that was good on Earth, and leave to history all that was bad. This beautiful planet Gabriel is now our home." Vance walked over and picked up a good-size box and returned to the colonists.

"Here is a tool for each of you." Vance started handing out a device as he walked down the aisles. "This, among other things, provides a chronograph reflecting the new seconds, minutes, hours, days, weeks, months, and years. You will note a difference in all of those units of measurements, I've just mentioned. It will take some time to get used to the difference, but it has to be. The device also acts as your personal communicator, location beacon, health monitor and computer. It has just about everything."

Vance looked down at his tablet. "The three of us thought it would be a good idea to rename the months of the year to better suit time as it is on our planet. This planet has just ten months. We further decided that the 19 of you should do the renaming. Don't want you to do it now; there's no hurry. Whenever you agree on the month's names, just let us know."

Vance again referred to his tablet. "The next order of business is dividing this group into four teams, or family units. We, along with behavioral scientists, psychiatrists, including our own Mary, have put together the groups we feel will work best together. These divisions won't come as much of a surprise, if any. Each team will consist of one male and four females. One team, Quinn's, just has three ladies for a total of four." Vance paused for a moment. "Each of you knew and agreed with the reasoning behind that division. If there is a conflict, or if a conflict develops later, we can mix and match." Again, Vance paused before continuing. "Team one is now Quinn, Lesley, Leda, and Maiko. Team two is Bob, Jennifer, Vijaya, Kathleen, and Ushi. Team three is Dan, Aidan, Amanda, Mary, and Leah. Team four is Tom, Eryn, Bonnie, Janet, and Tasha."

"You all know the guidelines that we've set out. All of you had a say in them. I'm not going to go over them right now, but I'll remind all of you that we don't want any pregnancies for at least the first two months. You all need to get settled in, both physically and mentally, before we start propagating. As circumstances dictate, we may lengthen that time."

"Another thing. As intelligent and mature as you all are, there may be problems with conflicting personalities, jealously, envy, and a myriad of other emotions. When one of these problems comes up, we need to deal with it right away… and I mean right away. So sound off. I don't care if it's you with a problem, or a friend—sound off to Mr. Gabriel or to me." Vance smiled, "We'll leave Dr. Isley out of it."

Everybody laughed.

"Thank you, Vance," Dale said sincerely.

During the following two weeks, they spent two hours a day on the flight deck watching recordings on the view screen. Vance, Alex, and Dale provided a running commentary of the history of the planet Gabriel. They saw the first recordings of Gabriel from the NORMAN, while still three light-years out. They viewed the first orbit, along with all data accumulated, from minutes to days, weeks to months, and years to centuries. These were the days that they would remember for all of their lives, and history would remember for as long as there was history. The days on the flight deck watching and learning about the development of their new planet were among the highlights of their lives so far.

They were encouraged to ask questions during these sessions, and being the brightest young minds gleaned from over five billion people, they did just that. They, during these sessions, came to know Alex and Dale as viable beings, not just computer programs. And the young colonists displayed a great deal of respect for the three extraordinary beings that guided their ship to their new home. They were in absolute awe of what Vance had accomplished single-handedly over the past 400 years. The record of the birthing of the two fawns Bambi and Bimbo brought raves and cheers. The encounter with the Grizzly Bear brought screams and expletives from most of the young women and Tom, and graphic expletives from the other three young men. Vance liked that part.

As the meeting was winding down, Tasha, the group's historian, held up her hand.

"Tasha," said Vance.

Tasha stood up. "We have come to an agreement on the naming of the months."

"Ah, let's hear them," said Alex.

"There were a lot of good ideas, such as naming the months after great people like you three and the rest of the original members of the WGC. Or nice names like Faith, Love, Charity, Hope, Peace, etc. but that didn't fly with everyone, so in keeping with the simple, 50-second minutes, 50-minute hours, 20-hour days, 5-day weeks, 5-week months, and ten-month years, we've named the months accordingly: Mo-one, Mo-two, Mo-three, etc. This is Mo-one 8, 0."

———

After a week of acclimation, Vance loaded the colonists into the smaller runabout that had now been reconfigured to seat 20 comfortably, with ten on a side. One seat would be empty. A port-holed canopy replaced the solid canopy that had been in place for the seeding programs. When aboard, all 19 colonists had a good view of their new home.

Vance piloted the craft from the hangar deck and headed on a course south toward the equator. Along the way he acted as a tour guide and pointed out various features of the landscape. Today, they would take in the western side of the Ring. The runabout could travel at over 2,300 kilometers per hour above 10,000 meters, or hover like a helicopter just centimeters above the ground. However, Vance wanted the colonists to see their new world, so he traveled at 1,000 kilometers an hour and just 3,000 meters above sea level. Occasionally, he slowed down to a crawl and dropped altitude in order to give everyone a better look at an interesting feature. At midday on this the first tour day, he surprised the youngsters by landing at a beautiful spot on a broad sandy beach 228 kilometers north of the equator. He wanted to give them a chance to stretch their legs and have a bite to eat. The temperature hovered around 88 degrees, and it was humid.

This was not a random stop. Vance had visited here several times in the past four hundred years. It was awe-inspiring. The main feature was a waterfall that dropped over 700 meters into a large pool over 120 meters wide extending out 160 meters from the base of the cliff. The pool in turn emptied into the ocean via a short boulder-strewn river. Vance had flown off his scheduled course one day over a 100 years ago to plant a few exotic tropical plants, trees, and flowers in this area. Over the past century, they had flourished and spread in this ideal climate; it was spectacular.

As the young colonists exited the runabout, Vance handed them a box lunch out of the cargo bay, much to their surprise. "Head up the river on this side, it's the easiest," Vance motioned with his right hand. After the last colonist headed inland, Vance attached a shoulder camera, grabbed a backpack and followed.

The expressions of delight began before they exited the runabout and got louder and more expressive as they worked their way inland. By the time they reached the pool, everyone was ecstatic.

Vance leaned against a massive boulder and enjoyed the enthusiasm his charges were displaying.

"Look at the height of the falls, they must be over 600 meters," said Bob.

"A bit over 700," said Vance.

"No shit?"

"Wouldn't lie to you."

Bob laughed, "No, sir, you wouldn't."

"Just smell those flowers," said Bonnie.

"Look over there," Janet said excitedly as she pointed to a spectacular flowering tree.

"After you finish your meal," Vance raised his voice to be heard over the roar of the falls, "feel free to explore the area... as a matter of fact, I think now is a good time to split into your groups. Each group can go a different direction, or not—your choice. I think you'll find it one of the prettiest places on the continent. I do require that each group carry a Taser and an Auratron. If you see any wildlife, record its aura. If you feel threatened, and whatever it is gets close enough, then Taser the shit out of it."

They laughed. All found a place to sit while they ate lunch and enjoyed the beauty of the area. Vance was pleased to see that they formed into their assigned groups automatically. When done, the four young men, with Quinn in the lead, walked toward Vance.

"In the backpack," said Vance before the young men said a word.

Dan took a step over and unzipped the backpack and handed out the Auratrons and Tasers.

"Any time limit here, sir?" asked Tom.

"There's no real hurry. I'd like to make it back to the NORMAN before sunset, so we have a couple of hours."

With the heat and humidity, it didn't take a couple of hours before the first group returned to the pool. Within 23 minutes all four groups were back. All were smiling; all were sweating.

Vance could see a few of the "kids" talking something over. After a couple of minutes, Quinn broke away from the others and walked over to Vance.

"Would you have any objection to us going skinny dipping, sir?"

Vance smiled, "Absolutely not. I'd have been kinda disappointed if you hadn't asked, but I want the ladies on the far left side of the pool, men to the right. No mixing."

Quinn smiled, "I understand. Thank you, sir."

Over the next three weeks, Vance flew his wards over the entire planet. A brief overview to be sure, but one that would be of great help in the future. All were now somewhat familiar with their new world. Vance made a point of stopping at least once a day in some unique spot for lunch. Sometimes they spent an entire day exploring a small area of a continent. During these trips, they also managed to capture the auras of dozens of animal species, much to Dale's delight.

Today, they were having their lunch by a good-size river in the central bush country of the Vast Continent. There was a pride of lions making a meal of a wildebeest about 250 meters off to the south. The group watched as jackals and vultures continually tried to make off with a scrap of meat only to be run off by a splendid male lion. He wouldn't chase them far before he stopped and returned to eat. But he wasn't getting his fair share of the kill and as time went on, it was clear that the lion was getting pissed. Suddenly, the lion chased a jackal directly at the colonists, but this time the lion didn't stop; he continued to chase the fleet-footed zigzagging jackal right at the colonists. The jackal turned off just before running through the group, but the lion did not. He was apparently dead set on mauling something for his troubles. Two of the women, Amanda and Janet, were the closest to him.

"Down," screamed Vance as he ran forward to put himself between the lion and the two women.

The girls dropped flat as ordered.

Fortunately for the girls, Vance just managed to put a blocking blow on the lion's rear hip, knocking him off-balance and causing him to hurtle ass-over-mane in a considerable cloud of dust. Vance's momentum also caused him to stumble and fall, but he did so in a roll that brought him back to his feet just three meters from the lion. The lion was up in an instant, facing Vance. The lion's huge fangs were bared and his ears were pinned to the side of his head as he sprang forward.

Vance jumped to the side and managed to plant a left hook to the shoulder of the pissed-off lion. The lion seemed unfazed by the blow. He spun and was at Vance again. This time, Vance did something that was unexpected by both the lion and the colonists. He thrust his right hand into the open maw of the lion and slammed the Taser into the lion's chest with his left. The lion went instantly stiff and fell to its side pulling Vance down with him. Vance after a brief moment pulled his arm and hand out of the lion's mouth and stood up, not taking his eyes off the prostrate cat.

"Shit!" was all he said.

The young people seem to be stupefied. None moved nor spoke, and none took their eyes off the scene in front of them. What in the hell had just happened?

"Holy shit!" It was Tom who was first to speak.

"Did you see that?" asked Quinn. "He knocked that huge son-of-a-bitch lion ass over teakettle."

The men in the group looked at each other with expressions that conveyed that this was a man never to challenge in any sort of physical contest—ever.

The ladies who were sitting stood slowly, and those who were standing sat down.

Vance stood over the lion as he quickly checked his right arm for damage. There was none. It had all happened too fast for the lion to bite down. The lion started to twitch a little. Vance stood his ground. In a few more seconds, the lion began to try to regain his feet. Vance didn't move. When the lion managed to stand up, Vance hit him with the Taser again, and again the lion stiffened and went down. Vance backed off a couple of meters and signaled the colonists to come over. After a moment's hesitation, they did as requested.

The lion's pride had quit eating and were all up, intently watching the dramatic scene unfold. A couple of big females started quickly trotting toward the colonists, but stopped after about 50 meters, clearly not sure what to do.

"Don't stand between him and his pride, but I want all of you to rub some of your scent on him."

"Why in the hell…" Dan started, but one look at Vance told him to just do as he was told.

Quinn was the first to walk over and rub his hands over the lion's face and mane. Dan followed within seconds, then two more and within a minute all had touched the lion to one extent or another.

"Okay, let's back off a few meters and let this big boy get up and go back to his pride."

They did so, and within two minutes the lion got to his feet. Clearly the fight was out of him. He looked at the colonists for a full 30 seconds and then shakily started limping back to his pride. He was clearly favoring his left front leg. The adrenaline had worn off and the punch that Vance delivered was now being felt.

"Damn, I hope I didn't break anything," Vance said as he was brushing the dust off his clothes. He didn't look happy.

His troupe started talking excitedly about what had just happened.

These young people had heard and read about Vance's bravery, intelligence, and physical powers for all of their lives. The stories were quite literally part of Earth's history, even before Vance became a SLF. Now they had just witnessed the legend in action. This incident would surely go down in Gabriel's history.

Vance looked around at his charges.

"With the exception of Quinn, not one of you people even pulled out your Tasers or got into a defensive position. I'm disappointed."

"But it all happened so fast, sir," said Ushi.

"Most of the time, that's the way shit happens, fast, so be ready for it," Vance answered. "Anticipate it. Protect yourselves and your friends. I can't be with you all the time."

The excited conversation stopped quickly. They'd just been chewed out by one of their heroes, and they knew they deserved the chewing.

Vance turned and walked up the river by himself, leaving the colonists to clean up the lunch site and stow gear into the runabout. When they were done, the 19 went into a huddle for a few minutes. The huddle broke up and the four men left the group and headed upriver in Vance's direction.

They found Vance about 200 meters upstream sitting on a large boulder looking across the river.

"Gentlemen," said Vance without looking around.

"Sir," said Quinn.

"I guess you're the spokesman," said Vance as he turned to face them. All four of the men looked a little sheepish.

"Guess I am, yes sir."

"Okay, let's hear it."

"We were just reprimanded and we had it coming. I can tell you that there isn't one of us who isn't embarrassed by our performance here today. We want to apologize."

Vance smiled. "Your apology is appreciated and accepted." Vance paused for a second. "Please take a seat, all of you." Vance waited until the four men were settled. "I have an apology to make, also. I've been sitting here thinking what would have happened if I had not been with you today. Even if you had handled everything perfectly, at the very least, one or more of you might have been injured… probably killed. None of you have my SLF quickness or power, to say nothing of my experience with violence. So, as it turns out I let you down, not the other way around. I did not anticipate. I did not provide you with enough training or equipment to keep you safe. That is going to be corrected. Each of you will be trained and will carry a firearm on your person when in an area that holds even the slightest danger. I'm going to ask Dale to work on a devise or weapon that is non-lethal but will effectively stop or detour an animal at a distance of fifty feet or more. As it stands now, we have to be way too close for a Taser to be effective. There is not an animal on this planet that is worth the loss or injury of any one of you."

CHAPTER 24

THE CAVE
MO-FIVE 5, 0

"That completes the survey of the cave structure," said Vance.

"It seems to be as solid as a rock," quipped Amanda, "Pun intended."

"Solid, gold-laden quartz, 266 meters thick at the top of the cave, and no fractures," added Quinn.

"The floor is a bit uneven but that won't affect the NORMAN. The landing gear will compensate for that," said Vance.

Five of them were standing about 110 meters inside the cave entrance. The cave could appropriately be called cavernous. Its measurements covered close to 15 acres, or approximately 230,000 square meters of area. It would make an outstanding warehouse/storage area. It was tight and dry, except for the huge freshwater spring-fed pool located at the far back. Grain and other perishables would be safe from damage from either weather or animals. The NORMAN could sit comfortably well back from the entrance and take up relatively little floor space because its landing gear could suspend it seven meters or more off the floor.

"So that's it then. We'll move the NORMAN in here, ASAP," said Vance. "Get her out of the weather."

"Might I make a suggestion, sir?" asked Vijaya.

"Let's hear it."

"The outside of the NORMAN is pretty dusty and grimy."

"I've noticed," said Vance.

"How about cleaning it up a little before we park it in here?"

"You must have a long handled scrub brush," said Lesley with a smile.

"I actually have a plan," responded Vijaya.

"Let's hear it," said Vance.

"Just before we move it in here, we find a rain storm and fly the NORMAN through it fast enough to blast off any grime that's on it."

"That is one excellent solution," said Lesley. "You did have a long handled brush."

"Agreed, great idea," said Vance.

They spent the next two days calculating the exact place to park the ship and laser-drilled seven two-inch holes through the cave's roof to run the cables for the communication antennas and sensor arrays. They needed the NORMAN's sensors to remain on line.

Vance was on the bridge talking to Alex and Dale.

"This will be the last time we fly the NORMAN for the foreseeable future," said Vance. "Let's put everyone aboard and take 'em for a spin."

"Agreed," responded Alex.

"How about circumnavigation?" suggested Alex. "A complete low altitude orbit?"

"Perfect," said Vance.

The next morning all 19 colonists and Vance were on the bridge. It was fairly close quarters for that many people, but not overly uncomfortable. They brought up the chairs from the flight deck and arranged them on the bridge as efficiently as possible. Bob, the engineer, figured out how to rig a restraining strap to hold not only the chairs in place but also hold the colonists in the chairs. The restraints wouldn't be high tech, but they would work for mild turbulence and weightlessness.

Vance was sitting in his captain's chair with a slight smile on his face. "Everybody comfortable?"

There was a chorus of affirmative responses.

"Bring the SMPE and MVAs on line," ordered Vance.

"Two minutes to full power," said Dale.

There was complete silence from the colonists. Their eyes were glued to the instruments and viewer.

"We have full power, Vance."

"Kick in the MVA and take her up, Dale."

The huge NORMAN started to rise slowly, gaining speed at a slow but steady rate. All on the bridge still had their eyes on the viewer, which was now divided into four screens, each providing a different view of Gabriel as the ship rose.

"Landing gear retracting," said Dale.

"Roger that."

"This is so exciting, I'm just about to pee my pants," Aidan whispered to Eryn.

"We're going to take her to 35,000 meters and circumnavigate the planet," said Vance.

"Yes!" said Dan, followed by a positive reaction from all on the bridge. None of the colonists had been in orbit while awake and they were anxious to see their planet from space.

It took only about four minutes to reach the desired altitude. They continued to accelerate at 1g as they leveled off and started their orbit around Gabriel. They stopped accelerating when their speed reached 28,000 kilometers an hour. They became weightless.

"Whoa!" said Leda.

"Holy crap," said Janet.

"Now this is a thrill ride," said Dan.

Bob's restraining rig seemed to work fairly well. Nobody floated more than a few inches out of their chairs… although a couple of the ladies were grasping for something more to hold on to.

"You've all done this many times," Vance smiled. "But you just slept through it."

The four pictures on the viewer became three. One facing forward and down and two displaying side and down views. What a great sight greeted the colonists! They could see the continents, the great oceans, and the abundant lakes and rivers. They could see the thousands of islands and the polar icecaps. As they came up on the screen, one or more would point out features they recognized.

They were about to start their second orbit as they sped over the center of the Vast Continent, when Vance said, "Let's slow her down and drop out of orbit, Dale,"

"Slowing down," responded Dale.

The ship changed its attitude to one of bottom first as the "brakes" were applied. The movement was so subtle that all they felt was the gravity returning.

"Speed at 5,000 kilometers, elevation 18,000 meters," said Dale, twenty minutes later.

"Roger that. Let's take it to 3,000 kilometers at 7,000 meters and hold there."

"Yes, sir."

"There are the Black Pearls," said an excited Tasha.

"Not too difficult to see why they were named that," said Tom.

"Here comes the Ring," said Dale.

As they passed over the Black Pearl Islands, their speed had reduced to 3,000 kilometers per hour. Just seconds later, the west coast of the Ring came into view.

"I can see the Home Bay," yelled Eryn as she pointed at the viewer.

"Wow, from this altitude it looks tiny," said Quinn.

"Compared to the size of everything else, it is," responded Bob.

"But there aren't many places, large or small, that are prettier," offered Aidan.

"Can't dispute that," answered Vijaya.

"Let's find a big storm," said Vance. "Need to wash this fine ship."

"500 kilometers south, we have a wet one," said Alex.

"Heading south," said Dale, "Dropping altitude, dropping speed."

Twenty-five minutes later, they were approaching the storm at 1,600 kilometers an hour at an altitude of just 3,000 meters.

"How fast do you think we ought to hit this thing?" asked Vance.

"All things considered, I think 200 kilometers ought to do it," said Dale.

"This might get a little rough, so I suggest you prepare yourselves as best you can," suggested Alex.

The NORMAN dipped under the heavy, low-hanging clouds and into the storm. They were immediately bounced around considerably more than expected. All held on to the arms of the chairs or the person sitting next to them, or both. It was quite a ride.

"Suggest we do a little spinning, Vance," said Dale. "A few RPM should get our backside polished."

"I'll leave that to you, my friend. Do whatever you think will get the job done."

The bridge, being near the center of the ship, lessened the effect of centrifugal force to almost nothing, but the colonists could tell they were spinning.

"Tilting the axis 40 degrees forward. Need to clean the top," said Dale. Two minutes later, "Tilting the axis 40 degrees back and lowering the landing gear. Let's clean her bottom."

Four minutes later, "I think that should do it," said Dale.

"Let's head home," said Vance.

Thirty-eight minutes later the NORMAN was landing on the same spot it had occupied since before the colonists were reanimated. Tasha, the planet's historian, suggested that many pictures from every angle be taken of the ship on this spot, before it was moved into the cave.

"And we need to get a picture of all of us standing outside with the NORMAN in the background. Future generations will want to see what everything and everybody looked like in the beginning of this planet's history."

After the NORMAN landed, the colonists couldn't wait to get outside and see how the ship looked after its bath.

"Oh my God," said Aidan as she practically ran down the ramp, "It's beautiful."

Bob was taking a close look at the massive landing gear. "Everything looks brand new. Squeaky clean without the use of soap—who'd a thought?"

All of the colonists were looking up at the ship, and walking away rapidly toward the cave in order to get the best look at the NORMAN from a distance. Even Vance had forgotten what an impressive sight the NORMAN was when she was new. She was a huge, shiny, sculptured bronze ball.

The picture session took longer than expected because Dale suggested that a small runabout be used to take pictures from various elevations and angles, some with the colonists, some without.

The time had come. Cameras were set up to record, for history, the mighty NORMAN being flown into the cave. It was a spectacular sight, the huge bronze ship moving very slowly across the flat ground as it approached the cave entrance. At first, from a vantage point of many angles, it didn't look like the mouth of the cave was big enough for the ship. But, as the NORMAN got closer, the perspective changed. There was actually close to 30 meters to spare.

Once 150 meters inside the cave, the NORMAN's landing gear was deployed and the ship settled down with the ramp side facing the cave's entrance. The flight deck's hatch was on the same side five decks up.

The inside of the cave, because it was in shade, diminished the NORMAN's bronze glow, and the sheer size of the NORMAN blocked a lot of the natural light that normally filtered quite a distance farther back into the cave.

"We'll need to rig some lights in here," said Quinn.

"Yes, we will," said Vance. "I'm putting you and Bob in charge of that chore."

"Yes, sir, we'll get right on it."

CHAPTER 25

HARVEST AND SEED
MO-SIX 19, 0

"We all know that we have hundreds of islands on Gabriel that have had little, if any, seeding. So we're going to prioritize these islands, divvy them up, and assign each team 25% of the area. The individual teams are responsible for the development of their islands. There are very cold islands to the far north and far south. There are sweltering hot islands around the equator, and hundreds of relatively pleasant ones in between. Each team has their share of each type," Vance took a second before continuing. "Common sense dictates that we start with the largest and most pleasant islands. However, if your team chooses to tackle one or more of the less desirable islands, that is your choice."

Tom raised his hand.

"Question, Tom?"

"Yes, sir. I've checked the ship's inventory. I don't believe there is a sufficient supply of the required seeds to even begin what you're proposing."

Vance smiled, "Good for you. And you're right. Our inventory has been nearly depleted of basic seeds. So, you fine young people will first have to harvest tons of seed that are presently growing on the continents," Vance paused. "This is going to take time. Each of our four runabouts comes with a harvesting attachment. You are going to have to study the specs and manuals and learn how to operate these machines. I expect the teams will interact with the other teams and share ideas and knowledge. I'd like to see harvesting start within a week," Vance paused a second, "Any questions?"

There were none.

Vance smiled to himself, *Jesus, it's nice to work with people that when you tell them something, you don't have to draw a picture.*

MO-SEVEN 2, 0

The runabout's harvesting attachments were remarkable pieces of engineering. When the attachment was in place, a small runabout resembled a hammerhead shark. The mouth of the harvester was seven meters in diameter, with the bottom edge displaying a sickle bar that looked like shark's teeth pointing straight forward. When engaged, the teeth moved so fast that they were only seen as a blur.

Grasses were to be harvested from the South Dumbbell and the southern hemisphere of the Vast Continent. This time of year, these areas were ripe with seed. Some of the grasslands and savannas on these continents enveloped tens of thousands of acres. The pilot of the runabout merely had to set the elevation at the height of the seed heads, engage the harvester and accelerate up to 70 kilometers an hour. Automatically, the runabout's navigation systems would guide the runabout over the contours of the land and around obstacles, such as trees, outcroppings, or even animals.

Sometimes, depending on the thickness of the seed growth, a runabout could fill its hoppers in as little as 30 minutes. Sometimes, it took hours. When the hoppers were filled, the runabout headed for the islands selected for seeding, broadcast their load and returned to harvest more. By the middle of MO-EIGHT, the colonists had managed to harvest and transplant over 30,000 kilos of seed. The NORMAN wouldn't be leaving on any more time-accelerating trips, so over the years the growth and spread of the grasses now depended on nature. But, that growth factor was offset somewhat because the colonists were able to seed at a much heavier rate than Vance had been able to just using the ship's stores of seed.

Harvesting seeds from plants and trees was a much more time consuming chore. In most cases, the seeds had to be gathered by hand.

MO-ONE, 4, 1

The colonists were again gathered on the flight deck of the NORMAN. All of them looked tan and fit. They had spent the past three months fine-tuning the planet's ecosystem.

The fact that all of the colonists seemed to enjoy this rather mundane work really surprised Dale. He thought that most of these bright people would surely find it tedious and boring. "But," Alex pointed out, "this world is like a personal creation to them. They have an immense pride in being a part of it."

"If I can have everyone's attention, we'll get the meeting started," said Vance.

Everyone broke off their conversations and took a seat.

"Several things to cover this morning. First, we have decided that each of you shall have an island of your own. We…"

Vance was stopped by a spontaneous applause.

"That's great!"

"Super."

"Wow!"

"We can pick our own?" asked Aidan.

Vance smiled, "Yes, you can pick your own. But since there are 19 of you, and Murphy's Law almost certainly will apply, some of you are bound to pick the same islands. So, we want each of you to identify at least three islands, and put them in your order of preference. In case of a conflict, a simple flip of a coin will decide who gets what. By the way, these islands will bear your name and remain in your family forever. You will not be living on your island, at least not for the foreseeable future. But, you will be able to develop it as you see fit. Plant what you want, stock it with whatever birds and animals you desire. Make it yours. All this, of course, is to be done in your pitifully little spare time. You will find three islands marked on the map that are already reserved for Dr. Isley, Mr. Gabriel, and me. The rest are open for grabs."

Vance let the excitement go on for a few minutes.

"We noted that there is a large island about 400 kilometers off the east coast of Vast, just north of the tropic zone, that seems to have had a considerable amount of attention. I'll bet that is one we can't have," Tom finished up.

"You'd win the bet. That's mine," said a smiling Vance.

"It's a beauty already," said Janet.

"Thank you."

"It looks to be about the size of Cuba," said Bob.

"Good eye. That's pretty close." Vance paused for a second, "Any other questions concerning the islands?"

There were none.

"Second on the agenda is propagation." Vance stopped to let everyone's mind-set change to this entirely unrelated subject.

There were some mixed emotions displayed here. It was clear that most, but not all, were excited about the prospect of having babies. Three women weren't smiling.

"There is only one thing to say here. And that is that you are now free to make babies. You have your family units, and we expect those to be exclusive. No further explanation is necessary. Your first babies will be conceived naturally. You will be surrogate mothers and fathers for the second child. We'll play it by ear past that. All this has been planned from the beginning, so there are no surprises here."

"Do we have to start right away?" Vijaya asked.

Alex got into the conversation, "That would be our wish, but certainly not a command. As you know, you were picked to be the mothers and fathers of this new world. You all enthusiastically agreed to be just that. However, it is possible that because of this strange new world, a completely new life, a myriad of unknowns, and perhaps a lot of insecurity, some of you may feel considerable trepidation when it comes to having children. I would think that would be a natural reaction." Alex looked at Mary. "Mary, is my take on this about right?"

"Yes, sir. Just about completely. You're very astute, sir."

"I've been around a long time, Mary." Alex smiled.

"Yes, sir, it's that 'with age grows wisdom' thing, I guess."

"Exactly."

"Well, as it happens, I am one of the people who is apprehensive and has a little anxiety here. And for all the reasons you have just stated. These feelings are quite natural. Studies have shown that when animals are relocated, or their environment is changed, they may take a season or two to start breeding again. But I'm confident that in our case it will be a relatively short period of time for those who are reluctant, such as myself, to come around."

"This old man thinks so too. But please talk this over among yourselves," suggested Alex. "Mary is obviously a perfect resource for you. She is you," Alex smiled. "And please be comfortable with whatever decision you make. Vance, I turn this meeting back over to you."

"Thanks for your help there, Alex. Sensitivity to human emotions is not my long suit."

This caused everyone to laugh, breaking whatever tension remained on the deck.

Vance smiled, "You know me well," he paused for a second. "There has been quite a bit of interest in building homes around the bay, which I personally think is a great idea. Wouldn't mind having my own place."

"Here, here," said Dan.

Alex's memory instantly shot back to the days of his Consortium meetings held at Gabriel headquarters in the late 1980s. Whenever Peter Joshua, a member of the Consortium and an original member of the WGC, heard something he strongly agreed with, he would raise his Martini glass and say, *here, here*. Alex smiled at the ancient memory.

"Ah, good," said Vance, "I have some agreement here. There are a lot of beautiful spots around the bay. We have detailed topographical maps of the bay and surrounding land. I thought we could take a boat ride tomorrow, get a look, and take some pictures from the bay side, and then coordinate them with our topographic maps. We'll locate 20 or 30 marvelous home sites and put the nine best in a hat and draw for them."

"Why so many sites and why draw nine of those?" Tom asked. "Why not five?"

"Good question. There are four family teams, Alexander Gabriel, Walter Gabriel, Jason Gould, Dale Isley and myself. So that takes care of the nine…"

"No offence Mr. Gabriel, but why would you, as an example, need a home site?" Tom was puzzled, along with the nineteen others.

"I'll take this one," said Vance. "Stored on this ship are many clones. Not the least of which are Alexander Gabriel, Walter Gabriel, Jason Gould and Dale Isley. When they are born and grow to manhood, they will have a premier spot on our bay in which to build their homes."

"Enough said, sir," said Tom with a big smile. "Enough said."

Vance nodded. "Also, along with the clones of all the original members of the WGC, there are clones of Teddy Oldaker … Stoddard, Colleen Gabriel, and Aidan Keefe, just to name a few."

"Aidan Keefe?" asked Lesley.

"She was Colleen's younger sister and . . . the only woman I ever passionately loved," Alex said sincerely, "The plan is that when I'm reborn, Aidan will be reborn two years later. I couldn't be with her in my past life . . . something I deeply regret, but my clone will be able to be with her in the future." They could see the sadness and hope in Alex's eyes.

If the women colonists didn't love Alex before, they surely would now. They had never seen this side of him.

"Was she as beautiful as her sister?" Lesley asked tenderly.

Alex said nothing for a moment, he was remembering. "By all accounts, Colleen was among the most beautiful women in the world. Aidan, in my eyes, was as beautiful."

This caused Vance to think, *my Lara will be in the second birthing too, by God,* but he said nothing.

"We're getting off the agenda here," said Alex, "Vance, I turn this back over to you."

Vance pulled himself out of his reverie. "We will reserve sites around this Home Bay of ours for those who made it possible for us to be here. This bay will be a place of great honor for them and for you. I'm sure there will be no disagreement."

There was no disagreement.

"In 18 or so years, we're going to have some very distinguished neighbors," said Mary on an up-note.

"That's a great thought," said Jennifer. "Wow!"

"Other than Quinn, and to a lesser extent, myself," said Dan, "few of us have any idea how to build a house. I helped my father build two of our family's homes, and that experience should help some, but other than that?"

"Quinn will obviously oversee the work," said Vance.

"May I?" said Dale.

"Sure."

"We have hundreds of home designs in our computer's memory banks, using all sorts of materials. Dozens of them are log designs, and all are really nice. These designs have full blueprints with comprehensive instructions. There are even videos showing how to do everything."

"We have, on the equipment deck, just about every tool you'll need," added Alex. "You wouldn't believe the brainpower and thought that was given to absolutely everything over a five-year span. This ship is the size it is for a reason."

"Don't tell me we've got a sawmill on board?"

"It's not very big, but we have one," said Dale, "Clever design, wait till you see it."

"We also have a glassmaker on board," said Vance.

"No!" said Quinn.

"Yes, the maximum size pane it makes is only a meter square, but we have one."

"However, before you can use it, you're going to have to mine and refine a bunch of tin," added Dale.

"Tin?"

"Can't make proper glass without tin. Melting points are the key. Briefly, molten glass is poured over molten tin, the glass spreads evenly over the tin because it is much denser than glass and flat as a pancake. The glass solidifies at a hotter temperature than tin, and then it simply slides off the top of the molten tin."

"We have an ore refinery aboard?"

CHAPTER 26

HOME SITES
MO-FIVE, 1

Within a week, the entire bay was subdivided into ten-acre plots; there were 36 of them, more than expected. All of the plots had wide bay fronts, and six of those also bordered on one of the three rivers emptying into the bay. These were clearly the most desirable, so an age-old method of selection was employed. The six on the rivers plus three spectacular plots on the bay were assigned a number one though nine; then the numbers were written on small pieces of paper and put into a small bucket.

"Okay, someone from each team come over here and pick a number from the bucket."

"After you, sir," said Lesley.

"No, we'll take whatever is left. You go ahead." Vance held the bucket up head high.

"Okay." Lesley walked over, reached up and in and retrieved a piece of paper. The others followed.

"Mind picking one for me?" said Alex, "I'm all thumbs this morning."

Everybody laughed.

"No problem." Vance pulled a piece of paper out, "This one is yours." He picked four others, "And this is Dale's, this Jason's and this is Walt's." He retrieved the last number for himself and sat the bucket down.

As the colonists read their number they looked up on the viewer where the map of the plots was displayed.

"Cool," said Kathleen, "Just the one we wanted."

Everybody began talking among themselves. Most seemed to be satisfied with their plots.

"If anybody would rather have a different plot, I'd be happy to switch with them," said Alex. "It will be at least 19 years before the future me will be able to build a home, and all of these plots of land are beautiful, so just speak up."

"All of you can trade if you want—there's no rule here," said Vance.

After a moment, Quinn asked, "Who has number five?"

"Alex does," answered Vance.

Quinn smiled, "Well, sir. Then we would like to trade with you."

"Done," said Alex. "What's your number?"

"Three."

"Would anyone rather have three than what they have?"

"As a matter of fact, three was our second choice," said Dan.

After a few minutes, three more trades were made and all seemed quite pleased with their plots.

"Okay, everyone has a family estate, or to be more accurate, a future estate. We still have a lot to do to this planet before anyone can build a home," said Vance. "However, the program for home building calls for a few steps to be taken right now. We need to accumulate building materials, specifically lumber. Most other materials can wait.

MO-SEVEN 1, 1

As one of the large runabouts was converted into a log hauler, the colonists, particularly Bob and Quinn, continued to be astounded by the brilliant designs of these machines.

"The finest engineering minds on Earth designed these contraptions," Vance explained. "And there is more to come."

"The forethought is astounding," said Quinn. "Every day I see examples of it."

"Well, you can thank our Mr. Gabriel for a great deal of it. He continues to give Dale credit for his mind-boggling contributions, but never takes credit for his genius in seeing and directing the big picture," said Vance. "Engineers design these machines, but Mr. Gabriel directed them to do it. He has a knack for putting the best people in the right places."

Fir and pine trees were abundant in massive forests all over the northern hemisphere of the Ring. A forest 32 kilometers north of Home Bay was chosen for the harvest. The oldest and largest of the trees were too big for the small lumber mill, so trees with a diameter of one meter or less were selectively cut and airlifted to the area just south of the NORMAN's landing site; the area that once served as the pastures for Gabriel's first animals.

Dan, Bob, and Vance did the heavy work. They used battery-powered chainsaws to fell, buck, and cut the trees into ten-meter sections. Bonnie and Leah volunteered to set chokers for the runabout. Vijaya, after training for a week, piloted the ship. The craft was able to lift three to five of these tree sections at a time and deliver them to the mill area, where they were purposefully stacked in pyramids seven meters tall and left to dry for a full year. After three weeks, the land south of the mill contained four-dozen such stacks.

In the meantime, Quinn and Tom headed for the South Dumbbell, where the largest concentrations of tin ore were found. The self-contained smelter machine sat in the cargo bay of the second large runabout. The power to run this machine was drawn from the runabout itself. They installed the mill right over a highly concentrated tin deposit. It was calculated that 12,000 kilos of this rich ore was required to produce 200 kilos of pure tin. This was twice the amount needed to run the glassmaking machine, but there was certain to be other uses for the tin in the future. It took a full month of heavy physical work to produce the required amount of tin, but they got it done.

MO-SEVEN 14, 1

Vance had just called the weekly meeting to order, when Jennifer stood up with a big smile on her face. "I have an announcement... Lesley is pregnant."

Everyone stood and enthusiastically cheered. All the women gathered around and gave big hugs and kisses to Lesley.

"Congratulations, Lesley," said Alex.

"Ditto," said Dale.

"Wonderful," said Vance as he nodded his head in approval.

"Quinn, congratulations. You're going to be a daddy," said Alex.

"Thank you, sir. I'm thrilled."

"Do we have a due date?" asked Mary.

"Not exactly, but we believe about the middle of next Mo-five," said Lesley.

"Anybody else?" asked Alex.

"We're working on it," said Tom with his typical straight face. "Mining tin takes a lot out of a guy." This time Tom smiled.

"Not that much," said Eryn as she jabbed him in the ribs with her elbow.

"Logging doesn't seem to weaken them either," added Leah as she shot a glance at Dan.

"Well, I suspect we'll be hearing more such announcements in the near future," said a clearly pleased Vance.

"Tasha, this is another bit of information for our history, not that you've been lacking events to record. You've been busy?"

"Yes, sir. I'm getting it all down and loving it. This is going to be the most interesting and rapidly progressive history ever recorded—if I'm any judge, and I am. Earth's history evolved over hundreds of thousands of years. It was slow, with lots of twists and turns and ups and downs. Many of the downs were caused by wars, starvation, disease, and natural disasters. This planet was started with most of the bad history eliminated, natural disasters notwithstanding. Quite remarkable."

CHAPTER 27

BUILDING MATERIALS
MO-NINE 22, 1

A huge tent was set up about 400 meters south of the cave on a large flat piece of land that was once part of the high-tech pasture system. Within the tent were the small lumber mill and the glass-maker. At the moment, Vance and three men were in the middle of turning those stacks of logs into usable lumber. The larger logs were being cut into dimensional lumber sizes ranging from the utilitarian 6 x 12's to 12 x 36 centimeter beams. The bark was stripped off the smaller logs and then turned so that the diameter of each was exactly 60 centimeters end-to-end and log-to-log. Each of these perfectly rounded logs was run through the mill, and a 12-centimeter flat cut was made the entire length of opposing sides to aid in sealing the walls. The notches required to lock in opposing walls would be cut on site.

Each family team had chosen a design for their homes and the lumber was cut to the dimensions that fit that specific design in order to allow for a minimum loss to scrap. By necessity, all of the homes were log designs, but they all varied in floor plan and size. With the exception of Vance's home, all contained ten bedrooms and six bathrooms. The kitchens were large enough to cook meals for up to 30 people. Enough space was left to add more bedrooms and bathrooms, if needed. These were designed to be homes for large and extended families.

Two women, Jennifer and Aidan, were turning out panes of glass and stacking them in a far corner of the tent for future use. Aidan was six months pregnant and Jennifer was five. This wasn't heavy lifting work but it was really hot working near the glass machine. That corner of the tent had no sides to allow for a breeze.

Back at the NORMAN, Lesley and Eryn were handling the day care facility. In their care were 11 babies, four boys and seven girls. Lesley and Quinn's son, Adam, was the oldest at four months. In order to keep track of future pairings, the surnames for the children of natural conception were based on their father's name. All of the last names for Quinn's children were Quinnson. Dan's children had the last name of Danson, Tom's would be Tomson, and Bob's offspring would be named Robertson. The mothers were identified by using the first three letters of their first names as the middle names of their children. For example, Adam's full name was Adam Les Quinnson.

"Keep it simple," said Vance, "and we'll save a lot of confusion later."

Of the colonist women, everyone but Janet was either pregnant or had already produced babies. Jennifer, the Ob-Gyn, had recently isolated and corrected Janet's fertility problem, so it was expected that she would now be able to conceive normally.

As of this date, there were 16 naturally conceived children on Gabriel. Next, the women would then become surrogates for the clones. A postpartum four-month period was mandatory before a clone could be implanted. Depending on the individual's physical and mental health, that period could be extended.

MO-THREE, 2

Vance was unnaturally animated as he paced from one side to the other of the large octagon-shaped gazebo built on the bay side of the cave. This gathering spot provided quick access to the cave while taking advantage of the view overlooking Home Bay. The whole area between the original landing site and the cave had been turned into a park of sorts. Trees were trimmed; some were removed and others planted in order to enhance the comfort and ambiance. A road of small river rock had been built from the ramp of the NORMAN to the full length of the park, a distance of just over 300 meters.

A month ago, Lesley had requested that she be given the honor of carrying Vance's beloved Lara. A grateful Vance instantly agreed. Now he was anxiously waiting for the word that the implanting of Lara's clone had gone without a hitch.

The actual implanting had been done in the previous week, but it would take a full week to determine if the implant was a success -- a week that seemed much longer to Vance. He actually considered shutting himself down, as he had on the long voyages of the NORMAN, but he was too responsible to do that. He needed to be with his "charges."

Vance looked back at the cave entrance just in time to see Jennifer walking out of the cave onto the broad path that led to the gazebo. Vance could see that she had a serious look on her face as she walked toward him. His heart sank.

She walked straight up to Vance and took both of his hands in hers, her somber face turned into one giant smile as she said, "She's real pregnant!"

Vance instantly let go of Jennifer's hands and put her in a tight hug. "You shit!... Thank you.... YES," he yelled.

CHAPTER 28

KIDS AND CLONES
MO-SIX, 20

It was a beautiful day and the Gabrielites were having a picnic. There were 119 people milling about the greatly expanded Home Bay gazebo. Only 20 of this number were adults; the other 99 were children between the ages of 5 through 19. No babies had been born for the past four years. A vote had been taken just over five years ago, and it was determined that the 15 ladies had done all that they should in populating the planet Gabriel. They each had an average of just over six children. There were 53 females and 46 males in the group of youngsters. Among these children were the clones of Alex, Vance, Dale, Lara, Colleen, Teddy, Aidan, Walt, Jason, Norman, and Marian. Of the clones, Norman, Marian, Walt, and Lara were the oldest; they were now 17. Colleen, Teddy, Jason, and Dale were 14, Alex and Vance were 7, and Aidan and Jason were 5.

There were many discussions about the problems that might arise when dealing with clones of famous people, such as: Would the clones feel special? Would they take advantage of the other children or demand special treatment? Would the knowledge of their heritage put additional pressure on them to excel at their original vocations? In the end, it was decided that all of the clones would and should carry their original names. Everyone agreed that based on the strength of character of these famous people, if their clones were raised properly, with no special care given, or heightened abilities expected, there should be no problems.

Mary suggested that they not be told of their complete history, their accomplishments, or their gifts until they reached the age of at least ten and maybe even older, depending on the child and the circumstances. "As an example, I don't think Vance should be told of his history on Earth. I have the feeling that he'll be as tough as a boot without any prompting."

This process necessarily invoked the study of nurture versus nature and was infusing all sorts of significant data into the debate. Tasha, the historian, and Mona, the geneticist, were having a field day—every day. It seemed that nature was winning the debate over nurture. The environment was just about identical for all of the children, yet their natural characteristics seemed to differ greatly and dominate their personalities.

Alex, of course, took great interest and amusement in watching his parents grow up. To see his mother, Marian, grow from a fun-loving, cheerful child to a beautiful, responsible young woman was wonderful. She was tall and lean with nearly straight black hair and blue eyes. And she was a natural organizer. She would always take the lead in putting an activity together for the young people in the colony. Alex hoped that she and Norman would, as they had in the past, become a loving couple.

Norman was a nice, low-key young man. With his light blond hair and blue eyes, he looked a lot like his son, Alex. He was well behaved and an excellent student. As he grew, he didn't change much. He excelled at anything mechanical. He loved taking things apart just to see how they worked, and never seemed to have trouble putting them back together. He was clearly fascinated by the engineering that went into the NORMAN. When he turned ten, he was told that the NORMAN's design was, in fact, his design. "REALLY?" was his excited response to that information. In the days that followed, he actually became full of himself and, for the first time in his life, began pissing people off with his attitude. He seemed oblivious to critiques and admonishments he received from his surrogate parents. Vance got word of this and sent for young Norman.

"Young man, we're going to have a little talk."

"Yes, sir?" As far as young Norman knew, none of the children up to this point had ever had "a little talk" with Vance. Norman was nearly shaking as he stood before Vance on the bridge of the NORMAN. To make matters worse, Vance was standing in front of the viewer and on either side of him were Alex and Dale both displaying stern expressions.

"Do you think you're special?" asked Vance.

Norman was a bright young man so he knew what his answer should be. "No, sir."

Vance looked at him with disapproving eyes. "Do you know what the worst thing you can be called is?"

Norman searched his mind but found no appropriate answer to this question, "No, sir."

"A LIAR!"

You'd have thought Vance had slapped the young boy judging by the way he recoiled.

"You want to try for a better answer to my question, young man?"

"Yes, sir." Tears were forming in his eyes. "When I found out I designed the NORMAN it made me feel… special. Maybe smarter than the other kids."

"That was a much better answer," said Vance while he held his stern expression. "But let me inform you of a few facts. First, you didn't design this ship, the man standing beside me here, his father did," Vance gestured to Alex, "hundreds of years ago. And the propulsion system was designed by this man," Vance nodded toward Dale, "Dr. Isley. Who, I might add, is not your friend, Dale." Vance paused for a brief moment. "What you are, young Norman, is lucky, not special. You have great genes in you, as does every person on this planet-every person, or they wouldn't be here. This is a planet full of people with great potential, and you are simply one of them. Do you understand?"

It was all the boy could do to not break down completely. He stood visibly shaking with tears streaking his cheeks, but he held his ground with his chin high and shoulders back.

"Yes, sir, I do."

"Then that will be all. You're dismissed."

Young Norman turned his shoulders and was about to run off the bridge when he stopped and turned back to face the three men who had just witnessed his humiliation.

"Sirs, I... am so... sorry for how I acted. I promise you that will never happen again. Mr. Youngblood, sir,... I'll never lie again... I promise." As humiliated as he was, tears flowed but he did not retreat.

If there was a person in the universe who respected bravery more than Vance, that person was yet to be identified.

Vance took Norman by the shoulders and pulled him into a bear hug and held him. "You are a fine young man. I have no doubt you will be one of the great contributors to this new world. I am very proud of how you've taken this dressing down." He released Norman from his powerful grip and stood back.

Norman looked Vance in the eye, "You can depend on me sir."

With that, young Norman turned and walked off the bridge.

Vance turned back to Alex and Dale. "There's a good one. He's brave, just like your father."

"I'm very proud of my father," said Alex. "Always have been."

From that point on, if a person were looking for Norman or young Dale, they need look no further than the ship. "Birds of a feather," was a common comment among the colonists. The boys' likes and dislikes were almost identical. He and young Dale spent all of the time they could on the ship, quizzing the ship's Dale for hours at a time—which he loved!

Walt, Alex's uncle, had a very different personality than his brother Norman. Walt was rambunctious and outgoing, but at the same time warm, friendly and big-hearted. He was bright, but not nearly as bright a student as Norman. To Walt, having fun was more important than studies, and because of that he required some supervision, whereas his brother required none.

Lara and Marian became best friends early on. They were the same age, same height, and possessed similar long-legged and short-waisted bodies. But their coloring was different. Lara had fair skin and bright red wavy hair and hazel eyes, while Marian was darker skinned, with dark hair and blue eyes.

Vance, through great force of will, treated Lara just as he treated the other children. Outwardly, he showed no special interest; however, the original colonists suspected that inwardly he paid close attention. As far as Lara was concerned, she was just one of the children.

Colleen, at 14, was still a bit gangly but was already a head-turner. Her alabaster skin was flawless; her emerald green eyes could melt the coldest of hearts. Her body was also breathtaking. Everything about this young lady was spectacular. All the older boys and the four adult men on the planet had trouble keeping their eyes off of her. Marian and Lara, as striking as they were, both took considerable offence to the attention given to this redheaded beauty. The situation was quite different in their first lives on Earth. Marian and Colleen had been best friends and married to brothers, whereas Lara had never met Marian and had only interviewed Colleen on a few occasions.

"All quite normal," said a smiling Mary. "Particularly for those two beauties. I'd be surprised if any of the females over age ten weren't a little bit jealous. That girl is stunning, and that isn't going change for the foreseeable future."

All 20 adults were quite interested to see whether or not Colleen would take a shining to Walt. In their past life they had been as close as any couple could be. They were considered kindred spirits.

Dale, at 14, was the outstanding student; his thirst for knowledge was nearly an obsession. His buddy Norman came in a close second. Although somewhat shy, Dale accelerated past all of his peers academically and, along with Norman, were the only youngsters allowed unlimited access to the ship's computers.

The ship's Dale was fascinated by watching himself grow up in such a warm and loving environment. His own personal childhood had been terrible. As a child, he was shuffled from foster home to foster home. When he joined Norman Research in 1983, his self-image was at rock bottom and he had completely withdrawn from civilized society. His personal hygiene was nonexistent, and he was pretty much a social outcast. His genius, however, could not be denied. By the time he was 22, he had earned doctorates in both physics and microbiology.

Dale's personal hygiene and attitude turned around six months after he went to work for Norman Research, when he ran head-on into Alexander Gabriel for the first time. This meeting was contentious to say the least, but the dressing down that Alex gave him concerning his hygiene and attitude was exactly what Dale needed. After that first encounter, he went through a remarkable change in appearance and attitude while simultaneously acquiring an affection and loyalty to Alex that would endure all of their lives.

Teddy, at 14, looked exactly like his predecessors: dark hair, olive complexion, large soft brown expressive eyes and huge white teeth. Wherever he was, it seemed to be a happier place when he smiled. He was, without question, a natural born entertainer. As soon as he became aware that his antics caused laughter, he found his calling. He loved making others laugh. He was, of course, Alex and Vance's favorite. He was a very funny young man.

It was with great amusement and interest that the adults watched the antics of the clones. Other than Teddy, Vance was their favorite to watch. He was born a fireplug weighing nearly ten pounds. He was cute at this young age with his thick black hair and low forehead. His brown eyes were sharp, but not cold like the older Vance's eyes could be at times. His eyes were, however, always moving, taking in and absorbing everything. He began walking at less than a year, which was definitely a detriment to Bonnie, his surrogate mother. He was strong and fearless. As he grew, he loved physical games and rough play. He proved to be too strong to play with boys close to his own age, so he joined the older boys' games. He didn't cry when he was injured, and most of the time barely acknowledged that an injury had occurred. As the years went on, even the older and bigger boys started to avoid the mighty Vance. Somehow, it always hurt when he made contact with them, but everyone agreed that he never hurt them on purpose, and he always showed sincere concern and apologized when he did.

His physical powers were clearly matched by his agile mind. He was sharp and quick. He studied long and hard to master whatever subject he was assigned; there were no half measures with this boy.

It was suggested that calling him Young Vance was going to be an ongoing problem, so it was quickly agreed that in order to keep track of the two, young Vance would take Vance's last name and be called Youngblood.

Alex, at seven, was the same age as Youngblood, but a completely different child. His hair was nearly white, his eyes were a striking blue, and he was of medium height and build. Alex was a purposeful little boy. He was an observer. He could be seen sitting on a stump or rock for long periods of time, usually near water, just looking around. What he was thinking was anybody's guess. Although there were four other children within a year or two of their ages, Youngblood and Alex were the closest and there was clearly chemistry between them. "Their relationship doesn't make sense—they are polar opposites," Mary said more than once.

"It was always that way with me and Alex," said Vance. "There is a deep core value, an understanding that we share. We do think alike in many ways. Our approach to a problem is unusually direct by most standards, and we always identify the same problems."

Aidan was just five, but what a cutie! There was no question that she was Colleen's sister. Her hair wasn't quite as red as Colleen's, but it was as thick. She had the same green eyes and alabaster skin. She clearly showed more of a wild side than Colleen had at that age, but time would tell if she would maintain that temperament.

Alex watched with great interest as Aidan grew up. He wouldn't be able to be with her, but his clone would.

Sunday was the meeting day, as it had been for 21 years. This was the day each week that the progress of the planet and all future plans were reviewed. Upcoming birthdays were announced and celebrated. It was a social day.

Adam was the oldest by less than a month. He was, predictably, the tallest of the naturally born, and pretty much ruled the roost over the other children.

Jason was, at 14, already tall and painfully thin. He had a dark complexion, dark eyes, and dark hair. Alex remembered that the first time he had met Jason in 1980, he reminded Alex of a Lebanese basketball player. In their past life, Alex and Jason were best friends, along with Teddy and Vance. It was Jason and Alex who developed Gabriel International and Gabriel Industries. Jason's brilliant leadership of Global Media was a major contributor to the WGC's takeover of the world, and it was Jason who took over the leadership of the WGC when Alex retired.

It was ascertained, after many meetings on the subject, that because of the way the children were raised and educated, and the amount of responsibility put on them at early ages, they would probably mature mentally far sooner than the children of Earth.

"Most of the youngsters will be mentally mature and responsible in their mid-teens," said Mary. "But we do need to put some sexual guidelines in place."

"Nowhere in history that I'm aware of has forbidding sex ever stopped teenagers from dabbling," said Lesley.

"You're right," agreed Mary, "but on the other hand, we don't want any pregnant 16-year-olds running around the colony."

"And the pairing of couples is critical," said Mona.

"I would suggest," said Vance, "that we start sex-education classes right away. You ladies instruct the girls on the rules; I'll instruct the boys. Number one rule is no sexual intercourse before the age of 16. Number two rule is to check the genetics of your planned sex partner. Certain pairings clearly cannot be allowed." Vance stopped talking.

"And?" asked Mary.

"And, nothing," responded Vance.

"There are just two rules?" asked Jennifer.

"Keep it simple. After I tell the boys what I'll do to them if they break either rule, we won't need any more rules."

"We have a great supply of 100% effective birth control implants that we can provide the girls on their 16th birthday. So Vance is right, we don't need any more rules," said Jennifer.

"Marriage?" asked Lesley.

"Because of the unique attributes of our small civilization, I don't think marriage is a good idea," said Mary. "At this stage, it could cause a number of problems and few, if any, benefits."

"As we are currently practicing genetic engineering, exclusivity would prohibit that," said Lesley.

"After our numbers grow, it's a subject that will certainly be back on the table."

"All agreed, no marriage for now?" asked Vance.

All were in agreement.

CHAPTER 29

VANCE AND LARA

It was clear from the time Lara entered adolescence that she found Vance fascinating. Everybody did, but her fascination was noticeably different. Only Alex, Dale, and the original colonists knew the history between the two, and only those people would be sensitive to the situation. But it was obvious to them that this young girl had a crush on this much older man. An older man who would never age past 36. Vance did nothing to encourage this youngster, and spent no more time around her than he did with the other children. Everybody remained in awe of Vance, but as the years went on, Lara's feelings continued to move to a different level. As she matured past adolescence, her attraction to Vance became more apparent. It was becoming challenging for Vance to avoid Lara as she grew mentally and physically; every day she looked and acted more like the beloved Lara he had left on Earth.

MO-TWO 5, 21

It was Lara's eighteenth birthday, and following a new custom, a coming-out party was thrown in her honor. She was the third of the clones, and the 19th teenager to be so honored. The celebration, as usual, was held in the gazebo above Home Bay and most Gabrielites over the age of 12 were in attendance.

Lara's peers, using a great assortment of vines, boughs, and flowers, decorated the gazebo delightfully. Everybody was dressed in their finest, which in most cases amounted to clean cotton pants and shirts. Fashion selection for the young was limited at best, but there were some exceptions. All original colonists were allowed to bring an extensive wardrobe on the trip. All of the ladies brought at least three beautiful dresses and gowns. They knew that they would never have access to fashion again.

It naturally became the custom for the mothers to lend a gown to their daughters for their 18th birthday celebration. Lesley was Lara's surrogate mother, and as such presented Lara with her emerald green silk gown. It took a few adjustments to make this beautiful garment fit Lara, but after the adjustments, fit her it did. The green color impeccably complemented her red hair and skin shade. Lesley had all the proper accessories for the gown, much to Lara's delight. She had never worn anything like this before, and she was ravishing.

Dressed in their finest, Vance and the original colonists, minus Lesley, formed a receiving line at the front of the gazebo and welcomed all the partygoers as they arrived. Vance had on his black tuxedo, complete with a ruffled fronted shirt accented with a royal blue cummerbund and bowtie, and black patent leather shoes. Vance's body was certainly not the ideal tall lean body that looked the best in a tux, but no one bothered to point that out.

As the guests walked through the receiving line and into the gazebo, they naturally formed into various groups. A small band started playing some lively old swing tunes from the 1930's and 40's on Earth. Teddy wasted no time and took Colleen by the hand and led her onto the dance floor. Teddy could really dance and Colleen was pretty good herself, but it was apparent that she had to make an effort to keep up with Teddy. It didn't take long before most of the other attendees joined in.

After everyone arrived and settled in, Lara, escorted by Lesley, came walking up the path to the gazebo. After spotting this beautiful young woman, those in the receiving line turned to look at Vance; the look on his face would have melted anyone's heart.

"Oh my God," Kathleen whispered into Tasha's ear.

Tasha whispered back, "He's done ignoring this girl."

As Lara approached to within eight meters of the receiving line, she spotted Vance and could see the way he was looking at her. She smiled brightly. It was all she could do to stay with Lesley for those last few steps.

Vance stepped out of the receiving line when the two women were three meters out and held out his arms. Lara didn't hesitate and stepped forward to embrace him. They wrapped their arms around each other; their faces just inches away.

Vance spoke first, "Hi Sweetheart. May I be your date tonight?"

Lara nodded, releasing a tear of joy from a corner of her eye. "Yes, sir, you may… and every night from now on."

In the following years Vance and Lara were inseparable. It was unusual to see one without the other. It was noted by all that Vance's personality became a great deal more relaxed. He wasn't as involved in the everyday working of Gabriel. He no longer needed to be made aware of all plans concerning the planet.

Since leaving Earth, his personality had softened considerably. But since he and Lara became a pair, it was rare to see him without a smile on his face. When together, they were almost always holding hands. She called him Hon, he called her Sweetheart.

MO-SIX, 33

Vance finally found himself with enough time on his hands to pursue his interest in his island and gorillas. He and Lara, with the help of Youngblood and some of his friends, started building a good-size home on the banks of a picturesque little river, which not coincidently was named Lara. This river flowed from the highlands on the west to the ocean on the east side of the island. The island already had a well-established ecosystem that three decades ago was designed and planted with the great apes in mind.

While the home was being built, Vance began incubating five gorillas; the usual one male, four females. All five were from different parents to help assure genetic diversity. Two months later, five orangutans were put into incubation. Eight and a half months later, the five gorillas were born. Most infants are cute but, to Vance's eyes, baby gorillas were the cutest. He acted like a kid with new toys. If he'd had cigars, he would have been handing them out.

He named the boy "Kong" and the female's names all started with the letter K. Kim, Karen, Kathy and Kristine. The five instantly became a handful, requiring as much care as a human baby—times five.

It didn't take long for Lara to realize they had a problem. "Hon, we're gonna need some help for the next couple of years."

"I've already put out feelers. I think we'll need at least two more people for this."

"You're an optimist, Mr. Youngblood," Lara smiled, "We've got five orangutans hatching in a couple of months."

Vance smiled, "And it's going to be at least two years before we'll be able to move them to the island."

MO-THREE, 43

The population of Gabriel had grown to just over 2,000 in the 43 years since the colonists were first brought out of stasis. All but a few people made their home on or around Home Bay. Two dozen or so adventuresome individuals set up small outposts on the Vast and Dumbbell continents to keep close track of the animals that interested them. And of course, the Youngbloods spent as much time as possible on their island with the apes.

As needed, the individuals living away from Home Bay had access to the runabouts. The runabouts were maintained in excellent condition, and were always available for emergencies or special occasions, or for occasional transportation to and from Home Bay.

There were some hardships on Gabriel caused by the lack of manufacturing facilities. Mundane products such as paper, mirrors, electric lights, bicycles, washing machines and toasters simply were not available. Those people born on Gabriel only knew of the existence of these products through stories recounted by the original colonists, by reading about Earth's history, or by watching movies that were stored in the NORMAN's computers. The lack of these products didn't bother most people—that was just the way it was.

Some products were being manufactured, and more products were being added as time went on and the population grew. Thirty-two years ago, a few talented individuals started making boots and shoes out of the abundance of leather. Others took to making furniture out of the diverse woods available. Still others made cloth out of cotton and wool by operating the small looms that had been brought aboard the NORMAN. School children made simple vegetable oil lamps out of fired clay.

The NORMAN's computers contained plans and instructions on how to build a foundry, and how to turn iron into much stronger and durable steel. Tools such as shovels, hammers, and saws were forged out of the abundance of iron.

Lacking a monetary system, barter became the method of acquiring manufactured products. Someone might trade a pair of boots for an oak dining room table, or they might barter their product for the labor of another. Values settled naturally within the system.

PART 4
THE VOUT

CHAPTER 30

VISITORS
MO-SEVEN 18, 45

"Vance, can you hear me?" came Dale's voice over Vance's home audio system. "Vance."

"What's up, Dale? Just got out of the shower."

"Need you at the NORMAN, ASAP."

"I'm on my way," answered Vance without giving the summons a thought as to its importance. If Dale called him to the NORMAN ASAP, there was a good reason. "Fill me in while I get dressed."

"Looks like we're getting company."

Vance stopped in his tracks, "One of ours?"

"No, I don't think so."

"Shit!... How far out?"

"120,000 Ks and closing fast—and slowing."

Vance started moving even faster. "Be there in ten."

Lara walked into their bedroom, "What's up, Hon?"

"Not sure, might be having visitors. I'm heading to the NORMAN."

"Is it the ship from Earth?"

"Dale doesn't think so."

"Uh, oh!"

"Want me to send a runabout?" asked Dale.

"No, keep everything under cover until we know what we're dealing with."

"Would you like me to involve any others?"

"Get a hold of Adam, Janet and Alex; have them prepare to head to the NORMAN."

"Will do."

"Anyone else in the ship or cave?"

"Yes, sir. Dale and Norman are in the lab showing some youngsters around. Youngblood is on the flight deck with a couple of young men doing some maintenance on one of the small runabouts, and there are a dozen or so taking inventory in the cave's store rooms."

"All right, keep everyone inside the cave and out of sight… contact everyone and tell them to get inside and stay inside until further notice."

Vance kissed Lara quickly, "I'll have my communicator on so you can monitor what's going on." With that, he ran out the door.

Their home was the southernmost area of Home Bay. It sat on a low bluff on the north side of the river, where Vance first spotted the animal tracks so many years ago. It was a ten-minute walk to the NORMAN, but Vance would not be walking.

"Dale," said Vance while running, "signal Youngblood to start putting a runabout in combat mode."

"Yes, sir. Got him started already."

"Two minutes out."

A minute and 50 seconds later, Vance entered the bridge and went straight to his captain's chair.

The viewer displayed a spacecraft of an alien design hurtling toward Gabriel.

"Slowing down," said Dale.

"Looks like it's going to orbit," said Alex.

"Can we get any readings on it?"

"Sensors can't penetrate the hull," said Dale.

"Down to 36,000 Ks per," said Alex. "Moving into orbit."

"Are we getting any communications from it?"

"There is considerable static that our instruments aren't deciphering. Don't know if they are trying to communicate."

"Hmm, what would we be doing if it were us up there?"

"Gathering intel," answered Dale without hesitation.

"I suspect they are not trying to contact us. The static is probably sensor probes."

"Agreed."

"Inform everybody to shut off all broadcast communication planet-wide until further notice. Face to face communication only."

"Yes, sir."

Three and a half hours later, the extraterrestrial ship had made two complete orbits of Gabriel.

"It slowed and moved into a geosynchronous orbit at 37,000 meters," said Dale.

Vance checked the coordinates. "Shit! It's directly over Home Bay."

"They know where we are," said Alex.

Vance continued to look at the image of the alien ship. "Would our sensors be able to pick up the NORMAN inside the cave from their altitude?"

"Yes, sir, but we couldn't see inside the NORMAN."

"But we would be able to spot and identify every living thing on the planet that are not inside the NORMAN, couldn't we?"

"Pretty much, yes, sir."

Vance sat in silence for a moment. "Are Adam and Janet heading to the ship?"

"Yes, sir."

"What are our sensors telling us about this ship?"

"Nothing on the inside, but I can tell you that the skin of the ship is made up of the same metal alloy as the artifact you found."

"Ah… I guess that shouldn't surprise us. Maybe they're a rescue ship," said Alex.

"I doubt that. We're going on 500 years on the planet."

"That would be a long time out for a rescue," said Vance.

"Indeed," said Dale. "Their home planet might be close, maybe one to three light-years from here, maybe closer."

"Right next door, relatively speaking," said Vance. "Alex, you have any thoughts on this?"

"No, other than to say that there is no reason to believe they are hostile. It seems likely that their civilization was here way before we were. It's also possible that they are the ones that seeded the original plants."

"That's a strong possibility," agreed Dale.

Adam and Janet entered the bridge 27 minutes later. Both had concerned expressions.

"What's up, sir?" asked Adam.

Vance nodded toward the viewer. "We have visitors."

Adam looked at the viewer, "Holy shit!"

"Oh my God," added Janet.

"Where is it?" asked Adam.

"37,000 meters straight overhead."

"Wow!"

"Any communication?" asked Janet.

"Not yet. But hopefully there will be. And that's your bailiwick."

"Damn, it's been over 40 years since I've thought about linguistics or the Rosetta program. Looks like now would be the time to see if it works."

"Rosetta program?" asked Adam.

"It's a universal language translator—we hope," said Janet.

"Oh, this will be interesting." Adam turned to Vance, "How big is the ship, sir?"

"Big," answered Dale, "It's about 200 meters long and 100 meters in diameter. Other than those disk-like outriggers, which are probably their propulsion system, it's a cylinder with rounded ends. Quite a practical design."

"Any visible weapons?" asked Adam.

"Nope."

"Have you tried to contact them?" asked Janet.

"No," said Dale.

"What do you suggest we do for getting that ball rolling?" asked Vance.

Janet thought about that for a couple of moments, "Use all mid-range frequencies, beam them directly at the ship, and send Pi."

"Excellent," said Dale.

"Why Pi?" asked Adam.

"It's a universal measurement. 3.1416. It can't vary, no matter where you are in the universe."

"Of course," said Adam.

"I suggest we use dots and dashes," said Janet. "Three quick dots immediately followed by a short dash, followed by one dot, pause a second, four quick dots, pause a second, one dot, pause a second, six quick dots followed by a long dash. Then keep repeating it. Hopefully that will get that ball rolling."

"Right away, Dale," ordered Vance.

"Already done," was Dale's response.

"You're fast," Vance said with a smile.

"I speed up when I get excited."

They all waited anxiously for a return communication. After 13 minutes, Dale reported that the probe signals were continuing but nothing more.

Vance got out of his chair, "Keep me informed. In the meantime I'm heading to the flight deck to check on the runabout's combat outfitting."

"You're preparing for a fight?" asked Adam.

"Absolutely. Plan ahead, anticipate—remember?"

"Of course. Sorry."

Adam, the first born on Gabriel, was now in his early 40s and himself a father of 19 children and 15 grandchildren. He was tall, not as tall as his father, Quinn, but just shy of two meters. He had sandy hair and dark brown eyes. He looked more like his mother, Lesley, than his father. He fittingly assumed the role of being the eldest of the colony's children. He was an exceptional father and an excellent role model for the youngsters that followed.

"Come with me. You're one of the few with enough time and experience on a runabout to qualify for combat. That's why I sent for you."

"I might point out that Youngblood is extremely capable with those machines," said Adam.

"I know." Vance smiled.

Vance and Adam headed for the elevator, leaving Dale, Alex, and Janet to man the bridge.

Vance and Adam entered the flight deck a minute later. They found one of the small runabouts stationed in front of the hatch with Youngblood in the middle of attaching the portside weapon pods. The top and starboard side pods were already in place.

"That's a runabout… my God," said Adam.

The runabout was being converted from a craft that looked like a flying bus with a slightly flattened top and an internal propulsion system, to something altogether different. The bus-like top with viewing ports had been replaced with a top containing two weapon arrays. One array held a heavy particle cannon, which might not be of any use. First, their sensors could not penetrate the hull of the alien ship, and therefore the cannon could not be aimed; and second, the heavy particles might not penetrate the hull even if they could aim it. The second array, located at the rear of the runabout, bristled with small missiles. The two side pods were positioned toward the front of the runabout and held 20 mm Gatling guns with 5,000 round magazines. Without Vance's insistence on being prepared these ancient weapons with a relatively short range would not have made the trip.

"Good morning, sir," said Youngblood.

"How's it going, Youngblood," said Vance as he looked at the runabout. "Never mind, I can see. You're getting this done in a hurry."

"Yes, sir. Been studying the tech manuals for this machine for some time now, just in case the need ever came up."

"Excellent," said Vance.

"Thank you, sir. I'll be done with this pod in a couple of minutes, then I'll get on the auxiliary power and external propulsion systems."

"We're here to give you a hand. Adam, take that lift to section 12 and pick up two auxiliary power systems. I'll help Youngblood put the finishing touches on the weapons."

"On my way." Adam ran over and climbed aboard the lift tractor and headed to the far end of the deck.

The conversion was finished 23 minutes later. The auxiliary power cell was installed inside the runabout just in front of the main power source, and the external propulsion systems were attached a few meters behind the Gatling guns. The runabout now appeared horribly lethal.

"Wow," said Adam, "how long did you say the engineers were designing the NORMAN and everything on it?"

"Five years, using the most farsighted and best brains on the planet. I was amazed at what they were designing when they were in the middle of it, and I still am. There is almost nothing they missed when they were designing, building, and outfitting the NORMAN."

"I don't know who or what that is above us, but I think if they take one look at this machine they will either want to flee, surrender, or be friends," said Youngblood.

Vance looked at his clone for a moment. "Do you think we ought to fly it up there and scare the shit out of them?"

"No, sir. I think that would send entirely the wrong message."

"Oh?"

"Yes, sir. If and when we have to take this machine out, we'll probably be at war. That is not a good scenario."

Vance nodded and smiled, "Right answer," Vance said with considerable pride.

"Vance," came Dale's voice over the intercom.

"Yes."

We're getting something. Better come on up."

"On my way." Vance turned to Youngblood. "Think you'll have any problem flying this thing in this configuration?"

"It might be a challenge. But if pressed, I believe I can manage."

"Get in the pilot's seat and make yourself as familiar with the ordinance as you can. Adam, you get in the copilots seat. Both of you go through as many simulations as you can devise and figure out how this thing will fly. Stay in there until I relieve you."

"Yes, sir."

"I'm heading back to the bridge."

Two minutes later, Vance returned to the bridge.

"What have we got?" said Vance.

Janet turned to face Vance. "They know what Pi is."

"How did they send it and what did they send?"

"Sent it on the highest frequency we broadcast on. They sent 3.141592."

"They added a couple of digits."

"Yes, sir. And we added a couple of more when we resent it to let them know we're on the same page."

"So we can assume they want to talk."

"Yes, sir."

"What next?"

"Spoken language. I'm going to send a voice message along with the digital of Pi on the established frequency. As an example, I'll send three dots followed by saying the word three and so on. Hopefully they'll do the same thing in return."

"The Rosetta program is open," said Dale.

Within a half an hour, Janet had sent Pi verbally and received the same back. The alien voice was higher pitched than Janet's and the language was certainly alien, but they had established a contact and some language. However, the fact that numbers were universal and the other verbal communication was in the abstract, it was going to take the Rosetta time to develop the data to allow communication.

"Can we send them a picture of us?" asked Vance.

"We could if we knew what they use as a viewer," Dale paused for a moment, "We might send what we commonly use as the viewing frequency and see what happens," said Dale.

"If they sent us such a transmission, would you figure out what to do with it?" asked Vance.

"I would recognize that a different and more complex signal was being sent. I would run it through every computer we have to decipher it. I would like to assume they would do the same thing."

"Might I suggest you do that," Vance said as he looked over at Janet, "Janet, your thoughts?"

"I'm a linguist. I know little about frequencies. But it seems like a logical next step. If we transmit pictures, we greatly speed up the Rosetta's learning curve. A picture is worth a thousand words, you know," she smiled.

Vance looked back at Dale.

"I'm on it."

"Pick a picture from the data bank that show a man, woman, and child."

"Yes, sir."

"After that, get a hold of Quinn, Bob, Dan, and Tom and have them join us here ASAP."

"Yes, sir."

Five minutes after the picture was transmitted to the alien ship, another transmission was sent to the NORMAN. This one contained a picture of three strange looking humanoids. The three were dressed in white form-fitting single piece garments similar to a jumpsuit. Their picture paralleled the one sent to them, depicting a man, woman, and child. The distinction between the man and woman was not as great as it was in humans. The female was smaller and finer, otherwise there was not much difference between the sexes. The aliens were a great deal thinner than humans and appeared to be hairless. They had small, fine noses, and wide, thin, nearly lipless mouths. Their large dark eyes were a contrast to their pale skin. Overall, they looked somewhat colorless.

Next to that picture, they sent the same picture superimposed in outline over the picture that the NORMAN sent. The aliens were nearly 30 centimeters taller.

The five on the bridge were stunned. They were actually looking at real aliens.

"Well, this picture shows that some people on Earth weren't too far off in describing aliens," said Janet.

"Maybe some of the outlandish stories of sightings and abductions were true. These people may have visited Earth."

"That would mean they could be hundreds, if not thousands, of years ahead of us in technology," added Dale.

"Hmm," mused Alex.

"Sir," said Janet, "If these beings had visited Earth in the past, don't you think they would already know how to communicate with us?"

Vance smiled, "That's a good point."

"It certainly adds to the questions."

"Janet," said Vance.

"Yes, sir?"

"You have your work cut out for you, learning their language and teaching them ours. The audio and video should help. We need to know what their intentions are, what they want, and what we can do for them,"

"Yes, sir. This is going to be great!" Janet was clearly excited.

"Any idea how long before we can carry on an intelligent conversation?"

"Well, they're obviously highly intelligent, maybe more so than we. So, I'd think in two or three days the Rosetta will have enough data to start a conversation. Once it has the basics it should gain abilities exponentially. Then we'll be able to say "welcome" in their language."

"What can we do to help?"

"Send Dale, Little Bob, and Norman here to help. They're our brightest. They might be a big help. They should be all I need."

"Done."

CHAPTER 31

LET'S TALK

Two days later, four people were gathered on the bridge in front of the viewer. Vance was sitting in the captain's chair with Janet standing on his right, Quinn to his left, and Adam standing behind the chair. All were dressed in the formal uniforms that had last been used on Earth just before the voyage started.

The two civilizations, over the past two days, had inputted enough data for the Rosetta program to begin translating words between the two languages. Once the basics were worked out, the Rosetta took over. Dozens of new words and descriptions were added by the minute. They were now ready to communicate.

"The translations will probably be slow and halting to begin with. But that shouldn't last long. The Rosetta will make adjustments quickly," said Janet.

"Are we ready?" asked Vance.

"In three seconds," responded Dale, "two, one."

An image appeared on the screen. There were six aliens, three sitting and three standing behind them. They appeared to be on their bridge. They were all dressed in the white jumpsuit that was shown on their first pictures. As close as could be determined, there were three males and three females.

Vance stood up and smiled, "My name is Vance. I, along with our citizens, wish to welcome you and your ship's crew to the planet Gabriel."

The alien in the center seat stood. "Thank… you. My name is… Callen. We wish to be your… friend… Vance."

"Then that is what you shall be, Callen."

The words were not yet flowing freely but the conversation was getting better by the second.

"May I ask your… race's name?" asked Callen.

"We are Human."

Callen nodded, "We are… Vout."

"We humans welcome the Vout to Gabriel."

Callen smiled slightly and again nodded, "Thank you, Vance."

"We are excited and delighted to make contact with you."

"We… feel the same. We are looking forward to. . . learning… more of you and your… world."

"This day will go down as one of the great moments in history," said Vance.

"…Agreed," said Callen as he looked at his fellow Vout, then back at the camera. "We would like to tell you how much we… marvel at what you have… accomplished on this planet over such a short period of time."

"Thank you. It has been a labor of love."

Callen paused for a moment. "Interesting choice of words."

By their demeanor those around him thought so, too.

Vance smiled, "How would you have described such an undertaking?"

Callen paused for a moment and smiled. "A splendid outcome to labors performed," Callen paused again, "your wording is better."

Vance smiled and nodded, "How do you know how long we've been here?"

"We have been visiting this planet for 1,600 of your years. We last visited just over five hundred years ago. You were not here at that time."

That's what we thought, thought Vance. "We must have just missed each other."

"Our last ship did not return. We were receiving a… communication when it stopped. There has been no other communication."

"Do you know what happened?"

"We suspect the… Malic destroyed them."

"Malic?"

"Another civilization. They are not friendly. They are to be. . . avoided when possible."

"Do these Malic come here?"

"Yes, they do, and another, and us."

"Another?"

"The Yassi."

"The Yassi... Are they friendly?"

"Yes, they are our trading partners and wonderful beings. We meet with them every two years to trade."

"We may want to talk about being your trading partners also."

"Yes, that would be our hope. You have, on this planet. . . Gabriel, resources that are rare on all but a few other worlds."

Vance said nothing for a moment. "Is gold one of them?"

Callen paused, "Yes, that is right."

Vance paused for a moment before continuing. "Tell me more about the Malic, if you will. Is their planet close by?"

"Four point eight light-years," responded Callen. "They are the most distant to Gabriel."

"How far are the Yassi and your planets?"

"We are one point two light-years, the Yassi are two point seven light-years, closer than the Malic but in a different direction."

"How long does it take the Malic to reach this planet?"

Callen said nothing for a second. "Nearly six years at full speed."

Vance nodded, "Would you like to come down here and meet person to person? We could get to know each other and work out a system of trade."

"We may do that, but we would like to get to know you better before meeting you in person. We are a. . . cautious people."

"That is sensible. Hopefully, we will be able to alleviate some of your concerns with a continuing dialogue from this distance."

"Thank you for understanding. I must tell you that we cannot spend too many hours at a time on your planet's surface. The gravity is too strong for our physiology. We use remote machines to extract the gold. We are usually here for six months mining the amount of gold we can carry."

"Perhaps we can help in that endeavor?"

Callen said nothing, and then the sound was cut off. Callen turned and talked to the man sitting on his right and the woman standing behind him. They responded in a way that appeared to be enthusiastic. The sound came back on.

"You are willing to let us extract valuable materials from what is now your planet?"

"We are aware of the abundance of gold this planet contains. We cannot imagine that you would take more than this planet can afford to give."

The Vout said nothing for a moment. They were apparently taken off guard.

"We are pleased by your understanding and generosity."

"It is our nature for the most part. And as new trading partners, you may have something that is of great value to us."

"That is possible," agreed Callen.

"If it would be more comfortable for you, might we come up to your position and enter your ship?" asked Vance.

"You have a transport that will allow you to do this?"

Vance smiled, "Maybe. We can get up there but I don't know if our smallest ship is able to enter your flight deck."

Callen said nothing for a moment, then turned to his fellow Vout as the sound went off. Vance assumed they were discussing the possibility of a personal visit and the ramifications. It was clear by the animation of the six Vout that there were several differences of opinion.

The sound came back on. "Some here have concerns concerning an unfamiliar race. They remain cautious. This is not meant as an insult, but your race looks more like the Malic than the Yassi or we do. That makes us cautious… my wish is that you understand."

"We do understand. Your caution is understandable. How can we to prove to each other that we are who we represent ourselves to be?"

Again Callen conferred with his bridge mates with the sound off. It was a full two minutes before he came back on with the sound. "We have a few who are specially trained to withstand the strong gravity of other worlds. They would be able to spend as long as three days on your planet's surface. Perhaps, if they met with you personally they will report favorably back to us."

The view being transmitted to the Alien ship suddenly switched to the image of Alex.

"My name is Alex, I am a computer program. But, at the same time, I am real. I would like to ask a question or two if I might?"

That seemed to confuse Callen and those with him on his bridge. The sound went off for a moment before it came back on.

"We do not understand what you are," said Callen.

"Are you seeing my image?" asked Alex.

"Yes, but you say you are not alive. You are the voice of the computer?"

"I am not the voice of the computer… I am in the computer. I was alive. We were able to transfer duplicates of all of my thoughts and emotions, all that I was mentally, into this computer. My actual body and mind remained on our home planet."

"We do not have such technology. We would be interested in learning much about this marvel."

"We can discuss that in the future," said Alex.

"We would be grateful."

"There are two of us that have our personalities in the computer. Dale is the other."

"May we see him?"

"Hello." Dale's image instantly appeared beside Alex on the viewer.

"This is a marvel—a true marvel," said Callen.

"Yes it is, even we think so," said Alex as his image reappeared next to Dale on the viewer, "I'm sure your civilization has creations that will amaze us as well."

"Yes, that is likely."

"May I ask a few questions?"

"Yes, Alex."

"Are you on a constant voyage of mining and trading?"

"Each crew only takes one voyage in their lifetime, then they retire on our home planet. The voyages last approximately 20 years ship time, 150 years planet time. We have 32 ships like this one. So, our home planet receives and sends out five ships a year. These ships bring back supplies that are not available, or cannot be created or grown, on our home planet. The rewards for the crews are a life of extreme ease for their sacrifice."

"In Earth's ancient history, we had similar voyages. But these were voyages on our seas, not in space. Though not nearly as long, the hardships were extreme."

"We have a similar history."

"How many planets do you travel to?"

"Twelve in all for this ship. Other ships travel to more and others travel to fewer."

"How many are inhabited by intelligent beings?"

"This ship travels to four inhabited planets, excluding our own. Of the four planets, only two, the Yassi home planet and now this one, have advanced intelligence. A small number of our other ships visit planets that contain intelligent life. Even then, most do not have advanced intelligence, such as ours, the Yassi, or yours."

"What do you regard as advanced?"

"Development of sophisticated technology like computers, complex medicines, and atmospheric flight; not necessarily space travel, which is a rare thing."

"Can you give us an example of a non-advanced civilization?"

"... Yes, the fourth planet, one that we rarely visit, is dominated by what you would regard as. . ." Callen paused, as if listening to some off-camera voices, "Dinosaurs."

"Dinosaurs! That is very interesting. Dinosaurs were the dominant animals on our home planet for 60 million years. It was speculated by many that had they not become extinct due to a massive natural disaster, they would have gained advanced intelligence. At what level of development are those you've observed?"

"They have a written language, primitive towns and commerce, and they have laws. They grow and raise their own food and have domesticated many animals. It seems they have shed their violent past for the most part. Their intelligence has gained ability at a rapid rate over the past millennia. They have the potential for future gains in technology."

"Do you interact with these beings?"

"We have observed them at close range, but have not dealt with them in any way."

Nothing was said for a moment.

"In the past, did you observe Earth and humans in the same way?" asked Alex.

Another moment of silence passed before Callen spoke. "One of our research ships, long ago, observed your species for just over 20 years before returning to our home planet. In those 20 years, your technology grew at a very rapid pace. At that time, we surmised that you would travel into deep space within 1,000 years. You have done so in half that time."

"There were reports of your visits," said Alex. "They were not believed by most. Many claimed to have been abducted and experimented on, but were branded as lunatics. Many suffered life-long ridicule, some went insane."

"We were not aware that physical contact was made with the humans. It was and is prohibited by our edicts and universal laws to interact or interfere with undeveloped intelligent beings. If this happened, it will be reported and the history of that research will be changed to reflect the disregard of those laws. Those who were praised for their research will now be seen in a different way," Callen paused for a second. "We sincerely apologize to you."

"All that was done a long time ago, and it is a history that involved neither of us as participants. No need to apologize."

"You are understanding. Thank you."

"I have a question," said Dale.

"Yes, Dale?"

"There was a report a long time ago of an alien ship crashing near an area known as Roswell on the planet Earth. It was rumored that five alien beings were killed and their bodies taken to a secret place. The government of that nation spent decades denying it ever occurred. Do you know anything about this?"

"Oh yes… it is a famous part of history known to all advanced civilizations."

"Really?" said Alex.

Callen seemed surprised that Alex would doubt what he had said. "Of course… I would not lie."

Alex's face displayed some confusion for a second, then changed to one of understanding. "Oh, I apologize Callen. The word `really' used in this context means I believed what you said, but was surprised at the information provided in your statement.

"Oh, I see. Interesting."

"Please go on with your story."

Callen smiled. "It was a small Yassi scout ship. It was a terrible tragedy for the Yassi. Even with all their technology, they could not determine what caused the crash."

"It was rumored that lighting was the most likely cause," said Dale.

"No, that would not have affected a Yassi ship. It had to be an internal malfunction. It was catastrophic. The Yassi mourned the loss of their people for a long time. The fact that they could not retrieve their companions is a sad part of their history."

"Why didn't the Yassi retrieve their companions before the Humans took them away?"

"They were too late. At the time of the crash, the mother ship was stationed on the other side of the Earth's moon. It would have taken too long to launch another small ship. They could do nothing without exposing themselves to the Humans."

"It seems they had already exposed themselves in the crash."

"That was an argument that was used at the time. But, as it turned out they did the right thing. Earth's government lied to its citizens, hid the ship and the existence of the Yassi, thus keeping the exposure to a minimum."

"Well, that clears up an old mystery," said Dale.

"We may have some record of those events in our computer's library. If we do, would you like them made available to you?" asked Alex.

"Yes, very much so."

"We'll do a search."

"Could the Yassi have taken their ship and companions back by force if they chose to?" asked Vance.

"Without question. But the Yassi would not do that."

"An action like that certainly would have changed history, for better or for worse," said Dale.

"Wow, who would have thought we would discover the truth about this thirty-two light-years from Earth," remarked Alex. "Incredible."

"Indeed," agreed Vance.

"I would love to see what the dinosaur race looks like. Do you have pictures of these beings?" asked Dale.

"We do, but by our standards they are quite ugly. We will transmit them to you."

A series of pictures came on the viewer, and everyone on the bridge was surprised. The dinosaurs were small, maybe a meter to a meter and a half tall, lean and colorful. They had large zebra-striped heads, but their stripes were red on a blue background. Their faces were somewhat elongated but not as much as a raptor's. Their eyes were large and yellow. Their mouth's contained no lips and their teeth were not exposed. There was only one picture that showed their teeth. They were short but sharp, much like a small shark. Their bodies looked to be something between a human's and a raptor's, with large strong legs, a short balancing tail, and nearly human-looking arms and hands. Their stance leaned slightly forward to offset the weight of the tail. They were wearing loose fitting clothes, but no footwear.

"Wow! They certainly look alien," said Alex.

"Fascinating," said Dale.

"Should we assume we are ugly by your standards?" asked a smiling Alex.

"No, you are interesting looking to us. You have so much diversity in appearance, where we have little."

"I thought that since we looked like the Malic, we would seem ugly to you."

"The Malic are ugly inside and out. They are short and blocky," Callen clearly hated the Malic. He looked to his right and said, "Send the pictures of the Malic." He turned back to the viewer. "A picture will tell you what they look like."

"We have an expression," said Alex, "One picture is worth a thousand words."

"We have a similar expression."

The pictures of the Malic came over the viewer. Callen was right, the Malic were ugly. The first picture was apparently one of an adult male with an outline of a male Vout superimposed over it, again to reflect perspective to the Human - Vout size.

The Malic appeared to be a little more than a meter and a half tall, just a little taller than the dinosaur race, with short-legged chunky bodies. The Malic had hair poking out from every opening in what seemed to be battle gear that they were wearing. Their eyes were dark and beady; their noses were little more than a couple of large holes in their big faces, and there were no ears visible. The most striking thing about their appearance was their teeth; they had long sharp looking canines protruding from the top and bottom of a large lipped mouth. They were clearly a predator species.

"They are truly ugly. But other than hair, I can't see that we resemble them at all."

"You are right, it is only the hair. We apologize for the comparison."

"We are not easily insulted. And there is no insult here."

Callen smiled, "Might I ask how we appear to you?"

Alex laughed a little. "You are thin, quite tidy, and very smooth looking to us. Just the opposite of the Malic."

Callen gave that little smile of his. "We like that description."

"Might I ask a few questions?" Vance interrupted.

"Yes of course, Vance," said Callen.

"We assume your race breathes oxygen?"

"Yes, all races breathe oxygen. And now, for the first time we will be able to breathe without assistance on your planet, thanks to your labors. . . of love."

Everybody smiled at that statement.

"Did you plant the vegetation that was here when we arrived?"

"No, the Yassi did that sixteen hundred years ago."

"Do the Yassi look similar to your race?"

Callen smiled, "They are also smooth and tidy, but they are smaller by half, yet stronger. Their planet, Yassi, is 2% more massive than

Gabriel, which accounts for their strength. Because of the oxygen levels, they also could now comfortably live on Gabriel."

"Could we see a picture of the Malic and Yassi ships, so we'll know which is which?"

"Yes," Callen looked off to the side. "First, we will show you the Yassi ship."

The viewer changed to a picture of a beautiful ship, gold in color, as was the Vout's ship. The Yassi ship was long and multi-hulled and looked almost like a massive trimaran yacht. It gave the impression that it was traveling at high speed even when sitting still.

"Wow! That's beautiful," said Vance.

"Is it ever," agreed Alex.

"They are a far advanced civilization," said Callen. "The Malic avoid them completely. The Yassi will not seek out the Malic, but the Yassi have advanced weapon technology and will destroy the Malic, if provoked. The Malic respect power."

"That's good," said Vance.

"We will transmit the image of a Malic ship so that you can defend yourselves, if and when they show up. Please make no mistake; you must be prepared for the Malic. They will take from you all they want and destroy all they feel is a threat to them."

Ten seconds later, a picture appeared of a ship that looked for all the world like a stack of four thick gray dinner plates turned upside down. The entire ship looked like it was adorned with weapons of varying descriptions.

"This is a Malic ship. We only know of three in existence." Callen paused for a moment. "We have had reports of only two for nearly five hundred years."

"Is that unusual?"

"There have been times in the past that no recorded encounters were registered for hundreds of years. We must assume that the third ship is out there."

"Are their ships capable of landing on this planet?"

"Yes, but it is vulnerable if it does so because it would take an hour for it to return to an orbit. They have dozens of smaller ships aboard that are much quicker; those are their main weapons."

"Can you tell us their weaknesses?"

Callen turned to his left and talked to the man seated next to him. Again, the sound went off. After a couple of minutes he turned back to the viewer, "We are discussing your question. I apologize for the delay, but we need a few more minutes."

Vance could see a red light blinking above the viewer. "Take your time. We'll shut off the transmission for five minutes."

The transmission was cut off and Alex and Dale's images appeared on the viewer.

"What's up, Dale?" asked Vance.

"The timing of their last visit. The alloy they employ. Our firing of the nuke on our way here is beginning to concern me greatly."

It only took Vance a second to make the connection. "Oh, shit!"

"Ditto," added Alex.

"Yes, I now believe it was us who destroyed the Vout ship. I believe we should tell them what happened and give them the artifact to verify our concerns."

"I agree," said Alex.

"First, let's see what they have to say about the Malic weaknesses," said Vance.

"This is terrible," said Dale.

"Do you think this information will cause the Vout to go to war with us," asked Adam.

"I don't think the Vout war on anybody. But it might cause them to abandon our new alliance."

"Or," said Janet, "they might be grateful for the information and might feel they can trust us because of our forthrightness. Such an admission should certainly demonstrate our openness and honesty."

"Adam, get down to the hanger deck. You'll find the artifact on the top…"

"I know where it is," said Adam.

"Good. Take it to the work bench and get ready to transmit its image to the Vout ship."

"Yes, sir."

Adam took off at a run.

Vance turned back to the viewer, "Let's turn it back on."

The viewer again displayed the six Vout. Callen appeared to be ready to continue their conversation.

"Vance, we are in agreement as to what information we can provide regarding the Malic weaknesses."

"We would be grateful."

"They are slow of mind. But, at the same time surprisingly cunning and absolutely ruthless. Other life, of any kind, means nothing to them. They have a belief that teaches that those species who are not Malic or do not serve Malic are not fit to live. For the most part, their technology was stolen or they would never have been able to be a threat to their neighbors. They were a subspecies on their home planet but were treated well by the superior beings called the Byuse. The Malic became dissatisfied with the order of things. Over many centuries, they propagated at an incredible rate, and in the end vastly outnumbered the Byuse. The Byuse were peaceful and gentle people who, like us, would not kill an intelligent being. The Malic rose up and destroyed them. The three ships the Malic have are the Byuse ships. They added the weapons."

"To get off the subject for just a moment. Did any Byuse survive?"

"Yes, both we and the Yassi have had colonies of Byuse on our planets for hundreds of years. They have contributed greatly to our civilizations."

"That's good to hear." Alex smiled. "Sorry for the interruption."

Vance continued the subject that interested him greatly, "Would your technology allow you to defeat them if you were forced into a conflict?"

"Our belief system does not allow the taking of intelligent life. However, it has been argued by many for a millennia that the Malic are not intelligent life, but still, there is this debate."

"What can you tell us about their weapons?" asked Vance.

"They employ four different weapons. One type is a simple projectile cannon. It is highly destructive and nondiscriminating. It is fired rapidly and covers a large area with powerful explosives. They use a much smaller projectile weapon that they carry with them. It is much more discriminating, and much less destructive. They have long-range missiles that can accurately propel a weapon with a large destructive force. These are large missiles, and each ship carries only two. Another is a heat generator. It creates waves of sonic vibrations that, given enough time, can melt solid rock."

"Do they have nuclear devises?"

"No, nothing nearly that powerful. They have uranium ore but not the refining technology. The Byuse managed to destroy that technology and a great deal of the refined uranium before the Malic took over their planet. The Malic ships have been operating on the remaining stockpiles for centuries. But we believe they will exhaust their supplies within the next several centuries. They have been looking for another source.

"How do you protect yourselves from the Malic?"

"We run."

"Run?" This was a concept that didn't fit into Vance's way of thinking.

"Their mother ships are not fast. They are heavily fortified and heavily armed, which adds greatly to their mass and makes them slow to gain speed. We simply leave when we see them approaching; they cannot catch us."

Vance thought about these revelations for a moment. "We are here, we cannot run."

"Exactly. So you will have to fight or they will take from you all they wish and give nothing in return. If you resist, they will destroy you if they can."

"How sensitive are their sensors? What can they detect and at what distances?

"We do not know exactly. We do not think they can analyze the chemical or metallurgical makeup of a planet from long distance. They can determine the makeup of atmospheres and they do have powerful telescopes that enable them to view small objects from a hundredth of a light-year away."

Vance was filing this information in his military mind; it was a part of him that hadn't been used for a long time. Vance now had many fortes, but his military training and experience were his oldest and most ingrained.

"Would they be able to detect our ship where it sits now?"

"No. We can just barely detect it ourselves. The amount of gold found within the quartz that is contained in your cave walls blocks or weakens almost all of our sensor probes."

"Ah, it is the gold alloy on the skin of your ship that is blocking our sensors."

"Yes."

"Do the Malic ships contain gold?"

"No, but they use a lead alloy that blocks sensors in a similar way."

"The purpose of both alloys is to block unwanted radiation, I assume," said Dale.

"Yes. The Malic have been trying for centuries to perfect our alloy, which is much lighter and stronger. And it is the gold they want from your planet… as we all do."

"How many Malic are on their ships?" Vance asked.

"It is our understanding that this number varies from ship to ship, from as few as four hundred to as many as a thousand. Both male and female—there is little difference in appearance."

"That fact is probably what makes them so mean," said Alex.

The Vout thought that was extremely funny. They lost their composure for a moment and laughed at length, as did the others on the NORMAN's bridge.

"Do you understand the Malic language?" asked Dale.

"Yes, we have a complete Malic program similar to what we just put together for your language."

"Can we get a copy of that program?"

"Yes, we will integrate that program into the one we are presently using. Between our program and yours, you should be able to communicate with the Malic."

"I assume that you also have the Yassi language in that program," said Dale.

"We will also provide that for your memory banks."

"Thank you," said Vance. "Maybe when the Malic show up, we can convince them to move along without the use of violence."

"We commend your intention, but they will have come from a long way; they will not want to leave without taking something of value from you."

"We will try to convince them that they will be destroyed if they attack us. Make them think that we have weapons that they cannot defeat."

"That belief will be the only thing that would stop them."

Nothing was said for a moment.

"How often do the Malic visit this planet?" asked Alex.

"Every 400 to 500 of your years."

"Do you know when they were last here?"

"We believe just less than 500 years ago. We believe they are now on their way here. In our last communication with the Yassi, they reported the Malic trajectory would bring them into this space."

"How much time do we have to prepare?"

"The Malic ships are much slower than ours, so we believe it will be about five years of planet time."

Dale's image returned to the viewer. "I apologize, Callen, but I must have a conversation with Alex and Vance."

"We'll wait."

The viewer was turned off.

"Now would be the time to tell them," said Dale.

"Alex?" said Vance.

"Agreed."

"Turn it back on," said Vance.

The viewer came back on.

"Callen, we have to tell you something; something that in all likelihood will not please you."

Callen's demeanor cooled noticeably. "What is it you wish to tell?"

"We have aboard our main ship two major protection systems. Systems that divert or destroy objects that are directly in our flight path. The first is passive. It is a generated magnetic field that extends out over 200 kilometers and deflects all debris of 3,000 kilos or less as we travel at high speed."

"We have a similar system."

Vance paused, "To handle anything larger than 3,000 kilos, we have a battery of nuclear devices. At the speeds that we travel, there is no time to judge what is in our path. These devices are launched automatically and at extreme speed."

Callen and his crew sat in silence displaying no emotion.

"Just shortly before we landed for the first time on this planet, one of our nuclear devices launched, destroying whatever was a threat to our ship. At the time, we assumed it was an asteroid or large meteor. We tried to analyze the debris field as we passed through it, however, we were not able to get a large enough sample. What we were able to detect was that the field contained some gold."

Callen leaned forward slightly, "Do you think now that you destroyed our ship?"

"There is more to tell. In that first visit to this planet, while I was seeding the largest continent, I came across a piece of metal stuck in the ground. I brought it back to the ship and we analyzed it. It is the same alloy as your ship."

The viewer went blank.

There was a momentary silence on the bridge of the NORMAN. Vance stared straight ahead while Janet and Adam looked around in confusion and concern.

"That's not a good sign," said Alex.

"No," agreed Vance, not taking his eyes off the viewer.

"What do we do now?" asked Janet.

"We wait," said Alex.

After thirty minutes, Dale reported that the Vout ship had not moved from its fixed position directly over their head. There were no comments from the others.

Eleven minutes later the viewer came to life. Callen and his crew were seated and standing right where they were before.

"Vance, Alex, Dale, we apologize for the delay in communication. We had much to discuss. We now have questions." No emotion was being displayed by any of the Vout.

"We'll answer any questions we can," said Alex.

"I felt you would," said Callen as he looked to his left briefly then back to the viewer.

"We have nothing that we need to hide from you," said Vance.

"Yes, I believe that," said Callen. "The first question is whether our ship would have been destroyed by a collision with your ship?"

"Without question," said Dale; "Had we not destroyed your ship with a nuke, if that is the case, we would have hit them at a tremendous speed. The resulting explosion would have made the nuke seem like a clapping of hands in comparison."

"Then, of course, we wouldn't be having this conversation," added Vance. "Everyone and everything involved would be space dust."

"That was the opinion of many of us," said Callen. "Second question. Do you still have the piece of metal?"

"We do. We are ready to transmit a picture of it if you wish."

"That would be helpful."

"Adam, you're on," said Vance.

Within seconds a picture of the long golden piece of metal was displayed on the viewer alongside the view of the Vout. Their interest was intense. They all began talking at once, losing some of the discipline that they had displayed up to this point.

Nothing was said for nearly a minute.

"Is there any writing on it?" asked Callen.

"Yes," answered Vance. "Adam, show the writing."

The camera moved to the far end of the metal. The writing came into view. Adam moved the camera slowly down the writing from left to right.

"Would you like a different view?" asked Dale.

"No, we have what we need. We will need a little time. Will five minutes be all right?"

"Of course."

The viewer went blank. Five minutes later, the viewer came back on.

"We now have an answer to an old question. That piece of metal is from one of our ships, but not from the ship that we thought we lost 400 years ago, the ship that you thought you destroyed. It is from a ship we lost to the Malic over 600 years ago. It seems that you have destroyed the third Malic ship. This piece of metal must have been aboard their ship when you destroyed it."

Nothing was said for a moment. Then Vance asked a question, "All things considered, destroying the Malic ship is probably a good thing, but that doesn't answer the question as to the location of your ship."

"We believe it does. The last message we were receiving from our ship was a distress message. The last words were, 'the Malic are…' We are now convinced that both ships were destroyed by your device. But there is a strong possibility our ship would have been destroyed by the Malic anyway."

Vance leaned back in his chair, clearly surprised. "Wow."

After a moment Alex spoke up, "I thought your ships could outrun the Malic."

"That has always been the case except for that one time 600 years ago. At that time, it was determined that the Malic managed a surprise attack. We cannot know what happened this last time."

"Perhaps their technology has improved. Maybe their speed has been enhanced."

"That is a most unpleasant thought," said Callen.

"It is. But, we will make our defensive plans accordingly," said Vance.

"Give us another moment," said Callen. The sound went off for a minute, then came back on.

"We want you to know that you have, in this short period of time, proven you are to be trusted and treasured as a friend and ally," said Callen. "We would be delighted to have you visit our ship anytime at your convenience."

CHAPTER 32

GOLD

Out of the over 80 Gabrielites who volunteered to assist the Vout in their gold mining on the Vast continent, 22 men were chosen. This was much to the delight of the Vout. The humans were much stronger and tougher than the Vout and were able to move equipment by hand that required the Vout to use a machine. This alone saved a great deal of time.

It was soon learned that it was the Vout and Yassi who, over centuries of gold mining, had carved out the massive cave that now held the NORMAN. The mountain that bordered the south side of Home Bay held one of the richest concentrations of gold on the planet.

The Vout used massive laser clusters to melt the gold away from the quartz ore. This effectively vaporized most of the quartz while increasing the percentage of gold contained in the remaining quartz ore from just below 10% to as high as 85%. A sophisticated machine then removed the remaining 15% of quartz and trace minerals, leaving pure gold. Because of the help of the Gabriel men, the holds of the Vout's ship were full of the precious metal two months ahead of schedule, allowing them to move the mining operation to the South Dumbbell. Two weeks later, the mining and refining of tin was completed and the Vout's requirements were filled.

There was, however, considerable damage to the mined areas. Left behind were three large pits in the northeast section of the Vast continent, and one large pit in central South Dumbbell. The South Dumbbell pit began filling with water even before the mining operation was finished. This was not a surprise; the miners were aware of a spring running fifteen meters below the surface.

"We'll have a small lake in the middle of nowhere. It will be of considerable benefit to the wildlife," remarked Vance.

The three new mining pits on the Vast Continent were up to 18 meters deep, and as large as 43 acres in area. When Alex viewed these pits, he asked the Vout if it was possible for their powerful lasers to carve a canal to a river 21 kilometers upstream, then from pit to pit and back to the river a few kilometers downstream. The topography was calculated and it was determined that Alex's idea would work.

The Vout were happy to oblige the request. Their lasers made short work of the project. In just shy of a week, a flat-bottomed, slopped-sided canal nine meters wide and two and a half meters deep was completed. It ended up covering a total of just over 36 kilometers in length as it wound around the low-lying hills. As an added benefit, the laser's intense heat melted the sand and rock into glass, which helped seal the canal and prevent a lot of water loss due to seepage.

On the day that the last seven meters of rock between the river and canal was to be melted away, hundreds of Gabrielites and dozens of Vout had taken up viewing positions on the low hills surrounding the area. At a fixed moment, a massive laser suspended from a Vout mining vehicle came to life, and in less than five minutes melted the natural damn; water from the big river immediately gushed into the new canal.

Everyone in attendance applauded, even the Vout, although applauding was not their normal way of showing appreciation. Their custom was to make a woo sound; the louder they wooed, the more appreciation it reflected. For this occasion, the atmosphere reverberated with the loud woos of the Vout and the clapping of the humans.

"This is going to be a great boon for the wildlife in the area," said Alex as he watched the proceedings from the viewer.

"We hereby name this string of three lakes "The Vout Lakes" in honor of our new friends," said Vance from a temporary podium.

"It will be interesting to watch the development of the area over the next few years," added Dale. "The river at this time of year is at an average flow; the amount of water released into the canal will increase and decrease depending on the seasons."

"How long before it fills the new lakes?" asked Alex.

"Don't know for sure without knowing the exact amount of water entering the canal, but I would think somewhere between three to four weeks."

The following afternoon Vance walked onto the bridge.

"I've asked the Vout for one more favor," said Vance.

"Oh? What?" asked Alex.

"We need four deep holes drilled with their laser. That gadget is something else. I would think they could cut a Malic ship in half with it in seconds."

"What holes?"

Over the five months that the humans and the Vout spent together, they became trusted friends and agreed to share technology. Some technology was withheld on both sides by mutual agreement. What was being withheld was not always told to the other party, again by mutual consent. It was agreed that what the other party did not know could not be coveted nor disputed. Dale, as an example, did not wish to share the formula or technology for Isleium or the SLF technology. The Vout were not yet aware that Vance was not human, and they didn't need to know. Maybe sometime in the future that technology would be shared. Vance withheld weapons designs, technology, and statistics on the armament that the NORMAN possessed. He didn't fear that the Vout would use that information against Gabriel or the humans, but if the Malic ever got their hands on it, it could be a disaster. Vance informed the Vout about the necessity of withholding this information, and they readily agreed.

When the mining and refining of gold and tin was completed, the Vout gifted the mining equipment, including the massive laser, to the citizens of Gabriel. They also provided technology for the mining and refining of many different ores. This undoubtedly would prove to be a boon in the future development of Gabriel.

"We have gotten the best of the trade," said Callen. "We owe a great deal more to the Humans in order to make this a fair trade."

It was Alex who spoke. "We don't know the value of these trades. And we truly appreciate your honesty."

"Trading partners must be open and honest or the system will collapse. We have taken a large amount of gold, the single most valuable metal that we know. In addition, we have also acquired a large amount of tin. Not as valuable, but still a rare metal. You have asked for very little… actually almost nothing."

"Uranium," said Dale. "Our ships and equipment are powered by it, as are yours. Our stockpiles have been reduced to less than 25% over the years. We have large deposits of uranium ore throughout this planet and the technology to refine it, but not the infrastructure to manufacture it."

"Ah, I believe we have something to trade," said Callen with a smile. He was clearly delighted.

"Good," said Dale. "We will not only need refined uranium but in specific weights and shapes."

"That is a fair request and one that we will honor," replied Callen. "If you will provide us with the specifications, we will produce what you require."

"Perfect."

"But, you will have to wait until the next Vout ship visits Gabriel. They will transport your uranium."

"Are you able to tell us how long it might be before their visit?" asked Alex.

"As soon as you provide the specifications, we will send a communiqué to Vout. We estimate it will be three years before our ship arrives here with your fuel."

During the time the Vout were visiting Gabriel, they sent a small shuttle daily with ten or so crewmembers to Gabriel's Home Bay. The planet Gabriel was, by their account, one of the most amazing places in the universe. The variety of plants and animals was astounding to them. They were like children at Disneyland. In the five months they were in orbit, they managed to visit every warm continent, and saw hundreds of animals they had never seen before, including most of the incredible variety of vegetation the planet now held. The flowers were of particular interest to them. They loved the beauty. Occasionally they would say, "Ah, we have something similar to that one." Or, "we have a tree that grows that straight, but much taller."

At the end of each day of their explorations, the Vout were invited to share a meal with the Humans. A young Gabriel nutritionist suggested that the Vout, due to their passive nature, might be vegetarians. She was right; they would eat fish, but not fowl or red meat. It was soon learned that the Vout loved spicy food. . . the spicier the better. Each day a different meal was prepared for that day's visitors. Each set of visitors was given the day's recipes and, when possible, seeds or plants from which the meal was made. When given the seeds for a dozen varieties of peppers and curry, the Vout nearly lost all dignity in their display of gratitude.

It didn't take long before some of the members of the two races were able to converse with one another. Janet and one of her daughters were the linguists of the group. They held classes each morning to teach the Vout language. The classes were well attended. Those who attended were given the privilege of eating with the Vout visitors, something that would give them stories to tell for the rest of their lives. The Vout would not return to Gabriel for at least three years, so these were times to cherish.

CHAPTER 33

PLANNING FOR MALIC MO-SIX 47

Vance and his crew had just re-entered Gabriel's atmosphere in one of the large runabouts. For the past few weeks, the runabout had been converted to a freight hauler. In this configuration, the runabout looked more like a streamlined boxcar than anything capable of flight. But it had done its job well in delivering large heavy materials to the planet's largest moon, 'Faith.' That job had just been completed.

"Before we take it back into the NORMAN, we need to get this ship washed," said Vance. "Is there a nice storm close by?"

"A good one about 210 kilometers south of Home Bay," Dale replied.

"Adjust course," Vance said to Youngblood.

"Adjusting course," Youngblood replied.

Two hours later the gleaming runabout slowly flew through the cave entrance and into the hanger deck of the NORMAN. Six men plus Vance exited through the front hatch and onto the flight deck. Their pressure suits were covered in a fine copper-colored dust from head to toe. Each carried his helmet under his arm.

"Gentlemen, let's get these suits clean, then hit the showers and head home," said Vance. "Nice day's work."

Thirty minutes later, a sufficiently clean Vance, dressed in comfortable coveralls, headed to the elevator and took it up to the bridge.

Alex and Dale's images appeared on the main viewer as he entered the bridge.

"Looks like it went well," stated Dale.

"It did. 10% gravity has its pluses and minuses. Hard to get a solid base to work from, but a hell of a lot easier moving big objects around."

"So we have four nukes set and ready for the Malic if needed?" asked Alex.

"Yes, buried with their rail gun boosters. And you can't see them, even if you were standing on them."

"Ready to put them on line?" said Dale.

"Turn them on."

"One."

In three seconds a row of red lights on the main computer's face came on, and in another second the top light turned green.

"Good. Two."

The second light turned green. This was repeated for the next two lights.

"All's perfect. What's next?" asked Dale.

"We need to put a long-range sensor array in a remote location. Vance paused for a second. "There's a small cave about two Ks south that might do nicely."

"Remote location?" said Alex.

"Yep. I'm assuming that the Malic will home in on our sensors and try to take them out. That's what I'd do. And, Dale, they need to be real and active."

"Of course," said Dale. "If we're not using them, they'll know."

"No doubt. But, we can use them without giving our location away."

"Short range microwaves should do it. We could use a narrow beam from the remote location to here. It would be undetectable, unless they flew directly into the beam."

"Perfect!"

"Along those same lines," continued Dale, "we had better add a large power source at the same location, for bait. Let me re-word that, a seemingly large power source. I'll bet we can design a beauty."

"That's the idea."

"What else?"

"If and when the remote sensors are taken out, we'll need backups."

"Agreed. We'll need to setup a second and third backup," said Dale.

"Have to have an evacuation plan. Need places that everyone can get to in a hurry. Preferably underground," said Vance.

"We have people scattered all over the Ring and close to four hundred in other parts of the planet," said Alex.

"The logistics are a challenge," said Vance.

"We'll need an alert system," said Alex.

"How much time do you think we have, Dale?" asked Vance.

Dale said nothing for a full minute. "Given what the Vout said about the main Malic ships, we should assume they are slow coming into orbit. Their mass versus power limits their ability to quickly slow down. Let's assume that they take twice the time to drop speed as we do. That fact should actually give us as much as eight or nine hours."

"Unless…" Vance stopped in thought for a second. "Unless they send out their smaller quicker ships before they get here."

"They could do that. And if they do, the alert time is cut in half, maybe less."

"That should still give us sufficient time to alert our people over normal channels."

"As soon as they drop to .05% of light, we'll send them a warning," said Vance, "to try to convince them that we'll have no trouble destroying them if they approach Gabriel."

"We have to assume they know nothing about us," said Alex. "How could they? They are heading here to mine gold. They probably haven't been here for at least 500 years, and maybe longer considering the fact that we destroyed what was probably their last ship to visit Gabriel."

"They're going to have several unpleasant surprises, that's for sure," added Dale.

"I hope they're surprised," said Vance.

"We were told by the Vout that they have excellent long-range telescopes, so they'll see the immense change this planet has gone through in a short period of time. Also, the last time one of their ships was in this sector of space, it was never heard from again. Given those two facts plus a dire warning not to approach, we just might deter them," said Alex, "It would work for me."

"I agree, that's a good possibility," said Vance. "Of course, that depends on them being able to do without the gold they've traveled seven light-years to get. I'll bet my pension that, at the very least, they'll send out a probe to test the waters."

Vance, aided by Youngblood, spent two days a week for the next two months training runabout pilots and crews on combat techniques. Vance was not a fighter pilot, so it was definitely a "learn as you go" training for everyone. An additional disadvantage was that the small runabouts were not specifically designed for fighting. They, when reconfigured, would be a formidable weapon, but not as effective as one designed for combat. At the end of the two months, Vance declared the training as complete as he knew how to make it.

CHAPTER 34

THE MALIC ARRIVE
MO-EIGHT, 49
1:30 a.m.

It was the darkest part of the night when a Malic ship was picked up by Gabriel's remote long-range sensors. Alarms instantly went off in specific locations around the Ring. Youngblood, Adam, three other pilots and 15 gunners headed directly for the NORMAN. Safety wardens were alerted, as well as the citizens who needed extra time to get to their shelters.

As Vance was running to the NORMAN, he was in communication with Dale and Alex.

"What's their speed?"

"1,300,000 kilometers per and slowing."

"What's their rate of deceleration?"

"About how we figured. Half as fast as we could."

"That's good news."

"How long before they get here?"

"Estimate eight hours."

"I'll be on the bridge in two minutes."

Two minutes later, Vance entered the bridge. "Is the translator on line?"

"Yes, sir," said Dale.

Vance sat down in the captain's chair. "Open all communication on the planet. I want everybody to know what's happening."

"Yes, sir."

"I'm ready to transmit."

"You're live," said Dale.

Vance nodded and began speaking. "This message is for the Malic ship that is presently heading toward our planet. You are not welcome in our space. If you approach any closer than 800,000 kilometers, we will destroy you." Vance made a cutoff sign to Dale.

"Transmission off," said Dale, while displaying a bit of concern. "Guess we're not going for diplomacy."

Vance looked at his dear friend, "Do you think the Vout would lie to us about the Malic?"

"Not at all."

"Then I believe we have no reason to be diplomatic. Quite the opposite actually. I believe these beings will take more notice of a direct lethal threat than any other approach."

Dale was pensive for a moment, then smiled, "You're right, of course."

Vance nodded at Dale and leaned back in his chair. "Now, it's up to them to fish or cut bait."

"It will take 90 seconds for our signal to reach them. Then I presume they will have a lengthy discussion as to their next move. I suspect it will be a while before we get a response."

"Youngblood reporting in, sir." Came a voice over the intercom.

"Your status?" asked Vance.

"All five runabouts will be reconfigured and ready to be manned in one hour, sir. We will mount up and deploy on your command."

"Understood, Youngblood. I suggest you and the men try to relax as much as possible. It will probably be about five hours before we go to full alert."

"Yes, sir. We'll be ready."

It was 25 minutes before the Malic responded. Their first words were, "Who are you?" The voice through the universal translator had a flat gravely sound.

Vance signaled Dale to open the outbound signal. "We are the Humans. We have taken and developed this planet as our own. We own everything on it and control the space around it."

Another five minutes passed before a response came through. "We have never heard of your race, yet you know of us and speak our language—how is this possible?"

"We will answer none of your questions. We strongly suggest you alter your course and head away from us."

Another communication came in 18 minutes later, "For centuries we have visited this planet, which you now claim, in order to peacefully mine minerals. We would like to work out a treaty to benefit both the Humans and the Malic."

"We are allies with the Vout and the Yassi. We do not wish to be an ally with the Malic."

This time, the Malic's response was quicker.

"So it is the Vout and Yassi who have poisoned your minds against the Malic."

Vance again made the cutoff sign.

"Let 'em stew for a while. What's their status?"

"They're still slowing at the same rate and still on a trajectory that will intersect Gabriel."

Vance leaned back in his chair as he brought up his hands and rubbed his temples.

"I haven't seen you do that since you became a SLF," said Alex. "Do you have a headache?"

Vance took his hands away from his temples. "No headache. Just trying to put myself in the shoes of the Malic. It's interesting though, to use a reflex from so long ago."

Three hours passed without any communication between the two races. Dale gave a status report every ten minutes. "If they don't alter course within the next 24 minutes, they won't be able to avoid coming inside the 800,000 kilometer barrier."

"Open the channel."

"You're live."

"We sincerely hope your civilization is not dependent on your return. You are within minutes of being annihilated."

Again the channel was cut off. Another two minutes passed.

"They are altering their course," said Dale. "Give me a second here."

No one said anything until Dale spoke up. "At their present deceleration and trajectory, they will come close to the 800,000 kilometer limit before they start heading away from us."

"Hum," said Vance.

"Also," said Dale, "they will pass just behind Faith on their way out of our space."

Vance's eyes narrowed. "How fast will they be going at that point?"

"At their present deceleration rate, about 50,000 kilometers per."

"They are going to get some good pictures of us at that speed and altitude," said Alex.

"Yes they are," agreed Vance.

"The Vout said they were crafty," said Dale. "It seems they're going to comply with our demand, but at the same time push it to the limit. They're gathering all the intel they can before heading out."

"That would make sense," said Alex.

"Yes," agreed Vance. "Youngblood?"

"Yes, sir."

Vance paused for a moment, "I would like you to man your ships. Something isn't right here."

"Yes, sir. We'll be ready to fly in two minutes."

"Roger that."

"What is it, Vance?" asked a concerned Alex.

"There's a rat in the crackers here, Alex. The Malic are giving in too easily, and that's not their normal pattern, according to the Vout."

"We just lost contact with them. They are behind Faith," said Dale.

Three minutes passed, then four.

"There they are," said Dale. "They're heading away and picking up speed."

"Oh wow," exclaimed Alex. "Guess we did scare them off."

"Hum," was all Vance said.

"Still picking up speed," reported Dale.

Vance continued to look at the viewer… saying nothing for a full two minutes. Suddenly, Vance sat forward in his chair, "Are they accelerating at full power?"

"One second… Actually no. By my calculations, they are only accelerating at just over half the rate they use in slowing."

"Heat up the laser and put it on line," commanded Vance.

"Heating it up," responded Dale.

"Youngblood, launch your ships, spread them out and head for Faith."

"Roger that."

"If you see anything that looks remotely alien, kill it."

"Yes, sir."

Within a minute, five small runabout fighters slowly flew off the flight deck and out of the mouth of the cave. As the runabouts passed the cave entrance, they separated and punched in full power. Their acceleration went to 4g within seconds.

"They're jamming our sensors!" said Dale.

"All of them?"

Dale said nothing for a second. "All but the telescopes."

"Put their ship on the viewer."

The picture changed to a highly detailed full picture of the Malic ship as it retreated. The ship looked like the pictures the Vout had provided, but with some additions. The ship had two very large missiles attached to the bottom and a different sensor array dead center at the top.

"Shit!" Vance had an angry look that Alex hadn't seen in a long time.

"Dale."

"Yes, sir."

"Put the nukes on line."

"Yes, sir."

A row of lights came on the main control panel.

"Can we direct the nukes using just the telescopes?"

"No, sir."

"But… I can calculate…" Dale abruptly stopped. "The Malic just launched something at us…"

"It's one of those missiles," said Vance.

"Looks like it's coming straight for us," said Alex, "Hopefully, it's heading for the decoy sensors."

"The missile isn't accelerating as fast I would have thought," said Dale.

"They don't have a rail gun as a booster," said Vance.

"Vance."

"What is it?"

"I think I can calculate close enough for a nuke to take out the Malic ship," said Dale.

"How?"

"We know the distance, acceleration and direction they were heading. If they haven't changed any…"

"Do it," ordered Vance.

The viewer switched to a split screen; one side still displayed the Malic ship, the other side was filled with a full shot of Faith.

"Ten seconds to launch… five, four, three, two, one. It's on its way."

A bright blue-white flash was seen shooting off the surface of Faith.

"Eight seconds to detonation," said Dale.

"Back off the view of their ship. Make it a ball size."

The screen went to a full picture showing the Malic ship the size of basketball in the middle. Two seconds later a spear-like light came in from the left of the viewer and a millisecond later, the picture went white. The screen stayed white for a full ten seconds before slowly fading to blue, then quickly to green and finally to red before revealing a view of empty space.

"Holy shit," said Dale, "That seemed massive."

"We, on the other hand, did use a rail gun as a booster," Vance said with a half-smile.

"Jesus," exclaimed Alex.

"Nice job, Dale." said Vance.

"Sensors back on line," said Dale. "Their missile will hit in five seconds. They are going for the decoy."

"Too late to take it out with the laser," said Vance. "Be ready to put a backup on line."

"Uh oh," said Dale. There are 15 small ships entering our atmosphere at high speed."

"Rat bastards!"

"How…?" asked Alex.

"They dropped them off behind Faith," said Vance, "Youngblood?"

"We see them. They're moving fast, sir."

"How fast, Dale?"

"3,000 kilometers per and they're coming straight at us."

"A little slower than the runabout's top speed."

"Yes, sir."

"They are out of range of the laser."

There was a sudden strong vibration felt on the deck of the NORMAN.

"The Malic missile," said Dale. "Sensors have been taken out."

"Powerful?"

Dale said nothing for a moment. "About a quarter megaton."

"That's big," said Alex.

"Backup on line," said Dale. "Putting the Malic fighters on the screen."

The Malic fighters were in five groups of three ships each; there was a spread of 260 meters between the groups. Dale began tracking the five Malic fighter groups represented by orange dots on the viewer, and the five-ship Gabriel group represented by green dots. The schematic behind the dots displayed their relationship to the ground.

"Surely they know their mother ship has been destroyed?" said Dale.

"Probably want some payback," suggested Alex.

"Maybe," said Vance.

The single five-ship Gabriel group split into two; Youngblood led the two-ship group, and Adam led the other, containing three. Either the Malic didn't detect the runabouts above and behind them, or they didn't fear them; they continued to fly straight at Home Bay.

"Adam," said Youngblood, "Little Tom and I will hit the three on the right, you take the next group inside."

"Roger that," replied Adam.

"Gunners wait until I give the word. With our weapons, we need to be close, and we're limited on ammo."

"Yes, sir," came a chorus of affirmatives.

"Sir?" said Youngblood.

"Vance here."

"We're gaining on them, but I'm afraid they will hit the coast before we get a shot off."

"Understood. Do what you can."

"Yes, sir."

Youngblood and his wingman, Little Tom, dove straight at the outside Malic group. Adam's three-ship group headed for the next group to the left.

The Malic ships suddenly dropped altitude as they passed over the Black Pearls, and within seconds they were approaching the west coast of the Ring.

"They're heading for the settlements," reported Youngblood.

The five Malic fighter groups altered their course as they lined up their targets. When they were a quarter mile off the coast, they opened fire with what seemed to be large caliber rapid-firing cannons. Homes and buildings on the coast north of Home Bay were torn apart in the explosions. A small settlement further north had a similar fate. Moments later Youngblood's group, having closed the gap to within 300 meters, opened fire on the Malic's right flank. Two of the Malic ships were hit and spun out of control. The third was hit but not critically and pulled up and left toward the next Malic fighter group. But that group had just lost two ships to Adam's runabouts. The remaining 11 Malic ships quickly changed altitude and direction. Now they were all heading toward the runabouts.

"Youngblood, lead 'em to us," commanded Vance.

"Roger that."

"Lasers on line," affirmed Dale.

"I guess now is not the time to point out that this laser was not designed as a weapon," said Alex.

"It wasn't, but we fixed it up a little. Now we'll see if our modifications work in a combat situation."

"There's not going to be a better time to test it."

"Not going to get much easier. They'll be coming straight at it."

"It's locked and loaded," said Dale. "Sighting for laser on viewer."

"I've got control," said Vance as he lightly gripped the joystick. "Let's see how straight I can shoot."

The viewer now displayed the sky above the laser. In the middle of the viewer was a simple crosshair sight. The five runabouts entered from the bottom of the viewer and were heading in single file at full speed straight through the middle of the crosshairs. Vance briefly tracked them with the crosshairs using the joystick then moved the crosshairs back to the lower center of the viewer. Three seconds later the first of the Malic fighters came into view, followed by five others.

The control and sighting modifications on the laser were designed to calculate speed, direction, and altitude. Now they were going to find out how well they worked.

Vance put and held the crosshairs on the lead fighter and pushed the fire button. A quarter meter-wide red beam hit the Malic ship and it disintegrated. The crosshairs quickly went to the second fighter and it exploded. The four that were following quickly changed course, but Vance destroyed two more before they got out of range.

Youngblood and his fighter group turned to engage the remaining seven Malic fighters. At the speed they were traveling, the gap between them closed quickly.

The Malic fighters moved to a side-by-side formation with 200 meters between them, And they began gyrating from side to side and up and down, making them tough targets.

"Spread out!" yelled Youngblood. He started firing his 20 mm Gatling gun. "See if you can get some missiles into those fuckers."

Within seconds, all five runabouts fired several missiles and were burning up thousands of rounds of 20 mm at the Malic. One Malic ship was hit by a missile and turned off in a steep bank. Two more were hit by Gatling fire, but they kept coming.

"Youngblood, head back this direction. We can cover you with the laser," ordered Vance.

"You heard the man," said Youngblood as he turned his runabout right and down. The other four followed him.

Before the Gabriel fighters could lure the Malic into the range of the laser, the remaining six Malic ships opened up with everything they had. Two of the runabouts were hit simultaneously, one disintegrated instantly, and the other became a ball of fire and dropped from the sky. The Malic broke off the attack before they came into the laser's range.

"Oh, God," said Youngblood as he watched eight of his dear friends die. Youngblood could see the Malic retreating. "Fuckers!" he yelled. He turned his runabout back toward the Malic. The remaining two runabouts turned to follow Youngblood back into the fray.

"Shit!" said Dale in an unusual display of alarm. "There's another missile heading at us."

"From where?" asked Vance clearly alarmed.

"North, northwest."

Vance quickly moved the crosshairs to the direction of the threat. A bright white dot could be clearly seen entering the viewer from the top. Even before the crosshairs were dead on target, Vance pushed the firing button. The laser's red line could be seen missing the missile but closing in as Vance moved the joystick. Two seconds later the laser and missile met. The resulting explosion was enormous.

"Where'd that missile come from?" Vance demanded.

"The same place that another one that was just fired came from," said an excited Dale. "There's another Malic mother ship in orbit over the North Dumbbell."

"How…"

Vance quickly located the missile and this time hit it first shot. This time there was no massive explosion; the missile was ripped in half and fell into the ocean.

"Rat bastards."

"The Malic ship is moving out of orbit… quickly," said Dale.

"Tell me when it will be safe to take it out."

"It's accelerating at top speed; they have seen all they need to see," said Dale.

"Open communication."

"Opened."

"Malic ship," said Vance.

Within two seconds, "We are leaving your space, Humans. We will not return."

Dale cut into the communication, "Vance, that ship deployed twenty more fighters. They're attacking the settlement on North Dumbbell. We have no protection for them from here."

"Malic, if you want to live for one more minute, you will recall all of your ships. If you do not, we will destroy you and them."

"Recalling our ships now… please let us leave peacefully."

"They're still bombing… wait, they are moving off. Heading to the mother ship."

"Youngblood here, sir?"

"Youngblood."

"We took out four more Malic ships but…"

"But?"

"…we lost two of our runabouts."

"Who…" Vance stopped talking. There had never been a doubt that Vance considered every living person on Gabriel one of his children. He became speechless for a moment.

"Adam and Little Tom's ships, sir."

"Adam… the first born. Any chance they… "

"No, sir. No…"

Vance moaned as he forced himself to get back to the battle. "Are the Malic still fighting?"

"No, sir. They broke it off a minute ago. They're retreating."

"Let 'em go. Don't want to lose any more men. We'll handle everything from here."

"We'd like to get a little more payback, sir." The rage and grief was apparent in his voice.

"Youngblood, follow orders," Vance barked. Then more softly, "The payback's coming."

A moment later, "Yes, sir. Breaking off engagement."

"How long before all the Malic are aboard the mother ship?"

"Ten minutes or so, I'd guess," answered Dale.

"How long will the mother ship still be in range?"

"Range?"

"For a nuke."

"But, Vance, they're leaving," said Dale.

"No… they are not."
"Agreed," said Alex.

CHAPTER 35

GREAT LOSSES

Each runabout had a crew of four, a pilot and three gunners. A total of six men and two women were killed in the two lost runabouts. The loss of fifteen additional citizens on the ground were added to those heroic eight, for a total of 23 Gabriel citizens dead. Sixteen more were wounded, four critically. In addition, two small settlements and a dozen homes were completely destroyed. Among the homes destroyed were three of the original homes built on Home Bay.

Vance was in a funk. He took all the losses as a personal failure. Protecting those in his charge was always Vance's greatest obsession, and in his mind, he had failed to do as he was charged. He went personally to relay the fate of the fallen to all of the parents. When he told Lesley and Quinn that they had lost Adam, their oldest and the planet's first-born son, they all broke down and Vance cried with them. It was one of the saddest moments in his life.

"I should have killed them as soon as they were in range. We were told they were evil." Vance was sitting in the captain's chair and clearly depressed.

Nothing was said for a few moments before Alex spoke up.

"Do you want my opinion?"

Vance paused a moment before answering. "Sure… always."

"You did exactly what you had to do and did it extremely well, as usual. Your preparations for the Malic kept the vast majority on this planet safe. If you think about the alternatives, you will know that you could not have killed the Malic in cold blood before they attacked us… that is not who you are."

Vance sat silently for several minutes before standing. "I'm going for a walk."

Ten minutes later, Vance was slowly walking up the south side of a river that emptied into the Home Bay. His home was in plain view, sitting up on the far bank above the river. He spotted Lara standing on their patio overlooking the rushing river. She smiled slightly as she waved to him. He raised his hand in acknowledgment and continued his walk. Within 20 minutes, he arrived at the place where he had encountered the bear, so long ago. The spot was marked with a large carved stone telling of that encounter. Next to the carved stone was a bench overlooking the river, where Vance sat down and put his face in his hands.

Thirty minutes later he heard a small noise and looked up as Lara approached.

"Hi, Hon." She walked up, leaned down and kissed him on the top of his head. "You didn't smile at me when you waved you know?" she said as she sat next to him on the bench.

"Sorry, sweetheart. It's been a horrible day."

She nodded as she took his hand in hers.

Vance returned to the bridge of the NORMAN two hours later. "Alex, Dale."

"We're here."

"Just want you to know that I'm going to quit feeling sorry for myself. You were right; I did what I could. Thanks for pointing that out to me."

Alex smiled, "That's what friends are for—to point out fucked up thinking by their compatriots, among other things."

Vance face showed a slight smile for a moment. "But the loss of all those fine people. It breaks my heart."

"All our hearts," said Dale.

"We lost more people in this battle than we arrived on the planet with," said Alex reflectively. "We've suffered terrible losses in the past and always survived; we will again."

MO-EIGHT 18, 49

Early in the morning, a memorial service was held for the 23 Gabrielites lost in the battle with the Malic. Most of the recovered bodies were laid to rest in the newly designated cemetery, the first on Gabriel. This memorial cemetery was placed on the east side of Home Bay, on a high hill with a picturesque view.

Headstones for the 14 recovered bodies were carved from the gold-bearing quartz. For those not recovered, a large monument was set in the middle of the 14 headstones, listing their names and dates of birth and death. The families of three of the recovered bodies wished to bury their loved ones where they had chosen to live; two were part of the North Dumbbell outpost and one was from the Vast outpost. This young lady had unfortunately been visiting relatives on Home Bay when the Malic attack occurred. None of the bodies of the runabout's crews were recovered. They had fallen into the deep ocean.

It was all Vance could do to maintain his composure while delivering the eulogy. As he recited each name, starting with Adam, he told a brief story of their lives. All Gabrielites personally knew each other; the total population barely amounted to the population of a small town on Earth. This was the saddest time in the history of Gabriel.

"I'm preparing a message to send to the Vout and Yassi," said Dale. "As per our agreement with them."

"Send a list of our dead. Many among them were friends with the Vout," said Alex.

"I will; the Vout will be devastated by the news."

"No doubt they will be," said Alex.

"They will be relieved that the Malic will never again threaten them," said Alex.

"Do you think we should tell them that we could have let the second ship escape?" added Dale.

"Give them a full report," said Alex.

"Agreed," said Vance. "We warned those ugly little bastards and we lost 23 people because we didn't take 'em out right away. They sealed their own fate, so fuck 'em."

"They may think we're barbarians," said Dale.

"Some will, maybe."

"I don't think they will," said Alex. "They know us."

CHAPTER 36

THE VOUT RETURN
MO-ONE, 50

It had been five years since the first visit from the Vout. Now in orbit over Home Bay was another Vout ship, two years sooner than expected. Apparently, the planet Gabriel had become famous through Vout communications, and subsequently through communications to the Yassi world. Callen and his crew predicted that the visits from the Vout and the Yassi would probably be a great deal more frequent than they had been in the past. Callen's last words to the citizens of Gabriel were, "Your labor of love will become the love of all in this sector of space. The Yassi know what you have done and what an industrious and honest race you are; they will want to visit. My crew and I want to thank you for putting a period of joy in our arduous voyage."

They would never see Callen and his crew again, but the friendship with the Vout was now well established.

This Vout ship, now in orbit, had a slightly different configuration than that of Callen's, but it was distinctly Vout, with its practical cylindrical body and exterior propulsion. This time there was no language barrier, and contact was established two weeks prior to their arrival. Their arrival was a time of celebration, and the people of Gabriel pulled out all the stops.

The Vout captain and crew were welcomed as visiting dignitaries. After Vance greeted the captain and his senior staff, he introduced the five who accompanied him as a welcoming committee.

The Vout captain, Sadda, said in English, "We have brought the trade items you requested," as he handed a manifest to Vance.

Vance thanked him in Vout. Everyone, on both sides, smiled in appreciation.

"Your English is excellent," said Vance.

"We've had many years to study your language, and are delighted to be able to speak to you directly. And might I say, your Vout is flawless."

"I've got a pretty good mind for that sort of thing."

Within the next two days the Vout delivered the uranium agreed upon in their trade agreement.

After an inventory was conducted and completed by young Dale and Norman, the ship's Dale addressed Sadda, "We thank the Vout for these valuable materials. It is of the highest quality, and fits our specifications exactly."

"About 5% more than was agreed upon," added Alex. "At our present rate of usage, this is enough fuel to last us for over 400 years."

And they provided me with two refills, thought Vance. *"Hell, I'm gonna live forever."*

Three days of visiting and banquets followed their arrival before beginning the work of mining gold and silver.

CHAPTER 37

HERE COME THE YASSI
MO-FOUR, 52

Just over a year after the last Vout ship left, the Yassi arrived for their first visit to Gabriel. As with the Vout, contact was established weeks before the Yassi went into a geosynchronous orbit above Home Bay. Their pending arrival was another cause for excitement and celebration for the citizens of Gabriel. What would this new race be like?

Days before the Yassi ship moved into orbit, their ship was being shown on all the viewers as it hurtled toward Gabriel. This ship didn't look like the picture that the Vout had shown them eight years previously, but it was, if anything, more beautiful.

"Just look at that," said Alex. "My God, I've never even seen an artist's futuristic rendering of a spaceship that compares to this."

"I wonder if form and function are the same here. I can't imagine that such beauty is created with a practical function as well," said Dale, "I would love to see the inside."

"Me, too," said Vance. "I'll see what we can do."

Three days later, the Yassi moved into orbit. Within two hours, a magnificent Yassi shuttle dropped out of the bottom of the mother ship and headed to Home Bay. All this was caught on Gabriel's telescopes and transmitted to all viewers. Similar to all the Vout and Yassi ships, this shuttle was a gold color, and the sculptured lines and use of glass was wondrous. The beautiful craft landed softly and silently in the park in front of the NORMAN's cave. Hundreds of spectators were gathered behind temporary lines while the welcoming delegates waited next to the landing site. Two minutes after the shuttle landed, a ramp lowered down from below the cockpit. A few seconds later, eight short and tidy looking beings walked swiftly down the ramp to greet their hosts. They were all dressed in dark green, wide-belted and blousy-legged pants that looked similar to those of Russian folk dancers. Their light green shirts looked stylish and comfortable. The Yassi, although similar in appearance to the Vout, were shorter, thicker, and a great deal more animated. Their eyes were large and green, and expressed a good humor and gentleness. Their noses were slightly larger and wider than those found on the Vout. Their jaws were larger and their mouths were narrower, but they had distinctive lips. Where the Vout were stoic, the Yassi seemed to be quite animated and relaxed, almost jovial. Where the Vout were colorless, the Yassi were quite the opposite. Those in the welcoming delegation were surprised.

Vance led the delegation of nine Gabriel seniors, including Lesley, Quinn, Bob, Tom, Janet, Jennifer, Vijaya, Dan, and Aidan. They were all now in their early seventies, but still looked to be in excellent physical condition.

The eight Yassi walked in single file, and each shook hands as they introduced themselves. Ergo, the Yassi's captain, after leading his crew past the receiving line, gathered them all in front of the welcoming delegation. At no time did their smiles fade.

The Yassi's hands were small, but not dainty; they seemed to have considerable strength. The shaking of hands as a greeting was believed to be unique to Gabriel, but by the time Callen and his crew left the planet it had become a new custom with the Vout; a custom that they had obviously shared with the Yassi. The Yassi had either adopted it, or they were simply displaying a respect for this planet's customs.

Once the introductions were over, Vance stepped forward, and in the Yassi language, he addressed the visitors. "We of the planet Gabriel wish to welcome the Yassi to our home. We are looking forward to your visit and hope we can make your stay here as joyful and productive as possible. We are pleased you are here."

The Yassi wooed enthusiastically and clapped.

When the wooing stopped, Vance continued, "As a token of our pleasure of your arrival, we have a gift for you to take back to your home."

The Gabriel delegation separated, allowing a wheeled cart to pass between them. Smiling happily, a pretty blue-eyed blond girl, who looked to be 11 or 12 years old, pushed the cart. She wasn't much taller than the Yassi.

"This piece of art was created by this young lady, Annie, who lives with her family on our largest continent. Annie, as you will see, is a truly gifted artist."

"Annie, show our new friends what you have created for them."

"Yes, sir." Annie said with an even bigger smile as she stepped forward and removed the bright green cover.

There sat a sculpture of a charging African elephant standing about a half a meter high with its massive ears held outright and trunk curled up to its forehead. It was cast of pure gold and weighed upwards of 13 kilos. Its long curving tusks were actually made of elephant ivory; ivory that was part of a broken tusk found in the Vast's savanna. The elephant was depicted charging around a clump of bushes, its head pointing toward a male lion that seemed to be in full retreat. The attention to detail was incredible. One could almost see the dust flying.

The Yassi quickly gathered around the piece of art and seemed overwhelmed with its beauty. They began applauding and wooing, in the same way as the Vout.

Captain Egro turned to Annie and addressed her in English, "Annie, words cannot express how wonderful your gift to the Yassi is to us. The creativity and skill in its making compares to the finest art we have seen in the galaxy. Please be assured that it will sit in an honored place in our finest museum of art. Millions of Yassi and thousands of Vout and Byuse will be enjoying it for millennia to come."

"Oh, thank you, sir. I'm so pleased that you like it. I was kinda worried that you might not."

Egro looked at his fellow Yassi, "I love these Humans. They are a wonderful species."

They all wooed loudly.

"So," continued Egro, "a millennia ago we had refined our machines as much as our intellect would allow. We began taking a great deal of interest in the appearance of everything. Our space ships are an example of this appreciation of art. They are not practically enhanced by their appearance, nor are they hindered. Such is the case with all we do. It keeps the mind active and creative. As a result, we live on a beautiful planet full of art in all its forms. You, of course, are invited to visit us at any time."

"Thank you. We will make that invitation known to all the Gabrielites," said Alex.

"The round trip will take…what… about 3 to 4 years ship's time?" asked Dale.

"Yes, about that," answered Egro.

"I'm certain that there will be a few people someday who would love to make such a trip," said Vance.

"You Humans have great skills at setting great order to living things. You selected a nearly barren planet and have developed it to one with biodiversity unequaled in the known sectors of space."

"It is our understanding that you, the Yassi, began this world's transformation nearly two millennia ago," said Alex.

"Yes, and that's all we managed to accomplish, just a start. But look what you've done in a quarter of that time." Egro waved his hands around in a big sweep of the horizon. "Truly wondrous."

As it turned out, the Yassi had quite a sophisticated sense of humor; a fact that didn't take Teddy long to discover. And it didn't take the Yassi long to make Teddy one of their favorites.

Teddy had studied the Vout and Yassi languages for several years and was fluent in both, as were most of the citizens of Gabriel. "Hey, if I can't speak their language, I can't amuse them," he had said.

As did his predecessors, Teddy had an uncanny ability to discover exactly where his audience's funny bone was located. Due to the cultural divide, it took him a little longer to find the Yassi's, but within a week he had it pinpointed and had them "rolling in the aisles." Soon, he spent as much time entertaining these little people after dinners as he was allowed. The Yassi, after the first "Dinner Show," recorded all future events where Teddy was involved.

The Yassi spent just shy of four months with the Gabrielites before continuing their voyage. As a parting gift, the Yassi left one of their magnificent shuttles. "We, being aware of the losses you suffered in the Malic attack, wish you to have this ship. By agreement, it is a gift from both the Vout and the Yassi."

Vance was clearly overwhelmed. "I don't know what to say. This ship is of such great value it is hard to accept."

Egro became serious for a moment, "You Humans are of greater value to us. You are such a welcome addition to this sector of space, our joy cannot be properly expressed."

Vance was clearly delighted with the Yassi. "We have established a lasting, trusting, and mutually beneficial relationship, but our delight at having the Yassi as our cherished friends is the best part of all."

PART 5
THE MARIAN

CHAPTER 38

THE RESCUE
MO-NINE, 53

Vance happened to be on the bridge of the NORMAN when a communication came in from the Yassi.

"Vance," said Egro, "we want to inform you that we have come across a Human ship just 330 million kilometers from Gabriel."

Vance snapped to attention. "Are they heading our way?"

"It is heading your way, but it is coasting… and tumbling."

Vance stood up quickly. "Tumbling?"

"We are sorry to inform you that this ship has suffered structural damage. We were not able to establish communication, nor have we been able to ascertain any life signs aboard."

"Oh, no," Vance went speechless for a moment; he sat back down. "This is terrible news… just terrible." Vance said nothing for a few more moments. "We have been expecting a ship for many years now. We've been concerned that something had gone wrong."

"More bad news," said Egro, "We were able to determine that it was damaged by a Malic attack. Most of the ship is intact, but its propulsion system is off-line or destroyed."

"MALIC!" Vance screamed; his face contorted in an expression of rage that no one had seen in hundreds of years.

"Yes, the explosive signature is distinctly Malic. They must have encountered the Earth ship before arriving at Gabriel."

"Ugly little…," Vance growled.

"The Earth ship would not have been prepared for any sort of attack," said Alex.

"Even if they knew what was going on, I doubt that they would have had any offensive or defensive weapons aboard," added Dale.

"No reason to," said Alex.

"Did you try to board the ship?" asked Vance.

"We did not. If it weren't tumbling, we would have made the effort. You will be more familiar with their systems and can possibly find a way to stop the tumbling. We do not want to risk further damage to the ship. We are transmitting visuals."

The viewer picture switched from Egro to one of the Earth ship.

"Doesn't look like the NORMAN."

"No, it looks more like five NORMANs hooked together."

"Egro, that ship is five hundred years ahead of us in technology," said Dale, "I doubt we will have much more insight into its workings than you will, but maybe together we can figure it out."

"We will assist in any way we can."

"If you will give us the coordinates, we will prepare our ship and head to your location."

"Coordinates are being transmitted."

"Give us a few minutes, Egro, so we can tell you how long we will take to get there."

"We'll wait."

"How long before we can join them?" Vance asked Dale.

"We'll need to take the NORMAN," said Dale. "We need a few hours to prepare it and reconfigure at least two shuttles. To reach the coordinates will take two and a half days at the earliest."

"Egro, can you wait two or three days?"

"We'll wait as long as you wish it. We will see what more we can do while we wait."

"Good luck with that," responded Vance, "and thank you."

"One more thing," said Egro, "There is a name on the ship. It says, WGC MARIAN."

Alex was clearly affected by this revelation. His image on the viewer displayed tears and a broad smile. "They named it after my mother."

There was no response for a moment, and then Egro said, "She must have been an extraordinary woman."

"Yes… yes she was."

"It's possible that there will be many in cryogenic stasis," said Dale, "Hopefully alive."

"We may be able to transfer them to the NORMAN, or maybe revive them on their ship and then bring them aboard the NORMAN," said Vance.

"Maybe we can repair their propulsion system," said Alex.

"Won't know anything until we get to the MARIAN," said Dale.

Nearly three days later, the NORMAN was just a hundred thousand kilometers from the damaged ship and slowing at 1g. Aboard the NORMAN were a hand-picked group: Youngblood, because of his exceptional abilities as a runabout pilot; Lesley and four other doctors; Bob, because of his gifts as a mechanical engineer; young Dale and young Norman, because of their remarkable minds; and twenty-five other young, strong Gabrielites to assist in any way that they could. They made certain that everyone on board was prepared for zero gravity when they arrived.

The NORMAN's sensors and telescopes had been gathering as much intelligence as they could before arrival. They could see the Yassi ship traveling alongside the still tumbling MARIAN.

"Looks bigger up close," said Dale.

"Wow. I'll say."

The MARIAN, other than her color, was very different from the NORMAN. She had five spheres instead of one. A large sphere, a hundred and fifty meters in diameter, was in the center with four spheres, each the size of the NORMAN, surrounding it. These smaller spheres were connected to the center sphere by thick spokes, each five meters in diameter and thirty meters in length. These were presumably passageways. These smaller spheres were in turn connected to the next sphere by narrower passageways. The overall width of the ship was right at 310 meters. She was huge.

"Look at that," said Alex.

They could see a single large hole, maybe five meters square, twenty meters down from the top. It looked as if it had been cut with a laser.

"Depending on the depth of that hole, if the ship is configured anything like the NORMAN, the damage to that location could have taken out all sensors, communications, and possibly even the bridge," said Dale.

"Wonder why there isn't more damage," mused Vance.

"A destroyed ship wouldn't be much use to anyone," suggested Alex.

"Shit!" said Vance.

"What?"

"I'm thinking… that the ship has been boarded," said Vance.

"Boarded?" Alex was alarmed.

"I'll bet that hole is big enough to fly a Malic fighter into."

"We need to get aboard," said Dale.

"How do we stop the tumbling?"

"We have a thought, sir," said Youngblood.

"Let's have it," responded Vance.

"Bob and I have been talking. We believe that if we take two runabouts and land them on opposite sides of the center orb, since its surface velocity is slower than any other part of the ship. Then we somehow lash the runabouts securely to the hull and apply thrust slowly and evenly in the opposite direction of the spin."

"That could work, but it could be dangerous," said Dale.

"Who's going to pilot the runabouts?" asked Vance.

"You and I, sir."

Vance smiled as he looked at his clone. He and Youngblood now looked about the same age; they looked like twins. "Did you happen to bring a lot of cable?"

Youngblood smiled. "Yes, sir."

"I'm going to need a little time to make a few calculations," said Dale. "We don't know the mass of that ship, how much strain the hull can take, how much strain the runabout can take or how much strain the connecting passageways can take. Added to those factors—are the small orbs all the same weight? At maximum safe thrust, how long will the operation take? That is just to name a few variables."

"Norm and I will get right on it," smiled young Dale.

The ship's Dale smiled in return, "Between the three of us, I'll bet we'll figure it out."

"Let's run this idea by the Yassi. See what they think," suggested Alex.

"Agreed," said young Dale, the ship's Dale, and young Norman in unison.

Egro's face was on the viewer thirty minutes later. "Your idea is simple and we concur, it will work. We have a bonding agent that you might use to secure your runabouts to the ship. Not knowing the resilience or strength of the hull, we suggest you fabricate eight plates of the strongest material you have available. Make them a meter square with your cable attached to the center of each. We further suggest that each of your runabouts have four of these, one at each corner. Our bonding agent has an interesting property; its consistency remains as a thick paste until it is sandwiched between two opposing surfaces. Once that is done, it hardens in seconds and cannot be separated. We suggest that whatever you choose to use for the plates should be something you will never need again."

"That sounds like just the ticket," said Dale. "How do we get that bonding agent?"

"We'll put together the ingredients and shuttle them over to you. It will take us about an hour."

"Perfect. In the meantime, we'll begin fabricating the plates."

An hour later, Vance walked onto the flight deck. Six of the colonists, including Youngblood and Bob were bent over working on the cable system. Scattered around the area were eight one-meter square plates made of aluminum alloy about three centimeters thick. Standing to one side and out of the way were four Yassi observing the fabrication.

"Where'd you get these plates?"

"Deck eleven. Actually these are part of Deck 11," answered Bob.

Vance nodded in understanding, "Are you sure they're going to be strong enough to do the job?"

"We considered bonding two of these plates together but 'the brain trust,' Bob, Dale, and Norman, said it wouldn't be necessary. The amount of thrust we will apply should not compromise a single plate," answered Youngblood.

Vance nodded his head in approval. Deck 11 was all but empty. It had been the storage deck for all the farm and heavy equipment. All that equipment was now in use in various places around Gabriel. "How long?"

"About another hour," said Bob. "We need to strengthen the areas on the runabouts where the cables will be attached. We also need to fabricate some type of release system that will allow us to get the runabouts detached from the MARIAN's hull after we're done."

Vance nodded as he looked around.

"Also, sir," said Youngblood, "we figured that we had better not let these plates just float around willy-nilly at the end of these short cables with the bonding agent on them. So when were ready, we're going to stiffen the cables with wooden slats like a splint in order to keep 'em pointed straight down. When we're ready, you and I will power up the runabouts, lift far enough off the deck to straighten the cables, attach the slats and apply the bonding agent to the bottom of the plates. Then we'll fly out and get in position over the MARIAN. When we're both in position, we'll drop straight down on its hull. It won't take much pressure to shatter the wooden splints and bond the plates at the same time."

"Nothing to it," smiled Vance.

"No, sir, nothing to it."

The operation went just as planned. Both of the Dales and Norman had programmed the runabouts to safely approach the MARIAN's hull at the same speed and direction as she was spinning. When both runabouts were in position, the signal was given and they both lowered to the MARIAN's hull at a speed of a quarter meter a second. They made nearly simultaneous contact, shattering the wooden slats, and within seconds the plates bonded to the hull. Now that the runabouts were securely attached to the disabled ship, they began applying the countering thrust.

"At maximum safe thrust, it's going to take approximately 18 hours to stop the tumbling," said Dale. "Watch your power output, listen for any signs of strain."

"Roger that," said Vance. "Youngblood, your men have enough food over there to last?"

"Yes, sir, and then some."

"In the meantime, we'll continue to try to make contact with the MARIAN's computers. I'm hoping that they are an offshoot of our Isleium computers," said Dale.

After two hours, Dale reported that he had not been able to make contact with the MARIAN's computers. You could hear the disappointment in his voice. "We'll keep trying. There is little else we can do."

Just shy of 19 hours later, the MARIAN was stabilized and the thrust was shut down on the two runabouts.

"Ready to disconnect?" asked Vance.

"Yes, sir. Just say when."

"How about now?"

"Disconnecting."

"I'm free," said Vance.

"Uh oh," said Youngblood. Right rear did not disconnect."

"Drop back down," interjected Bob. "Jar it a little."

"Dropping down… Ah, we're free."

"See you back in the NORMAN," said Vance.

"Roger that."

"We want to congratulate you on a job well done," said Egro.

"Thank you for your help, Egro. That bonding agent was perfect for the job."

"So it seems."

Twenty-two minutes later, both runabouts were sitting on the flight deck and the temporary modifications were being removed by the young Gabrielites.

"Let's clean up and you take a rest before we head over to the MARIAN."

"Yes, sir. We could use a shower."

Three hours later, Vance, Youngblood and two young Gabrielites, Johnnie and Al, loaded into a single runabout. They each had on pressure suits with various tools attached, including handheld computers, automatic pistols, and shoulder-mounted cameras. The helmets contained two floodlights, one on each side. These suits were also equipped with small jet packs to aid in mobilization. Vance's SLF body wasn't affected by being exposed to a complete vacuum, but the deep cold would stiffen up his frame.

"Opening the hatch," said Youngblood.

"We're on our way," said Vance.

"Please be careful flying into that hole," said Dale. "I can't detect any booby traps, but that doesn't mean they're not there."

"Going to go very slowly. We will only put our nose in about five meters. Should have plenty of clearance. It's the only access to the interior of the ship. Once we get inside, we'll see if we can open an outside hatch."

Very carefully, Youngblood eased the runabout into the hole left by the Malic.

"Let's see if we can set an anchor," said Vance.

"On it," said Johnnie. He released the anchor cable with a grappling hook on the end.

"Need it to hook on something solid," said Vance.

"Yes, sir."

After the cable was let out ten meters, Johnnie retrieved it. It caught on nothing. He let it out 12 meters and retrieved it. Still nothing. After several tries to secure the hook, Vance's patience gave out.

"I'm going out the hatch to find something to hook onto."

"Yes, sir. Lowering the hatch," said Youngblood.

Seven minutes later, Vance had carefully exited the runabout. He took the hook in hand and pulled it into the MARIAN's interior. The floodlights on Vance's helmet starkly lit the damage done by the Malic lasers. It was extensive. "*Sumbitches!*" It took Vance several minutes to find a strong stable spot to attach the anchor.

"Hooked up. You can take out the slack now."

"Yes, sir."

Twenty-three minutes later, the four men were floating weightless on Deck four, which was, in fact, the bridge. There was little visible damage, except for the hatches at the top and bottom of the stairs between the third and fourth decks. The electronic latches were cut off with a laser. Once on the bridge, all they saw was the degree of the Malic's thievery. The deck had been stripped of all computers and all other technology. It was nearly an empty shell.

"Are you seeing this, Dale?"

"I am."

"You had no chance of communicating with the MARIAN's computers, because they're not here."

"So I see."

"Can the stasis pods survive without power or computers?" asked Alex.

"They can if they are still frozen," answered Dale.

"Let's find them," said Vance.

"Yes, sir," said Youngblood, as he headed to the stairs.

The four jetted themselves single file through this intact hatch and down one flight, entering what was obviously the medical deck. It was pitch-black except for the light provided by the pressure suit's floodlights. The deck was in surprisingly good shape, except for three bloody, dead bodies floating aimlessly around the expansive deck. All were dressed in destroyed pressure suits. Two were missing limbs, one was missing most of his head. They were Malic.

"Holy Shit!" said Vance.

"Holy shit is right, sir," agreed Youngblood, "Who could have done this?"

"No fucking idea, but you can bet your ass I'm going to find out. We need to search each deck thoroughly as we head down. Everyone, draw your weapons."

"Over here," said Al.

Vance looked across the expansive room and spotted Al pointing at a table. The table had someone on it. Without hesitation, he and Youngblood jetted in that direction. They stopped just short of the operating table. Both recognized what was strapped to the table. It was a tall man without a pressure suit. He was missing one arm and the body was nearly torn in half just above the waistline. He was dead.

"Holy shit!" said Youngblood. "It's a SLF."

"I'll bet that's what accounts for the dead Malics," said Al.

"No bet there, but what strapped him to the table… and why?"

Vance took several minutes just staring at the SLF.

"Vance," said Dale.

"Yeah, Dale?"

"Is there any damage to the head?"

Vance gently turned the body over, giving it a close inspection. "Not that I can see."

"Is the power source intact?"

Vance turned the body in order to see inside the exposed chest cavity. "Looks like everything is there, but ripped up."

"Bring him back to the NORMAN with you."

"Roger that." Vance turned to the other three, "Keep your weapons handy as we keep searching."

On the far side of the deck they came across a bank of seemingly intact computers. They were switched off.

"I'm liking this," said Dale.

"Me too. Want me to turn them on?"

"Run your camera from top to bottom and side to side first. I want to be sure we're doing it right."

Two minutes later, Dale said, "I think we've got it. Nothing has changed that much over the centuries. Push the three green buttons on the far right. That should bring the main frame on line. We'll leave the supporting computers off for now."

Vance did as requested. Nothing happened.

"No power," said Dale.

"Of course not. Shit!"

"Got so excited to find computers, I forgot the obvious," said Dale. "That's one for the books."

Vance smiled, "Maybe we shouldn't tell anybody."

"I won't if you don't."

"Agreed." Vance turned to his men and ignored the smiles on their faces. "Let's keep looking."

"We need to find a power source," said Dale.

"Heading down to the next deck."

The next deck was packed with all manner of sophisticated machines and tools. There was no noticeable damage here.

"Go to Deck twelve. That's the middle of the ship, and should be where the engine room and power is located."

"Roger that."

The four jetted themselves down and entered the massive engine room.

"It's the engine room alright," said Vance.

"Should be power there," answered Dale. "Head to the center of the deck."

"On our way."

They hadn't traversed more than 12 meters when they made a grisly discovery.

"Holy shit!"

There, suspended in a weightless state and scattered over a large area of the deck, were more than a dozen dead Malic.

"That SLF was busy," said Youngblood.

"Found some weapons," said Johnnie from the far side of the deck. "Not anything I've seen before."

"Bag 'em and bring em."

"Yes, sir."

"Looks like the main power here," said Al.

A minute later all four men were gathered around what had to be a huge generator.

"What do you think, Dale?"

"Not sure what makes it tick, but it's sure not what we use."

"It looks as if it was in the process of being disconnected from everything," said Youngblood.

"Looks like the Malics were going to take it with them when the SLF fucked up their plans," observed Vance.

"Do you think you can put it back together?" asked Dale.

"I sure couldn't," said Vance, "but between Bob, Norman, young Dale and you, maybe. It doesn't look like anything has been destroyed or cut."

"They wanted this machine intact, not broken," suggested Youngblood.

"Any radiation leaking?" asked Dale.

Vance checked his personal computer. "No."

"Hmm," said Dale.

"We'll finish up this deck and then head back to the NORMAN… Dale?"

"Yes, Vance."

"Have you seen enough of this machine to have an idea as to how to hook it back up?"

"I'd like more info before we get there. Leave one of the men there, and I'll direct him around that thing in order to get more images while you're checking out the other decks."

"You got it."

Vance looked at the two young men. "Al, you're it."

"Yes, sir."

"Youngblood, Johnnie, let's take a look at the rest of the decks." Vance paused a second, "Al, we won't need any distractions, so you and Bob pick a different channel to communicate on. We don't need to hear you."

"Roger that."

"Stay alert, men. There could be some live Malics still on board."

They jetted themselves down one deck; it was a warehouse. It was stacked from deck to ceiling with interlocking crates. They could see two sophisticated forklifts and several other machines, some with wheels, some with tracks. They spent the next 32 minutes going up and down every aisle. There was nothing out of place.

The three then headed down to the next deck; it was the hanger deck. Hopefully, this deck contained an illusive power source. There were six small ships here, all of them about the size of the small runabouts, but different in appearance. The three men did a quick look in every direction; the deck was apparently unscathed.

"Dale."

"Yes, Vance. This is great… just great. If we need it, I'll bet those runabouts will provide some power."

"Agreed. But right now we need to get the hatch open. Any ideas?"

"Unless you can find an old fashioned hand crank, you're going to need to get the power on line."

"We will look for a crank."

"Found one," said Johnnie.

"You're kidding?"

"No, sir. Right here." Johnnie was holding on to part of the ship's superstructure next to the hatch to hold him in place. He was pointing to his left using his pistol as a pointer.

Vance laughed. "500 years ahead of us in technology and they have installed a hand crank?"

"Yes, sir, a simple backup system," smiled Johnnie, just as a chunk of the beam he was grasping was blown away only a few centimeters from his hand.

There is no sound in a vacuum, so there was no sound to follow or warn them. Vance was the quickest to respond. He spun himself around holding his pistol with one hand in his line of sight. He saw nothing on his first spin. "Move it, you two. Get behind something. NOW!"

On his second spin, he spotted what had taken the shot at them. He nearly dropped his pistol. He quickly lowered his weapon. There on the other side of the hanger just a meter to one side of the last runabout was a tall man holding on to the runabout for support with one hand, the other held a weapon that was now pointed straight up.

The man was wearing a pressure suit, but no helmet. He didn't have to wear a helmet. He was another SLF and he was smiling.

Vance quickly lowered his weapon. "Don't shoot, men, I believe this is a friend."

The SLF continued to smile as he attached his weapon to his chest rig and effortlessly propelled himself toward the three pressure-suited men.

As he approached Vance, he held out his hands, palms forward signaling for help to stop his forward motion. Vance grabbed him.

This SLF was tall, at nearly two meters.

The SLF could now see inside Vance's helmet. He eyes got big and he mouthed the words, *Vance Youngblood?*

Vance gave a quick nod.

The SLF was clearly stunned; he remained wide-eyed for several seconds before gathering his wits and motioning for the three to follow him. The three nodded in unison. The SLF turned and, using a bulkhead for leverage, propelled himself off in the direction of the back of the hangar. The three followed using their jet packs.

The SLF led the way into a small room, and when everyone was inside, he closed the hatch and pushed a button. The three could feel the atmospheric pressure coming up. When the red light above the hatch turned green, the SLF said, "You can remove your helmets now."

Vance had his off first. "I cannot begin to tell you how happy we are to see you."

"Sir," said the SLF, "I can assure you that any pleasure you have at seeing me pales in comparison to my joy at seeing you. I thought I was to be alone forever. Now to be standing here in the presence of Vance Youngblood is. . . I have no adequate words to describe it."

"Your name?" asked Vance as he put his hand forward.

"Troy, sir, Troy Miller," he said as he took Vance's hand and shook it vigorously.

"Troy, may I introduce Johnnie and Youngblood."

Troy looked closely at Youngblood as he shook his hand, "Are you a clone, sir?"

"I am."

"You look exactly like you," Troy said with a smile. Then he turned to Johnnie.

"Johnnie, you seem to be the only one I don't recognize. But I'm very pleased to meet you too."

"Same here, sir."

"I'm sure we'll have plenty of time to talk later, but right now we have a lot of questions and a lot to do," said Vance.

"Yes, sir."

"First, are there any more Malics aboard?"

"Malics?"

"The ugly little bastards that attacked this ship."

"Didn't know what they were called." Troy paused a second, "No, sir, not alive."

"Good."

"The little rats swarmed into this ship like ants. There must have been over a hundred of them. Gary and I stayed low until we figured out what they were up to and then worked out a plan to annihilate them."

"Go on."

"But they worked fast. They had the bridge cleaned out before we got at them."

"We saw that. And we saw what I assume was Gary."

"Yes, sir."

Troy stopped talking for a few seconds. "He was my dear friend and I will miss him. We took turns overseeing this trip."

"I can relate to that," said Vance.

"Yes sir, and you did it alone."

"I was never alone. Alex and Dale were with me."

"Yes, that's right, you had Alexander Gabriel and Dale Isley with you. I'd forgotten in all this excitement. Are they still with you?"

"They are, and you'll be talking to them soon."

"That's… remarkable." Troy paused for a moment. "We had a few friends in the main computer also."

"They may be lost," said Vance.

"Not sure. I don't know if they managed to transfer to another computer before the main computer was removed."

"We'll find out," said Youngblood.

"How did you and Gary manage to kill and drive off the Malic?" asked Vance.

"The Malic were clumsy and slow in their pressure suits; we are not. We caught up with them on the propulsion deck; we were taking them out nearly as fast as we could pull the trigger, but somehow a couple managed to get behind us."

"Yes, they seem to find a way to sneak up behind their target, but go on."

"Gary was hit and lost an arm before I could get a clear shot. We killed most of them on that deck before the rest escaped. We caught up with them on the bridge and finished them off, but not before Gary was killed." Troy stopped for a long moment. "Sorry, sir,"

"We know what it is to grieve, Troy. Take a minute."

"I'm okay, I… I was devastated when Gary was destroyed. I took him to sickbay to see if there was anything I could do to bring him back, but there was no power and no computers. There was nothing I could do… except mourn."

"We'll be taking him back to the NORMAN with us," said Youngblood.

"Good… the NORMAN is here? Oh my God… the NORMAN!"

The three were surprised at Troy's reaction.

"Guess the NORMAN is ancient history to you," said Youngblood.

"Something akin to one of Columbus's ships to you. I can't wait to see it."

"You'll see it soon enough," said Youngblood, "It's alongside us right now."

"The NORMAN?"

"The NORMAN," answered Youngblood with a smile.

"Go on with your story," said Vance.

"The computer was gone. I had no one to talk to. I had no idea what it was to be truly alone. At first I tried to clean up the mess that the Malic left. I threw dozens of their bodies into space. Then I tried to seal the ship off from the hole in the hull, but couldn't without power."

"I had to shut myself off after a few months, I felt myself slipping into a deep depression; I was going insane. I wanted to stay awake and oversee the MARIAN but… I don't know what switched me back on."

"How long have you been reactivated?"

"Right at 28 hours now. How long was I switched off?"

"Around three years, assuming our encounter with the Malic was shortly after they attacked you."

"Three years." Troy thought about that for a moment. "How did you find me?"

"We didn't. A new friend found you and contacted us."

"A new friend?"

"You'll see."

"Your wakening corresponds with our attaching the runabouts to the MARIAN's hull. That change in status quo probably triggered your reactivation."

"That would do it. I thought the Malic had come back to finish the job. I was looking forward to killing as many as I could before they killed me."

Vance nodded in approval. "Did you have nukes aboard?"

"Nukes? Oh, you're referring to atomics, yes, sir. We had ten in the top of this sphere, just as you did on the NORMAN."

"Did you use any?"

"No, sir."

Vance said nothing for a minute. "Are there any humans in stasis?"

"Yes, sir, just over five hundred. All in the outer spheres."

"Five hundred!"

"Yes, sir."

"What's their status?"

"I believe most are fine for now. But the Malic broke into four stasis pods and took the people."

"Rat bastards."

"Those four young people were special, as are all aboard the MARIAN. They'll be missed."

"I have no doubt," said Vance. *We sure missed Terri*, he thought.

"Vance?"

Vance held up his finger requesting a pause for a second. "Yes, Dale."

"Inform Troy that we destroyed the Malic ships and tell him that we need the hatch open ASAP."

"The ship that attacked you has been destroyed along with everything in it."

"How?"

"They attacked Gabriel; that was a mistake," Vance said matter-of-factly.

"Apparently they didn't know who they were dealing with," Troy smiled, "or, as history has recorded, you would have said, 'They didn't know who they were fucking with.'"

"They sure didn't," said Youngblood with some pride.

"Continue with your story," said Vance.

"Yes, sir. When we caught them on the propulsion deck, the little bastards were trying to steal our main power generator."

"We saw that."

"I believe we can put it back together," said Troy. "Nothing seems to be damaged."

"Then that's what we'll do."

"Vance."

"Yes, Dale?"

"Ask what powers the MARIAN's generator."

"What is the generator's power source?"

"Nuclear fusion."

"Fusion! That's great!" Dale was clearly excited. "Can't wait to look at the specs."

"You will soon enough," Vance turned to Troy, "but right now, let's get the hatch open and get some help in here."

"Yes, sir."

Troy had no trouble using the hand crank to open the hatch. Twenty minutes later, the two runabouts were parked and secured to the flight deck.

"What the hell?" said Troy as a beautiful Yassi shuttle flew silently into the hanger deck.

"Pretty, isn't she?" said Youngblood.

Troy's confusion was obvious. "Your technology has come this far?"

"Not ours," answered Youngblood.

"What?"

"Watch."

Three Gabrielites in pressure suits quickly secured the Yassi shuttle to the deck. Two minutes later, the hatch dropped down and four little beings in magnificently crafted pressure suits floated down feet first and settled on the deck. "Come on, I'll introduce you to our friends and allies."

"Oh, my God!"

"First thing we need to do is to get this ship sealed up," said Vance. "Second is to get the power reestablished."

"Repairing the hatches between the third and fourth decks should seal everything from Deck four and below," said Bob. "Then we can tie the power supply from the runabouts to the main grid and bring the atmospheric pressure up to normal levels so we can take off the pressure suits."

"OK, you, young Dale, Norman, and Troy, assist and direct the power generator re-installment."

"Exactly."

"Might I offer one of our best engineers to aid in that endeavor?" asked Egro.

"Your help would be much appreciated," said Vance, "but you have already taken a lot of time out of your scheduled voyage. We can't ask you to take any longer."

"You are not asking, we are offering. The time saved in our mining operation by using the human's help more than makes up for any time spent now."

Vance smiled, "Thank you."

The two races got to work. Most decks of the MARIAN were not involved, but the bridge, flight deck, medical deck, and engine decks became a frenzy of activity.

Some of the computers used in other sections of the ship were disconnected and reinstalled on the bridge deck. Most didn't fit as well as the originals, but they were modified and did the job. The Yassi were masters at technology, and when the combined intelligence of both Dales, Norman, and Bob couldn't quite figure out a problem, the Yassi produced the solution with little trouble.

"Kind of humbling, isn't it?" Norman remarked to young Dale.

"Yes, but I keep telling myself that they've been at it a thousand years longer."

Another team of Yassi worked in space, replacing the section of the hull that had been cut away by the Malic. Their patching materials came from NORMAN's Deck 11. The deck's floor plates had sufficient strength to do the job, which they completed in less than four hours with the help of the bonding agent.

"We believe you can now pressurize the entire ship," Egro informed Vance.

"We can't thank you enough. Now we will be able to see what the Malic took out of the top four decks."

"We are in your debt," said Youngblood.

Egro smiled broadly, "We will have stories to tell when we return to Yassi. They will write books and put on plays for centuries using our adventures with the Humans. It is we who wish to thank you."

"All the same, we are grateful. The Vout and the Yassi will forever be part of our history. A wonderful part." Vance laughed, "Teddy has enough material to last him a lifetime."

"Ah, yes, Teddy. We wish we could take him with us—what a wonderful mind and kind spirit in that man. We will be showing his performances to appreciative audiences for decades to come."

"He is a treasure. No one would deny that," agreed Vance.

Two hours later, a small team with Youngblood in the lead inspected the top four decks of the MARIAN. They were nearly intact except for the nukes. They were all gone. When Youngblood reported the loss to the ship's Dale, he seemed relieved.

"I thought I was going out of my mind," he said. "The explosive force when we nuked the Malic ships seemed many times larger than I anticipated. Now I know why. They were many times bigger. Five times larger to be exact."

"I shudder to think what hell they could have created with those nukes," said Alex. "They probably would have used them on us, but I doubt they had time to figure out the technology."

While the top four decks were being inspected, another team led by Troy, Vance, and Lesley inspected the four outer spheres. They found them to be in pristine condition, except the destroyed areas where the four stasis pods had been attached.

"These people are taller than we are," said Lesley.

"Yes, over the centuries, humans continued to get taller. We finally had to do some genetic engineering and selective breeding to stop the trend. The average man was over two meters and women weren't much shorter."

"Wow," said Lesley.

"And you will soon note that there is much less diversity in hair and skin color. The races have melded together."

"That's not a surprise," said Vance.

"But the good news is that we have five hundred and eight humans to add to Gabriel's population," said Lesley with a big smile. "I can't wait to see what their reaction will be when they see their new home."

"Before that can happen, we gotta get them there."

Two days later, with dozens of people working nonstop shifts, the ship MARIAN was restored to a condition which allowed it to proceed to Gabriel.

"Is everybody ready?" asked Vance.

"Affirmatives," came from various parts of the MARIAN, NORMAN, and the Yassi ship.

"Captain Troy, you have the helm."

"Starting main engines."

To offer technical assistance, young Dale was on the MARIAN's bridge with Troy, and Norman and Bob were on the engine deck. Both positions would normally have been handled by the ship's computer personalities. A dozen other Gabrielites were stationed around the rest of the ship, with about half on the engine deck.

"All systems running normal," said young Dale as he scanned the bridge's instruments.

"All smooth so far," said Norman. "No grinding or screeching."

"We're ready to move," said Troy.

"We'll follow you," said Vance.

"Rolling her to vertical," said Troy.

The massive ship slowly started revolving to a vertical position.

"I would have thought she traveled in a flat plane," said Johnnie.

"There is no atmosphere in space, so drag isn't a consideration," answered young Dale. "She travels with her top forward just like the NORMAN."

"Here we go," said Troy.

The MARIAN began moving at about a quarter g to start. Those on the MARIAN could feel the gravity coming up. They settled down on the decks.

"So far, so good," reported Norman from the engine room.

"Going to half g."

CHAPTER 39

BACK TO GABRIEL
MO-NINE 7, 53

Troy, of course, had been completely schooled on reviving the MARIAN's colonists, as had Vance with the NORMAN's colonists. He left the bridge in Youngblood's hands while spending two hours instructing Lesley and her team on the reanimation protocols.

"Vance, we're going to start bringing some of the colonists out of stasis right away, starting with those who have expertise in this ship's design and manufacture, as well as the computer experts. We'll be starting with the stasis pod designers. We can use their help now, no point in waiting until we get to Gabriel," said Lesley. As she was reporting to Vance, she and Troy were walking down a long row of stasis pods and Troy was checking off the names and pod numbers of the desired colonists on his handheld pad.

"They'll come out of stasis a lot quicker than we did. The technology has improved tremendously. I'm impressed. We may have as many as a hundred people up and moving before we reach home."

"Affirmative," said Vance from the bridge of the NORMAN.

"Once we reanimate the stasis techs, we won't need Troy's help. He can get back to the bridge."

"Roger that."

Three days later, the MARIAN went into a geosynchronous orbit above Home Bay. She had undergone a complete systems check while traveling to Gabriel and was ready to enter the atmosphere within an hour of going into orbit.

Because of her massive size, the MARIAN was clearly visible to the naked eye from the western side of the Ring. This historic occasion was being broadcast to all of the viewers on the planet. Everybody living on the western side of the Ring was outside looking up, and those who could make it were at the actual landing site.

"Take her down, Captain," said Vance.

"Yes, sir. Applying power and slowing."

As the MARIAN slowly dropped through 1,000 meters, its extensive landing gear began to lower. There were four struts on each of the four outer spheres, and six on the large center sphere. At the end of each strut was a pad ten meters square to spread the massive weight of the ship as she settled on solid ground. She slowed as she approached the surface; by the time she was a few feet from the ground, she was nearly stopped. Other than the breaking of twigs and crushing of small rocks under the pads, the MARIAN was nearly silent as she gently touched down on the surface of Gabriel. The landing gear on all five spheres adjusted in length to fit the topography of the landing site. She would sit absolutely horizontal. The ship settled on an area that had been hastily cleared to accommodate this massive ship; an area located just south of the NORMAN's traditional landing spot.

At the landing area, there were nearly a thousand Gabrielites anxiously waiting for this ship's arrival. This was a truly momentous occasion. This ship held the last of the Earth's Humans; the last survivors of a lost world. How would they differ in culture and attitude from the humans who were born and raised on Gabriel?

The applause was enthusiastic and continuous. It seemed like every recording device on the planet was there to capture the moment.

"Look at the size of that thing!"

"I'll bet she's five times the size of the NORMAN."

"Closer to six I think."

"How many people are on board?"

"Did they bring any animals?"

"Look at that," said a man as he pointed upward.

He spotted the NORMAN on her descent. At the moment, it was just the size of a BB to the human eye, but it was growing quickly as it dropped toward Gabriel. This was the bright bronze sphere that itself had left Earth hundreds of years in the past. This was the spacecraft that had brought life and civilization to the planet Gabriel.

Two minutes later, the NORMAN landed on its designated spot just 80 meters north of the MARIAN. Again there was sustained applause. What a sight, what a day!

The main hatch of the NORMAN lowered within minutes of its landing and Vance and his crew walked down to great applause. As they waved at the crowd, they stopped and looked up. There in the sky above them was a Yassi shuttle heading down to land.

"Every time I see one of their shuttles, I marvel," said Vance.

The Yassi shuttle landed just west of the NORMAN. Its crew, including Egro, were now walking with Vance and his crew toward the MARIAN. As they walked under one of the MARIAN's connecting tunnels, the ramp from the large center sphere began to lower. By the time they took up a position at the bottom of the ramp, Lesley, her team and the rest of the Gabrielites walked down and joined them. Thirty seconds later, with Troy in the lead, 104 Earth colonists, walking four abreast, came down the ramp. All were dressed in beautifully designed and tailored jumpsuits. All were smiling brightly as they looked around and waved to the applauding and whistling crowd. There was an even mix between men and women. All of them seemed taller than the Gabrielites, and a good percentage seemed to be a close match in hair and skin color. There were a few exceptions. When the last of them stepped off the ramp onto the soil of Gabriel, Vance stepped forward.

"We of the planet Gabriel welcome you to your new home."

CHAPTER 40

THE GATHERING
MO-TEN 6, 53

For the past few days, people had been assembling from all over the planet to attend this historical gathering. Hundreds of people had yet to meet the new arrivals or see the sight of the NORMAN and the MARIAN parked side by side. The incredible spectacle dominated the landscape.

MO-TEN 7, 53

It was a beautiful afternoon and upwards of 100 people were sitting, auditorium style, in rows of ten under the roof of the open-sided gazebo near the NORMAN's cave. An additional 1,500 gathered around the edges. Half of those assembled under the gazebo's roof were the new colonists from the MARIAN. The other half consisted of the original colonists and their first born. Ten Yassi sat in the front row. The mood was clearly festive.

Sitting at the head table were Vance, Jason, Lesley, Youngblood, young Dale, Alex, and Norman. Troy sat in the center seat. A large viewer was set up just behind the head table so that the ship's Dale and Alex could be seen and heard. For the few hundred people who could not make it to the site, cameras recorded and transmitted the event to every part of Gabriel.

The people under the cover of the gazebo and on its fringes chatted excitedly as they waited for the meeting to begin.

At the appointed hour, Vance stood, and as he did the chatter ceased within seconds. He looked around, smiled, and began addressing the assemblage.

"This is a truly momentous occasion. We have here among us—Earthlings."

There was spontaneous laughter mixed with whistles, applause, and wooing.

Vance paused for a moment before continuing, "Earthlings from an Earth far in the future from the one we left so long ago. An Earth that sadly no longer exists." Vance again paused. "But, as the NORMAN did centuries ago, the MARIAN now brings to our home planet marvels in life and technology. Because of the MARIAN, we can now add over 500 human beings who will contribute greatly to our technology, culture," Vance smiled, "and gene pool."

Again the assembled clapped, whistled, and wooed.

Vance paused before continuing. "Had the Yassi not discovered the MARIAN, all life and technology aboard the MARIAN would have been lost forever. As it turned out, the loss of life was minimal. The loss of four colonists and one SLF is, of course, not trivial, but it isn't catastrophic," Vance paused and looked directly at the Yassi, "We Humans owe a debt to the Yassi that cannot ever be repaid. There are no words that adequately express our thanks—we will never be able to thank you enough."

With that statement, everyone stood, and applauded, and wooed as loudly as they could. The Yassi stood, and with their broad smiles bowed their heads in unison toward Vance.

Vance bowed his head in return and then waited for the applause to stop and the audience to sit before continuing.

"There was a great deal of technology stolen by the Malic, but most of it is not permanently lost." Vance smiled slightly, "Troy tells us that many of the people on board the MARIAN helped design and create much of what was stolen, and we will be able to recover a great deal of it. I would now like to formally introduce Troy Miller, the last Chairman of the Board of the WGC."

Half the crowd didn't know that Troy was in fact the last Chairman. The MARIAN's colonists started clapping immediately, but there was a few seconds pause before the surprised Gabrielites joined in.

Vance smiled and looked to his left, "Mr. Chairman, I'll turn this meeting over to you.

Troy stood up from his position at the head table.

"First, I want to say on behalf of myself and the MARIAN's colonists what an immense pleasure it is to finally be with you on the planet Gabriel. There are actually no words to describe it… there simply can't be."

This statement caused a sustained applause. Troy waited until the applause subsided before continuing.

"Just a short note here. I would like to be simply addressed as Troy. I am no longer Chairman of the WGC, I am now a proud citizen of Gabriel."

This statement was quickly greeted by appreciative applause.

Troy smiled and nodded, "To actually be sitting at the head table with the people responsible for the creation of the WGC, so many centuries ago, is absolutely indescribable. I'm here with the most famous people in history, actually the most famous and revered persons in the history of planet Earth. Imagine yourself standing among Plato, Socrates, Da Vinci, Newton, Einstein, Washington, Jefferson, and Lincoln. If you can imagine that, you would only be half as impressed as I am. I have never felt so humble. So, please… just Troy.

I am told that we have with us in this gazebo all of the original NORMAN colonists. Again this is incredible, just incredible. Each of your names is… or was known to all peoples of the planet Earth. The original twenty, as you have been referred to over the centuries, have had dozens of biographies written about each of you." Troy paused for a moment to let this information sink in. "In addition, hundreds of thousands of children were named after you; thousands of schools bear your names; statues were erected in all parts of the world in your honor. It is hard to express the awe and respect in which we, of the MARIAN, hold you. But here you sit… I'm nearly overwhelmed." Troy paused to maintain his composure. "You couldn't know over the centuries how much your fame grew, because you weren't there.

But I'm sure you'll be interested in reading about yourselves in the MARIAN's extensive library." Troy smiled brightly.

"Alexander Gabriel, Jason Gould, Dale Isley, and of course Vance Youngblood, were considered by all to be the saviors of the world. There was no one person or group of people who came before or after you who even came close to your incredible accomplishments. It was accurately determined centuries ago that if anyone of these four men had not existed, if they had not been part of the WGC team, then there would be no human beings left in the universe."

The crowd was on their feet clapping furiously. Up to that point, only the MARIAN's colonists had any idea that the original twenty colonists had that kind of fame or stature on the Earth of the past. It was clear that the Yassi were also impressed, and they wooed loudly. Finally, the applause subsided and Troy resumed.

"Now, I'll report on the more mundane; work to repair the MARIAN is coming along nicely. Many of the designers and builders of the MARIAN are among the colonists, and were the first people brought out of stasis. These are brilliant people and I'm confident that the MARIAN will be functioning at or above 90% within a month.

Troy looked around the gazebo, "Many of you here have opened your homes to us, and everyone from the MARIAN is overwhelmed by your hospitality. Nevertheless, we have decided to leave the remaining 400 people in stasis until such time as housing accommodations can be made available. On a very personal note, I'm told that my dear friend Gary can be repaired, and will probably be able to function at over 80% of normal."

That statement brought loud applause.

"Thank you. I know that you will find Gary a delightful man and a great asset to Gabriel." Troy paused for a moment; "Aboard the MARIAN there is a great deal of technology that you are unfamiliar with, but that I'm certain you will enjoy. As an example, there is a textile mill. This self-contained machine produces hundreds of yards of cloth a day, any color and any print, out of almost any kind of fiber."

There was spontaneous applause, particularly from the women in attendance.

Troy smiled, "Thought you would like that one."

"We have a loom, but it only works with cotton and wool," said Lesley, "and, we can have any color we want—as long as it's off-white."

That brought laughter.

"Go on, Troy," said Vance with a smile.

"There are hundreds of high-tech, hydrogen-powered fuel cells stored in the MARIAN's warehouse. Fuel cells were being developed and used before the NORMAN's voyage, but the technology has grown exponentially. They were used on Earth as the primary source of energy for over 300 years, powering just about everything from factories to motorcycles. And, of course, hydrogen production is easy, inexpensive, and clean." Troy paused for a moment. "However, I must point out that the main power for the MARIAN is nuclear fusion. We could not store enough hydrogen to make the voyage. Fusion, or fission in the NORMAN's case, is the only practical power source for space travel. Fusion reactors will eventually replace fission reactors as power sources.

All diseases have been eradicated, mostly as a result of gene and stem cell therapy. Those two therapies were also used to lengthen life. The average life of a human is… was 120 years…" Troy abruptly stopped talking.

No one said anything—they waited.

"Sorry, I let my thoughts shoot back to the loss of our planet. The loss of two billion people."

Vance interrupted, "Let's all stand and give a minute of silence for reflection on the loss of our home planet and all the life left on it."

After that minute, Troy finished telling of the wondrous things that humans came up with over the past five centuries. He told of new vegetables, new sports games, and new teaching methods. Crime, he reported, even the most minor crime, was rare and almost always attributed to mental illness. He credited The WGC for laying the groundwork for success in that social arena.

Troy smiled, "The MARIAN is a huge ship with nowhere to go. There is no cave big enough to store her. But she is a huge asset and should be used as such. As an example, there is a large hospital containing the latest medical technology. A complete library, research labs, and production factories that you won't believe.

So, it has been decided by the brilliant people here at the head table to make a permanent place for her near where she presently sits. If, however, for whatever reason, she might be needed, either in space or somewhere else on the planet, she is always available."

CHAPTER 41

LITTLE RAT BASTARDS
MO-TWO 14, 54

"Vance, are you close to a viewer?" asked Youngblood.

"No, but I can hear you."

"We have a report with video coming in from a logging detail up in the north woods."

Vance knew it must be important or Youngblood wouldn't have contacted him. "What do they have?"

"They have a video of three Malic."

"Alive!"

"Yes, sir."

"Send a runabout to pick me up."

"I'll be on my way in five minutes."

"Bring a portable Rosetta translator with you."

"Have it in my hand."

"Holy shit," said Vance 30 minutes later as he watched the video on the runabout's viewer.

"As you can see, sir, they are running away from our men. The men didn't have any weapons with them or they would have taken them out."

"Glad they didn't. I'm looking forward to seeing these rat bastards up close and personal. They aren't very fast, are they?"

"No, sir, really short legs, but they look quite agile."

"One of the guys got an Auratron image, so we know where they are."

"Excellent!"

A few minutes later, the runabout landed in a clearing that was presently serving as a logging camp. Within a minute, Vance exited the small runabout followed closely by Youngblood. Both had backpacks draped over one arm and equipment in the other.

Two young men came running over to meet them.

"Peter, Samuel," Vance greeted the two.

"Sirs," they nearly said in unison.

"Where are they?"

Samuel turned and pointed northeast. "They're about two clicks away, up in the hills, in the thick woods. Their signal weakened all of a sudden, so I'm guessing that they must have gone into a cave."

"Any place to land the runabout in that area?"

"No, sir. This is as close as we can get."

"Take these." Youngblood handed Samuel a rifle and a protective vest. Vance handed Peter, the larger of the two, a vest and what looked like a small rocket launcher and a backpack with four missiles. Each missile had a different colored tip.

Vance and Youngblood had sidearms.

"Let's go," said Vance and headed off up a long rise toward the northeast. The forest was thick with pine and fir in this area, which made the going a bit slow.

They kept checking the Auratron as they moved up the hill, and crossed a fair-size creek, stepping from stone to stone. The signal stayed at about 60% strength for most of the hike, but started getting stronger as they got closer to the cave.

As they were heading up a boulder field at the bottom of a large rock outcropping, Peter called out, "There's the cave, sir."

About a hundred meters further up, on the side of the outcropping, was the narrow entrance to a cave.

"How deep is the cave?" asked Vance.

"Sensors show no more than 30 meters, sir."

"Okay, let's be cautious here. The video didn't show any weapons on them but that doesn't mean they don't have 'em."

"Yes, sir."

The four men spread out and advanced cautiously, moving from the cover of one boulder to another until they were no more than 20 meters from the mouth of the cave.

"They are as far back in the cave as they can get," reported Peter.

"We're not going in there," stated Vance. "Give me the Rosetta."

Youngblood took off his backpack, unsnapped the flap, reached in and pulled out the translator. He quickly covered the ground between his protective boulder and Vance's.

Vance took the translator and turned it on. He adjusted the setting to Malic and pointed the speaker at the cave.

"You three Malic in the cave. If you come out unarmed within the next 60 seconds, we will not hurt or kill you. After that time, we will burn you out. This is your only warning."

Within ten seconds a grating voice yelled out, "How do we know that you will keep your word?" The translator worked perfectly.

"Because I gave it. We are not low life, lying pieces of shit like the Malic. We keep our word. You have 30 seconds."

Vance called over to where the two young men were, purposefully leaving the translator on. "Peter, do you know how to operate that rocket launcher?"

"Yes, sir."

"Load it with an incendiary and point it into the cave."

"Yes, sir," Peter said enthusiastically.

Within two seconds, the grating voice screamed, "We will come out. Please wait."

A few seconds later, the first Malic appeared.

"Jesus, they're ugly," said Peter.

"Put your hands above your heads where we can see them," said Vance.

The Malic did so without hesitation. The other two followed five seconds later. Apparently, they were waiting to see if the first one was killed before revealing themselves.

"Keep them covered. If they move even a millimeter, kill them." Vance paused for a moment, "Youngblood, watch our backs."

"Yes, sir."

Vance stood up from behind his boulder, a drawn pistol in one hand, the translator in the other. The Malic didn't move and they didn't take their eyes off of Vance.

"Keep your hands above your heads and walk down here."

The tallest Malic said something to the others that wasn't loud enough for the Rosetta to translate, but all three began walking single file down toward Vance, stopping in front of him.

"You are even uglier than your pictures, and I wouldn't have thought that possible," Vance said into the translator.

Peter and Samuel looked at each other and smiled slightly. Their leader was not known to mince words.

The Malic did not respond. They had their beady black eyes glued to Vance. They had never seen a being like this. This being was powerful looking; not like the Vout, or the Yassi.

"Are there any weapons in the cave?"

"Yes," replied the tallest of the three who was just over one and a half meters in height.

"Are there any traps set for us inside the cave?"

The tall one hesitated for just a brief moment before saying, "No."

Vance's head cocked just a fraction. "You are lying." Vance holstered his pistol, took a step forward and slapped the Malic on the side of his head. The Malic was knocked off his feet and sideways into a large boulder and he collapsed, writhing in pain. Vance's face held a look of disgust as he wiped his hand on his pants.

Vance turned to the next tallest Malic. "Are there any traps in the cave?"

"Yes," came an instant reply.

"Go into the cave and disarm them and bring them out here... now!"

"Yes." The Malic turned and ran up and into the cave.

Five minutes later, it reappeared with straps over his shoulder carrying three bags and weapons of some sort in each hand.

"Stop. Drop the weapons right there."

The Malic dropped the weapons as if they were hot.

"What is in the bags?"

"Explosives."

"Are they armed?"

"No."

"Take them out of the bags and spread them out on that rock so I can see them." Vance pointed to a flat rock just a meter in front of the Malic.

The Malic that Vance had slapped started to get up.

"Stay on the ground, face down," Vance commanded, "you," he pointed at the third Malic, "get on the ground next to him, face down."

Both complied without hesitation while the other continued to remove the contents of the bags and spread them out on the flat rock.

"DOWN!" yelled Youngblood as he jumped behind a boulder and began firing his pistol down the hill.

Vance was down in an instant, but Peter and Samuel stood for a moment before diving for cover. Something hit Peter in the leg before he was safe and he shouted out in pain as he stumbled behind a small boulder.

"I've got it pinned down about 90 meters below us," yelled Youngblood, "off to the left."

Vance did not take his eyes off of the three Malic. The third had frozen in place. The two on the ground were up on their knees behind a rock looking over the top.

"You up there, come down here."

The Malic quit spreading out the explosives and headed down quickly. "All three down on your faces. If you move, you will die."

They did as told.

"Samuel, keep them covered. Any one of them moves, kill em."

"Sir."

"Peter, what's your condition?"

"Got shot... have a hole in my calf, sir," came a pained reply.

"Can you handle it yourself for a minute?"

"Yes, sir, I think so."

Vance turned the Rosetta translator around to face down the hill.

"This is to the Malic down the hill. Drop your weapon and show yourself and no harm will come to you."

"Not until I kill you, Human."

Vance's left eyebrow raised a little. "Peter, can you still operate the rocket launcher?"

"Yes, sir."

"Load a high explosive in it."

"Yes, sir."

"Youngblood?"

"Yes, sir."

"You're sure he's pinned down?"

"Absolutely."

"Peter, when you're ready, say so."

"Need a minute, sir. Need to stop the bleeding a little more."

"Take your time, we've got him stuck."

A half a minute later, Peter rose up and leaned across the boulder in front of him with the launcher resting on his shoulder. "Just show me where to shoot."

"Youngblood, soon as I say, put a round where you'd like to see a rocket hit."

"Peter, watch where the bullet hits and fire the launcher."

Vance looked down the hill, but couldn't see the Malic. He talked into the translator. "Malic, unless you're out in the open, unarmed, within seconds, you're dead."

"SHEMISM YOU!" screamed the Malic.

"I believe that was a negative," smiled Vance. "Take it out."

"You ready, Peter?"

"Yes, sir."

"Here goes." With that Youngblood took carful aim and fired his pistol into a large boulder that was just two meters behind a smaller boulder. Peter saw the bullet strike and took aim at the same spot and pulled the trigger.

It took less than a second for the rocket to cover the short distance. The explosion was thunderous and the sound reverberated from the surrounding hills for a few seconds. But the Malic didn't hear it. He was in a dozen or more pieces scattered over an area 15 meters square, along with a good chunk of the boulder and a lot of pine boughs.

Vance reached into his backpack and retrieved a coil of heavy cord. "Samuel, tie their hands behind their backs." He handed him the cord.

A couple of minutes later, the three Malic were securely bound.

"Now let's take a look at these ugly little bastards."

They were truly ugly. Their beady eyes were like sharks, just cold black. Their "fangs" were long and protruded out of their mouths and over their bottom lips about 20 millimeters. The smallest of the three had much smaller "fangs." Their hair was dark brown, long, tangled and matted. It stuck out of every opening in their uniforms. They seemed to be nearly as hairy as a chimpanzee. There were just small holes instead of ears and the same with their noses. They were bare footed and bare headed.

"Not only ugly, but they stink," said Youngblood.

Twenty-four minutes later, after inspecting the remains and bagging a small piece of the dead Malic, the four men and three remaining Malic headed down the hill. At the back of the procession, Vance carried Peter piggyback while Samuel led the Malic, and Youngblood followed with pistol in hand.

"The stench of these little bastards is overpowering," said Youngblood. "My eyes are starting to water."

"You should be grateful that you don't have my sense of smell," said Vance.

"I am, believe me, I am."

"They're going to stink up the runabout," said Peter.

A few minutes later, they came to the creek they had crossed earlier.

"Stop," said a smiling Vance, "Let's wash them up a little."

Samuel also smiled, "Got some soap in camp, sir."

"Get it," said Youngblood. "Bring three bars if you have it."

Vance carefully sat Peter down on a fallen long and sat down next to him. "How's the leg?"

"It hurts, but I'll live, sir."

Youngblood kept watch on the Malic while Samuel went for the soap.

"Youngblood, untie their hands."

"Yes, sir." Youngblood handed the rifle to Peter and proceeded to untie the Malic. When he was done, he rinsed his hands in the creek. "Jesus!"

Vance took the translator out of his pack and turned it on. "Get those uniforms off and get in the water," Vance ordered.

"We don't like to get wet," said the tallest Malic. "We can't swim. We are afraid of deep water."

Vance smiled, "Good. That will make this even more fun. Now get those uniforms off and take them into the creek with you."

The Malic looked frightened and began talking rapidly among themselves. They didn't move.

Vance didn't say anymore as he set the translator down next to the log. He stood up, walked over to the tallest Malic, picked him up by the collar and crotch and threw him head first into the middle of the creek as if he were a spear.

When the Malic managed to get his head above water, he screamed in terror as he flailed in the water. The other two quickly began to remove their uniforms.

Vance walked back to the log and retrieved the translator. "Now you two wade into the creek with your uniforms in hand and sit down in the water. You, the dumb shit in the water, get your uniform off and sit down, it's not deep."

"Jesus," said Youngblood, "that one is a female."

Vance shifted his gaze. "Holy shit, it is. Now that's the stuff nightmares are made of."

"Oh my God," said Peter.

The two stripped Malic slowly put their feet into the creek, testing every centimeter before proceeding.

"Move faster, or I'll move you," said Vance.

The two did as they were told and reluctantly joined their companion in the center of the creek.

Samuel came running back with bars of soap in each hand and a large towel draped over his shoulder.

"Hand it to them."

Samuel walked from rock to rock until he was able to hand the soap to the Malic. They took it as if they had never seen soap before.

Each put it up to their noses and sniffed... and then sniffed again. They seemed to like the smell.

"Now scrub every inch of yourselves with that. Head, feet and ass. I'll tell you when you're done."

Again, the Malic didn't move.

"If I have to come in there and do it for you, I'll hold your heads under water until I'm done."

"Can we stand up?" asked the female.

"Yes."

They all gratefully stood but clearly didn't understand what to do. Samuel yelled, "Hey!"

They turned to look in his direction. He started miming the scrubbing process. He started rubbing an imaginary bar of soap all over his body, from his armpits to his feet, including his crotch. He dipped down as if to rinse and then did the same to the top of his head. It was pretty funny.

They got the idea and started taking what may have been, and probably was, the first bath of their lives. Youngblood and Samuel demonstrated how to wash each other's backs, and how to wash their uniforms. The Malic complied. In the end, it looked as if the ugly little bastards were about to freeze solid.

It took a full 45 minutes and three complete washings later before Vance felt they were sufficiently clean. He told them to get out of the stream. They didn't have to be told that twice.

"Hang your uniforms on those branches to dry," Youngblood pointed to leafless branches of a fallen tree.

Samuel demonstrated how to use the towel.

They toweled off and stood there shivering. The day was warm and the sun was shining. Within fifteen minutes they had completely dried.

They looked at each other curiously. It seemed likely that they had never seen one of their own clean. With their hair clean, it was much lighter and more of a reddish brown. It also fluffed up and made them look much fatter. They actually started touching and smelling each other.

"I think they like what they see and smell," said Vance.

"I believe you're right, sir," said Youngblood.

A group of people, including Troy, were watching a viewer on the deck of the NORMAN. They were watching the three Malic sitting in a holding cell that had been put together just for them.

The Malic had gone through a physical change, not voluntarily to be sure. The tallest and most belligerent one had attempted to bite one of the guards, and would have succeeded had the young man not been extraordinarily alert and adept with a Taser. As a consequence, all three were tranquilized and had their long canines cut back to the length of their other teeth.

The female and the shorter male did not take kindly to being horribly disfigured because of their companion's actions. The two banded together and beat him to within a millimeter of his life. As a result, the whipped Malic now sat in the corner of the cell, fangless, with a full 20% of his body wrapped in medical dressings.

"Those are vicious little rats," said Vance. "They put a lot of pain through that fucker's nervous system."

"Yes, they did. It took our docs a little time to put him back together," smiled Youngblood. "If they'd still had their fangs, he would be dead."

"I don't think he's the boss anymore," Dale observed.

"The question is, what to do with them," said Alex.

"That is a problem," responded Vance. "We could simply execute them."

"Vance, my friend, I've known you for centuries, and I know you wouldn't execute these creatures. As far as we know, these are just lowly soldiers following orders."

"Put them on an island," suggested Youngblood.

"Island?"

"We have hundreds of developed uninhabited islands. Maroon them on one with the tools they need to survive, and let them fend for themselves."

Vance thought about that for a brief moment, then nodded.

CHAPTER 42

WORLDWIDE NEWS HOUR
MO-TEN 20, 99
16:00 Hours

The weekly Worldwide News Hour's familiar format had been changed for this momentous event. This was New Year's Eve for the first 100 years of the planet. The normally one-hour weekly program was expanded to include all of this historical evening's activities.

The opening scene was not the usual shot of the two amateur news anchors, Bob Gertan and Brandon Zobro, sitting at a desk in front of a viewer, but instead it was an interior shot of the NORMAN's cave.

The cave had been creatively and colorfully decorated inside and out. The NORMAN was the centerpiece as it sat majestically in the middle of this massive cavern. Even at this early hour, there were thousands of people milling around. A band was playing lively music on the good-size stage, built especially for this event. Everybody was in a festive mood.

The picture switched to the two newsmen sitting behind a desk on a temporary set built in front of one of the NORMAN's massive landing struts. In their actual lives, Bob was a wheat farmer and Brandon ran a small mercantile store. Both had, a few years ago, volunteered to replace the original "Newsman", whose health had begun to deteriorate. The show normally consisted of a weekly update of the planet's activities—births, deaths, new constructions, marriages, things like that. The two had good chemistry and humor, and managed to bring a little more entertainment to the show, which otherwise was quite flat. There were few people on the planet who did not watch the show.

The picture went to a single shot of Brandon.

"Well, Bob, I don't know how many people we have as an audience tonight. It seems to me that everyone on the planet is here in the Home Bay area, and not watching their viewers at home. What a party this is shaping up to be."

"There is no question that this is by far the largest gathering in the planet's history. As of today," Bob looked down at his notes, "Gabriel's population is 17,520 and I believe that we are expecting as many as 10,000 of them as attendees this evening."

"So, we may still have an audience," Bob smiled.

"Probably there will still be a few watching, even taking into consideration that there are dozens of parties taking place all over the planet."

The picture switched to Bob. "We're going to use this first hour of our broadcast, while things are still relatively quiet, to give a brief review of planet Gabriel's first century."

"Now would be a good time to point out that we have installed about half a dozen large viewers in strategic spots around the cave so that anyone located in a remote area can still see what's going on."

"It's been just over 19 years since the first scheduled news program was produced on Gabriel," said Brandon, "Somewhat before our time, Bob."

"Not too much before. We were in our teens."

"Yes, I guess we were. At any rate, we have a wonderful array of recorded events to show the citizens of Gabriel, and we'll attempt to present them in an entertaining and informative way."

"Take a look at this."

The viewer's picture changed to the first recording of the planet's surface, a recording made from the NORMAN while it was still three light-years out. The planet's surface seemed to be completely void of foliage, but the blues of the oceans and the colorfully stratified bare land made a fantastic picture. Beautiful music began playing in the background.

"These recordings come from the archives of the NORMAN," Bob said in a voiceover. "This is Vance Youngblood's first vision of Gabriel. Wow!"

"But, by their own accounts, Vance, Alexander Gabriel, and Dale Isley were ecstatic to find this planet," added Brandon, "They had been searching in space for 32 years at this point."

The picture changed to a closer shot of the planet's surface, as the NORMAN orbited.

"The only green you can see here were thin areas bordering the water. Not much, if any, vegetation on the planet at this point," said Bob.

"This is one of my favorite pictures, Bob. It's taken from Vance's shoulder camera as he first set foot on the planet. This gives me the chills."

"Can you imagine what he felt?"

Excerpts from that first walk, including the dialogue between the three men were seen and heard. As these scenes were playing on the screens, many of the celebrants in the cave began to group around the remote viewers.

"Now here's a recording showing Gabriel taken 100 years later, just before their second landing on the planet's surface."

The picture changed to show a planet with a great deal more green visible.

"That's a 100 years planet time, Brandon, just 11 years ship time."

"Yes, of course. And look at the change; how the green spread for hundreds of miles from nearly every water source. Incredible."

"To think that just one man, even a SLF, could seed an entire planet single-handedly is nearly unimaginable."

"It's recorded that he never stopped working, not for a single minute while the NORMAN was on the planet's surface."

"And here we are nearly a 100 years after that, with another huge change visible on the planet."

The picture changed again and again as the reporters continued their narrative. At times, the conversations between Vance, Alex, and Dale were heard along with pictures of their discussed subjects.

"It should be pointed out that all this occurred prior to year one. Year one comes later."

"Okay, here comes one of my favorite scenes," said Brandon.

The scene was that of Vance's encounter with the grizzly bear. It included the responses of both Alex and Dale.

"That was incredible, just incredible," said Brandon.

"I love Dale's reaction."

"In 2104 ship's time, the NORMAN took off on its last time-acceleration trip. Here you see the planet's surface as they entered orbit nearly 100 years later in 2114; ninety-five more years had passed on Gabriel."

The picture was from orbit, and clearly showed well-established forests, plains, and deserts. It showed the oceans, seas, lakes, and rivers.

"Our brilliant production manager edited the following recordings in split screen to show everyone what is on the surface as they pass over Gabriel in orbit."

The music continued as the two anchormen said nothing for a full 15 minutes. As the picture from orbit came to the west side of the Dumbbell Continent, the motion of orbit slowed, and on the split screen was a scene of a beautiful river flowing through a forest of pine. The orbit recording sped up and then slowed again, showing snow-covered mountain peaks to plains with massive herds of bison.

"You can see areas where the forests and grasslands have burned over the decades. That was a huge fire on the North Dumbell about eight years ago. Just starting to green up again."

"Lost a lot of animals in that one. But, we're assured by those who know that their numbers will come back."

The program continued showing wildlife, lakes, and plains in the split screen. As the orbit went over the oceans, it slowed and the split screen showed schools of a variety of fish, kelp, and coral. As it traveled over the Vast Continent, scenes of elephants, prides of lions, vast herds of plains animals, and birds of every description were displayed. The Vout lakes were shown along with the multitude of animals and birds that now made these artificial lakes their home. It took 16 minutes to finish this segment of the program. The orbiting picture faded, and a picture of the news anchors returned.

"Wow, we live on a beautiful planet," said Bob.

"We do, but now we continue our history lesson. Eighty-four years after the NORMAN left the planet Earth, 19 of the original colonists were brought out of stasis. Sadly, one, Terri Diggs, perished in the process."

The picture changed to a rear-view shot of a dark haired woman dressed in a blue jumpsuit walking down a ramp into a grassy field.

"This is a recording made by Vance's famous shoulder camera of the first Lesley walking off the NORMAN and onto the surface of Gabriel for the first time. She was the first human to walk on the planet."

"What an incredible piece of history."

"Indeed that is, and here's another," said Brandon.

The picture went to one of Vance and the 19 original colonists sitting on the flight deck of the NORMAN.

"They, at this moment, were being addressed by Alexander Gabriel and Dale Isley; this was the first meeting held by humans on the planet."

"Look how young they are."

"It was during this meeting that they were told of the Earth's destruction."

"By the way, anyone can access these historical recordings through their viewers. As you know, our schools' history classes use them all the time."

"It was also on this day that the New Calendar began. It was the first day of year 0," said Bob. "That was exactly one hundred years ago today."

"It was later on in that year when the famous encounter between the lion and Vance occurred. Unfortunately, as the story goes, no one had the presence of mind to record the encounter. But the event sure made the history books."

"One of the great stories… school kids just love it."

"Here is a recording of the colonists working on the original lumber mill and glass maker. All of the lumber for the original homes was manufactured at this mill. This is the same site where the MARIAN complex now sits."

"You can see Vance working alongside some other colonists in the background, there on the right."

"We are going to skip ahead a few years to the year 20. Here we show recordings of the colonists and their offspring having a picnic. Fortunately, the great historian Tasha recorded all of the children. But for the sake of time, rather than show you all of them, which amounts to just under one hundred, we thought you would enjoy seeing the more famous ones. We'll start with the oldest and work our way down. The first are the clones of Norman and Marian Gabriel at 17 years old."

The two were talking animatedly with each other. You could tell they were close friends.

The picture centered in on Norman first. He was tall, blond, and gangly. All in all, he was a handsome young man.

"The original Norman was the engineer who designed the starship NORMAN. And that basic design is incorporated into the starship MARIAN."

Next came a picture of Marian. Tall, brunette, and beautiful.

"Boy, is she a beauty," said Bob in voiceover.

"More than a beauty, Bob, she was Alexander's muse in a lot of ways. Many books have been written describing her numerous abilities and influence on her son. The starship MARIAN was named after her for more reasons than just because she was Alexander Gabriel's mother."

"Next is Walter Gabriel, Uncle Walt to Alexander Gabriel. You can sure tell he and Norman are brothers. He, along with Alexander, Vance, and Jason Gould were the creators of The WGC."

The pictures continued with the two newsmen commenting in voiceover.

"Here is Lara Lane, and wow again. She became Vance's wife about three years from the date these recordings were made."

"That's some head of hair on the girl!"

"History shows that Lara and Vance were truly soul mates. We'll get into their relationship a little later in this program," said Brandon.

"Apparently she was the exclusive reporter for the WGC, that's how she and Vance met."

"Which also means that she is another case of beauty and brains."

"Speaking of which, we're now going to show you the 14-year-old clones of Colleen Keefe, Teddy Stoddard, Jason Gould, and Dale Isley."

The recording started with Colleen in a group of other young people. She was clearly amused with Teddy's antics, and interacting with the others. She was wearing cutoff shorts and a halter-top. The picture zoomed in to show her from the chest up. She was laughing and smiling brightly, clearly having a good time.

"Well Bob, there are no words to describe this girl… and she's just 14."

"This is truly a case where a picture is worth a thousand words. Oh my God! That could be the most beautiful woman ever born."

The picture moved to Teddy. He had his eyes on Colleen—as did all the boys. Teddy slowly turned his head to look into the camera's eye; he had contorted his face and crossed his eyes. It was a hysterical expression.

"And of course, the famous Teddy. This young man went on to become an intergalactic superstar," said Brandon. "Still is. He's cloned every 50 years."

"Thank God for that. What a talent."

The camera moved to Jason. At 14, he was already close to two meters in height and thin as a rail. He looked more serious as a young man than the others.

"Jason Gould. A media genius on Earth, and President of the WGC after Alexander Gabriel retired. He's credited with shaping the opinions of the majority of the Earth's citizens before the WGC's world takeover. His efforts, both before and after the takeover, resulted in making the takeover a great deal more palatable for the majority of Earth's citizens."

"And last, but in no way least, is Dale Isley."

Brandon laughed a little. "He looks to be about half the height of Jason. He's just a little guy."

"With a huge brain. It has been said that he is probably the most brilliant human being in history," added Bob.

"Couldn't argue with that. He is also one of those people selected to be cloned every fifty years."

"Now, we are going forward to the year 45. That is the year that the Vout came to visit for the first time."

"These are the first recordings of the Vout ship as it was stationed in orbit over Home Bay."

The screen filled with a view of the Vout ship.

"That sure did get the Gabrielites' attention."

"But, what a positive moment in time. A benevolent alien race came to mine gold and became our great friends and trading partners. Without the Vout and Yassi, we wouldn't have many of the modern conveniences we enjoy. We'd have the technology, but not the manufacturing facilities. We still lack many things, but our industry is catching up to our technology at a rapid pace."

"We've all been brought up with knowledge about the Vout and the Yassi. We have interacted with them all of our lives, but the Gabrielites of that time weren't even aware that other species existed."

"They handled that first encounter nearly perfectly. I've watched all the recordings of those first meetings many times over the years, and still marvel at the intelligence and diplomacy they employed."

"Bright people."

"It was during this first encounter with the Vout that we learned about the wonderful Yassi, and the evil Malic."

"It was fortunate that the Vout arrived here before the Malic. Had they not, the outcome of our battle with the Malic could have, and probably would have been quite different."

"As it was, Gabriel lost 23 of its citizens in that first encounter with the Malic. Among them was Adam, the first human born on Gabriel, and the son of Lesley and Quinn."

"That was a devastating blow to the colonists. They lost more people in that battle than they originally brought to the planet."

The picture switched again.

"In the year 52, the Yassi arrived for the first time. Take a look at these recordings."

The viewer showed the first Yassi shuttle as it came down from the mother ship and landed on the hill next to Home Bay. It showed the eight Yassi coming down their ramp to meet the Gabrielites.

"This is what the Gabrielites first saw of the Yassi. It is no wonder why we love these little people so much… they are just a joy."

"It was the Yassi, a short time after they left Gabriel, who came across the disabled MARIAN adrift in space. Without that discovery, the MARIAN, its colonists, and its technology would have been lost forever."

"And that includes several of my ancestors," said Brandon.

"Probably everyone on the planet, except the clones, have genes from the MARIAN colonists," added Bob.

"Not only did the Yassi find the MARIAN, but they were instrumental in providing technical support and help in making repairs to her. I'm sure the Gabrielites would have gotten the job done without them, but it would have been a great deal more difficult."

"Now, here is the recording of the captured Malic. These three are the only Malic ever to be seen by humans. The first recording shows them while they still had their long canines. The second shot is after their canines were removed."

"Removing their canines didn't make them look any less ugly, but it did make them look much less vicious."

"They are hideous."

"They were marooned on an island close to the equator. It has a climate that couldn't be tolerated by humans, but it was to the Malic's liking. The female gave birth after a year or so, and that made four. As the story goes, they adapted well to life on the island, but Vance was never comfortable with them being on the planet. The Yassi made an offer to return them to their home planet and Vance accepted. A year later, they were gone."

"As an amusing side note here, it is said that the Malic requested soap to take with them."

"I wonder if that single thing changed the Malic? Maybe introducing soap to a malicious civilization made them easier to get along with."

"We may never know."

"Well, back to our story," said Brandon. "Gold was clearly the currency of this part of the galaxy, and it naturally followed that it became Gabriel's currency. It didn't take long before gold began to replace a good percentage of the planet's barter system, which to an extent did and still does work well."

"An ancient proverb from Earth says that "money is the root of all evil," and it proved to be a huge problem for Gabriel's people," added Bob.

"That's right. Where the barter system caused few problems, gold created greed and envy. The lust for gold damn near brought Gabriel's progress to a halt."

"Seems just about everybody started mining gold to the exclusion of most everything else; after all, you didn't have to grow, build, create, or barter if you had enough gold."

"It didn't take long before Vance, Alexander, and Troy had to pass a law to curtail an individual's right to mine gold. Apparently, this law went against everything these men believed in, but there was no choice. In this instance, free enterprise needed to be curtailed."

"That's right," said Brandon, "after much thought, a major portion of the gold mined using the Vout laser is distributed. Each year, one kilogram of gold is given to each citizen, regardless of age."

"What the individual or family elects to do with it is up to them."

"That's right, and for the most part this decision has worked quite well."

"It also didn't take our leaders long to realize that we needed the gold broken down into specific weights. A stamping machine was designed and built to produce five different weights of coins. Since then, this new 'coin of the realm' is used for nearly everything. To purchase products and services made on Gabriel, or to purchase a great variety of goods from the infrequent visits of the Vout and the Yassi."

"In effect, the Vout and Yassi ships became Gabriel's super stores; they trade products such as state of the art viewers, personal movers, boats, high-tech tools, art, medicine, and many things that cannot be grown or manufactured on Gabriel. As the years and decades pass, the list of items that Gabriel is unable to produce becomes smaller."

"So, in the past hundred years, as this wonderful pictorial reveals, Gabriel continues to develop, and the population has grown exponentially. Based on the present rate of growth, it is estimated that in another 100 years, our population will reach over 600,000."

"Most of our original colonists have passed on and become a cherished part of our history."

"However, as of this date, there are still three alive. The oldest, Lesley, is 124 years old. She was the first human to set foot on Gabriel… remarkable. Quinn and Leda are 123."

"All three live in Lesley's original home under the loving care of their great grandchildren, and all three are said to be quite active—all things considered."

"On a truly sad note, in the year 79, Vance's beloved wife, Lara, passed away. She was only 76. She had a fatal allergic reaction to an orchid, of all things. Vance, of course, was devastated. He ordered that all orchids of that variety should be destroyed and never grown again on Gabriel. Then, he became a bit of a recluse. In the following year, he announced that he was going to switch off for a few years. That was 20 years ago and he hasn't been seen since."

"He is still in his ready room aboard the NORMAN."

"However, prior to going into stasis, Vance recommended that Troy take over his job of overseeing the planet, and Troy has done an excellent job for these past 20 years."

Bob smiled, "Of course, managing a planet of less than 20,000 people shouldn't take much effort compared to what he was managing—a world of over two billion. It is safe to say that he may be overqualified!"

"It must seem to him as if he's the mayor of a small town."

"Interesting to note that the planet Earth's population was an astounding seven billion and growing before the WGC took control. One of their nine goals was to reduce the world population to no more than two billion. When the NORMAN and its colonists left Earth, the population was still above six billion. Clearly the WGC's goals were accomplished in the centuries that followed."

"Seven billion! That's hard to comprehend."

"It certainly is. Okay, we're going to take a long break here. Our cameras will continue to show what's going on in the cave throughout the evening. We'll come back on the air at 19:30 and we'll have a little surprise for you."

19:30

As scheduled, the viewers switched back from filming crowd scenes to the two newsmen.

"Wow! What a party." Bob looked and sounded as if he might have had a beer or two in the preceding hour.

"Getting hard to walk around. If there are only 10,000 people here, I'd be surprised; the cave seems full to capacity."

"We are just minutes from an announcement that, to our surprise, has managed to be kept a secret."

"The crowd isn't paying much attention to us now. They're having too much fun eating, drinking, and dancing. This is great."

19:45

A warning buzzer sounded from inside the NORMAN and ten seconds later, the NORMAN's substantial loading ramp began to slowly lower. Everyone who was under or near the ramp moved out of the way. All cameras turned to record whatever was going to happen. A minute later, the ramp touched the cave floor with a soft boom. The huge crowd went silent. Those people closest to the NORMAN kept their eyes on the ramp. Those in other parts of the cave turned to watch the viewers.

Nothing happened for a full minute; no one made a sound. A voice came over the intercom loudspeaker. "We would be grateful if all those people who are close to the NORMAN's ramp would please back off about ten meters."

Anyone close to the NORMAN did what was asked.

Seventeen seconds later, five men dressed in the formal blue jumpsuits that the original colonists wore came walking down the ramp. They were recognized instantly. They were Alexander Gabriel, Norman Gabriel, Walter Gabriel, Jason Gould and Dale Isley.

The applause was immediate and sustained.

In a voiceover Bob could be heard saying, "These are the last clones of these five remarkable men to be born."

"It hadn't occurred to anyone at the time, but now on this 100th anniversary of Gabriel, their ages coincide closely with what their ages were when the NORMAN left Earth nearly 600 years ago," added Brandon.

"You don't suppose someone actually planned it that way?"

"Probably not, but I wouldn't put it past them."

The five men stopped at the bottom of the ramp, turned and looked up inside the ship. Within seconds, Vance came walking down. He was dressed as they were in a blue jumpsuit.

"Oh my God!" exclaimed Brandon. "That's Vance, the SLF. Oh my God, I've never seen him before."

"I did when I was about ten," said Bob. "All of us kids thought he was a God."

At the sight of Vance, the applause stopped. The cavern went silent for a brief moment before the surprise sank in. Then came the applause, the whistles, the woos and the sounds of joy as the six men stood side by side in a straight line, with Vance in the center. Vance's face held a slight smile. The six bowed slightly. The applause increased.

The six turned to look up the ramp as two more beings started down. They were a Vout and a Yassi dressed in their traditional garb, a white jumpsuit for the Vout and colorful shades of green for the Yassi. The crowd went wild.

"Holy crap!" said Bob. "We didn't know about this."

"This is the first time these three races have been together at the same time."

"This is historic."

"This will be a New Year's Eve party that will never be forgotten."

EPILOGUE

MO-ONE 4, 100

Vance had spent the first few days of the new year in an emotional reunion with his 85-year-old clone, Youngblood, and Youngblood's 74-year-old wife, the second Lara. The loss of his Lara was nearly as fresh today as the day he put himself into stasis; however, after the reunion with Youngblood, Lara II, their children, grandchildren, and great grandchildren, he began coming out of his grief.

MO-ONE 9, 100

Vance was sitting in the captain's chair of the NORMAN carrying on a conversation with the images of Alex and Dale.

Vance was smiling, "Knowing that Youngblood's children are Lara's and my children, our families, gives me a warm feeling."

"Genetically identical," said Dale. "They are your children without doubt."

Vance's eyes clearly held mixed emotions, some sadness, but mostly love.

"When you see the hairline and shoulders on most of the males, especially little Jeep, there can be no mistaking where the genes came from," added Alex.

The combination of Vance and Lara produced offspring that were somewhat abnormal in body configuration. The boys were taller and slimmer than Vance or Youngblood, but for the most part they had his shoulders and hair. Unfortunately, the girls produced by this pairing didn't have the beauty of their mother. They were quite handsome, but slightly blocky rather than pretty and slim.

"How do you like the changes in and around Home Bay?" asked Alex.

Vance smiled, "There's a nice increase in population. Sure seems strange not knowing everyone… and those I do know have aged some."

"About 20 years," said Dale.

"Just about." Vance smiled. "Our present population still wouldn't populate much more than a good-size small town on Earth."

"That's true, but in another century we'll be able to populate a good-size city."

"As we agreed, won't it take about three more centuries to reach our maximum population of 200 million?" Vance asked.

"At the present rate, about 280 years," said Dale.

Vance nodded. "By the way, I like the way you've set up the little town at the bay entrance. Well done. Beautiful boardwalk, nice little stores with some great products. The pub located right on the point is, for lack of a better word, perfect. Great place for adults to gather. Great view." Vance paused for a second, "Wish I could taste the beers they're serving; they sure look good."

"John Carlon's place. He is one of Lesley's great grandsons, believe it or not. Makes a lot of his own beer. Others supply him with their own special brews."

"Nice place."

"Your tour around town caused quite a stir," said Alex.

Vance smiled, "I noticed. Kind of felt like one of the rock stars of old."

"Your chair at Carlon's will probably become a shrine," added Dale.

"Shit, I hope not." Vance seemed reflective for a moment. "I'm going to spend a month or so traveling around Gabriel catching up on the planet's progress. Then, I'd like to spend some time on my island—if it's still mine?"

"It will always be yours," said Alex. "And wait until you see the gorillas and orangutans."

"God, I'd nearly forgotten about them." Vance paused to reflect for a moment. "After 20 years, the place is probably overgrown."

"Hardly. There has been a team of caretakers there since you went into stasis. I think you'll find it quite the same as the way you left it."

"Oh? Thank you. That means a lot to me. I haven't been there since…," his voice trailed off.

"Wasn't our doing," Alex quickly jumped in, "there were so many volunteers we had to have a drawing to select the winners; we ended up limiting the time spent on the island to two years per volunteer."

Vance nodded while he smiled. "I'm looking forward to seeing my gorillas, and… Lara's orangutans." His smile faded slightly as he thought of Lara.

This time Dale came in, "When would you like to head out?"

Vance looked at Dale. "Tomorrow morning works for me."

"We'll have a runabout ready."

MO-ONE 10, 100

It wasn't a runabout that waited for him on the flight deck, it was a magnificent Yassi shuttle with its ramp invitingly down.

"Wow," said Vance, as he did every time he saw this craft. He boarded with a smile. "Could have done with one of our old runabouts you know," he said to the viewer located below the cockpit window, as he settled into the captain's chair. A custom chair had replaced both the Yassi pilot and copilot's chairs. There was no room for a copilot.

"We know, but you deserve the best," Alex smiled. "The cargo hold has some stuff that needs to be taken to some of the settlements. So, if you don't mind, while you're there… "

"No sweat," said Vance, while he scanned the instruments. The instrumentation was completely foreign to Humans, but Vance had no problem learning and following the instructions given him by the Yassi.

"Okay then, bon voyage," said Alex.

In the following month, Vance managed to spend from two to three days at each settlement, much to the settlers' delight. No one under the age of 20 had ever seen Vance in person, but everyone except the youngest knew his entire history. He was truly a hero in every sense of the word.

None of the settlers, young or old, had been inside the Yassi shuttle; many had seen the outside as it sat displayed on the flight deck of the NORMAN, and most had seen pictures of its interior. So much to the surprise and delight of everyone, Vance took the time to give all the settlers, young and old, a ride in it. A ride in this shuttle with Vance Youngblood at the helm was an experience that they would cherish the rest of their lives.

MO-TWO 8, 100

"I'm on my way to my island," Vance informed Alex and Dale.

"We think you'll find it in fine shape. Have fun."

Vance came in for a soft landing 40 minutes later on the tidy lawn that sat between his home and the Lara River.

Vance exited the shuttle with a fair-size duffle in each hand. He stopped as soon as his feet hit the grass, and looked first up the river, then down. He smiled to himself as he started up the lawn toward his home.

He managed to open the door without dropping the duffels, and stopped just inside. It was exactly as it was left 20 years ago. The furniture, fixtures … everything was the same.

"Hum," he said aloud.

He looked toward his bedroom, half expecting Lara to come out to greet him. But, there was nothing but silence. His heart sank a little.

He carried the duffels to the bedroom, nonchalantly dropping them on the bed. He'd put things away later. As he returned to the kitchen to get a glass of water, he spotted a note on top of the counter.

We're in Section 3. Please join us, sir.

Vance nodded to himself. *Okay—Good.*

He headed to the back door on the far side of the kitchen. The wall on the right side of the door had a row of pegs holding a small array of umbrellas, gloves, and hats. His old straw hat was still hanging on its peg. He smiled briefly before realizing the peg next to it was empty. He stood for a moment looking at that empty peg. Lara's favorite old hat wasn't there. He took his old hat off the peg, put it on, and walked out the door.

Section 3 was where he and Lara, 75 years ago, had released the first of the gorillas, Kong and his ladies, and it was there they could occasionally find them and their progeny as the years passed. Since that time, many more gorillas and orangutans of varying genetics had been introduced.

Section 3 was a delightful two-kilometer walk upriver from the home. It was a short hike that he and Lara had always enjoyed. The trail, over the decades, had become a well-established walking path. For about half its distance the path bordered the river, the rest meandered through thick vegetation.

Vance was inside Section 3 for 100 meters before he began hearing some activity coming from the clearing up ahead.

As soon as he entered the clearing, he spotted a young woman in her late teens intently hammering some siding to a shack of some kind. She was a tall, slender young lady with olive skin and short dark hair under a bright red scarf. Vance didn't recognize her, and assumed she was part of the extensive gene pool that the MARIAN had brought to Gabriel.

She didn't see Vance approaching, and continued to give the piece of siding some serious whacking.

Off to Vance's left came another noise. Vance turned just in time to see another young lady walk into the clearing about 30 meters away. She was carrying a young gorilla on her hip. She stopped when she spotted Vance. Then she slowly slid the young gorilla off her hip, setting it on the ground. Her eyes never left Vance's as she released the small ape. This young lady had long red hair under an old straw hat. This young lady's eyes were filling with tears as she started walking rapidly toward Vance.

"Oh, Jesus," Vance said softly.
"Hi, Hon. Welcome home," she said.

THE END

CPSIA information can be obtained at www.ICGtesting.com
Printed in the USA
BVOW04*1643171113

336254BV00002B/2/P